Hi Judy.
Enjoy my Book
Love
Mary Ann
Berkshire

Twice Dead

Mary Ann Berkshire

PublishAmerica
Baltimore

At the specific preference of the author, PublishAmerica allowed this work to remain exactly as the author intended, verbatim, without editorial input.

ISBN: 1-4241-9082-7 (softcover)
ISBN: 978-1-61582-503-5 (hardcover)
PUBLISHED BY PUBLISHAMERICA, LLLP
www.publishamerica.com
Baltimore

Printed in the United States of America

I want to thank my husband Jerry, my #1 fan and critic.
My daughter Raquel, my computer expert.
Martha, who put the commas and periods in the right place.
Jackie my #2 fan and very good listener.
I love you all

Chapter 1

God, I have to have a cigarette! I just have to have a cigarette. I usually do when I'm in a stressed out situation. I quit smoking a year ago, so you'd think the urge wouldn't be as strong. Old habits die-hard.

I knew there was one more wayside before the town of Hartger's Grove. I decided to pull in and collect my thoughts; maybe I'd find a cigarette at the bottom of my purse. No such luck. In one of my health conscious moments, I decided to clean house and toss every cigarette.

The wayside was empty. It was late in the afternoon and not yet summer so this was a normal scene. I parked my banana yellow V.W. convertible in a parking space. The car was a rental. I had wanted a more sedate color like red.

I had been down this highway many times yet had never pulled into this particular wayside. It took the death of my beloved teacher and her secretive book to bring me back to my adopted hometown. Hartger's Grove was my hometown, not by birth but by choice. The years I spent here were my high school years, the time in my life when I found love and true values, Most of all the cherished friendship of Miss Beatrice Wilkes, my sophomore counselor, and biology teacher. Next to my grandparents, Miss Wilkes was one of my favorite people.

During my college years I tried to write her as much as I could, but with each passing year the letters between she and I became less frequent and farther apart.

After I graduated from college and found my first job teaching biology to high school sophomores, I wrote her about this new chapter in my life. I thanked her for instilling in me the confidence that I could be anything I wanted to be.

I didn't realize how infrequent her letters to me were becoming until one day they stopped altogether. I haven't gotten a letter from Miss

Wilkes in the past three years. I remember her last letter; I could read the anxiety between the lines. In the letter she mentioned a book. She seemed adamant that, upon her death, the book should be in my hands and that I destroy it immediately. She did not give me the name of the book, but wrote that when I found it, I would know that it was the one she referred too. This seemed strange to me and not at all like Miss Wilkes.

I felt guilty about not keeping in contact with her. My life was busy with teaching, but she was my friend and I chastised myself for neglecting her. I made a promise to myself that I would visit her as soon as possible. Time goes so swiftly. One day you receive a dreaded phone call telling you that your friend is gone forever. Death waits for no one.

I did not realize how long I had been sitting in my car until I heard the air horn of a semi trying to coax a whitetail deer across the highway. I turned the key in the ignition, put the gear in reverse, and backed out of the parking space. Within seconds I was once again on the highway. With each passing mile I was closer to my past and the search for Beatrice's book of mystery.

Chapter 2

I entered Hartger's Grove from the southwest corridor. This led me passed my old high school and the Catholic Church that Grams and I had attended every Sunday.

Nothing has really changed since I left Hartger's Grove ten years ago. There are a variety of stores that help keep a small town going. Craft shops, with the magic word Amish, printed prominently on their signs, entice tourists. There is the Hartger's Grove Gazette, our local newspaper. The Java Cup Café, where if you didn't like reading a newspaper, you could hear it first hand from the town's retirees. Gramps and his "committee", as I used to call them, would spend a good part of their morning discussing local and world news. There is also an assortment of five or six fast food restaurants that have sprung up since I left.

The town is just beginning to wake up after a long winter that is so prevalent in this central Wisconsin town. It will soon welcome the summer people who have cottages or lavish homes that surround the lakes in the area.

My grandparent's farm is just a mile from town. After I graduated from high school I moved back to Milwaukee for my college years. My grandparents got their wish to move to Florida in the winter. They now refer to themselves as snowbirds because of their grey hair and the fact that they fly south for the winter. At any rate their farm is closed except for a few horses that a neighbor girl keeps in the stable. Her name is Katie. She is a high school student who watches over the farm, as well as her horses, which are stabled on my grandparent's farm.

My sweet, wonderful grandparents. They were more like parents to me than my real ones. My parents were social butterflies that didn't have time for their only child. When they drove me to the farm that last time, I somehow knew this stay wasn't a mere two-week vacation. They kept telling me that they were giving me the better of two worlds. It didn't do any good to argue with them. When you're 13 years old, you don't have much of a platform to stand on. My parents and I both shed tears. I felt as if I was being abandoned. As far as my folks were concerned, I heard that happiness would do that to some people. My friend Natalie cried some real tears. After all, we had planned great adventures this last summer before high school, but life does go on. Now as I think back to that time I realize they did me a tremendous favor by leaving me with my loving grandparents. My grandmother understood how I felt so she gave me enough love to take care of me, and an army of kids. That's the way she was.

I pulled into the driveway and got out of the car. Gosh, it was good to be back. I didn't realize how much I had missed the farm. I hadn't been back to the farm in ten years, but I didn't stay away on purpose. When the school year was over, I also taught summer school, so I didn't have much free time. My grandparents always made time to come and visit me. My granddad would say, "I had to come and see how my favorite granddaughter is doing." I would always remind him that not only am I his favorite, I am, his only grandchild.

It was nearly dusk when I took my bag out of the trunk of the car. I found the house key under the mat and let myself in. The house needed an airing since my grandparents had been in Florida the last four months. Its funny how a house changes from a home to just a building when nobody is living in it. I put the teakettle on for hot chocolate. While the water was heating, I opened a couple of windows, changed the bedding, and unpacked my bag. I am only going to stay for three days. The school semester is almost over, and it will be time for exams. I have to get my kids ready for them.

I sat down at the dining room table and looked out the big picture window. I noticed how the fields were turning from winter brown to the light green of spring. Spring and fall were my favorite seasons. I thought how Miss Wilkes was going to miss this and once again I felt sad that I hadn't kept in contact with her. She was sixty when I first met her in my sophomore year. At that time, I thought sixty was ancient. Miss Wilkes did not seem that old. There was something youthful about her. It's like her birthday said she was sixty, but her body language, her gentleness, her way of explaining life in general was anything but old. She was the kind of teacher that made a young person believe in herself in everything she did. After I received the call about Miss Wilkes death, I was in shock. In my head I added up the age she would have been and it came to seventy-three. It seemed like she would be here forever. I hadn't given Miss Wilkes book much thought until now. Why was she so adamant that I find it? Surely she must have had a close friend that she would have confided in. Miss Wilkes was an excellent teacher but a very private person. She loved her students, yet we were never invited to her home as some of the other teachers often had. So what was so important about this book that I had to destroy it as soon as I found it? As soon as the funeral was over, I would go over to Miss Wilkes house and try to find this mysterious book. If I didn't find the book, what then? How was I to get into her home? All these questions made me very uneasy. If only she told me the title, it would make it a lot easier to find. Then again, I'm probably worrying for nothing, and it would be sitting on her kitchen table just waiting for me. I always did make mountains out of molehills.

Chapter 3

The body of Miss Wilkes was in state at Vormen's and Son funeral home. It was the town's only mortuary. It served Hartger's Grove, all the surrounding towns and rural communities that were not fortunate enough to have this kind of establishment in their own area.

I stood in line to view the body. Vormen's was as I imagined it to be. The funeral home had wall-to-wall people. Beatrice did not have any close family, but she had touched the lives of so many of her students. Like me, they were here to pay their final respects.

Along with her former students came many people from town, as well as the town's gossips. Beatrice was not a social butterfly. She taught school and that was her whole life. She never married, but the gossip mill said there was a secret beau who paid a visit to her quite often. All eyes watched for any male mourner who stayed a little too long at her casket. They also mentioned that when Beatrice was younger she had taken a year off to care for a sick relative. Maybe it was true. Maybe it was pure gossip. Whatever the story, being a romantic, I hoped she'd had a beau and that they had been in love.

As I got closer to the casket, I could not believe what I was seeing. There lay Miss Wilkes, but then again it wasn't her. I listened to the voices around me saying how marvelous she looked, how young, and how she looked as if she were just sleeping. She indeed looked very young. I had heard that Vormen's did a good job with cosmetics, but younger by twenty years was a stretch of the imagination.

The burial was at the town's Union Cemetery. The sky was a dismal gray with a light mist falling to the ground. If there was a perfect weather for a funeral, this was it. It seemed like the whole world was crying at the death of Miss Wilkes. A canopy was erected over the gravesite and what protection it didn't give, an abundance of black umbrellas did. Vormen's had everything for the deceased, and a lot more for the survivors. Black umbrellas with the name of Vormen's and Son printed in gold lettering were provided for the mourners to take home if they wished too. My family never had any dealings with Vormen's except to pay final respects to dear friends who had passed on.

Grandma had mentioned to me that the women of the Vormen family were rather arrogant because of their money and beauty. They were in charge of many civic and social functions. The town's newspaper would have their pictures on the front page. That would be the only time I would hear my grandmother complain,

"Humph, there they are again, Mrs. and Miss American Beauties."

I would just chuckle when I would hear her say that. It sounded funny coming from her. Grams also mentioned, with a twinkle in her eye and a secretive tone of voice, that Lewis Vormen was quite the ladies man in his younger days.

While at the funeral I did some socializing. It was good to see so many of my classmates again. We all agreed that it was too bad it had to be under these circumstances. They suggested going for a late lunch after the burial to talk over old times. As much as I would have liked to, I only had two days before I had to be back in Milwaukee.

I was listening to Father O'Malley's final words over the casket when I felt someone staring at me. I looked up and saw a very familiar face. A face so sweet that at one time I thought I would marry the boy it belonged too. His football uniform was now replaced by a police officer's uniform and worn with great pride. It was a cool misty day, but I still felt my face getting rather warm when I read his lips as they said, "Amanda Harding, I still love you."

I cleared my throat and tried to concentrate on what Father O'Malley was saying, but my thoughts kept coming back to Aaron Fischer, the star quarterback of Hartger's Grove high school, my knight in shining armor. The young man, who on our graduation day, said he would wait for me forever.

It was then that I noticed the woman clinging to his arm. It was Anne Bradley, a former classmate and a royal pain throughout high school. Anne always wanted Aaron for herself. By her adoring looks at him, it appeared she had succeeded. After Father O'Malley said the final prayer, the casket was slowly lowered into the ground. I softly whispered my goodbye to this wonderful person. Upon turning, I collided with Aaron. His arms went around me in a big bear hug. Oblivious of the other mourners, we hugged for what seemed like an eternity. I opened my eyes and I could see Anne glaring at us. For a brief moment I had forgotten about her. I pulled myself out of Aaron's arms and started to turn away. He caught me by the arm and looked concern as he asked me what was wrong. He didn't wait for an answer, but instead asked me to meet him at the Java Cup Café. I shook my head no.

"Amanda, I need to talk to you. It's important."

I thought it over and then looked at Anne. Aaron saw me and then it dawned on him that it was Anne who was holding me back.

"Please Amanda, meet me at the Java Cup Café. There are so many questions I would like to have answered."

I still did not give him an answer. Taking my hand he said,

"I will be at the Java Cup Café if you decide to join me. I hope you do."

I returned to my car and thought about Aaron. It seemed like yesterday when we were a twosome in high school. Where there was one of us, there was the other. We both knew that college was in our future, but so were marriage and a family. So what happened to change all this? Maybe it was being apart for so long and finding a whole new and exciting world. Aaron studied police science in Chicago and became an officer on their police force. We wrote a lot of letters in the early years stating our undying love. Before we realized it, the letters turned from our undying love to just news between good friends before the letters stopped altogether. Now seeing Aaron at the gravesite and reading his lips, I felt my old feelings for him rekindle. I have not seen him for ten years, but just a hug and a few spoken words brought back the sparks that I had thought were extinguished long ago. I was not surprised to see Anne Bradley at his side. Ever since high school she was out to have Aaron as her own. It looks like she finally won. Although my stay here in Hartger's Grove is going to be short, I decided to join him at the Java Cup Café.

Chapter 4

When I entered the café, I spotted Aaron at a corner booth. He stood up and waved to let me know he was there. Without saying a word, he reached for my hand and had me sit on his side of the booth. This felt like old times. I wondered how many times we had met here while in high school. It was just past noon and there were a few customers who lingered over their lunch. I recognized a few of the people and nodded hello.

Aaron asked if I was hungry and I said "No, not really." We just ordered coffee. Aaron and I were both silent until the waitress set our coffees in front of us. Aaron was the first to speak.

"Amanda, I think you have gotten more lovely with the passing years. I didn't know you would be at Miss Wilkes funeral. When I saw this beautiful woman across from me with her dark halo of hair and dark eyes, I felt as if I had died and gone to heaven. It was you Amanda Harding, my Angel from the past." Although ten years have past since we last saw each other, he had been on my mind many times. I was surprised by his feelings, but then again, maybe not. I was the one who had stopped writing to him. I suppose I could blame it on my busy college schedule and later on my new job in teaching. To be perfectly honest with myself I just wasn't ready for the seriousness of romance like we had in high school. I wasn't ready for marriage and family. I needed to be away from the small hometown cocoon and sample life in the big city. After I stopped writing to Aaron, I still received a few letters from him. He asked me what was wrong. One weekend he came up from Chicago to visit me and I pretended not to be home. I did not have the common courtesy to face him. Even now, I could not look at him. It hurts to see the sadness in his eyes and the many questions that need answers from me. There is so much to say, but where do I begin except to apologize for the past. He noticed how uncomfortable I was so he changed the subject to Miss Wilkes funeral, and said how everyone in Hartger's Grove was going to miss her. Before we knew it, it was time for a change of waitresses.

Aaron asked me to join him for a late dinner and I accepted. He was to pick me up around eight that evening.

When I got back to the farm, I felt excited. It was wonderful seeing Aaron again. The whole time we were at the café he never mentioned his involvement with Anne Bradley. I decided that Anne being with him at the funeral was just as he said, "A friend doing a friend a favor." I still didn't trust her intentions, but then why should I care? I have no hold on him.

Aaron came at eight on the dot. Punctuality was one of his many fine traits. We drove slowly to one of the fine restaurants that were situated on a big lake. It was a beautiful dining place with rustic turn of the century décor. The hostess sat us at a table near one of the big windows overlooking the lake. The misty rain, which had been falling for most of the day, had stopped but the dark sky looked as if more rain could be on the way. I sighed with contentment as I let the warmth and coziness of the restaurant's atmosphere seep into my body. Aaron smiled and said

"I must have picked the right restaurant. I haven't seen you so relaxed since high school."

"I agree you made a very good choice in choosing this place. Remember when we were in high school and we would always drive by and say that some day we would like to have our wedding reception here."

I hadn't realized what I'd said until I noticed the same sad look on Aaron's face. It was a look that I had seen earlier in the day.

"I'm sorry Aaron. Sometimes I don't think before I speak."

Aaron just nodded and began looking over his menu. I looked at my menu. However, sometimes it's hard to read when tears threaten to spill out onto the menu. I had hoped Aaron would not notice, and that the waitress would take her time in coming for our order.

It was the middle of the week and past the prime dinner hour so there where few diners. After giving our order, I had a chance to notice that we were in one of the restaurant's smaller dining rooms. All the tables were set with white linen and napkins. In the middle of each table was a lit lantern that made the silverware and water glasses sparkle. Aaron took my hand in his and said,

"Romantic isn't it?"

"Yes it is. It didn't dawn on me how totally relaxed I feel until you mentioned it. It's funny, but when I was driving into town yesterday, I actually started looking for a cigarette, despite the fact that I haven't smoked in over a year."

"I didn't realize that you had smoked."

"When you're in the big city, you pick up some bad habits."

As the candlelight flickered on Aaron's face, I wondered how many times I had seen his face in my thoughts and dreams. His thick sandy blonde hair was worn longer in high school, but even now in its military style cut, it had lost none of its waves. The tan on his face made his blue eyes all the more bluer, like the sky on a sunny day. The smile lines at the outer corner of his eyes were a little deeper, perhaps from being out in the sun. Knowing Aaron the way I do, I like to think it was because he was just delighted to be alive and happy. Across from me sat Aaron Fischer, the boy I loved every day in high school. As a woman, I lost track on how important he was to me. Aaron smiled one of his melting smiles that I remembered so well. How I longed to say "Lets go home and make up for all the lost time, and let these ten years melt away as if we were never apart." He must have read my mind because he said,

"Amanda, did you ever wonder what our life would be like now if we had gotten married right out of college? You were always in my dreams as a beautiful loving wife and mother. I see myself showing you and our kids off to everyone who looks our way. Amanda, I know it's been ten years since we last saw each other, but I remember the love we shared as if it were just yesterday. I guess I was hoping you felt the same way. Maybe I'm moving to fast for you. I know you have your life in Milwaukee, but I was hoping that if you feel like I do, you would move back to Hartger's Grove and we would get to make up for the ten years we lost.

I looked at the earnestness on Aaron's face. I realized right then and there that those ten years were melting away by seeing that loving look on his dear face and his warm hand holding mine. Was this possible? Was somebody up there giving me a second chance to fine true love again when I so carelessly threw it away the first time? It would be so wonderful to be with Aaron again, but until I find the book Miss Wilkes was so obsessed with, I could not go on with my own life. Deep down I had a feeling that this was not just an ordinary book.

I didn't have to answer Aaron for the waitress arrived at our table with our salads and Aaron reluctantly let go of my hand. The topic of me staying was not brought up again until after dinner, over coffee. He once again took my hand in his and said,

"Amanda, I don't want to push you into an answer today I just want you to know how deeply I still care for you. I will give you all the time you need to make your decision. I know there is something on your mind and I think until you have the answer there will be no room for me or our future."

I wondered to myself how I could have spent ten years without this man in my life. Can love be refueled in a single day? True, I had never forgotten him. I would see him walking down the street only to realize in disappointment that it was someone who looked very much like him. It was then that I made my decision for the night. I picked up my bag and taking hold of his hand, I bent over and whispered in his ear.

"Let's go home."

I wondered why the days are so long and nights so short, especially this night with Aaron. We had never made love in high school although at the time it seemed to be the thing to do. We came close so many times, but something always stopped us. Tonight was different. It was as it was suppose to be Aaron and me, a soft bed, and a night breeze whispering through a partially opened window. Somewhere in the night I could hear the tiny pond creatures singing to their lady loves.

The dawn came too soon. I knew Aaron had the early shift, but I didn't want him to leave. I needed him for the love and warmth he had offered me so freely. I also needed him for the strength he could give me, but I was too afraid to ask for. He sensed my mood change. He sat on the edge of the bed and pulled me close saying,

"Last night I asked you what was bothering you, but you wouldn't say. At first I thought I was pushing you too fast, but now I think there is something else. Is there someone else in your life? Is that why you stopped writing to me? If there is, please tell me and I will fight for you. Tonight was beautiful and I want this to last for the rest of our lives. I'm not leaving you until you tell me."

I looked up at him and ran my finger slowly across his lips, those lips I couldn't get enough of last night. I was silent for a moment; stunned at his outpouring of love, and that he would do anything to have me back. Truly, I don't deserve this wonderful man but I will try and make up for the way I treated him. He is my sweet, wonderful Aaron.

"Talk to me, Amanda."

I looked up into those trusting blue eyes, and I wanted to cry for pure happiness.

"Oh Aaron, no, I don't have anyone else. Deep down I knew there was only you, there always seemed to be a void in my life. I was too afraid to find out that there might be someone else in your life." I threw my arms around Aaron's neck

"Please Aaron don't ever let me go." This time I did cry as I heard a deep sigh from Aaron.

Aaron had to leave for home to change into his uniform. Before he left I asked if I could get into Beatrice's home to retrieve what she had promised me. Aaron shook his head no and explained that the police did not have a key to her house. He did not know who did, so I would have to wait until her distant relatives came to take inventory.

"I'm sure her relatives will give you what Beatrice promised you. Sweetheart you're just going to have to wait. I'm sorry I know you have to get back to Milwaukee, but there is nothing I can do at this time."

Before I could nod my head in consent, Aaron gently laid me back down on the bed and once again gathered me in his arms, the issue of Beatrice completely forgotten.

"Amanda, if you only knew how many times I thought about you all these years. After you stopped writing me, a part of my life seemed to disappear. For a while I tried to fool myself by thinking that we were trying to establish our future, for the sole purpose of building our lives together afterward. Somehow, fate brought us together again in the form of Miss Wilkes."

Aaron and I talked for a little while longer, reluctantly he said he had to leave, but we made a date to meet at the Java Cup Café for lunch. After Aaron left, I lingered in bed a while longer, and thought about all he had told me, and about his feelings for me. I now knew Aaron was what I wanted and needed to make my life complete. As Aaron had said maybe Beatrice's funeral was fate in disguise.

Chapter 5

Beatrice's house was a ways out in the country, five miles northwest of Hartger's Grove. I didn't realize that she had lived so far out. Her nearest neighbor was a Miss Gertrude Greyson, who lived a mile from her. I parked my car at the bottom of the long driveway. I wanted a good look at the painted lady, Beatrice, always talked about.

Beatrice's house was two stories high and very quaint. Its main color was white with a green and burgundy trim. If you looked real close you could see it needed a lot of loving care. This was strange since Beatrice was always so fussy about her appearance and she always spoke so highly of her home. What could explain the neglect of her house?

I circled the house and tried some of the windows to see if I could get in. It was then that I noticed a broken window next to the back door. Hmm, this was strange. Why didn't Beatrice have this replaced? I didn't like this at all. Had Miss Wilkes been ill before she had died? I couldn't recall anyone at the funeral mentioning she was sick. Everyone said how young and pretty she looked. If I could get into the house, maybe I'd find if there had been a problem. The broken window made it a lot easier for me to get in. I wondered if Aaron would consider this breaking and entering. I noticed glass on the floor; there must have been a break in since Beatrice died. I proceeded carefully through the first floor of the house. The prowler could still here, but nothing else seemed disturbed. In fact, the presence of all the dust and cobwebs made it look like nobody lived here in quite a while. This was indeed strange.

I began to chastise myself for not keeping in touch with her. She was trying to tell me something in her last letter. It was not like her to be vague, "Damn, I should have known there was something wrong, but what?

I had reached the top floor. I looked down the hallway and saw there were three rooms on this floor. Opening the first door I found the room to be completely empty. I continued down the hall to the second room, which was a very small bathroom. That left only one more room, which had to be a bedroom. I was about to reach for the doorknob, when I heard the distant rumble of thunder. I hesitated for a moment; I never did like the sound of thunder as it always sounded so ominous to me. I would have to hurry or be caught in a downpour. I had to find the book here, if I didn't, that left the basement to search, and I didn't particularly want to go down there.

With deep resolve I entered this last room; it wasn't empty like the first one but full of bedroom furniture. I looked around to see if the book was in plain sight, I wasn't that lucky. Beside the usual bedroom furniture there were a desk and a swivel chair, I ran my fingers tenderly over the desk and wondered how many hours Miss Wilkes must have spent going over school papers. I still couldn't believe she was gone. I wasn't much of a friend to her toward her last remaining years, but I promise you, Miss Wilkes, I will not leave this house until I find that book of yours.

Everything was very dusty, which made this more of a mystery to me; this just didn't fit Miss Wilkes personality. The wind was picking up as I heard the windowpanes rattle; I started to whistle to calm my nerves. I began to hurry as I looked through every nook and cranny in the room, but came up with nothing. I had almost given up when I spotted a book on the vanity table. It was so obvious, I couldn't figure why I hadn't seen it when I first came into the room?

I opened the book and realized that it was a diary, Beatrice's diary. I flipped through a few of the pages and noticed the date of the entry was October 15, 1999 almost three years earlier. How very strange that a woman like Miss Beatrice Wilkes would keep a diary. This was such a frivolous thing for her to do, and that was one thing she wasn't. Miss Wilkes life was all about her students; she never had a beau, although at the funeral I did hear some whispers that someone saw a man visit her quite often. I started having a lot of questions about Beatrice, like how come she looked at least twenty years younger? Why the neglect of her house, when at one time she took so much pride in it? Who broke the back window and why wasn't it fixed? This was all so very strange, but maybe the diary would shed some light on it.

I noticed the bad weather was getting closer. I took the book and retraced my steps leading me back to the stairway. I wanted to get to my car before the weather broke.

I was halfway down the stairs when I stopped. I felt a sudden chill that made the hair on the back of my neck stand up. I took a deep breath and slowly made my way down the rest of the steps to the first floor. I could feel Miss Wilkes presence in her house and it wasn't a happy one. I looked over my shoulder as if expecting to find someone behind me. "Oh come on Amanda, you don't believe in ghosts now do you?" I shook my head in disbelief at what I was thinking; I'm supposed to be a sensible person and teacher just like Miss Wilkes. It was then that I realized what I was saying and I repeated it, "Just like Miss Wilkes." We were human beings and not always perfect. Maybe this thought would get me ready for what I was going to read in the diary, if I did indeed read the diary.

Before I got to the back door I could hear the splatter of raindrops against the windows. I wanted to make a mad dash to my car, but it was parked at the far end of a very long driveway. I would be soaked by that time, as I watched the rain come down in torrents. Like it or not I would be here for the duration. With the rain came the darkness. I switched on a lamp next to an easy chair, I was glad the electricity was still on. I found myself talking to myself as I said "There now, Amanda, doesn't that feel better?"

I settled down into an easy chair and stared down at the book on my lap. Dare I read this book? If I did, I felt like I was prying into Miss Wilkes private life. On the other hand, maybe I could solve the mystery of what happened in this house and find out why Miss Wilkes was so adamant on me finding this book. I took a deep breath and begged forgiveness from Miss Wilkes as I slowly opened the book. Again a low rumble of thunder resonated through the house. I wonder if the thunder set the mood of the diary.

The first entry was dated:

May 17, 1961

Dear Diary,

I guess that's how you start one of these books. I have never had a diary, not even as a young girl. I feel silly starting this at my old age, but I do desperately need a friend. The years come and go so quickly that it is hard to believe that on my next birthday I will be 32, with no prospect of ever falling in love and getting married. I guess you can call me an old spinster schoolteacher.

My whole life is children, don't get me wrong, dear diary, I love them, but they are someone else's children. I love children and teaching, but after today I find this is really not all that fulfilling. There is something missing in my life.

I put the diary down and closed my eyes; it was as if I could feel the sadness and her deep loneliness. I wanted to cry for Beatrice. I wondered if I wasn't following the same path. Here I was twenty-eight and still not married. I, too, have many children, but they are other people's children. I didn't have much of a social life. The date I had with Aaron was the first in a long time. I sighed and began reading the entry dated May 17, 1961.

I'm writing this late at night because I can't sleep. After the Mayor's funeral today, I went to the drug store and purchased this book. I am a private person so I don't know how much I will tell you, my new friend.

Signed, your new friend,
Beatrice

The next entry was:
May 18, 1961
Dear Diary,
Today I am very, very happy. He is the reason I bought this book. I met him yesterday and I can't stop thinking of him. I am like a schoolgirl with her first big crush. Lewis, Lewis, even his name sounds wonderful to me, can this be happening to me? His dark eyes are so electrifying. His mouth so sensual and his hands were so warm and firm as they held mine. Few words were spoken between us. It's amazing how touch speaks volumes. We met at the Mayors funeral; Lewis is in partnership with his father-in-law at the mortuary. We talked for just a few moments; he had mentioned that he had heard a lot about me and what a great teacher I was. I wondered if my face turned red as he continued to hold my hand as he spoke to me, I hope not. His last comment, in a whispered tone, was that he was going to call me soon. I cannot believe that I'm looking forward to his call. I know that he is a married man. I also know that his wife is beautiful and that she comes from money. Dear diary I wish you could tell me what to do.

Beatrice

I laid Beatrice's book down; I could not believe what I was reading. Now I really felt guilty about reading her diary. Being a little inquisitive I turned to the next page. This entry was dated

May 21, 19961
Dear Diary,
Lewis phoned me this evening; he wants to meet me at my home. I don't know what's the matter with me. I didn't even hesitate when I said yes. Maybe this means nothing, except that he wants to be friends.
Beatrice

May 25, 1961
Dear Diary,
Why does Lewis have such an impact on me? He came over last night. He told his wife Serena that he had to work late at the mortuary. Lewis said that she loathes funeral homes and only goes there when forced by her mother Lila. I am not the type to lie, but it feels so good to have someone that seems to care for me. I never realized how lonely I was until I met Lewis. In this short space of time he has filled a void that a roomful of students could not fill. I told myself that if our friendship goes beyond this point I would end it immediately. I hope to God I have the strength. He was a perfect gentleman, we sat across from each other as we talked about my teaching career and he told me funny little stories about the people he deals with. He liked my home and the fact that it's away from the hustle and bustle of our little town. When he talked I watched his mouth and facial expressions. It seems that everything about him is so sensual, even the way he moves, I have the crazy notion of being more than just friends. Something in my mind keeps telling me that I'm not that type of person. Sometimes loneliness over comes common sense.

He stayed for just a short while. Serena is expecting their first child and needs more hand holding then usual. He asked me if we could meet here again. I didn't hesitate to say yes. I walked him to the door. As he turned to go he ran his fingers gently down the side of my face. I could not help but shiver, he then pressed his lips to mine in a light kiss, and before I could open my eyes he was gone.
Beatrice

May 26, 1961
Dearest Diary,
I'm afraid I wasn't a very good teacher today. I wonder if my students noticed my daydreaming. After Lewis left, I ran to the mirror and stared

at my lips. I still could feel his lips on mine. He didn't say when he was coming over or that he would call, but I hope it is soon. Where is the Beatrice who, in her childhood, was taught strong values? Can one man change her over night?

Beatrice

June 1, 1961
Dear Diary,
These have been the longest five days of my life. Lewis finally called today. I just came home from school when I heard the phone. I was out of breath when I answered; he laughed and asked me if I was the new school track coach. Oh, it was so good to hear his voice. Before I could answer, he told me he would be here at 7 P.M. That only gives me an hour and a half to get ready.

Love, Beatrice

June 10, 1961
Dearest Diary,
I know I haven't written you these past ten days, but my life has been very busy with school and Lewis. School is out for the summer, but I'm teaching summer school. Summer school is much harder. There is so much to teach in a short space of time.

Lewis's funeral home has been exceptionally busy. He comes at 10 in the evening, but I don't care as long as I get to see him. He has been coming over almost every evening. He has told me a lot about his marriage, which never should have taken place. I asked him if his wife would think it unusual that he gets home after midnight? He said that now that she is in her late pregnancy, she's usually in bed by 8. Talking about her and her coming baby makes me feel guilty and sad. Guilty, because I'm in love with her husband, yes I'm in love with Lewis. Sad, because he's someone else's husband and I can't have him for my own. We haven't made love yet, but I know it's only a matter of time.

My conscience tells me I should stop before it's too late, but I'm afraid it's already too late.

Goodnight dear diary

Chapter 6

I was so engrossed in Beatrice's diary that I didn't notice somebody else in the room until I heard her voice. "Honey, what are you doing in Beatrice's house?"

At the sound of her voice I jumped up from the chair, sending the diary to the floor. "Honey, don't you know that you can't be in here unless your Beatrice's relative?" I stood staring at a little old lady who looked to be in her 90's. She had a kindly face and a twinkle in her eye. She reminded me of a little elf. Before I could answer she continued,

"You haven't answered me, are you a relative?" I shook my head no.

"I see that you have her diary."

"You know about her diary?"

"Of course I do, honey"

I also noticed that she used the word "honey" a lot, which gave her more character. I told her that I had known Beatrice for many years. I also told her how adamant Beatrice was that I have this book after she died. After I told her my story about the diary, she introduced herself, and told me her name was Gertrude Grayson, and how she came to know Beatrice. She said that she knew about the diary but that she'd never read it. She figured it was none of her business. She wanted me to read it in its entirety, and then we would discuss it. Just then a deep male voice said

"Well Amanda, I see you just couldn't stay away from here. Gert, both of you will be in big trouble if some other police officer finds you both here. This place is off limits to you both."

"Aaron how did you know I was here?"

"I am a cop, remember?"

"Now Honey, don't be angry with us. Come to my house, I'll put some coffee on and we'll have it with some of my homemade cookies."

"Miss Greyson, you're changing the subject." Aaron said disapprovingly.

"Aaron Fischer, I knew you when you were a twinkle in your folk's eye, and what is this Miss Greyson business? It's Gert to you or are you that angry with me?"

Aaron stared at her for a minute then started to laugh, which broke the tension.

"Gert, I could never stay angry at you, you are one in a million."

It was then that Aaron saw the book.

"I take it that you found the book?"

"Yes I did." I replied

"Is it as valuable as you thought it would be?"

"Yes, maybe more than I realize."

"Well good, now we all can leave. Beatrice's relatives could be here at any time."

I picked up the book and told Gert that I would drive her home. I was about to go out the door when I turned to Aaron and mentioned the broken window. He said he noticed it when he came in and that he would make a notation about it.

It had stopped raining, with the exception of raindrops that dripped from the trees. As we got to my car Aaron reached for my elbow,

"Since you missed your lunch today I'll pick you up for dinner at 7, and we can continue where we left off."

Aaron said, with a twinkle in his eye and a quick kiss. I didn't like his authoritative sounding voice, but I figured it went along with his job. I just nodded my head yes. Gert raised her eyebrows but didn't say anything. She was a tiny lady about five feet tall and full of spunk. It was amazing how fast we became friends, once we found we had Beatrice in common. Aaron's eyes twinkled when I kissed him goodbye. Gert asked me if that was an apology kiss, I just laughed. When we got to Gert's house I asked her if I could come in for some of those cookies she had offered earlier. She was glad to have company, and as if she could read my mind, she said she was anxious to see my reaction to the diary. As she was making coffee, she said,

"Honey when are you and Aaron going to set the wedding date? He loves you, you know."

I looked up at her in shock,

"How do you know he loves me? You just met me for the first time today."

"I'm an old lady of 93 and I have known Aaron all of his life. I've seen him when he was happy, which is most of the time, and when he was about to get his butt whipped for misbehaving. He comes from a good family just like you do. True, I have never met you but I've have heard your name a thousand times from Aaron. His face would always soften and had a glow about it when he said your name. Today I could see how protective he is of you. I don't know what happened to come between you, but I hope it's all straightened out. I hope you have the same feelings for him because, if you don't, please leave tomorrow and don't come back. I want him to get on with his life."

I put my arms around Gert and said,

"Don't worry Gert, I do love him, but I have to leave tomorrow, to end the school year, but I will be back, I promise you."

We both hugged each other, I suddenly felt very light-hearted. I looked at Gert and said that we should go on with the reading of the diary.

June 15, 1961

Dearest Diary,

Remember when I told you that Lewis and I have not made love yet? Well we did tonight. It was beautiful and wonderful. It was everything I had dreamed it would be. He could not believe that I was still a virgin. I am so glad he was my first love. Oh diary, I love you, I love everybody, I'm so happy. There is only one thing that bothers me. Lewis wants to meet me at the funeral home tomorrow night at ten. I guess I'm a little squeamish about meeting there, but as long as I can be in his arms, I'd meet him anywhere. Dear diary, I can't believe I'm turning into this kind of person, what is happening to me? I'm very tired; I didn't realize making wild beautiful love could make one so tired.

Goodnight and sweet dreams

Beatrice

Gert and I looked at one another with the same questioning look. Why would Lewis want to meet at the mortuary? Gert was the first to reply that maybe he didn't like to travel so far each night, after all Beatrice did live far out of town. Whatever reason Lewis had, I was beginning to dislike him more with each passing entry of the diary. The next entry would tell us more, but do I really want to know more?

June 17, 1961
Dear Diary,

Again I ask you, what is happening to me? Is this what love does to me? Does this happen to everyone or just to people who are starved for love? I really don't know, but I think Lewis has a spell on me. I would do anything for him, anything.

Last night I met him at the funeral home. It was a very dark night; the moon was hidden behind some clouds. The wind was becoming stronger, as if it were brewing up a storm. I was becoming a little uneasy. I didn't like the situation I was in. I checked my watch and I was five minutes early. I made a vow that if Lewis was not on time I was going home; maybe my conscience was getting the best of me. I waited in my car until I saw Lewis's car come down the driveway, it was ten o'clock on the dot. We both parked behind the home so as not to draw attention. The funeral home was a mile out of town and its closest neighbor was the Union Cemetery. Lewis is a very cautious person. He got out of his car and offered me his hand. He told me not to be afraid and that he would be at my side. He did not put on the foyer lights. Lewis said that he knew this place like the back of his hand. Just holding his hand gave me strength. Diary, I don't know if I should tell you any more. I should feel ashamed, but we love each other so how can it be wrong? Lewis took me down a long flight of stairs. When we reached the lower level it was then that he put on the lights. He must have felt me tremble because he took me in his arms and whispered how much he loved me, and that he would never hurt me. He showed me some of the rooms that were on this level. I think it was to put me more at ease with the surroundings. He then took me into the showroom of caskets. I stood in the doorway unwilling to go any further. Lewis urged me to come closer. As he stroked the lining of the casket, I felt as if he was caressing me. He spoke in a soft whisper, using a coaxing tone of words. I felt paralyzed, my whole body rigid with fear. I have never been in a place like this. He sensed my fear, and took me in his arms once again. I murmured that we should have met at my house instead of here. He didn't say anything for a moment; he knew I didn't like being there. He sighed and then led me back to the stairs that led to his office. He mentioned that most people don't feel relaxed in this kind of atmosphere and that he brought me here prematurely. When we entered the office,

Lewis started looking over invoices that were shipped with a new casket that had arrived that day. I stood close to him. The only light was coming from a desk lamp, but my eyes were adjusting to the darkness. He turned toward me so suddenly that if he hadn't grabbed me I would have toppled over. Dear diary, I could see those beautiful eyes of his and feel his warm breath on my face. His hands worked magic as they moved to my shoulders and then slowly down my blouse to its buttons. I couldn't breathe for fear of breaking the spell, as he slowly began to unbutton my blouse. I should have stopped him but I am weak when it comes to him and his kisses. The kisses never stopped as he led me into another room, which was next to his office. I felt as if I was drowning. He started whispering words of love, telling me that he was going to carry me up to the stars and when we were through I would never fear this place again. I did forget where I was. In the darkness and stillness of this place he made me float up to the heavens only to come gently down to earth. The words of love were exchanged often between us.

Pleasant dreams my diary

Beatrice

I put the book down on the table and looked at Gert. She had the same dumbfounded look I must have had on my face.

"Gert I can't believe what I just read. She was my teacher, my mentor; I never thought this of her She always appeared calm and serene. I never thought she had this underlying intensity."

Gert got up from her chair and went over to the kitchen sink and looked out the window. She stood there awhile, before drawing herself a glass of water. When she turned around her face was once again composed.

"Honey, don't be so fast to condemn her, that's what life is all about. Love does many things to a person who has never felt that emotion."

"But in a funeral home? That's bizarre."

"I admit that it's a strange place, but Lewis was not your average man. He was just a nice young man of twenty-six who had the misfortune of marrying into the Costner family."

"Why do you say misfortune? Grandma said they were one of the leading families of the town."

"Sure they were, why? Because they had money and when Lewis came on to the scene fresh out of mortuary school, Ben saw in him a working partner in the funeral home business. He was a young man who could take over a lot of his workload. Serena, Ben's daughter, saw a handsome, young man who would be a perfect match to her beauty. I don't think love ever entered the picture for her."

I looked at my watch and saw I still had two and a half hours before my dinner date with Aaron. Gert poured me another cup of coffee, which made it about nine cups. I looked at her and asked her to tell me more about Lewis so I could understand Beatrice's adoration of him. Gert once again sat down on her chair.

"Honey, did you know that some of the most important conversations were spoken around this kitchen table? My husband Elmer, rest his sweet soul and I would talk and talk about all kinds of things. Maybe to some people it wouldn't be as important, but it was to us. Beatrice would come and keep us company, especially holidays, and then we would have more conversations. Here you are, another generation, and here we sit and talk."

I was anxious to get back to reading the diary. I began to think that Gert knew more about Beatrice then she was willing to say.

"Gert, did Beatrice tell you what was going on in her life?"

Gert paused for a couple of seconds and tool a sip of her coffee.

"Yes and no, now as I hear in her diary I think she was too embarrassed to tell us. After all Lewis was a married man, and they were having an affair in a funeral home. That was something you don't tell your friends, even good friends. I personally think that her never being married, and not having a close-knit family, gave her a tendency to be a very private person. You just never knew what Beatrice was thinking. Could you imagine what her life would be like if this leaked out? That was the 1960's and she was a well-liked teacher, her kids looked up to her. Beatrice would have definitely lost her job, and probably not been able to find another in this county. Then there was Lewis. He probably would not have as much to lose because I'm sure the Costners would cover for him. Like I said, love was never in his marriage. It was just a big façade. For Beatrice, meeting Lewis was the biggest event in her life. To her, he was a man of the world, good looking, intelligent, and even at thirty-two he was on his way to making a small fortune. When Lewis found out that he was to be a father, he decided to play the biggest bluff of his life. Like Ben Costner, Lewis was a hard worker who thought he deserved more recognition. After five years of working side by side with Ben, Lewis still didn't have his name along side his father-in-law. His expertise with handling people "dead and alive" drew praise. Lewis's sense of style was gaining recognition in other communities. The night of the mayor's funeral was the night Lewis and Beatrice met, was the perfect time to play his bluff.

The mayor's funeral was going to be a big event for the Costners. The Mayor was well liked by many. Lewis knew his funeral would draw many dignitaries from surrounding communities and this would be too difficult for Ben alone. Ben wanted Lewis to handle it, but Lewis refused. He told Ben that he needed a vacation. Ben was shocked that he refused him. It wasn't until the eleventh hour that Lewis gave in, but only when Ben promised to put his name next to his on the sign. Ben hesitated and Lewis started to walk away. Ben called out his name and told him that his name would be on the sign when he retired. Ben hesitated and again Lewis started to walk away. Ben called out to him and told him that within three months he would have his name up there in lights next to his. Lewis did not like waiting three months, so he planned to keep after him."

"Gert you do know more than you said. How did you find out? Did Beatrice tell you the whole story?"

"In my many conversations with Beatrice she would sometimes let things slip out."

"Gert you amaze me, tell me more."

"Not so fast. Honey, I can only tell you so much. The rest will have to come from the diary."

"My time here is running out. I have to head back to Milwaukee tomorrow and get my kids ready for their exams. Aaron is taking me out for dinner tonight. I missed lunch today and if I miss this dinner tonight I might not get to see him for another ten years. I guess this mystery will have to wait until I come back."

Gert raised her eyebrows and folded her arms across her chest.

"Are you coming back for Beatrice's sake? Or is there another reason?"

I put my arms around Gert. I only knew her for a few hours but I felt like I knew her forever. I now have two grandmothers in my life.

"I do owe Beatrice, and there is another reason, but I'm not going to tell you until I come back."

I looked at my watch and decided it was time to go. I left the diary in Gert's care. She promised me she would not read it until I came back. I gave her a big hug and she wished me a lot of luck with my other "reason." That Gert, sometimes I think she is a mind reader.

Chapter 7

I was dressed and ready for my date with Aaron, fifteen minutes ahead of schedule. Instead of wasting God's precious time, I decided to start packing. I would be leaving early in the morning. I promised my principal that I would be back for my afternoon classes. I kept thinking of the past two days and how events were turning more and more into a mystery. To tell the truth I don't even know why I thought it was a mystery. Beatrice wasn't shot, knifed or strangled to death. The police evidently weren't called to the scene of her death so there was no foul play involved. Everyone who saw her in the casket said she looked as if she was just sleeping, so why do I, a high school teacher, think something's not kosher? Just then I heard a car pull up into the driveway. It was Aaron. I grabbed my sweater and flew out the door. I hate to keep people waiting. It was then I saw the car he was driving.

"Aaron, where did you get that beautiful car?"

There in the driveway sat a fire red mustang convertible.

"Do you remember Caleb Somers?"

I shook my head no.

"He was the guy everyone called a nerd. He was in my gym class, and He was always hanging around us guys. I felt sorry for him, he never seemed to fit in."

The image of Caleb started to materialize as I ask Aaron

"This is his car?"

"Well he's not a nerd anymore. After high school, he went to the police academy with me. After a couple of years as a cop, he wanted more. He went back to school and became a lawyer.

"Is he married?"

"No, he's a confirmed bachelor who could have his pick of any girl in town."

"So what are you doing with his car?"

"Caleb had to go to Los Angeles to a special seminar. He lets me use his car when I have a very special girl I want to impress. He also mentioned that this car is really a chick magnet."

I had to admit the car and the driver impressed this chick. Aaron held the door open for me and asked if I minded the top being down. It was a lovely May evening and I wanted everyone to see who was sitting next to handsome Aaron in this lovely car. The car and Aaron seemed to be a perfect match. I told him I didn't mind and that I would move a little closer to him if it became cooler. He smiled that wonderful smile of his, and said he thought it was already cooling down. It was so wonderful being with him that I could have kicked myself for letting all these years go by without him. Aaron turned the car onto the state highway and after a couple of blocks headed south out of Hartger's Grove.

"Where are you taking me?"

"I hope you're hungry, and you should be after missing lunch today. I never forgot how you loved roasted duck with orange sauce."

I looked at him questioningly. Aaron saw the puzzled look on my face.

"Don't you remember our graduation night? I took you to this romantic restaurant and you ordered duck? When you left for college you kept writing about how you love duck but couldn't afford it on a student allowance."

"Yes I remember, but maybe it wasn't so much the duck as it was the company that night."

"I was hoping you would say that Amanda."

I sighed in contentment. Life was so great. Aaron took hold of my hand and it was warm and protective. Just then I mentioned to him that I thought the weather was getting a little cooler, he patted the seat next to him, and I moved closer to him. We made small talk the rest of the way.

The restaurant was situated in the midst of a huge stand of pine trees. To get there we had to drive a half-mile of winding driveway, which was lovely. I realized how sentimental Aaron was; he even reserved the same table we were sitting at on graduation night.

We ordered our dinner and Aaron ordered the wine. I settled back against the chair and studied Aaron. The ten years had matured him to the point of making him more handsome, if that could be possible. With the rest of his fine qualities, I had wondered how he escaped the clutches of other women. As if reading my mind he asked me if I had a beau in my past. I thought a moment before I answered,

"There was someone in my life, but he was missing some of the qualities I thought were important in making a good marriage. I was busy with my kids to have much of a social life. I found out that they were not just my kids at school, but they were also my family. I strived to be so much like Beatrice, and that took a great deal of my time. I really didn't realize how fast the years were going by until I came to Beatrice's funeral. What about you, why aren't you married?"

Aaron looked down at his utensils before answering.

"I was engaged to a girl from Chicago. We had the wedding date set, but she didn't like the fact that I had planned to move back to Hartger's Grove. I convinced her to give living in a small town a try, she agreed. When she met Caleb and found out that he had been a cop who became a lawyer, she was really impressed. She became obsessed that I follow his footsteps. I told her how I loved this town and its people, and I wanted to be their protector, but she just couldn't understand. Eventually we parted ways, I think deep down you were always on my mind. After we broke up she decided to try for Caleb, but he wasn't interested. When I saw you at Beatrice's funeral, the love I had for you came bubbling up to the surface, like Old Faithful, the geyser."

"What about Anne Bradley? From the way she looked at you, I would say she's in love with you."

"Anne? She's my fellow police officer. I had a couple of dates with her but we just didn't click."

The waitress came with our dinner. I found that I was very hungry. I heard from someone that clearing the air with someone you love will do that to you. My duck and Aaron's steak were out of this world. I like to think it was seasoned with friendship, love, and happiness. What a beautiful combination.

After dinner and a couple of after dinner drinks, I told Aaron that I really had to get back to the farm. I had to be up early to head back to Milwaukee. When we pulled into the driveway, Aaron turned off the ignition and turned to me and asked,

"Do you know what I would like to do next?"

I had an idea, but I wanted to hear it from him, so I just shook my head and said,

"I know we skipped dessert at the restaurant, and I don't have any food in the house, so I can't imagine what you would want."

I tried to keep a straight face as I watched his,

"Do you remember when we were in high school we used to talk about exploring your grandparents hay loft in the old horse barn? We never did because for fear your folks would find us in the tide of passion. Amanda, there is nothing stopping us now. How about it Amanda…Hmmm?"

It took but a second to respond.

"I'll race you to the barn!"

It took a few minutes for our eyes to become adjusted to the darkness. There was a full moon but the barn was so well made that it didn't allow much light in. I could hear the horses snort and shuffle their hooves as Aaron spread a blanket he found in the back seat of his car. I commented that he must have been a boy scout. He came so well prepared.

"Aaron, I feel absolutely silly doing this in a barn when we have a nice soft bed in the house, besides what are these horses going to think?"

"Do you know what they are going to think? See that gelding in the doorway? He's thinking what a lucky stud I am. Now come here woman, let me love you like you've never have been loved."

He took my hand and we both fell into the hay, laughing until I could feel the tears trickle down the side of my face. Then there was silence as we looked into each other's eyes. We knew what was coming next, but we wanted to savor the moment. I could feel Aaron drawing closer, his warm breath gently fanning my face. It was when our lips met that I heard Aaron whisper "Amanda, marry me." I wanted to shout "Yes" but his kisses took my breath away. Little by little our clothing came off. I could feel the night air caress my body. Aaron never stopped kissing me. I felt like I was drugged. I was floating to the ceiling. I kept thinking that this was what heaven must feel like; I didn't want him to stop as I strived to become one with him. He pulled me on top of him. His chest was wet with perspiration. I felt myself wanting to scream, to laugh, to cry, and then it happened. It was like fireworks on the 4th of July. They exploded all at once for Aaron and I. I wondered how long did it take, a minute, an hour?

Aaron pulled the blanket over us. He nestled me closer to his heart. This is where I belonged. I thought of Beatrice's diary, the part where they made love in the mortuary, and how she too, felt like she was riding to the stars. In that moment, I knew this barn will always be special to me.

I awoke to feel Aaron tickling my nose with a strand of hay.

"Did I tell you how beautiful you look tonight?"

"No, you didn't" I replied. It was then that he started to tickle me and I was very ticklish, he remembered that from our high school days.

"Ok, ok you did tell me that I was beautiful, lovely, drop dead gorgeous, and cute as a button."

"Amanda, didn't you say you had this nice soft bed? Besides I think we're keeping the horses awake."

He helped me down from the hayloft; we had one blanket between us. I started to put my clothes on when Aaron stopped me.

"Why are you putting them back on? They will come off as soon as we're in the house. Come on I'll wrap this blanket around you, Miss Prim and Proper school teacher."

"Humph, I did fit that title two days ago, now see how you corrupted me? What about you Mr. Police Officer, the moon is full and we're on a busy highway, somebody is bound to see us."

"Amanda you worry too much, besides, if we get arrested, I know a good lawyer friend who will plead our case."

I shook my head; another quality I'd forgotten about Aaron was his sense of humor. Before I could say another word Aaron made the fifty-yard dash though the barnyard to the house.

"Hey, wait for me!" I yelled

"Come on slow poke, I'm freezing, and the house is locked."

"Serves you right Mr. hot shot." I called back as I slowed up my walk to a crawl.

We laughed a lot that night and by the time the sun started to peek over the horizon, I found out that I enjoyed being a wild carefree creature, out of school. I took a shower and tried to comb the hay out of my hair. It was a good thing I had started to pack the night before. Aaron awoke and beckoned me back to the bed.

"I can't, Aaron, no matter how good looking and sexy you look to me. I promised my boss that I would be back this afternoon. Besides, I will be only gone for three weeks, and then if you want, we can pick up where we left off."

"Pick up where we left off? Amanda, do you realize how much I want you and need you in my life? Doesn't marriage come into your mind or at least an engagement ring?"

I could not believe how angry Aaron became.

"Aaron, why are you so angry? Of course I want a ring and marriage. I thought that when I came back we could talk marriage at that time. Ten years is a long time to be apart. We should plan to have this summer together to get reacquainted."

Aaron looked at me for a long time before he slowly got out of bed and walked towards a chair where his jacket was lying. He pulled out a long white envelope and said, "Sweetheart, it seems to me that we have become very well acquainted these past two days, I don't want to take a chance on losing you again. There will be an opening this fall at the high school. I took the liberty of getting an application. If you fill it out now, by the time you come back you should know if you have the job. Besides when they hear you are one of Miss Wilkes protégés you'll definitely get the job. Please, open the envelope."

I took the envelope from him and opened it. It was then that a ring fell out. I slowly picked it up. It glittered and sparkled in the morning sun. It was breathtakingly beautiful.

"Oh Aaron, it is beautiful, it's exquisite." was all I could say before I started to cry."

"Amanda please be my wife, my one and only, and the mother of my children?"

I looked down at him; he looked so serious and yet so comical with hay sticking out of his hair, on bended knee, in just his shorts.

I hesitated for a moment to let his question sink in. I knew Aaron would ask me to marry, but somehow I thought it would be later in our courtship. I could see he was getting a little worried by my hesitation. It was then that I threw myself into his arms and cried, "Yes, yes I will marry you!"

He pulled me down on the bed, and what started last night, started once again.

"Amanda, do you know I think you're definitely a hussy."

"Yes I am, but this time I have a ring of approval."

Chapter 8

My students were happy to see me. They all agreed that it seemed like I was gone a month instead of three days. Everyone noticed my ring. The girls ooh'd and ah'd, the boys wanted to know who the lucky guy was. Of course everyone wanted to know when the big day was going to be. They asked if I would be leaving Milwaukee to live in Hartger's Grove. I told them that Aaron and I hadn't set the date yet, and that I would be leaving after school lets out, to live in Hartger's Grove. They could not fathom leaving a city to live in a small town. The questions went on and on. It was a good feeling to be back with my kids. In September there would be new students. A teacher touches so many lives, how very fortunate we are

I counted the days till I would be back with Aaron. I missed him so much. I had gotten a phone call from Grams, asking how the farm was holding up. Before I could answer, she asked me if I could watch it for the summer. They were going to make a side trip to Alaska to visit some friends, and would not return home until August 1st.

"I hate to impose on you like this, but our friends are getting older and we have to see them while we can. That's all our friends seem to do, is sit and read and talk about their last surgery. Gramps and I are going there to shake them up a bit. I hear they have some fabulous casinos there as well as golf courses, that sounds great don't you think?"

I told her there would be no problem. I also told her about my engagement to Aaron, she was speechless, but only for a moment.

"You mean that wonderful boy you were going out with in high school? The one I liked so much?"

"Yes that's the one."

"Isn't he in the military?"

"No, Grams he's a police officer in Hartger's Grove."

Grams was just delighted about Aaron and that he was a police officer, which meant we would be living in her town.

"Have you set the date? What does your mother say? Maybe I should just come home and help you plan your wedding."

"No we haven't set a date and we will not get married before you and Gramps come back. I didn't tell mom yet, but I will before I head back to Hartger's. Grams, I have so much to tell you about Beatrice's funeral and about Aaron, but I have to go for now, this phone call is costing you. I'll see you in August. Give Gramps a big kiss and hug for me."

Before she could say anything else, I hung up. I love Grams more than my own mother. How they could be mother and daughter is beyond me, they are so different. I never understood how my mom could send me away for four years. It was the best thing that could have happened to me, but at the time I didn't realize it.

Aaron called me just about every day. He would say that he wanted to hear my voice and that it was not just a dream that we were together again.

I had canceled my lease on the apartment. It always expired on the last month of the school year. I also turned in my resignation to the school board, hopefully, I would have that job in Hartger's that Aaron was so assured I would get. Living on the farm for the next couple of months solved a lot of problems. Grams came though again.

Exams came and went. My kids and I were busy cleaning out our desks and lockers. It would take a couple of days to grade papers. It was at this time that I was notified that I would have to come in for an interview at Hartger's High. It looked like the job was mine and I would be teaching the eleventh grade. Instead of a wedding shower, my friend Natalie threw a packing and cleaning party. There were a lot of hugs and tears all around.

On the last day of school and my very last day in Milwaukee, I decided to put the last box of books into my car. My kids had been very helpful all that morning, not once did I have to carry anything to my car. Lord only knows if there will be enough room for me to drive.

I stood at the front of my classroom and looked around. The six years that I was here went so fast. The room was now empty of students, maps and books; yes, I'm going to miss it here.

It was past noon when I said my final goodbye to the principal and my fellow teachers and headed for the front parking lot. It was then that I noticed a police van with a group of my students surrounding it. I quickened my pace as I wondered if there had been an accident. I noticed my car was missing, panic started to set in.

"Here she comes." yelled Nancy Evers, one of my students
"Surprise Miss Harding!"

Surprise wasn't the word for it. There in the middle of my kids stood Aaron in his police uniform with the biggest grin on his face.

"Miss Harding, aren't you surprise? We got you a going away present. All of us kids put our money together, we hope you like it."

They handed me a big package wrapped in brown paper and twine, but on the package sat a very fancy bow. Nancy, who was one of my most animated students, exclaimed that Aaron had furnished the paper and twine, but the girls supplied the bow. I looked at Aaron and saw the love and admiration in his blue eyes and the words "I missed you." on his lips. Life is truly wonderful.

"Come on Miss Harding, stop flirting and open your gift," Billy Sty yelled over the heads of my other kids. I noticed one of the boys was busy polishing Aaron's police badge that was pinned to his well-pressed shirt, and the girls were staring at him in adoration. I thought I overheard one of the girls say, "Boy, is she lucky." Yes I sure am. I was a little embarrassed with all the attention and of course this didn't escape the boys.

"Hey, Miss Harding, you made a nice catch." After that a camera was brought out and a lot of photos were taken, some posed, some candid. Aaron brought out scissors and cut the twine. One of the girls warned him to be careful so as not to ruin the gift. As the final wrapping was removed, I stared down at the most beautiful oil painting of my Arabian horse, which my grandparents had given me the first month of my four-year stay with them. They told me they would supply me with the hugs and kisses, but my horse would give me the friendship and freedom to ride the wind.

I was speechless the portrait was beautiful. It's coloring was the exact duplicate of my horse "Tohamis." She was a dark bay in color with a sprinkling of dapples on her sides, which showed in the sunlight. She had a white star on her forehead that was partially hidden by her forelock. The portrait made her look so real, that you almost felt the wind caressing her mane and tail. The artist captured her white marking on her left hind foot. Her head was posed high as if she were blowing into the scent of spring.

"Do you like it Miss Harding? Hey guys, she has tears on her face, is something wrong Miss Harding?"

"Don't be stupid, she's crying because she's happy, right Miss Harding?" asked Nancy Evers

I took an armful of kids, and through my tears, kept mumbling my most heartfelt thanks. Just as I thought I had reached my last student, I inadvertently reached Aaron and was about to hug him. It was hard to see though my tears. When I heard one of the boys call out "Hey Miss Harding, he just bought the paper and twine, we gave you the gift, no fair hugging him."

Everyone started to laugh at the remark Aaron handed me his handkerchief so I could wipe the tears and blow my nose. I looked fondly at my students and asked,

"How did you kids get this photo of my horse?"

"Well Miss Harding, you always talked about your horse, so we asked Miss Natalie to get a picture of your horse, and she did, but she had to be sneaky about it. Mrs. Crawford the art teacher did the painting," replied Nancy.

I just shook my head in wonderment. What wonderful kids, I will truly miss them. Aaron looked at his watch and mentioned that it was time to go. He was working the graveyard shift, but he was concerned about me driving one hundred and thirty seven miles in my old car. He had volunteered to bring a prisoner from Hartger's to Milwaukee for a court date. My students were in on the surprise. With their help and the help of my fellow teachers they put all my belongings into the police van.

Once again the goodbyes were painful, but I knew there would be a two and a half hour drive back to Hartger's Grove, and I knew the kids were anxious to start their summer vacation. So, after more hugs from my students, we all went our separate ways to whatever life hands us.

I looked up at the principal's office and saw him waving goodbye. Most of my fellow teachers were standing in the main entrance waving and throwing kisses. Once again I could feel the warm liquid trickle down my cheeks and realized that parting was indeed, such sweet sorrow.

Chapter 9

I kept looking in the rear view mirror at the school. It was getting smaller until it disappeared from view when Aaron turned the corner and headed down the expressway. He reached over and took my hand.

"Hon, are you having second thoughts about us getting married?"

"Oh Aaron, never, I just feel bad that I let those ten years slip through my life. It was my decision that we became just friends. When you asked me to marry you, for an answer, I just stopped writing to you. Oh Aaron I'm so sorry for all those wasted years."

I looked over at Aaron: it was then he said, with a twinkle in his eyes,

"I know how you can make it up to me."

I looked at him questioningly.

"Since we are still in the big city, we could go to the court house and get our marriage license, how does that sound?"

I thought it over for a moment, if he only knew how much of a wonderful idea it was, but then I saw Grams face and I couldn't deprive her out of being at our wedding. She did so much for me all these years. I told this to Aaron and being a sweet wonderful man, he understood, but remained persistent.

"Amanda, I just have another idea. We could marry and have a family started by the time your grandparents come back from Alaska. I think she would certainly forgive us when she saw that there would be a great grandchild to love."

"Oh Aaron, I think you and Grams are going to get along just fine."

The two and a half hour drive passed quickly. We talked about my last days at school and he told me what was going on in Hartger's since I had left three weeks before. I asked him how Gert was. He said she was as feisty as ever, but she misses you and is anxious to get back to your little adventure. Aaron looked at me suspiciously

"Amanda, what are you and Gert up to? Is there something about Beatrice that you're not telling me?"

I looked at him very innocently and with my fingers crossed told him that we were reading that book we had gotten from Beatrice, and that it was very stimulating for both of us. Aaron's eyebrows rose skeptically.

"A 93 year old woman and a 28 year old woman find the same book stimulating? I find that rather hard to believe."

"Well why not? Beatrice was a very intelligent woman and why wouldn't we find the same book to our liking?"

I was hoping Aaron would not ask me the name of the book, so I changed the subject quickly.

"There's a MacDonald's, let's stop for a hamburger. I'll treat since you came all the way to Milwaukee to pick me up."

We received a lot of wondering looks when an officer escorted me out of the police van

We arrived at the farm around five P.M. Aaron helped me unpack the van and we stored everything in Gramps basement except for my clothes. As I headed for the bedroom closet, I could feel Aaron right behind me. I laid the clothes on the bed so I could locate some room in the closet, then I felt Aaron's hands on my shoulders. He turned me around to face him, and said,

"I'll take the police van back to the station, bring back my own car and come back here to keep you company, how does that sound?"

All the while Aaron was talking his face and lips were so close to mine. His offer was so enticing, and the bed so near that if I moved an inch we both would topple onto it. As much as I wanted to, I knew he would have no rest before he went to work on the graveyard shift. I took a couple of deep breaths and led him out of the bedroom. I would probably be kicking myself for the rest of the night, but I could not let Aaron go to work without sleep.

"I can't let you come back, you have to be back at work in six hours. You need your rest, so as much as I want you to stay, you can't."

"Amanda, you look so irresistible and it's been over a month since we've been together, how can you say no to my offer?"

I slowly pushed Aaron towards the door, my knees getting weaker with each step.

"Okay, I can take a hint, but I'll see you around noon, if not sooner." replied Aaron

After an enticing kiss and a sharp salute, Aaron turned and walked to the van. As he opened the door he turned and said,

"You know, there have been reports of bear and coyote sightings in this area, are you sure you don't want me here to protect you?"

I shook my head and blew him a kiss.

"Goodnight, Aaron, I'll see you tomorrow, sweet dreams."

"You know I'll have them," he said with a wink and a wave.

After Aaron drove off I stepped back into the house, and finished unpacking. This really amazed me, I never considered myself a clotheshorse, but seeing all this accumulation of clothing made me wonder if I had enough closet space.

After awhile I decided to take a break and phone Gert. I was hoping she didn't go to the casino. Gert, had mention that a bus has been picking her up and driving her to a near by casino, which she really loved. From what I gathered she was frugal with her money, but it was the friendship of Roger the bus driver, and the social aspect of being with people her own age. I was glad she was getting out of the house. Her phone rang three times before she picked up the receiver. She sounded young and feisty; you'd never believe she was ninety-three years old.

"Hi Gert, its Amanda."

"Honey your back, are you here for good?"

"Yes Gert I'm here for good."

"Honey, you don't know how hard I prayed that you would make the right decision. Aaron is such a wonderful young man, and he's just right for you."

"Aaron and I are getting married, but we haven't set the date yet."

"What are you waiting for girl? I hear that one of the girls who work with Aaron is batting her eyelashes at him."

"Gert we just met again after a ten year absence. We have a lot of catching up to do, besides Grams want to be here to help with all the details, and I can't cheat her out of that."

"If you don't mind a suggestion, I think a summer wedding would be just great."

I just laughed; I think her and Aaron were made from the same mold.

"Gert, can I come over tomorrow morning so we can pick up were we left off on the diary?"

"Why certainly, why don't you come for breakfast so we can start early."

I agreed to be there at seven thirty the next morning. I was hoping she would have said around nine but Gert was from a farming family and even seven thirty was getting a little late for her, so I didn't push it. I was anxious to once again get back to Beatrice's diary. It's been almost a month since Gert and I last read it, but it seems longer than that.

After exchanging a few more pleasantries, I hung up the phone. I was at a loss for something to do. My thoughts turned to Aaron. It had only been an hour since he left and I felt like something was missing from my life. Gert was right, what are we waiting for? No, its not we, its me. What am I waiting for? Everything was moving so fast in my life. The death of Miss Wilkes, was a shock to me, meeting Aaron after ten years and the rekindling of my feelings for him, Aaron's marriage proposal, which happened so soon after we again met, and my leaving Milwaukee before I even found out if I had my new teaching job here in Hartger's.

I was always the cautious type, so this was so unlike me. Beatrice's diary was a shocker to say the least. I probably shouldn't be reading it, but there was something strange about her death, and I felt that if I finished reading her book I would find the answer. Yes, everything that happened is enough to make my head spin.

I sat down in Gramps' easy chair and thought about my next step in my life. It was then I decided that tomorrow would be the first day of a most glorious life. I'm getting married to the most sweet, wonderful, handsome, compassionate, and sexy man in the world. If I missed any other beautiful descriptive words it was purely by accident. Furthermore the wedding date would be set as soon as possible.

I took a deep breath and decided that tomorrow I would have a candlelight dinner for Aaron. We could set the wedding date and discuss wedding plans. Suddenly I felt very light hearted and full of energy. I decided the house needed a good cleaning, and just maybe if I had the time I would plan on what I was going to wear. No, I'm going to take time, because this was going to be an extra special evening for Aaron and me.

Chapter 10

The alarm clock went off at 6:30. I had my clothes laid out; all I had to do was shower, brush my teeth and comb my hair, and I was out the door with a half hour to spare. I was at the back door when I remembered I had to call Aaron. There's certainly no rest for the wicked, I mumbled to myself, as I raced back into the house. I dialed the department number when a sugary sounding voice said,

"Good morning, Hartger's Grove police department, Officer Anne Bradley speaking, how may I help you?"

The voice didn't sound familiar, but her name sure did.

"Good morning, this is Amanda Harding. I would like to speak to Officer Fischer, please."

"Amanda, is this really you?"

Before I could answer, she went on in a very fake accent,

"I do declare it is you, I wanted to talk to you at Miss Wilkes funeral but there were so many others who wanted to talk to me so I really didn't get the chance to say hello. After awhile I wanted to catch your eye, but you two where so engrossed in each other, but Aaron did apologize for leaving me the way he did. That Aaron is such a sweet boy."

I wondered where she picked up the southern accent, and as far as Aaron was concerned he was no boy, but all man and I should know, I was almost tempted to tell her that, but I called to speak to Aaron and not her.

"Anne, please may I speak to Aaron before he leaves for home?"

Evidently she didn't get the message because she went on as if I didn't say a word to her.

"Everyone here is talking about our new school teacher, and here we are chitchatting with one another like the old friends we are."

I held the phone away from my ear and wondered what planet she was from. I knew that Aaron was about due to finish his shift, so as soon as she took a breath I again asked to speak to Aaron.

"Why sure, Sugar, you know I surely do enjoy working with him, I even rode in a squad car with him, we had so much fun. He really is a sweet guy and so good looking, why he reminds me of a younger version of that actor who stars in the series, "Dead Zone," don't you think? We are taking bets here at the station to see what girl will lasso him. She will definitely have the catch of the department. By the way Sugar,

There she goes again with that sugar.

"Is this business or pleasure? Oh shoot, he just left by the back door, I'm so sorry Sugar."

"One more sugar and I'm going to throw up," I thought to myself.

"Would you like to leave a message? I can give it to him tomorrow morning; I'll be working with him all day, isn't that wonderful?"

Evidently, Aaron kept his personal life to himself and she didn't know we were engaged, or maybe she did know and was up to her old tricks again like when we were in high school Anne was a very vindictive person.

"Hello? Hello Amanda, are you still there?"

"No, there is no message, I'll just call him on his cell phone, thanks Anne," for nothing, I thought to myself.

With that I hung up and dialed Aaron's car phone. Somehow my day that started off well was slowly going down hill. I remember Gert telling me about some girl batting her eyelashes at Aaron; could she be talking about Anne? When I thought about it, any girl could fall in love with him. He had all the fine qualities you could possibly want in a husband. He was kind, gentle, considerate passionate and has a great sense of humor. On top of that he was handsome, in a movie star way? Humm, maybe like the actor Anne mentioned, only in a more rugged sort of way. Before I could think of another hundred words to describe Aaron, he answered his phone. I could feel myself getting warm just listening to his voice.

"Hello?"

"Hi Aaron, its Amanda."

"Well good morning Sugar."

I groaned when I heard him say sugar.

"How's my favorite girl this morning? Did you sleep well? I sure hope you did, because I want you full of energy, energy enough to handle me tonight."

"Aaron, Honey I've got a surprise for you but I need time to fix it, so would you please come over at 7 for dinner instead of noon?"

I hated to put him off, but I did need a day to get ready.

"Hon, you don't have to surprise me. I only need a couple of hours sleep; I can come over at 11 and help you with the surprise."

"Aaron, please, do this for me. I want to show you how much I appreciate you picking me up from Milwaukee."

There was silence at the other end of the line.

"Besides you need your sleep, you hardly slept at all these last couple of days." I said pleading with him. I crossed my fingers hoping he would understand, finally he said,

"Well, okay, Amanda, I'll give you the day, but I want you to know how much I love and need you, and I would do anything for you. I don't think I'll be getting much sleep because you are always on my mind."

After Aaron hung up I made a promise to myself that I would make it up to him that night. I reached for my bag and headed out to the garage. My granddad had an extra car, which he said I can use whenever I need to. "On a farm you always need two cars," was his favorite saying when Grams would push him to sell it. I always felt good when thinking about them both. I could feel my happiness pill kicking in.

Chapter 11

I was barely in Gert's driveway when she came running out of the house, that woman never ceased to amaze me. After a lot of hugs she put her arm around my waist and led me into the house. I had stopped at the local baker shop and bought some sweet rolls to finish off our breakfast. It was a custom Grams always had when I was living on the farm. If we did not have them for breakfast, we then had them in the evening with coffee.

Over breakfast, Gert kept asking me about the time I spent in Milwaukee. I filled her in about the gift my students gave me and about the cleaning and packing party my friend Natalie gave me. I also told her how hard it was to leave everything that was familiar to me in such a short space of time. Gert interrupted me and said,

"Amanda, honey, you have one of the brightest futures a girl could ever want, you have Aaron. If I was 62 years younger I would fight you for him, and I would make sure I was the winner."

I was silent for a moment when Gert and I started to laugh as we talked about ourselves rolling on the floor, fighting over Aaron, while he sat like a king with a smile on his face to see who the winner would be. I think it was at that time that I promised myself never to look back.

I told Gert about my plans for the evening with Aaron and that we were going to set our wedding date over a candle light dinner. I didn't tell her about my nightwear fashion show. That part came to me while I was driving over to Gert's. I was planning a surprise Aaron would never forget. I did tell her that I had to leave at noon so I could go food shopping and shopping for other necessities. I told Gert to remain seated while I cleaned off the table and did the dishes. I was just about done when Gert went to get the diary. She asked me if I would be more comfortable reading it in the living room. I thought for a moment and said,

"Gert don't you know that some of the most important conversations where held around this table?"

She laughed at that and opened the book to the entry we left off on, dated June 17, 1961. We reread the entry of the 17th; it was when Lewis took Beatrice to his funeral home for the first time. We didn't know what he really had in mind for her. Did he fully intend to seduce her there and if so why did he show her the casket room? After he saw how uneasy she was about being there, he took her back upstairs to his office, where they did make love. I thought about Aaron and I in the barn and how that barn became a special place for us. I wondered if that's how the funeral home seemed to Beatrice after she made love to Lewis.

According to the entry a whole week had gone by before she again wrote in her diary.

June 24, 1961

My Beautiful, beautiful diary,

I am so much in love; I could climb the highest mountain and shout it to the world, "I'm in love with Lewis Vormen,' but I can't, it's only our secret. I know Lewis will never leave his wife for me. This bothered me at the start, but now I feel that as long as I have half of him, I will be satisfied. What would be the alternative? I'd be just another very lonely spinster schoolteacher.

We have been together for over a month, and I'm so thankful to Lewis. Thankful? That is an unusual word to use, but yes I'll say it. Without him I would never experience love, not just sexual love, but the love that makes me feel so happy when I think of him and so suicidal if I'd lost him. I realize how empty my life would be without him. If I could only have a child, my life would be complete. I'm not telling Lewis about my secret longing, it would upset him. Serena is about to have his baby and he often says that one child is more than enough for him. Well my diary, I'm going to close for now. Thank you for listening.

Love, Beatrice

Gert shook her head and said how all alone Beatrice sounded, you almost wanted to be there for her and put your arms around her. I agreed with Gert, but I also thought Lewis a user. He wanted it all, a wife and a mistress on the side. After a little more discussion we continued on to the next entry.

June 30, 1961
Dear diary,
I am so shaky, I don't know if I can even think clearly. I met her today. I met Lewis's wife, Serena. As long as I had never met her, I fooled myself into thinking that what Lewis and I were doing would be ok, since its not hurting anyone. Serena was like a fog that appeared ever so often in our conversation, no face, no body, just a name, but I was so wrong. I was standing in line at the checkout counter of our food store when I heard her laugh. I looked up and saw her entering the store with her mother Lila. Serena is beautiful, even in her eighth month of pregnancy she glows. She spied me and walked over I thought I would faint. My hands gripped the shopping cart. She introduced herself and asked if I was the high school teacher everyone was exclaiming about? If I said yes or no, I don't know if it mattered to her because she'd went on talking as if she never asked me a question. She went on to say that she hoped I was still teaching when her child started high school. Serena was about to leave when she looked me right in the eye and laughingly warned me to behave myself since I was a teacher and we had to set a good example. Oh diary, I'm so ashamed of what I've gotten myself into. I just wanted to crawl into a hold and hide. I learned to hide my feelings because of being alone all these years, so when she gave me a quick hug, I just nodded my head. If somebody had just seen our exchange they would think we were friends. Diary, I don't think I will see Lewis tonight. Serena is not a fog anymore.
Beatrice

I looked at Gert and said,

"Gert, I think you know more than you're telling me. I know Beatrice didn't suffer a normal death. Please tell me anything you can about Beatrice."

Gert pondered this request for a minute, and then asked me if I wanted another cup of coffee.

"Gert, sometimes you're exasperating."

"Honey, I will give you some answers but not today, your time is almost up."

I looked at my watch; it was 11:30. It would take me about 20 minutes to get home.

"Ok Gert, but I'm coming back tomorrow morning and I would like some answers."

I really didn't want to sound so harsh, but I was getting desperate for answers about Beatrice's death. The more I knew about Lewis, the more I knew that Beatrice didn't have to die when she did.

"You, young lady, will not get any answers until you tell me your wedding date."

"Gert, you can certainly change the subject." I said laughing. We then hugged each other goodbye.

Chapter 12

Aaron is a meat and potato man so I bought pork chops and the rest of the trimmings that went along with a pork chop dinner. I also went to our Wal-Mart to see what they had in Fredric's of Hartger's Grove, lingerie that is. They didn't have much of a selection, but what they did have, didn't leave much to the imagination. I decided on a red nightie. I was always partial to red; it went well with my dark hair. I stopped at a liquor store and the clerk was very helpful on what kind of wine goes well with pork

It was 5:00 p.m.; I had the table set with Grams best dishes, glasses, and utensils. For a finishing touch I put long tapered candles on the table. I stepped back to give the table a once over, it looked like a dining table I had seen in a women's magazine. The meat was simmering and the peeled potatoes were on a low flame. I had purchased a chocolate cake, just in case we get to that part of our dinner. The table and food looked and smelled great now it was my turn to get ready.

I took a leisurely bath and splashed on my favorite perfume. Since I loved red I decided to go all the way from dress to shoes in red. I stepped back and looked in a long mirror. I felt like the girl in a diet commercial, somewhere the song "Lady in Red" popped into my mind and I started to hum it. I was never good at remembering song lyrics.

Aaron arrived 15 minutes early, carrying a bouquet of red roses with white baby's-breath. He gave a long low whistle and said,

"Surely I have died and gone to heaven, I see an angel in front of me. Amanda, you look beautiful."

He set the flowers on the table and walked towards me, arms outstretched. I slipped into his arms, his fingers pushed up my chin. I was staring at his blue eyes; slowly his lips kissed my forehead, my eyes, and the tip of my nose. My legs turned to jelly as I slid my arms around his neck. His gentle kisses turned firm as his tongue sought mine. Suddenly he stopped, his breathing ragged, he held me away from him and said,

"God Hon, we've got to get married soon. I'm going crazy constantly thinking of you. Since you came back into my life all I can think of is your lovely face, your dark hair, and flashing dark eyes. I want to make you mine forever, not just for a night."

I felt tears trickling slowly down my cheeks, as I tenderly touched his face. Aaron took my hand and placed it over his heart. It was then I heard myself say,

"August."

"What did you say?"

"August is a lovely month to get married." I said

"Oh baby, you don't know what your words just did to me!"

He started laughing as he swung me around. It was then I could smell the chops burning.

"Oh my God the meat is burning."

We both rushed to the stove to rescue whatever was left of the meat.

"Move aside wife, I'll save the day" he laughed and looked at me in wonderment.

"Did you just hear what I called you? Wife, wife, God I love the sound of it.

We started laughing and kissing but this time the kisses were not out of passion but of happiness. The evening was lovely, the meat wasn't as burnt as I thought, and the flowers made a beautiful centerpiece. We even got to the chocolate cake, which he ate with gusto.

After clearing the table we decided to have the rest of our wine on the porch. It was an old fashion porch, which wrapped around the front and side of the house. Gramps had built it and it fit this old farmhouse to a T. It was well into June. In Wisconsin the weather could be warm with a hint of a hot summer ahead, or on the cool side leaving everyone asking, "When is summer going to get here?" Tonight, the weather was a little on the cool side so we snuggled close. Katie, the teenager who boarded her horses on our farm, came over to feed and groom them. With a twinkle in his eye Aaron made a remark about them taking over our favorite barn. I turned a little red thinking about that special night. Katie saw us sitting on the porch and said,

"Hi Aaron, hi Amanda, beautiful evening isn't it? Amanda I saw you at Miss Wilkes funeral, but you were so busy talking and hugging a certain someone, I didn't have a chance to talk to you." before I could say anything she went on,

"I heard you are going to be our new high school teacher. Maybe I'll be lucky enough to have you this year; I'll be a junior in the fall. Well, I have the gang to feed; they love that new pasture grass in the spring."

With a quick wave, she turned and walked over to the barn. The horses all walked single file in back of Katie. She was a born equestrian. Katie was only eight when she started riding but she had a knack even then.

"Word sure gets around fast, next they will be talking about our wedding." I looked at him questioningly; again he had that same twinkle in his eyes.

"Well, Sweetie, when I heard that you got your job, I told Anne and I guess she fueled the gossip mill, you know how small towns are. Tomorrow they will be surprised again, when I tell them a certain beautiful young lady will be marrying a certain lucky guy in August."

"Oh, are you going to tell Anne? She'll be shocked since she didn't know we were engaged."

I know I must have sounded catty, but when I think of her sugary voice, my blood begins to boil. Aaron looked a little surprised at what I said.

"Anne knew we were engaged, I told all the guys at work."

I told him about the conversation with Anne and how she enjoyed riding in the squad car with him and the fact that all the girls were making a bet on who would be the lucky one to lasso him, almost implying that she could be the lucky one. Aaron laughed and then said,

"Well I do declare my new wife to be, sounds a little jealous." He started tickling me and I started laughing and squirming away from him.

"Stop it, Aaron, Katie will be coming out of the barn at any minute and since when did you pick up that fake accent?"

With a wink he said, "Why from Anne of course."

This time I was the one who straddled Aaron to put a chokehold on him. About that time Katie came walking passed the porch.

"Show him whose boss Amanda."

"Hey Katie I thought you were on my side!"

"Only if you tear up my speeding tickets," replied Katie.

"No way kid, don't you know speed kills?"

Katie climbed into her old beater of a car, waved and hollered,

"Suit yourself Aaron, beat the heck out of him Amanda." with a wave she drove off.

Things quieted down on the porch, when Aaron took a pocket calendar out of his wallet.

"Ok, my little wife to be, let's pick a date when I can make you legally mine."

We both decided on the third Saturday of August. It would give me a week and a half before school starts. I would have to go and be assigned my classroom, and meet the principal and my new fellow teachers. Aaron and I would be going on a very short honeymoon. My major was in biology, when I decided on that choice I did it because of Beatrice, I wanted her to be proud of me. I taught juniors in Milwaukee and I would be teaching the third year of high school here as well. I told Aaron that I would call Father O'Malley first thing in the morning and set up as appointment so we could meet with him, we both want a small wedding. Aaron's parents are wonderful people. When Aaron told them we were engaged, they gave him hugs and said it was about time. I suggested to Aaron that we all meet and discuss our plans, after Father O'Malley okayed the date for our wedding. I decided to contact my parents ASAP about our upcoming wedding. I almost dreaded that.

It was starting to get dark, so we decided to go in and do the dishes. Aaron asked if there was any more wine, which there wasn't, so he offered to go to the liquor store. I knew he wanted to get out of doing dishes so I gave him my blessing, besides I figured I would need the wine after I talked to my Mother. He gave me one of his melting kisses and left. As soon as I heard him drive away I dialed up my parents' house. Dad answered, and after a few endearments he went to get Mother. I always favored my dad more then my mom, but I did blame him for his lack of assertiveness where Mom was concerned. Our conversation was brief, I told her about my upcoming wedding and the date. I also told her that it would be a small wedding, with Father O'Malley officiating. She sounded somewhat disappointed. Mother always wanted me to marry one of her best friends' sons, it didn't matter that I didn't like him. She always said that love grows on people, I wondered, at the time, if that's how she felt about my dad. She then asked me if I would get married in Milwaukee, so one of her monsignor friends could marry us, again I told her no. As a last remark she said that she thought Grams had too much influence on me. I chose to ignore the statement. I mentioned I wanted Dad and her to meet Aaron's parents and we would discuss the wedding plans. She didn't say anything for a moment, and then gave me a date that would be convenient for them. I told her fine, and that I loved her and Dad and that I would be seeing them in less than a week. I let out a sigh of relief just as Aaron entered the house with the wine.

"Quick, I need a drink!"

"What's the matter, Hon? I know you must have been talking to your mother."

"Yes, we set the parents meeting for next Sunday. You will have to get hold of you parents and see if that date is ok with them."

Aaron opened the bottle of wine while I started the dishes. I didn't realize how late it had become until I saw Aaron start to yarn.

"Gosh that wine made me a little drowsy. I really shouldn't be driving until this passes," he said with a sly look.

I looked down at him sitting in the recliner, I looked at my watch, and it was 11 o'clock and said,

"Oh Aaron, I'm so sorry I've kept you so long. I was rather hoping you would spend the night, you can sleep on the sofa and I will cancel my nightwear fashion show and have it when you are more alert.

"Whoa... what did you say?" He pulled me down on his lap and asked me "Now, my little vixen, repeat what you just said."

"I was hoping you could spend the night."

"No the other part."

I pretended that I had to think what I had just said to him.

"Oh the fashion show! I just want to do a survey to see what kind of sleepwear you'd like on me."

"It's a miracle! I'm not tired anymore, when does the show start? Woman you never cease to amaze me. You know I must have read your mind because I just happened to have my police uniform hanging in my car just in case."

"You are indeed a very clever man." I replied.

Room by room the lights were turned off. So as the neighbors would not wonder why Aaron's car was here all night, he put it in Gramps garage. I was glad Gramps had a three car garage, Grams would sometimes grump about Gramps putting his tractor in the garage, and that it would scratch up her car. Gramps would just pinch her on her cheek and tell her that his tractor was putting class into their garage, since the tractor was a John Deere, and in his eyes that was the best tractor ever.

Aaron pulled me on the bed beside him, and asked me about the fashion show. I didn't want to tell him what it was all about so I just told him to be patient, besides I didn't have my courage up to snuff.

I looked at his face and saw him trying to hide a grin, his dimples getting deeper; it was then that I decided to give him the show of his life. I asked him if there was any wine left, there wasn't much left, so I went to the refrigerator and took out a can of beer instead, no I took out two cans of beer; I decided I would need reinforcements. I closed the blinds in all the rooms, I really don't know why I did that, since the bedroom blinds would have been sufficient. Maybe I needed the time for another beer, I noticed I was on the second can and I just might need a third. When I went passed the bedroom to the kitchen, Aaron was slipping out of very tight jeans, I didn't realize he had such cute buns. Oh my gosh what was I thinking, this wasn't my first time with Aaron, but the other times where in the dark or under the covers. Oh Lord what did I get myself into? It must have been the wine I drank; I wondered how many glasses of wine did I drink? Where was that other can of beer? I wasn't a drinker, an occasional glass of wine at dinner with friends but hardly ever by myself. Golly this second can went down even faster. In my fuzzy mind I counted how many more cans I had seen in the refrigerator. I think there were six left. It was then that I heard Aaron's voice asking me when the show would start. Yes, another beer wouldn't hurt. I told him I'd be there in a few minutes between gulps of can #3. It's funny how alcohol gives you that false confidence. I had my red nightie hiding between towels in the linen closet. As I took off each piece of clothing I started to sing "Lady in Red" over and over. I only knew the first line, and I think I heard Aaron ask if I was alright. When I put on the nightie, I looked into the mirror and struck a provocative pose. I slowly opened the door, and stuck my arm out in a come to me motion. I then flung open the door the rest of the way and proceeded to the bed in a hip swaying motion that I had seen some movie star do in an old movie. I could hear Aaron's wolf whistle. He threw back the covers and I could see him reaching for me, everything moved in slow motion. All of a sudden, the lights went out! Sometime in the night I could feel the bed sway. To me, it wasn't a bed, but a ship, that was sailing on rough seas.

Chapter 13

The dawn came too early, and it was going to be a clear sunny day, too sunny for me. I tried opening my eyes, but it hurt to do that. No it wasn't my eyes that hurt, it was my head. I never had a hangover before but there is a first time for everything. I kept hearing a man's voice singing in the distance. Oh no, he's singing "Lady in Red." I have to find the radio and shut it off. Where is Aaron? What must he think of me? He'll probably call off the wedding thinking that he would be marrying a bimbo who drinks like a fish. Oh my head!

"Well good morning my wife-to-be, my super sexy, hip swaying, lady in red. I brought you some coffee."

There stood this six-foot hunk of a guy dressed in his well pressed uniform, his badge picking up the early rays of the morning sun. He was like a knight in shining armor holding out a steaming cup of coffee to me, a poor wretch of a stripper. I could just die a thousand, no make that a million, deaths.

"I'm so sorry; I wanted it to be an extra special evening for you."

"Oh Honey it was, you were great and sexy. I saw a side of you that I will always remember."

When Aaron made that comment I started to cry. I can just hear him tell our kids and then grand kids about their grandma who has the nickname "The Red Swinger." I fell back on the pillow and pulled the sheet up over my head, and started to hic-up. Aaron pulled the sheet back and said,

"Hon, I have to go to work. I hate to leave you like this but I'm leaving you a glass of water with two aspirins, and a cup of coffee if you want it. I'll call you later this morning to check on you."

He kissed me on the lips and again called me beautiful as he left. He was being so kind to me, I don't deserve him. I could smell his aftershave; he was so…so clean smelling. All of a sudden the green-eye of jealousy picked up its blonde head and said in a southern drawl.

"Good morning, Aaron Sugar, oh you look so handsome and smell so yummy. Come a little closer so I can guess the brand of cologne you all are wearing, why it's the brand I bought you for your birthday, how wonderful. What, you are going to marry that outcast from Milwaukee? You poor sweet man let me comfort you. She didn't even make you breakfast? She what? She had a hangover, oh I feel so sorry for you. Why don't we jump into your squad car and go have some breakfast at the Java Cup, or better yet we can go to my apartment for a quickie...breakfast."

Then I could hear Aaron replying, "I thought you would never ask."

Oh I felt so awful; I could not believe all these things were happening to me, even jealousy. I have to pull myself together and then I thought of Gert. I was supposed to be at her house by 7:30 and it was already 7:10. I'll call her and see if I can come after breakfast. I couldn't move too fast because the room was starting to spin. She answered on the third ring. With luck she still didn't have the breakfast started, she must have sensed I was feeling under the weather and felt sorry for me because she said I could come whenever I was ready. I hung up and tried to decide the next course of action. Aspirin, then a shower, and maybe some toast and tea.

An hour and a half later I arrived at Gert's. As soon as I entered her house she told me that Aaron called looking for me, she said he sounded worried about me. She also asked me why I was wearing sunglasses when it was clouding up to rain. It was amazing how fast the weather changes in Wisconsin. I hadn't even noticed that the sun had disappeared. I took off my sunglasses; Gert took one look at me and said that she would get me a couple of aspirins. She had me lay down on the couch and covered me with an afghan that she had made. After a kiss on the forehead, she left me to my misery.

A couple of hours passed when I awoke to thunder and the rain bouncing off the metal roof. Sometime in the midst of sleep, I had heard the phone ring. I opened my eyes and saw Gert sitting in an easy chair knitting. I slid my legs off the couch and realized how much better I felt.

"Feeling better honey?"

"Yes I am, but I'm very hungry."

"I bet you are, go and freshen up and I will make lunch."

With her kind concern I could once again feel the warm tears slide down my face.

"Oh Gert, I don't deserve you or Aaron, I ruined what was to be a beautiful evening. Then I come to your house and cry like a baby, and now you are waiting on me hand and foot just like Grams used to when I was a child."

"Nonsense child, that's what friends are for." She said that she would bet any money that I hadn't ruined Aaron's evening. She also said if I wanted to tell her what happened, I could tell her over lunch. As I repaired my make-up, I thought about what she said and decided to tell her. I figured that at 93 years of age she had probably heard it all.

Gert and I just sat down to lunch when a squad car pulled into her driveway. Aaron stepped out of it and headed for her house. Gert chuckled and said it was lucky she didn't have any close neighbors because there would be gossip galore, with the police being here all the time, and a handsome one at that. Gert called for him to walk in before he had the chance to knock. H e looked so breathtakingly handsome.

"My two beautiful girls together, how lucky can a guy get? I was just passing by and thought I would drop in for a cup of coffee."

His eyes kept searching my face; despite my makeup he could still see the dark circles. He told me he had some good news. He laid his hand across mine and told me that he had gotten hold of Father O'Malley and that the third Saturday of August was fine with him and that we would have to come for marriage classes. It was still raining, but inside my heart, the sun had just come out. Gert clapped her hands in joy and said that one evening soon she would have a celebration dinner for us. A short while later I walked Aaron out to his car, he wrapped his arms around me and said softly,

"I loved that red nightgown of yours, I think it would look great on you on our wedding night. But then maybe it wasn't so much the gown, but who was wearing it."

He then gave me one of his drowning kisses and drove off. I stood there watching his car, until it disappeared, unmindful of the rain hitting my umbrella.

"There now, don't you feel better? He loves you despite whatever happened last night. He called two times while you were sleeping, asking how you were. He wasn't just passing by, because I know his beat is on the other side of town."

I told Gert what happened the night before, picking my words carefully. I told about the candlelit dinner, about the two bottles of wine plus three cans of beer that I had consumed, but I did not tell her about my red nightgown, that was Aaron's and my secret. I told her that I was not a drinker and that it must have hit me like a sledgehammer, I even told her about Anne Bradley and the jealousy I felt because of her. Gert never interrupted me but I could tell she was trying to keep from laughing. She asked me why I was jealous of Anne Bradley?"

"Gert, why am I jealous of Anne? Fist of all, she has a figure to die for; she is blonde, and most men love blondes. She is in very close contact with Aaron on a daily basis; she always liked Aaron from the first day of high school till the present day. I think she became a police officer so she could be close to Aaron. When I saw her at Beatrice's funeral, she could not stand close enough to Aaron, and the look she gave him was like an invitation into her bedroom. Are those enough reasons to be jealous?"

"Amanda, I really don't think you have to be jealous of anyone. Aaron only has eyes for you, I really don't know Anne well but I do know women like her. It seems she would like you to believe that there is something going on between Aaron and her. I'll tell you something else; jealousy can break up any relationship. It can eat away until there is nothing left, I speak from experience, but that's another story. From what you told me about her, I would say she is playing a game with you, and if she wins, well… don't let her win. Enough preaching for today, lets get on with Beatrice's diary."

We both took our favorite chairs preparing ourselves for a long afternoon of reading and discussion. We discussed Beatrice's last entry of June 30th and how she accidentally ran into Serena in the grocery store. I looked at Gert and said,

"Can you imagine how she felt, coming face to face with the wife of the man you're having an affair with? Serena looks her right in the eye and tells her to behave because she is a schoolteacher who has to set a good example. It was almost as if Serena had an inkling of what was going on."

Gert shook her head in disagreement, then replied,

"You have to know what kind of person Serena is. She wasn't the type to play a cat and mouse game. Serena would go right to the jugular. Lewis was her property, the Costners owned him lock, stock, and barrel, or so they thought. After being with them, Lewis became as crafty as they were, perhaps more so."

"Gert, yesterday, I mentioned that I thought you knew more about Beatrice than you're telling me. I will be getting married in less than two months and I will have to get ready for that, plus school will be starting soon after, so time is limited, please help me out here. Beatrice did so much good and I have let her down these last three years of her life. I believe you're holding back some of those missing pieces of the puzzle. If I was a gambler, I would bet my bottom dollar that Beatrice did not die a normal death, and that maybe it wasn't even her in the casket."

Gert looked guilty when I said the last sentence. I saw her face pale and her hands shake. She got off her chair and went to the kitchen window and stared out into her yard. I was beginning to realize that she always did that when she was in deep thought or about to say something profound. She turned to me after a few minutes and asked me if I really wanted to know all the details, no matter how sordid? I said, yes, in a quiet tone of voice.

"All right Amanda, but first you have to know something about the Costners, starting with Serena herself. She was the Costners only child. She was almost everything you could want in a little girl. Serena had beauty and brains and knew how to use them to her advantage. The one thing she was missing was love. Love was not given freely in the Costner family. Her mother, Lila, was vain and unforgiving. Serena's father was a workaholic who had little time for his family, except to bring home a nice big paycheck. At the time, Costners was the only funeral home in Hartger's Grove and surrounding areas, and because of this, Ben Costner had a lot of work.

It was Serena's eighteenth birthday when her father heard of a young man just out of mortuary school. Lewis graduated in the top ten of his graduating class, was twenty-six and had great potential. Ben had heard of him from one of his colleagues at the graduate school. Lewis also heard that Ben was interested in him and that he had a beautiful daughter named Serena. Like any red-blooded male he was struck by her beauty and flirtatiousness. Serena's mother, Lila, was not happy with the whole situation. She wanted all the money the funeral home brought in, but if Serena married Lewis, Lila would have to share the money. Lila had other plans for Serena. She saw the immediate attraction between the two young people, but this was not in her plan.

There was one particular young man whose father ran a very successful real estate company and Judd Landis would be the heir apparent to this firm. In Serena's senior year, she was crowned prom queen. Her date was Judd Landis. Her mother was ecstatic. Serena's father wanted her to go to college in the fall. Her mother wanted a marital partnership of Costner and Landis.

Fate has a way of changing lives. The martial partnership was not to be and neither was college. Serena's mother had to settle for second best, which she wasn't used too. Since nobody in town knew much about Lewis, Lila became his P.R. person. In a way Lila was a con artist, if she lost one way she would find a way to save the situation. She would tell all the ladies at the beauty shop and bank, which were her two favorite places, how wonderful and talented Lewis was, and how much in love Serena and him were.

It didn't take much P.R. since Lewis was a handsome and very likeable young man, who had a way of handling people "dead or alive." Six months to the day they first met, Lewis and Serena announced to the family and the town's people that they were to be married.

The Costner/Vormen nuptial was the biggest wedding Hartger's Grove had ever seen. Lila saw to that. There were eight bridesmaids and eight groomsmen; many of the men were classmates of Lewis. Lila made sure that the newspaper editor was there to record the event, from the church, to the reception, and to the young couple leaving for their Hawaiian honeymoon. Yes, it was a lovely day in Hartger's Grove.

They say love is blind and it didn't take Lewis long to take the blinders off. Serena wasn't the kind of wife Lewis wanted, but he would some day inherit the very lucrative business. He decided he would just wait it out. Serena had a lot of her mother's bad qualities, vanity for one, too demanding for another, and just plain spoiled. What Serena wanted, she received.

Ben eagerly looked forward to his young son-in-law's help. Lewis had a way of soothing the women when their spouses died, almost to the point of underhanded flirting. If the widow's marriage hadn't been too happy, the widow would pick up the vibes almost immediately. Lewis was also very good at the art of mortuary cosmetics. He impressed upon the customer how important it was to look not just good, but beautiful or handsome (whatever the case may be) to the very end.

Lewis talked Ben into buying a more expensive line of caskets. He convinced him that people should be made to feel guilty if they buried their loved ones in a plain wooden box.

Serena's mother's life was money, and after awhile she saw Lewis as a great asset and he did make the money roll in. Lewis's motto was "It's always best to plan ahead. Put your money in a trust fund with us. Pick out your casket now and save." Lewis had all the right selling gimmicks and it paid off.

Every Friday morning, Lila went to the bank to put in the week's receipts and then proceeded to the beauty shop where she would brag to the town's gossips about her son-in-law. The way she talked you would think this was an on going love relationship, but it was not mutual. Lewis knew the real Lila, the moneygrubber, the vicious, and selfish person who was only happy when she had money in her hand. Her daughter was following in her footsteps. Lewis loved money and what it could do for him. So as not to feel guilty about it, he would argue with himself, he would often think that if he had a loving wife, money wouldn't mean as much to him.

Chapter 14

It was just after their fifth wedding anniversary that Lewis met Beatrice. The town of Hartger's Grove's mayor passed away and the funeral was to be at Costners. "The place to be laid" was Lewis's secret motto. It was a huge funeral since the mayor was well liked by his constitutes. The town gossips watched with well-trained eyes. They gave sympathy to the family, yet noting who they were and what they were wearing. Lila played her part to a T, sitting next to the bereaved wife and family. She offered any help she could, even to the point of getting more Kleenex for them.

Lila seldom came to the funeral home. She came only when she wanted to make an impression on a family of the deceased.

The mayor's funeral was where Beatrice first met Lewis. He spied Beatrice as soon as she walked into the room; Lewis always had an eye for pretty women. When they saw each other there was electricity in the air. He had heard about the young schoolteacher, who was a hit with all her students. He went over to her and introduced himself.

Maybe if it had been another time, and if he'd had a real wife, things might have worked out differently. Fate, once again, had a mind of its own, and Lewis just knew he had to have Beatrice. He saw qualities in Beatrice that Serena lacked. Serena was far prettier but shallow. Beatrice's face was intelligent, soft with compassion and animated when she spoke. Lila watched Lewis converse with the young schoolteacher but she wasn't worried. The woman was no comparison to her daughter Serena's beauty."

Gert stopped talking, looked at her watch, and then poured us another cup of coffee. I too looked at my watch, it was almost 2:30 and I knew Aaron would be getting off his shift in an hour. I wanted to check with him about our meeting with his parents. I was so happy he got in touch with Father O'Malley, which took one task off my hands. I was also pleased that

Gert let me in on what happened between Beatrice and Lewis, but I had another question for her.

"Gert, was that Beatrice's body in the casket?"

Again Gert was silent, when she did speak it was just one word, "No."

"Whose body was it? I asked excitedly. Gert walked over to one of the recliners in her living room and beckoned me to do the same, and then she began again.

"It was one of the worst rain storms of the season when Lewis's son, Ronald Allenton Vormen made his entrance into the world. By this time Beatrice and Lewis had been seeing each other about two months. He insisted that they always meet at the funeral home. Because of the storm, the power and phone lines were down. Ben took Serena to the hospital and stayed with her until the baby was born. Once Serena was settled into her private room, Ben decided to chance the bad weather, and go down to the mortuary to check on Lewis. He didn't recall any new bodies coming in. He also thought that Lewis should know that he had become a father.

Ben let himself in; he had to push the door closed because of the intensity of the wind. The funeral home foyer was bathed in darkness, except for the flashes of lightening that lit up the room. The darkness didn't bother Ben; this was his real home for a great many years. In this place, he was away from the constant nagging of Lila. God how he hated that woman, he wondered if he had ever loved her.

Ben had been in this business for over twenty-five years, he'd spent a lot of nights there until Lewis came and told him that he would take over. It was a struggle at first but finally he decided that Lewis was right and that maybe he should start enjoying life.

Ben was very pleased with Lewis's work; the young man had certainly proven himself in the five years since he had joined forces with Ben. They not only had the town's people but clientele was also coming from farther away. Costners now had two chapels under one roof to service the people. Ben thought about Lila, and the trouble they'd had with her about taking out the loan for the new addition. She didn't want to spend the extra money, but Ben figured that, once the loan was paid off, she'd be happy again.

Ben was slowly making his way to the stairwell when he heard a muffled sound. At first he thought it was the wind, but then he heard it again, this time it sounded more like a moan. Thinking that Lewis might have fallen and been injured, he quicken his pace down the steps. By the time he was at the bottom of the stairs he hurried over to the casket room. Once there he pushed open the swinging doors and stood there for a moment. When his eyes adjusted to the dark, Ben thought he saw movement in the center of the room. He slowly inched his way around a few of the caskets that were in his way. What he saw made his whole world come crashing down upon him. He grasped his chest and staggered toward the coffin. Ben reached out his hand to grasp the box. The pain was like a vise, twisting and tightening every muscle in his chest. He couldn't breathe, he tried to talk but no sound came forth, except a grasp as he slowly collapsed to the floor.

Lewis picked up his head and opened his eyes. Drops of perspiration beaded his forehead and bare chest. A hand reached up to pull him back to her waiting lips. Thinking that the storm was playing tricks on his hearing, he continued his trail of kisses, slowly traveling from her lips and down her throat. Oh she was so delicious, he ran his hands down the length of her body, making her squirm and then push up into his hard body. Suddenly he heard that faint sound again, like air hissing out of a tube. He abruptly stopped kissing her and laid his hand gently across her mouth to silence her. He rose up to his knees and with one long leg stepped out of the casket. What his eyes didn't see, his foot found what he had heard. Lewis picked Beatrice out of the casket and stood her onto the floor. Their naked bodies were bathed in sweat and started to shake as if in shock. His father-in-law lay on the floor, eyes wide open, with his mouth opening and closing like a fish gasping for air. Lewis knelt down to find a pulse and it was very weak. He ordered Beatrice to go upstairs, get dressed, and go home, and that he would call her later. Lewis could see she was scared. He took her in his arms and tried to comfort her."

Gert stopped talking and lowered her head. I was about to ask Gert if she was ok, when she looked at me and said,

"I think its time for you to go home, honey."

"But Gert, I can't go home at this stage of the story."

"Yes, you can go home. Aaron will not be happy with us if we keep him waiting again, besides I'm not feeling well, I have a headache."

When I heard that, I realized how hard I was pushing her. I put my arms around her and thanked her for what she did tell me.

We agreed to meet the following morning, but first after breakfast, if I hurried I could see Aaron at work. We were going to a movie later that night.

As luck would have it, I just got to the station on time. Aaron was walking to his car and didn't see my car pulling into the parking lot. I was just about to call his name when Anne came running out of the building and over to his car. She put her hand possessively on his arm as they stood there talking and laughing, and then she handed him a bag. He then got into his car and she blew him a kiss as he backed out of his space and out of the parking lot. He hadn't seen me, and I was glad. He might have thought…. oh I don't know what he would have thought. Gert's words came back into my mind about jealousy, and how it could ruin a relationship, but damn it, that Anne makes it so difficult not to be jealous.

The farm was only ten minutes from the police station, by the time I was walking into the house, I heard the phone ringing, and it was Aaron.

"Hi Hon, were you running, you sound a little out of breath." Before I could say anything he continued in a teasing voice, "Okay, you don't have to say it. I know, just hearing my voice takes your breath away."

Aaron didn't know how right he was, not only that, but the sound of his voice made me feel weak in the knees.

"Are we still on for the movies tonight, or would you prefer to stay home, have some wine, and maybe you could even show me that dance you started last night?"

I started laughing,

"Sorry Aaron, I'm all danced out for this week, but maybe we could have some wine after the movie."

After more small talk, we set the time for the movies and planned on having hamburgers at a drive-in near the theater. We had to drive 37 miles to see a movie; Hartger's Grove was a small town, too small to have a theater. We didn't mind the drive, since it was a straight drive on a nice highway. I changed my clothes and applied new make-up, I still had a half hour to spare, but that was okay, since I wanted to rehash some of the things Gert told me about the Costner family. The last thing Gert mentioned was Beatrice being in the casket with Lewis, which shocked me. Lewis was certainly a smooth talker. If I could remember correctly, Beatrice was afraid to be in the funeral home at night. Now she was making love in a coffin. That's hard to believe. Lewis could probably talk anyone into buying the Brooklyn Bridge. Beatrice would have to be truly in love with him to do that. I wondered what I would have done if Aaron suggested something so macabre.

It was then that I heard Aaron's car pull into the driveway. I looked out the window, expecting to see his older car; instead he was in the "red chick mobile." I raced to the door just as he was about to knock; I threw my arms around him and almost knocked us over in doing so.

Aaron started to laugh, I love hearing him laugh.

"Wow, this is some greeting."

I told him I do this to all the guys who drive up in a red mustang convertible.

"Oh so you like me just for my car?"

"Mm yes, but there are a few hundred other qualities I like about you. Besides that's not your car, it's Caleb's."

"Maybe, maybe not." was Aaron's reply.

"That's a strange answer." I said

"Well I thought maybe I could buy it. When we start a family, we could trade it in for a eight-passenger van. If you continue to wear that red nightgown, we should fill that van in no time."

I could feel my face getting rather warm; I wondered what went on after I passed out, I was too embarrassed to ask.

It started off as a wonderful evening; just being with Aaron does that to me. Then we got to the movie theater, and that's when it started.

Before the movie started, we decided to go to the concession stand and buy some popcorn.

Suddenly I heard this squeal and a fake southern drawl. I made a metal note to ask Aaron were she picked up the accent when she was born right here in Hartger's Grove.

"Aaron, Aaron, Sugar I haven't seen you in all of five hours. Fancy meeting you here in this little ole theater, isn't it a small world?"

With that greeting she gave Aaron a great big hug. I kept thinking about what Gert said about jealousy, and that helped tone down my feelings.

"Amanda Harding, my, you certainly have changed since I last saw you. Being a schoolteacher with all those kids around does take a toll on ones looks. But aren't you lucky to live in an age where we have all those wrinkle remedies? Oh, I do declare since we are all going to see the same movie, why don't we all sit together? Aaron, Sugar, do you remember when you took me to a movie, now let me see what was the name of it?"

Before she could say another word, Aaron took me by the arm and said, "Sorry Anne, Amanda and I want to be alone; we have ten years to catch up on."

With that comment, Aaron and I walked into the dark auditorium. I happened to turn and glance at Anne and her poor date. Anne stood there with her mouth hanging open, saying to her date, "Well can you imagine that, and just today I gave him some of my home-baked cookies…humph."

I didn't say anything to Aaron about seeing him and Anne in the parking lot, but it does look like I have some competition in the sweets department.

The movie was great but on the scary side, which gave me all the more reason to cuddle up to him. Ever so often I could feel Aaron's eyes on me, he would then lean over and kiss me. As we left the theater we walked arm in arm over to the car. It was a beautiful evening, in the low 70s, with a hint of a breeze. Aaron stopped abruptly, muttering under his breath. I looked around to see what the problem was and found it.

I saw Anne standing by the car, running her fingers, with those long fake nails, over the hood of the mustang.

"Hi Sugar, is this your car? If it is you'll just have to give little ole me a ride in it. I just love convertibles."

Aaron turned to me and said guiltily,

"I was going to keep this a secret until later tonight when we were alone, but I think that now is as good a time as any. Amanda this is my wedding gift to you. As of this morning the license and title to this car are in your name."

I didn't know what to say as Aaron gave me a deep devouring kiss, and then handed me the keys. I looked over at Anne, but all I could see was her backside as she pulled her date away from us.

Aaron opened the driver's side of the car and ushered me in. His blue eyes twinkling in the dark night and those beautiful smile lines deepening.

"Oh Aaron, I love it, but this car must be very expensive, are you sure we'll be able to afford it?"

"Honey, nothing is too good for you, and yes we can afford it, the car is paid for."

I put the key in the ignition and the car came to life, I didn't realize this car had so much power.

We had just entered the house when the phone started to ring.

"I looked over at Aaron, "Who could be calling at this hour?

"Hello? Hi Grams how are you? Are you okay? Is Granddad all right?"
"I was just going to ask you the same question. I've been trying to reach you since early this morning. Granddad and I are just fine; we're in Seward, Alaska, enjoying ourselves. You didn't answer me, are you alright?"

"Yes I'm just fine."

"How is that fine young man of yours?"

I looked over at Aaron and winked,

"I probably shouldn't say this because he might get a big head, but he's just great. I was at Gert's house during the day and then Aaron and I went to a movie."

"How is Gert, I just love that little old lady, is she as feisty as ever?"

I laughed at that and said she was probably more so.

"How did you get to meet Gert?"

"After Beatrice Wilkes' funeral we met and have become great friends."

"Oh I'm so happy to hear that I know Gertrude will take good care of you while we are away. Now tell me, have you set a wedding date? You know I think October is a lovely time of the year for a wedding."

That was the question I dreaded, I turned to Aaron and motioned for him to open the bottle of wine. I figured I'd need it after I told Grams the wedding date.

"Well I heard that August is also a fine month, especially the third Saturday of August, so that's what Aaron and I decided." I said in a rush.

There was silence for a second, although I thought I could hear Grams thinking, and I was right.

"Now let me see I'm getting tired of traveling, so if Gramps and I came home by mid-July there should be enough time to arrange a wedding shower and help you with other plans. What did your mother say?"

"Well you know Mom." I said with a sigh.

"Say no more; sometimes I wonder if they mixed up the babies at the hospital, but she looks so much like her father, we had to claim her."

I started laughing; we were on the line for a few more minutes then decided that the call was costing Grams a fortune. After assuring Grams that there will be enough time for her to make plans for my shower, we hung up with "Give my love to Gramps"

Grams and Gert was definitely a couple of my favorite ladies. Aaron was sitting in the recliner, holding two glasses of wine.

"Are those both for me?" I asked laughingly

"Nope, you just get one. Come over here and sit on my lap, you look so delicious standing there, that I wanted to carry you off to the bedroom and devour you."

I settled onto Aaron's lap and took a sip of my wine.

"It didn't sound like your Grams gave you much of an argument about the wedding date?"

"Well, first of all, we're going to have to find an apartment as soon as possible. They are cutting their vacation short and will be coming home by mid-July."

"What's wrong with my apartment? You can move in with me."

All the while Aaron was talking he kept kissing my neck sending shivers down my spine.

"Aaron, get serious, I can't move in with you, how would that look to everybody? I can just read the town's newspapers, "Small hometown school teacher caught in wild sex games in boy friends apartment.""

"I hope they mention that red nightgown of yours I would be the envy of all the guys at work." added Aaron. As a matter of fact, just this morning your neighbors, Jake and his wife, you know the one who spends her day gossiping, well they saw me leave here this morning, asked if I had a good night, I said I had one of the greatest. He then gave me the thumbs-up sign, and his wife fainted."

"Aaron they didn't, you didn't!" I replied, horrified

"Ok, ok we'll go apartment hunting." he said leaving it at that. I looked straight into his dreamy eyes to see if he was joking with me about Jake and his wife, Aaron can joke with a very straight face, but his face was deadpan serious. We'll probably be married fifty years and I'll still wonder if that's what happened. We were quiet for a while, enjoying each other's company and the fine wine, when my thoughts turned to Beatrice. This is how she must have felt about Lewis, only for her there would never be a wedding, and she never could tell the world about her feelings for him, how very sad. Gert told me that Lewis was a very handsome man, tall with thick black wavy hair, and eyes that were dark and smoldering. He definitely sounded like a ladies man. From what Gert could remember Beatrice was not his first affair, but Beatrice thought that she was the only one he truly loved.

"A penny for your thoughts Babe, you have such a serious look on your face."

"Oh I was thinking about Beatrice and wondered what her last three years where like."

"I think her life was just fine. She and Gert were great friends."

How I longed to tell Aaron all I knew about Beatrice, maybe someday.

"Did you see Beatrice around town?"

Aaron's forehead wrinkled a little, then he said,

"Come to think of it, I didn't. From time to time I'd see Gert and I would ask her how she and Beatrice were doing. She'd say they were like two peas in a pod and doing great. I told her if they needed help I'd be there in a second. Both ladies were very independent people."

"Can you tell me what Beatrice was doing since I left town? Like when she retired, was there a party for her? When she died did they take her body to the hospital and perform an autopsy? Who paid for her burial?"

"Whoa Honey, not so fast, why all these questions?"

At first I didn't know how to answer Aaron's question without making him suspicious. I had to take it slow and easy. I really hated deceiving Aaron.

"Beatrice really did a lot for me. I had gotten a letter from her, it sounded so different from all the rest of her letters. It was vague, something was bothering her and that was the last letter I received from her. I should have followed through but I didn't. I chalked up the letter to being written on a bad day."

"It probably was, but she didn't want to bother you with it, after all she knew how busy you were in Milwaukee. She figured you'd write her when you had the time. Honey, I think you are too hard on yourself."

"Aaron you still didn't answer my questions."

"No, there wasn't any retirement party for her, a letter was sent from her to the school board requesting no party. I suppose it would be hard enough for her to say goodbye to her students and fellow teachers without having to go though it again in a very public place. From what I gathered, Beatrice was a very private person. As for her death, Gert called Vormen's when she found Beatrice dead on the floor. After pronouncing her dead, Lewis and Ronald took the body to the funeral home. Since she was the town's beloved teacher the burial was at their expense. The rest is as you saw it, any more questions?

"Oh, I have a ton of them. "Aaron, didn't you think something was strange when you saw her house that afternoon with Gert and me?"

"Men don't look at a woman's cleaning ability like women do. I was just in hurry to get Gert and you out of there before another officer found you there."

After listening to Aaron, I figured I'd better stop asking all these questions, and made a promise to myself to find the truth about Beatrice's death. I changed the subject quickly,

"Aaron it's too bad you didn't bring your uniform along, you could have stayed here tonight."

"We police are always vigilant, always ready."

With that, he left the house and went to the trunk of his car, my car. He pulled out his uniform and swaggered back into the house.

"At your service, Mademoiselle." he said with a deep bow. I just nodded my head and beckoned to him with my finger. No words were needed; he knew what room to go to.

There was no fashion show, no dance, no two bottles of wine, and no three cans of beer. We undressed each other very slowly, showered with many kisses in-between, and then came the sexual love. Every time we make love, it's greater than the last. From lust to gentle love, how could it get any better?" I wondered to myself.

We both fell asleep in the early hours of the morning. My last thought was that poor Aaron would not get enough sleep again. When the alarm went off, we both made a seven-yard dash to the bathroom. We were going to flip a coin to see who got to take a shower first. Before I could say boo, Aaron pulled me into the shower stall with him, saying we were saving money on the electricity and water. How could I argue with that, but the shower did take longer then usual.

Chapter 15

I got to Gert's house just as she was putting the coffee on.

"Your house smells so delicious, what are you baking?"

"I'm done, I baked an apple coffee cake, it's too hot to eat yet, but we can have it for lunch, maybe a handsome cop will drop by."

"I certainly hope he does", I thought to myself, once again thinking about last night.

I asked Gert how she was feeling and I again apologized for pushing her so hard about Beatrice.

I knew this had to be hard on her, after all she and Beatrice were best friends. Gert probably thought she was betraying Beatrice's confidences. We made small talk for the next hour I told myself that I wasn't going to push Gert, and that I would let her start talking about Beatrice if she was so inclined.

I told her about Aaron's wedding gift to me, I also mentioned us bumping into Anne Bradley at the movie theater, and what her reaction was when Aaron gave me the car as a wedding gift. I think she could have burst a blood vessel.

"Honey, you will not have to worry about Aaron and Anne. Aaron is as loyal as they come and he loves you with all his heart."

It was Gert who brought up Beatrice's diary. We again got comfortable in her living room. I decided to take it slow and easy with her. I wanted her to set the pace, as she opened the diary,

Diary,

I hate you, I hate myself, and tonight, I even hate Lewis. Oh God, why did I do this?? I am so weak when it comes to Lewis. I went over, to Gert's house, I was hysterical. I think it took me twenty minutes before I calmed down. I don't know what Gert thought, because I didn't tell her everything, but I will tell you.

It must be the worst rainstorm of the season. I met Lewis at the funeral home; I would go to the ends of the earth to be with him. Our lovemaking

started in the side room off his office. It was at that time the high winds knocked the power lines down. I didn't care; I was safe in his arms. He had mixed us some drinks. I'm not accustomed to drinking and I lost track of how many I had consumed. After awhile Lewis said he had a surprise for me. He took my hand and walked me through the funeral home and down the stairs to the lower level. Everything seemed so out of focus, I felt light headed. I started to giggle; it was then that I realized that I was drunk for the first time in my life. It gave me a warm feeling in the pit of my stomach. I wrapped my arms around Lewis's neck; I didn't ever want to leave him. I was starting to do things to him I've never thought I was capable of. We were naked and I started to rub my body up and down his. As I kissed his chest, the hair tickled my nose. Again I started to giggle. I felt so free; I loved the way I felt. Lewis sensed my mood; he took my hand and led me to the room of caskets. I froze, but only for a moment. His voice was low and husky sounding, slowly coaxing me farther into the room. I couldn't see his face, but I could feel his warm breath on my face, and then on my breast, he whispered provocatively, all the while sliding his hands up and down my arms saying,

"Beatrice, my darling have you ever wondered how it feels to make love in a casket? No you probably haven't, you are my sheltered butterfly, my innocent angel. I will tell you how it feels, the lining feels like the finest silk, the pillow, so soft and luxurious."

I didn't say a word as he lifted me off my feet and laid me gently into the casket, he told me it was his most expensive model. He started to kiss me again, over and over until I thought I would go insane for wanting him to join me in this silken bed. No matter how hard I begged him to satisfy this ache inside me, he just stood and watched me as I twisted and turned searching for love and the relief that I knew would come. It was a long minutes, later before I felt the weight of his warm muscular body come down on mine. He held my hands above my head and started moving his body slowly...slowly. Somewhere in the distance I could hear the thunder and wind that whistled though the air vents, I could also hear harsh breathing and soft mewing sounds, were these human sounds coming from Lewis and me, I wondered? Minutes seemed like an eternity and I could not hold back any longer. The explosion shook my whole body over and over, I heard myself crying for the relief that came after it. Oh it was so heavenly to feel this way. It was not long after that Lewis quickened his thrusts that drove deeper and deeper into me. All of a sudden he stopped, he picked up his head as if he was listening for something, but all I could hear was muffled thunder. Again I put my arms around his neck and tried to pull him down on me, I wanted him here with me. A minute or two passed and again it seemed that Lewis was listening to something that was beyond my hearing. He raised his head, this time telling me to stay put. It was then that I felt fear travel though my whole body. He put one leg out as if feeling around for something, and then he got completely out of the casket before I heard him utter a course. I asked him what was wrong. That's when he told me he found Ben lying on the floor, and that he might have had a stroke or heart attack, his words were like cold water being thrown at me, he sounded so harsh. My body started to shake, the warmth of lovemaking and liquor all but disappeared. Lewis helped me out of the coffin and took me into his arms. He told me not to be scared, that I should go up to his office and dress. I asked him about what would happen to Ben. He said he would take care of Ben and that I shouldn't worry.

Dear Diary, I really don't know how I got to the office, fear had left me, but now shame came in heavy doses. I finished dressing and started to walk out into the pouring rain and wind. It felt like needles against my skin. I didn't care; I just wanted to be cleansed of all my shame. I got into the car and started the engine, and just sat there. With time the shock passes, and then tears start, a whole lifetime of tears.

I started driving aimlessly. I had wondered if the rain or my tears came faster. I don't know how long I was driving, but I found myself in front of Gert's house, and I was still crying. To tell you the truth I cannot remember what I told Gert. Gert's comforting words made me cry all the more to the point of being hysterical. It is only now, hours late, that I can tell you, my diary. Despite the consequences, I hope that Ben does not die; this would only weigh heavily on my heart.

Beatrice

Gert looked at me after reading Beatrice's account of that night and said "Beatrice didn't tell me too much of what happened and I didn't push her. I figured she would tell me in due time if she wanted too. The next day I went to the hospital to visit a sick friend from our church. I knew something happened to Ben from what Bea said, so being part of the ladies auxiliary I took it upon myself to see how bad Ben Costner was. He was definitely in intensive care, and I only could see him though a window in the door."

"What is wrong with him, was it a heart attack?" I asked,

"He suffered a massive stroke. He laid there as if he were dead, except for his eyes; they were wide open and looked as if they had seen something horrible. I will never forget the look on his face. They had Ben wired up to life support systems, and all you could hear was the whirring and beeping of the machines that kept him alive. To help Beatrice, I went there every day and gave her a report on Ben. I also told her that Serena had a baby boy on the same night Ben had his stroke. Her face became deathly pale and she ran to the bathroom where I heard her throwing up. She hadn't seen Lewis since that night, and at the time I did not know if that would be a temporary situation or not."

"Did Ben recover? Did Serena ever really find out what happened that night?"

"One of my casino friends worked at the hospital, as a matter of fact she worked the day shift on Ben's floor. She had mentioned to me that everyone at the hospital had very little hope for Ben's recovery.

It was a couple of months after all this happened that Beatrice appeared at my front door. She looked very tired and had dark circles around her eyes. She looked as if she hadn't slept much since it all happened. I invited her in and asked if she wanted some coffee. She was quiet for a while then took a deep breath, it seemed as if it took a lot of effort to talk. She then told me that she was taking a leave of absence from teaching and was going out East. It seems she had an elderly aunt who was ailing, she felt it was up to her to be the caregiver to this poor woman. She then said that she would be leaving as soon as possible and asked me if I would take care of her home while she was gone."

"Did she give you a phone number and address?"

"Beatrice said she would give me a phone number as soon as she got there, instead she sent me a post office box number. The whole story sounded so strange, but after what she had been though I figured she just wanted to get away for a while. Ever so often she would call me and we would talk for a few minutes. Beatrice would ask me how Ben was doing but not once did she mention Lewis. It seemed to me that chapter of her life was closed forever, but it wasn't".

"What do you mean Gert, about it not being closed?" I could see Gert was getting a little uneasy, and since it was about time for lunch, I told her I would treat her for lunch and a ride in my new wedding gift.

When we got to the Java Cup Café it was very crowded. We did manage to get a small table for two; I could see why Gramps liked coming here. It had atmosphere, and almost everyone knew one another. If you listened very close you could here the local and world news and of course local gossip over a never-ending cup of steaming hot coffee.

After putting in our order, Gert asked me how my wedding plans where coming along. I told her that my best friend Natalie was my maid of honor and that I was going to meet her on Saturday to pick out our dresses for the wedding. I mentioned that Caleb was going to be Aaron's best man. Gert knew Caleb's parents and a little bit about Caleb himself. She thought he was a good person, but a little flamboyant, and what he needed was a good girl to settle him down. I was secretly hoping that Natalie and Caleb would get together. I told Gert that Grams was coming back early to plan a wedding shower. Gert laughed and shook her head. She asked me if we started apartment hunting yet, and I told her no. It was then that she astonished me by saying, that I was spending too much time on Beatrice. I was surprised to hear her say that.

"Gert how can you say that? Don't you want to get to the bottom of this to find out who killed her?"

"Amanda, nobody said she was murdered. As far as the police are concerned it's a closed case. You, Amanda, are the only one who thinks otherwise."

"If it's over and done with, why do you always seem so uneasy when I asked you certain questions about Beatrice? No I won't quit, if you want to help me get over Beatrice, then tell me everything you know about her. I let her down while she lived, but maybe I can help her find peace."

I had just finished my tirade, which I had promised myself I would not do to Gert, when I heard this fake southern accent.

"Well look it here, if it isn't the blushing bride to be. Hmm what are you eating? Oh I wouldn't touch that with a ten-foot pole, calories, calories, and more calories. You will never get into your wedding dress eating that. Of course they do make larger dress sizes now, for the older bride. Well I better get going, I promised Aaron I would bring him back his lunch, goodbye you two, Oh, take it easy on dessert!"

That's all I needed, to bump into Anne Bradley, and just when the waitress brought our sandwiches loaded with French fries. Gert looked at me and said,

"She doesn't like you very much, does she?"

"That's the understatement of the year. Gert, why does she have that fake accent? I know she married a man from Louisiana, but she was only married six months before she came back to Wisconsin."

"I think she has a lot of insecurities, but she tries to cover them up with this fake accent. She married a very rich man, but I think she would give that up in a minute if she could only have what you've got."

"Gert didn't have to tell me what a treasure I have.

Lunch passed all too quickly. We drove the back roads to Gert's house; the scenery was so breathtaking that she really enjoyed riding in my new car. We drove past Beatrice's house where we noticed a "for sale" sign on the front lawn. Gert sighed and said rather sadly,

"Now I know Beatrice will never be back." I covered Gert's hand with my own in consolation.

When Gert and I returned to her home, I could see a new determination in her. She sat in Elmer's chair, and I took the easy chair across from her.

"Are you comfortable, Honey?" I nodded my head yes.

"Amanda, you seemed obsessed that I tell you everything about Beatrice, so I'm going to tell you everything that I know. Then I want you to tell me if you still think she was murdered. Lets see where was I, oh yes, it was two months after Ben's stroke that Beatrice left town. I didn't know how long she would be gone, but I missed her from day one, she was like a daughter to me. I would go to the hospital to keep check on Ben's progress. But you know something funny? Lila and Serena were never there, just Lewis. I found this out from Marge my casino buddy, who was a nurse on Ben's floor. All the staff thought this was a little odd, but something even more odd was how Ben reacted when Lewis visited and spoke to him. From all medical aspects Ben was in a coma. Marge was in the room when Lewis came in and said, "Hello Ben." Marge was standing behind Lewis, she said Ben's eyes opened wide and his chin started to quiver, and it was almost like he was trying to say something. Marge saw how upset Ben was so she asked Lewis to leave. It was two weeks later that the doctors told the family that they could do no more for Ben and that they should pick out a nursing home for him. That day Marge called me and told me about the scene

Lila made. She screamed that she would never put him in a nursing home because it would cost too much money. She said she would take him home and hire a nurse to take care of him. Lila walked up to Ben's bed, with a sneer on her face, told the doctors to unhook him from all the machines. This whole operation was costing too much. Normally you would need a legal paper to do this, but the Costners were big people in this town, so the doctors did what was requested. Well Lila didn't have to worry about a nursing home or nursing care. After Ben was removed from life support, he steadily went down hill. At two in the morning Dr. Hiller called Lewis and told him that Ben would not see the morning sun, and that the family should come immediately. An hour later Lila, Serena, and Lewis arrived. Nobody shed a tear; they just stood next to his bed and stared down at him. Ever so often Serena and Lila looked at their watches and Lewis just kept yawning.

Right around this time a strange thing happened. Ben tried sitting up, his eyes filled with something akin to anger. Slowly Ben raised his arm and pointed a finger at Lewis, his mouth twisted as he tried to say something. Then his arm came down and with a final shudder he was gone. Lila let out a loud sigh and walked out of the room, followed by Serena and Lewis. Marge said that one of the nurses on duty that night could have sworn that she'd seen a smirk on Lewis's face."

I shook my head and said

"I cannot believe what a cold and unfeeling family Ben had. I'll bet Lewis almost had a heart attack when Ben pointed his finger at him."

"I imagine he did get startled for a minute or two. The funeral was held two days later, and of course it was a big turn out. Lila played the grieving widow to a T, expounding on the virtues of her deceased husband. Less then a week after Ben was laid to rest, Lewis had the Costner sign torn down and a bigger sign that read "Vormen & Son" erected over the mortuary."

"But his son was only months old, why would he put it on a sign at this stage of the game? When he becomes of age he might not want to become a mortician, what then?" I asked rather puzzled.

"According to Beatrice, Lewis always planned for the future, and he could be very persuasive. No one could say no to Lewis, except Ben."

"When did Ben refuse Lewis?"

"As you remember Lewis wanted his name up in lights with Ben's, but Ben said no, not until he retired or died, whatever came first. It was probably Lila's decision as much as Ben's. Lila did not want to share anything concerning the funeral home, not even its name."

Chapter 16

"A year went by before Beatrice came home. It was the end August and school was about to start. The days were still very hot, but the nights were getting cooler. Somehow you knew fall was just around the corner without looking at the calendar. I was baking a peach pie for my Elmer, when the doorbell rang. I opened the door and there stood Beatrice, looking radiant and more youthful then ever. There also was a calmness about her that she didn't have before. We hugged each other and laughed and hugged some more, it was so good to see her again. I told her to come in, but she hesitated. She looked back at the car and then she said she had a surprise for me. She went back to the car and opened the back door and started fussing over something. She straightened up and began walking towards me. It was then I heard a tiny baby cry. If I hadn't been holding onto the porch rail, I would have fallen over in surprise. It was then that she introduced me to Sarah Anne Wilkes, the most beautiful name for the most beautiful baby I'd ever seen."

"Gert, Beatrice had a baby? Why didn't you tell me this sooner? Where is she now?" I asked excitedly. It was then I noticed the sadness in Gert's eyes.

"You went to her funeral."

I felt like I had just been punched in the stomach.

"Gert, what are you saying? If that was Sarah, what happened to Beatrice?"

"Patience Amanda, that's another part of the story and if you'll just calm down I'll will tell you.

Sarah was a complete shock to me; in the phone calls I received from Beatrice not once did she mention that she was pregnant. There never was an ailing relative, but Beatrice had to leave because she was an unwed mother and schoolteacher. This was the sixties, and in those days that was looked down upon. Of course it was Lewis's baby. I ushered Beatrice into the living room where she lay the baby down on the couch. She took the little blanket off the baby so I could have a better view of her. It was then that I noticed something wrong with her. She was beautiful, like her, you could tell that she was going to have dark curly hair like her mother and a little turned up nose and a tiny rosebud mouth. She was almost perfect except for her eyes; they were dark brown almost black. To look at them was to look into emptiness. She cried, but that was all the emotion she would ever have. Beatrice noticed that I knew something was wrong and she then filled in the rest of my unasked questions.

Shortly after Sarah's birth the doctors told Beatrice that Sarah would never be normal. She would never have the emotional response we have. She would never laugh or coo, she would not be able to go to school because her learning capacity would only be that of a child of barely two years of age, if that. The only emotion she would have was to cry if she was hungry or hurt."

By this time I was crying for Beatrice and how fate had dealt her another bad hand.

"I know how you feel Amanda, I felt the same way. Beatrice looked at the sadness and pity on my face and explained how lucky she was to have this baby, because she was to be her baby forever. I asked her if she was going to tell Lewis about Sarah. She said that she had given this some thought. She decided that she would in case she needed monetary help in the future, or if Sarah had a medical problem she might have to give the father's name. She told me that she had to go back to teaching and asked if I could watch Sarah while she was at work. She said she hated too impose on me but she had no other choice. Elmer and I never had any children, so I was all to happy to do it for her, besides it would be like watching my own grandchild. I told that to Beatrice and I could see the relief on her face as she thanked me over and over. She did tell Lewis about Sarah, and at first he didn't take it very well. I think he was afraid that this might slip out and he would be ruined. He thought about it for a while and then accepted the fact that Sarah was his, she did look so much like him. He saw Sarah very little, but the money, in cash, came every month like clockwork. There was only one stipulation and that was Beatrice was never to tell anyone, except me of their affair. If she told anyone else the money would stop immediately, and he would deny everything. He would get away with it, because there was no DNA testing at that time. That was fine with Beatrice, she didn't really want anyone to know, or to share Sarah with Lewis."

Gert and I took a coffee and cake break. We needed this time to clear our minds. Aaron did come over in mid afternoon. It was wonderful to see him.

I was thankful that I had him and not another Lewis. After an hour break, Gert wanted to get back to Beatrice, so we once again sat down in her very comfortable chairs and Gert began.

"The years went by; Sarah was a well behaved child. Having a mother who was an exceptional teacher helped Sarah's intellect advance to the two-year-old stage. She did not speak like we did, but she had her own vocabulary. She would say mo for Mom, wa meaning water. Beatrice even managed to potty train her, she would say we, for that. Sarah was so sweet, so quiet that your heart, would automatically go out to her, she was like an angel.

The years were not only going fast for us, but for Lewis and his son Ronald as well. I got all my information from Marge, who now turned into my daily phone partner. I couldn't tell her I was babysitting and loving every minute of it, although in the summer I had more free time since Beatrice declined to work during summer. She wanted to spend more time with Sarah, besides with the money that Lewis gave her; she did not have to worry about bills. I just told Marge that my Elmer wasn't feeling up to par and that I should stay at home with him. I hope the Good Lord forgives me for that lie. Marge always told me all the gossip, since my casino trips where pretty nil by now, but Beatrice needed me. One day Marge mentioned that she heard through the grape vine that Lewis was having a lot of trouble with Ronald his son. He was about done with college and his father had signed him up for mortuary school. He had good marks despite the fact that he was lazy and a playboy, who squandered his father's money. It was all Serena's fault, she had babied him and had given him everything he wanted, nothing was too good for her son. Marge had also heard that Lewis threatened to cut him off from his inheritance if he didn't fulfill the funeral home sign of Vormen and Son. So off to mortuary school he went, but just barely passing in his grades. I think he was punishing his father.

While Ronald was in mortuary school, Lila passed away. She had as big a funeral as Ben's after all she did belong to a lot of civic clubs. Serena, was playing the grieving daughter, it was quite the show. Everyone knew there wasn't much love in that family, but they wanted to sit in on the sideshow. Even Ronald was there, playing doorman to all the people who came. He looked just like his father, good looking and a flirt. I often wondered if there would be another poor woman who would have the same fate as Beatrice. If there was,

I'd never heard of her. One thing I did notice was that Ronald paid an unusual amount of attention to his mother. One would think he was her husband instead of her son.

My Elmer really loved Sarah. When it was summer or days that Beatrice did not bring Sarah, Elmer just moped around the house. It was like he lost all sense of priority when she was around. I was always happy when school was back in session. It was around this time that I noticed Elmer's health was failing. He didn't like doctors, so he very seldom went to one. One night his left arm went numb and it was hard for him to breathe, I told him that he was a stubborn old coot, and that I was calling the ambulance. He went to the hospital; they put him in intensive care where he died three days later. He had a massive coronary. I thought my life had ended along with Elmer's. He was my everything for fifty years. I didn't know how I was going to live without him always getting in my way. Life did go on with the help of Beatrice, Sarah, and my buddy Marge."

I could tell this was wearing on Gert so I told her that maybe we should stop for now, although I really wanted her to go on. She must have sensed my feelings because she said she wanted to get this out of her system, as well as mine, she said it was her wedding present to me. In a way I think she was glad to be sharing this burden with me. So she went on.

"I had to have Elmer laid out at Vormen's. Lewis knew that I knew about Sarah and that I was taking care of her. When it came time to pay the funeral bill he waved his hand and said it was all taken care of. I would not hear of it! Elmer was sold on insurance so there was plenty of money to bury him, besides after what Lewis did to Beatrice; I wanted nothing more to do with him.

Lewis realized he was getting old and had no real love since Beatrice, so he started to phone her. She would have nothing to do with him. One day Lewis stopped by my house, looking distressed. Lewis mentioned that he went over to Beatrice's home to pay her the money for Sarah. Nobody answered his knock and the door was slightly ajar. He called out to Beatrice, but nobody answered. He walked in and saw Sarah sitting on the couch rocking back and forth, saying "no mo" "no mo" over and over again. It was then he saw Beatrice lying on the floor dead, apparently dead from a heart attack. There was no evidence of foul play. I grabbed my jacket and starting running to Beatrice's house when Lewis grabbed my arm and stopped me. He said she was taken care of. I asked him what he meant. He told me since she died of a heart attack there was no need to take her to the hospital. Instead he took her body to his funeral home and cremated her. I looked at him in shock, I could not believe what I was hearing, and suddenly I thought of Sarah all alone in the house. Panic set in. I had to get to Sarah and fast; she had never been alone in her life. Sarah had to be petrified by now. Lewis called my name sharply,

"Gert we have to figure out what to do with Sarah." he said. I told him not to be concerned, that I would take care of her in my own home. He also told me that he would type out a letter of resignation to the school board. Beatrice was seventy years old, so she was retirement age. The school board would not think too much of it except that it was rather sudden. He would also mention in the letter that Beatrice was again going out East to see family. Yes, Lewis had it all planned out. In the days that followed, so many questions crossed my mind, but I was an old lady of 90 who now had the extra burden of caring for a woman-child. I had no time to get the answers I needed. I thought that in his way Lewis loved Beatrice and would never physically hurt her.

Once I settled Sarah in my home, Lewis started to talk money and how much he was going to pay me. At first, I wasn't going to accept the money. I had stocks, dividends, plus my social security checks and I lived very frugally, except for my occasional casino outings. Lewis insisted he pay me in case Sarah got sick and I needed extra money. So I agreed to take the money.

At first I didn't realize how major this undertaking was going to be for me. Sarah was a forty-year-old woman. A woman nobody knew existed except Lewis and me. Sarah knew me and I think loved me, if she had indeed that emotion in her. When we got to Beatrice's house that day, Sarah was still sitting on the couch rocking back and forth. She came willingly with us and for the next three years she was the daughter I never had. The only sad thing was the fact I could never take her out in public, Sarah looked just too much like Beatrice, and people would see the similarity almost immediately. I was glad I lived out in the country where very few cars ever traveled. Sarah loved my garden, which was her playground.

This spring Sarah came down with pneumonia and I just couldn't snap her out of it. She was forty-one when she died and it was her funeral that you went to. That's the whole story; do you still think there was a murder, Amanda?"

I could not answer her; the whole story was too much to take in. I told that to Gert. I thanked her for telling me, even though it brought back so many sad memories.

It was almost dinnertime and Gert asked me if I wanted to stay, but I excused myself. I knew she must have as big a headache as I did. I told her that I had to go home to digest what she had told me. Tomorrow, Natalie would be here and we would be looking for dresses for the wedding, I told that to Gert, and then gave her a big hug good-bye.

Aaron was not coming over tonight, and I was rather glad. After this afternoon I really didn't feel much like talking. Aaron had to work an extra shift since a couple of guys called in sick. Katie came over to ride her horse; she waved, and then went right over to the barn. I put on some soup for my dinner and put a slice of bread in the toaster. There was some wine left from the night before, maybe that would help to relax me. I took my meal and wine into the living room. Listening to Gert telling me about Beatrice was like being on an emotional roller coaster. I would have loved meeting Sarah, but that was not to be. I didn't feel much like eating, but the wine went down smoothly.

The phone rang it was Aaron. I get butterflies in my stomach every time I hear his voice. Today was no exception.

"Hi Babe, how is my favorite girl?"

"Great, now that I hear your voice." I replied.

"You sound tired, did Anne upset you today?"

I had almost forgotten about our chance meeting at the café.

"Oh, so she told you of our meeting." I'll bet she didn't tell him how bitchy she was towards me.

"Yes, how were your fries and hamburgers, she said they looked big and tasty. She also mentioned that you got a little testy at Gert."

"Boy, she doesn't miss much does she? Honestly I really don't like her." I said, probably sounding rather catty but I was too tired to care.

"Do we have to have her on our wedding list?" I asked

I disliked putting Aaron on the hot seat like that. Remembering Gert's wisdom about jealousy I apologized.

"I'm sorry Aaron, of course she'll be invited with the rest of your fellow officers."

"Amanda, do you want me to come over after my shift? I have the feeling there is something peculiar going on, although I don't know what Gert and you could possibly be up to, that would make me think that."

"No, please Aaron, I'm alright it's just…it's just I heard some disturbing news about Beatrice today and it's got me down a little. I'll be fine by tomorrow after a good nights' rest, besides Natalie is coming from Milwaukee in the morning and we're going shopping for wedding dresses."

"Hon, I just got a brainstorm. Why don't I round up Caleb and we can all go out for dinner tomorrow night?"

"That sounds like a good idea. I'm sure Natalie won't mind, especially once she meets Caleb."

I felt my spirits lifting after talking to Aaron. He told me how much he missed me since he saw me earlier today, and how he was going to remedy the situation when we got together. Like I said, he is a very sexy guy.

When I went to bed, I lay there thinking of what my next course of action should be. Part of me reminds me that I have a wonderful wedding to plan, of which I'm way behind schedule. The other part says there is still something not right about Beatrice's death. When I think about it I think my answer lies at the funeral home in their records, but that will have to wait until Monday.

Chapter 17

Natalie came to town early. I had just brewed some coffee and she brought the sweet rolls. We decided to eat a very light breakfast and then later, go for lunch. Why does shopping and eating go hand in hand for women? I came to the conclusion that it was a social thing taught from small on.

It was so good to see my very good friend again. It really hasn't been so long since I last saw her, but she is like a sister to me. I told her how wonderful Aaron was and how every day I'd find something new and fascinating about him, and how they all added up to him being Mr. Wonderful. She asked me if I laid Beatrice to rest. I couldn't answer her, but I did tell her it would be very soon. She frowned and said that she didn't like the sound of that. If she only knew my plans.

Shopping went very well; we found gowns for both of us in the second shop we visited. Natalie had beautiful auburn hair, so we picked out a black gown, which showed off her hair and trim figure. Natalie hadn't found Mr. Right yet, but I was hoping her luck would change when she met Caleb. I tried on my wedding dress, and held my breath when I looked in the mirror. I could not believe what I was seeing. I was transformed from a very ordinary looking woman to a storybook princess. I wondered if there was something magical about wedding gowns. Our shopping went so well that we decided to order the flowers, too. I decided not to tell Natalie about our dinner date with Aaron and Caleb until later in the day. Knowing Natalie the way I do she would be a nervous wreck the rest of the day.

As we looked over the menu we decided to eat light. What Anne said about calories must have hit home with me, darn her. When I looked at the menu and read all the scrumptious entrees, I thought, Oh heck you only get married once, and this was a celebration, so let's eat up. Natalie and I ordered desserts to go with our meal, "Here's looking at you Anne." I thought to myself.

During lunch, Natalie brought up the subject of Beatrice. At first I didn't tell her too much, but I did tell her about Sarah and how she was mentally handicapped. Natalie was close to tears when I told her that. So I switched the subject and we talked about Anne Bradley for comic relief.

That evening, as we dressed for dinner, Natalie was a nervous twit, just like I knew she would be. She kept looking in the mirror and asking me how she looked, lamenting that she wished I had told her sooner about Caleb. She kept asking me if I thought Caleb would like her. Natalie was very shy, and the sweetest person I know. I just hugged her and told her he would have to be crazy and blind not to love her. Finally the guys arrived, but in separate cars,

Natalie looked at me in panic, and said,

"I thought we were all going together."

"Natalie just be your sweet charming self and you will bowl him over, I guarantee it." I replied

She looked lovely in her emerald green dress, which brought out her Irish heritage. I've known Natalie since grade school and I've had never seen her looking lovelier than right now, she was absolutely stunning.

The evening was a complete success. Once Caleb took one look at Natalie, I knew she had nothing to worry about. I asked Aaron whose idea it was to come in separate cars. He had a sheepish look on his face and admitted that it was his idea.

Aaron picked out the Rustic Inn on the Lake. It was where we went, the evening of Beatrice's funeral. Because it was now the busy tourist season, we had to wait at the bar until our table was ready. After about an hour and three drinks we were escorted to our table. The conversation flowed freely, all the intimidation Natalie had felt earlier disappeared and she was her sweet natural self. I could see Caleb admiring her as her eyes sparkled in the candlelight. After dinner Caleb and Natalie were the first ones on the dance floor. Aaron whispered in my ear,

"They make a cute couple, who knows, maybe we will be going to their wedding next year."

"Do you know something Aaron? You are a regular matchmaker."

"And who was our matchmaker Amanda?"

He didn't wait for an answer but he said,

"I think Beatrice had a hand in ours." he took my hand and kissed it.

Natalie left for Milwaukee the next morning. Caleb picked her up for breakfast. I could see Natalie was walking on air. I would start a conversation but it was like I was speaking a different language, she was in her own little world. Finally I said,

"Natalie. Earth to Natalie?"

"Are you talking to me?"

"I am, if your name is Natalie."

We both started to laugh.

"I know what you are going to ask me. Yes, I had a wonderful time, and I like him very much and yes he's coming to Milwaukee to visit me, and P.S. he is as great as he looks and a good kisser. I'm hoping that by the time of your wedding we will be very good friends."

After Natalie left I tidied up the house. This was the day for the parents get together. The day our wedding plans were to be finalized. Aaron and I knew what we wanted for our wedding; it was just getting it across to my parents. In a way I wished Grams were here to handle my mother. Don't get me wrong I love my mother but I love Grams more. Mom is a perfectionist, a social butterfly, and a snob. My dad goes along with anything my mother says or does. Sometimes in his own way, he would apologize to me by saying,

"Sorry Honey, I have to go along with what your mother says, I have to live with her."

I heard that many times in my youth. By God I was going to make sure my wedding was going to be the way Aaron and I wanted it, not my mother's way. On the other hand, Aaron's parents were sweet and affectionate people. When Aaron and I where dating in high school I would very often go to his home, his mom was always baking or cooking and asking me to stay for dinner; I would call her the June Cleaver of Hartger's Grove.

My parents were punctual as usual. Aaron and his parents arrived shortly after. I must have had a million butterflies in my stomach. I could see Mom scrutinizing Grams house. It was an old fashion farmhouse with four bedrooms but it spelled HOME in capital letters. The kitchen was large and at one time they had a lot of field hands eating in this room. The dining room window looked over the horse pasture with its white and green fences. The whole place was a warm and relaxing place to come home to.

After I introduced everyone, we sat around the dining room table to discuss where we going to hold the reception and how big a wedding it was going to. Aaron and I already decided that there was to be one bridesmaid and one best man, and that we were only going to have one hundred-fifty guests. This was the part I had to make clear to my mother as I said to her,

"Mom, that means seventy-five people from our side, and seventy-five people from Aaron's family. When I told her that, I thought she was going to hit the roof.

"Oh no, no, your father and I have a list of at least two hundred people." she said, as she pulled a sheet of paper from her attaché case. Yes, I said attaché case. Mom works for a CEO of a large company and that is part of her uniform.

"Did you say seventy-five people? That is a joke, why I would invite that many from my office plus friends, and family that would certainly come to two hundred people."

In a way I could see why she would want a large wedding. Aaron and I were the only children on both sides, and for mother, this was the only party, to her it was a party, she was ever going to give. I could feel a headache building. I told her that Aaron and I would have to talk about it. I felt myself caving into her demands. It was funny but it was as if I could hear Grams' voice saying, "Stick to your guns Amanda, it's your wedding not hers!"

"Oh the other hand, Mother, I think a hundred and fifty guests are enough. Most of the people you would invite I wouldn't not even know, and Aaron and I are paying for the wedding."

"Well if its money you are worrying about, your father and I will pay for the whole affair."

"No Mom, a hundred and fifty guests it will be, and that means seventy-five from our side."

I could feel Grams patting me on the back, but my mother was not done.

"I think you should be married in Milwaukee and have your reception at the Milwaukee Museum, I went to a lot of affairs there, and they were tastefully done."

I looked at her and shook my head.

"Mom, Hartger's Grove is going to be my new home, and this is where I'm going to be married."

At this point my mom got up from her chair and said to my father,

"Well Dear, I don't even know why we came here. The children obviously have their minds already made up. Come Steven, I think you and I will be leaving. This was just a waste of our time. It was nice meeting you Mr. and

Mrs. Fischer; I hope you're not as disappointed as we are. Amanda let us know a week before the wedding when you want us at the church."

"Mom, please don't go away angry."

"Amanda you're my only child and I had big plans for your wedding, but I never expected this. Living in a, excuse the expression, hick town, miles away from any big city, certainly has made you small minded. I am definitely crossing off my working associates; I don't want to be humiliated by a small town wedding. Goodbye Amanda, come along Steven."

Dad looked back and just shrugged his shoulders. I was just glad Aaron and his parents didn't hear mom's last discourse. I shouldn't have been feeling so bad, but I was. I thought Mother would feel good about me marrying a wonderful man like Aaron, but I guess Mom will never change.

I must have looked a little dejected when I walked back into the room, because Aaron put his arm around me and said that my parents would think it over and come over to our way of thinking. Aaron then said that if I wanted a larger wedding it would be fine with him. My precious Aaron, I gave him a hug and told him that if there were only Father O'Malley and us it would be enough for me.

Aaron's parents gave us their list of guests. We took them over to the Rustic Inn to check out their banquet hall. They loved it immediately. It just so happened that there was a cancellation for that day so it was available to us. It only took us minutes to sign a contract and put down money for the reception. The more we made plans, the more excited I was getting, and everything was falling into place.

We were going to treat his parents to dinner, but they had a previous commitment, so we said our goodbyes. The restaurant gave us menus so we could pick out the entrees that we wanted for the wedding. I asked Aaron if he would like to come over and we could go over the rest of our lists. He looked at me and said

"I thought you would never ask."

It was so good to be home again and I did think of my grandparents' house as my own home. It was like a safe, quiet haven to me. I knew we would have to go apartment hunting very soon. I mentioned that to Aaron and he slapped his forehead and said,

"Oh, my gosh, I almost forgot to tell you, you know Mike from my department? Well his wife is expecting their third child, and they just bought a house. Right now they are living in a two bedroom, first floor apartment. I saw it and it looks just right for us. Of course it had a lot of toys lying around but then we'll have to get used to that right, Hon? As a matter of fact we probably should start practicing on how to have babies, so after we are married we'll know how. How does that sound to you Amanda?"

I laughed and said, I like the practicing part but I think the school board would prefer that I worked at least a year before I apply for maternity leave."

"Ok Hon, I'll settle for the practicing part, but we are close to twenty-nine and we want to grow old with our kids."

I had never thought of my biological clock ticking away, but I decided we will just have to put it in God and Mother Nature's hands. I did say to Aaron that, if I become the Lady in Red, would that be satisfactory for tonight?"

That night, our lovemaking was better then ever. It had been a trying day for me as far as my parents were concerned. Who ever said wine was a way to relax, never tried lovemaking. As I lay in Aaron's arms, I mentioned how wonderful it was this time, and how could that be, since we were the same people, in the same bed, sharing the same intimacies as before, in the quiet haven of this bedroom?

Aaron looked down at me and gently swept my hair off my forehead.

"Don't you know the answer to that, my sweet?"

I shook my head in reply.

"It's because we are more in love each day. In the short space of time since we found each other again, we are finding out each other's weaknesses, and strengths. That makes us love each other more, and that shows up in our lovemaking. Imagine when we are married fifty years and have made love a million times, it will still be better than the last time."

With that statement I put my lips on his and whispered that maybe we should try again. Aaron was right; it was better than the last time.

Chapter 18

The next morning at breakfast, we both decided to take Mike's apartment. I relied on Aaron's good judgment. If Natalie was walking on air after being with Caleb, so was I, for a very different reason.

After Aaron left for work, I lingered at the breakfast table over a cup of coffee. Today, I decided to put my plan in action, but first I had to go over to Gert's house and see how she was. I also wanted to tell her about my eventful weekend. As I drove over to her house I put the top down on my convertible, it was such lovely weather. Nothing could get me down today, even Anne Bradley saying "calories, calories."

As I had hoped, Gert was also in good spirits, and I intended to keep her that way, so I didn't tell her my plan. When I got to her house I asked her if she'd had breakfast, she said "Yes, but it was a light one." I told her to grab her purse and that we were going to put money down on an apartment. Then we were going to the Java Cup Café for a hearty breakfast, it was going to be my treat, and I wasn't going to take no for an answer. So off we went to enjoy the beautiful Monday morning. After doing my errands and eating a hearty breakfast we went to visit some of the craft stores in the area. All the while I was telling Gert about my weekend. About the meeting of Natalie and Caleb and how well they seemed to click, and that, just maybe, we will be going to another wedding next year. I told her about the dismal meeting with my parents. She told me that I did good, sticking to my guns. If I did give in there would always be another thing and still another, and before I knew it, it would be her wedding and not mine. Gert was right, but it still made me a little sad. I got Gert home a little past one. I walked her into her house. She asked me what was the next item on my agenda. I was a little evasive with her I didn't want to worry her, so I made up a little story about running more errands for the wedding.

As I drove over to Vormen's, I tried talking myself out of it. It would have been so easy just to end it here and now and walk away. Something inside me said there was something very wrong. I would be letting Beatrice down if I didn't get to the bottom of this.

I parked my car next to the handicap parking space and walked confidently to the front door. As I walked into the dimly lit foyer, a faint fragrance of flowers surrounded me like a mist. I wondered if Beatrice had the same feeling when she entered this building. It was then that I felt a presence beside me and heard a male voice.

"May I help you, Miss?"

"I certainly hope so. I would like some information on a burial trust for my grandparents."

Lewis Vormen must have been in his early 70's with thick salt and pepper color hair. He was tall and still very good-looking.

"Who are they and who are you?"

"I am Amanda Harding. My grandparents are Frank and Emily Peterson. Right now they're in Alaska visiting friends, but they will be home by mid-July. They asked me to get all the information for them, and then they will come in and discuss it with you."

"Peterson… Peterson, is that with a son or sen?"

"That would be son. They have a farm on Hwy 62."

"Is that the farm with the green and white horse fences?"

"Yes, that's the farm."

"They really have a beautiful place; I can tell that a lot of work has gone into it."

"Thank you, I'm sure my grandfather would love to hear that. He works so hard to keep it that way."

After a few more minutes of idle chatter, Lewis led me into his office and held out a chair for me. He then left to go into the next room to get the information I requested. While he was gone I frantically searched his office, I only had minutes to find keys that would help me get into this place. It was then, that I spied several keys on a key ring few were identical. I took one of them off the ring. In the corner I saw a huge filing cabinet. I quickly went over to it, opened the drawer that had U.V.W. printed on the front of it. As I was about to open the file I heard Lewis footsteps. I quickly sat down and tried to look bored. I hoped I did a good job of acting. He offered me a set of papers, and then as if he read my mind he asked me if I would like a tour of his mortuary.

"I know a lovely young woman like you probably would prefer to be with her beau, but if you like, I would love to show you my mortuary. Frankly I'm very proud of my state of the art establishment. When your grandparents come back you can tell them all about us."

He offered me his arm; even at his age he still hadn't lost any of his flirty ways. As he gave me the ten-dollar tour I studied his facial features. I could see why Beatrice fell for him. Whatever his age he still was a striking man, his eyes were dark and penetrating and when he talked of his funeral home, I could see the passion in his eyes. He kept his trim shape, which made his designer suit fit prefect on his body. He was also, very arrogant. Yes, he really must have been a lady-killer in his younger days. I wonder if that is a poor choice of words?

After he showed me the two chapels, he put on the sound system that played any type of music the family of the deceased would like played. Lewis then led me down to the lower level to the casket room. I couldn't help but think of Beatrice and I shivered. He put his arm around me and seemed to pull me a little too close for comfort towards him. I pulled away pretending to show interest in the casket in the middle of the room. I had a hunch that could have been the one that fateful night.

"Oh this is a beautiful casket. It must be very expensive. The interior is like silk and the pillow is so very soft."

"She is grand, isn't she? Nothing is too good for our customers, and you certainly have excellent taste, young lady."

I asked him if these caskets have names or serial numbers, in case my grandparents would be interested in this particular model.

"It's the Coventry five-thousand, she is the top of the line," he said with pride in his voice.

I asked him what the price would be. Without blinking an eye he said,

"My customers usually don't ask. They see the beauty of it; they know it's the last thing they can buy for their loved one. They usually do not see the price until they get the final bill after the funeral, but if you really want to know, it's 15,000 before tax."

I was shocked at the cost,

"Isn't that rather underhanded of you, to do that to these grieving people?" I know I shouldn't have said that to him, but he looked so arrogant and he was so wrong. I had to let him know how I felt about it, but I could tell I put him on the offensive. He shifted his weight from one foot to another and he seemed to have lost some of his friendliness towards me. Before he could answer, I asked him if he sold a lot of the Coventry five thousand.

"But of course, my son Ronald and I are excellent sales people." Con men was a better choice of words, I thought to myself.

We by passed the embalming room. In a way I was relieved and in another way I was disappointed. I really wanted to know the whole layout of this place, before I came back at midnight. It would be a lot easier on me if I knew each room.

Lewis escorted me back up the stairs to the front foyer. As we went though each room I tried to memorize it because I would be doing this mostly in the dark. If I could just confide in Aaron and have him come with me. First Aaron would raise the roof and then he probably would think I'm crazy, maybe he would be right. Am I beginning to doubt myself? I turned to Lewis and thanked him for his time, he held my hand and said

"You are a very lovely woman Miss Harding, it's too bad my son Ronald could not be here to meet you, he has an eye for beautiful things."

I pretended to be flustered at his comment, and for good measure I said that my grandparents would certainly be interested in his trust fund. I could feel his eyes watching me as I climbed into my red mustang. I only hoped I had sounded convincing.

The day passed very slowly. I prepared my clothes for the evening. If I was to blend in with the night I had to wear everything in black, slacks, sweater, socks, and shoes. I felt like a cat burglar. I checked everything twice, but I forgot where I had put my gloves and flashlight. After a frantic search of the house I finally found them on my bedroom dresser. So just to be sure I checked everything over again.

Aaron called just before dinner, asking me if I wanted to go for a sandwich. He was on call tonight, so he couldn't be far from the station. At first I was going to refuse, but then I thought it would make the time go a little faster, so I told him yes. He would pick me up at six, and after a few loving words we hung up. I then thought, "What if he wanted to stay overnight? How was I to let him down gently?" After some thought I decided that I would pretend to be a little under the weather. I hated lying to Aaron, but after tonight everything would be back to normal, I hoped.

We went to the Java Cup Café, it was Monday night and there weren't many customers. The weather had changed; earlier in the day we had sunny skies, which now turned to dark grey clouds with a light mist. It seemed like we would have a lot of rain this season, but sometimes a rainy day or night seemed relaxing. I also noticed the wind was picking up, as if it was bringing in a change of weather for the next couple of days. That's the way the weather is in Wisconsin. I had hoped the bad weather would hold off until morning. I would hate to go to Vormen's in a bad storm.

As Aaron and I ate our food, I kept glancing out the window and then at my watch, this did not go unnoticed by Aaron.

"Amanda is something wrong? Are you feeling ill?" he had a worried look on his face. "You hardly touched your food. If you don't feel well I can take you home, before the storm breaks, and I'll stay with you."

Aaron started to get up from his chair; I grabbed him by his arm.

"No, Aaron, I'm fine really, it's just that I don't like what the wind is bringing in. Since I was a child I was always apprehensive about storms, it's time I get over this fear. Please sit down and let's finish our meal."

Aaron once again sat down but looked at me with concern on his face. Sometimes I was too good of an actress, I almost blew my plan. I really wasn't hungry but I pretended that my sandwich was delicious. On another day it probably would have been. I again made a promise to myself that after today I would never put Aaron though this again.

After dinner, Aaron drove me back to the farm. Since the weather hadn't gotten as bad as I'd thought, I asked Aaron if he would like to sit on the porch for a while. Gramps built this porch with a huge overhang that protected people in weather like this, so it was prefect for tonight. We sat on a two-person swing and put his arm around my shoulders. He asked me if I was warm enough, and I replied "yes" I commented on how I love to see the wind run its fingers through the tree branches and ruffle its leaves. I laid my head on his shoulder and thought to myself how wonderful it was going to be, married to him.

"Penny for your thoughts, Amanda."

"I was just thinking how wonderful it's going to be, being married to you. In the past I never gave marriage much thought. It always seemed so far into the future. I was always so busy teaching school that I didn't realize how fast the years were going. Then one day this beautiful man came back into my life. When I saw you standing there and I read your lips, the ten years that we hadn't seen each other just melted away."

"What did my lips say, Amanda?"

I looked up at him and said,

"Amanda Harding, I still love you. I don't remember what Father O'Malley said over Beatrice's grave. I just kept thinking about you. Maybe I shouldn't tell you this, because I don't want you to get a big head, but to me, you will always be my knight in shining armor."

I looked into Aaron's eyes and even through the deepening shadows I saw more love in them than the sky had stars.

"I will always love you, Amanda."

If he said anything else, I don't remember, because I was drowning in his kiss. Just then somewhere in the recess of my mind I could hear a beeper going off, it was Aaron cell phone.

He mumbled a few choice words before answering it. There was silence for a few seconds with Aaron nodding his head in agreement, and then he said he would be right there, and clicked off, then he turned to me and said,

"Hon, there is an emergency out on the highway, a semi and a school bus collided. I don't know how bad it is, but they want every available man. I'm sorry, Babe, but I have to go. I'll call you later." With that, he was gone in a flash, disappearing into the dusk. For the rest of the evening, I paced in front of the television, listening for any word on the accident. I hoped it would not be serious, and that Aaron and everyone involved would be okay.

Chapter 19

It was after the ten o'clock news that I decided to get dressed and go over to Vormen's funeral home. I was pretty sure there would be no one around at this time of night. There was a brief news flash about the accident, but it was too sketchy to really know what was going on.

The weather had gotten worse; you could hear the distant rumble of thunder. As it lit up the sky in the distance it looked as if there was a war that was getting closer. I lamented, "why couldn't this bad weather have waited till morning?"

I drove slowly to Vormen's. The wind had picked up in its intensity and the lightening and thunder were now over our area. I parked in the handicap space, which was closest to the front door. I shut off my headlights and let my eyes get adjusted to the darkness. I buttoned up my jacket, not so much for the coolness but because I was scared. "I'm not going to back down." I kept repeating this over and over; "This will all seem like a bad dream in the morning." I had the key in my pocket and I took it out. I checked the flashlight again to be sure it was still working, it was. My eyes were now adjusted to the dark. I looked at the surrounding area, the cemetery with all its soldiers of stone, some square, some round, others were praying angels, and still others were little lambs sitting on beds of stone. It was then I saw a flash, like someone running, only to disappear behind the mortuary. The storm and circumstances were making me see things. I had to get a hold of myself; it was probably just a deer. I did not get out of the car. I locked the car door and took deep breaths. My hands felt clammy; I wish I had remembered to bring my gloves, but in my rush I had forgotten them. After a few minutes and seeing nothing else moving, except for the trees and bushes, I reasoned to myself that I better get on with this, otherwise I'll be sitting here till morning.

I unlocked the car door and put the keys in my pocket, in case I needed them for a quick get away. I ran up to the front door and put the key in the lock. I turned it, but nothing happened.

I felt moisture on my upper lip. Maybe this was the wrong key. Just because there were several that looked the same, doesn't mean they were for the front door. My hands started to tremble as I tried the key again, this time pushing the key further in. I heard a click; I turned the knob and slowly opened the door. All of a sudden a strong gust of wind caught the door and me. It felt as if a giant hand was flinging me. I quickly closed the door and once again let my eyes get adjusted to this new darkness.

It was so quiet; I tried to imagine this place in the morning sunlight, with a lot of people around. But reality checks in and I'm alone. I didn't want to spend any more time than I had to in this place, so I tried to remember the building design. As I did, I talked out loud to myself, and then I tried whistling. Maybe I should sing; that would scare any body to death. Oh, that was a terrible joke.

What was I looking for? What did I hope to find out about Beatrice? Even if I did find Beatrice's records, Lewis probably lied about the circumstances surrounding her death, and how would I prove that? It was too late to turn back, I'll have to see this thing all the way through. I remembered the office was to the left of the front foyer. I was glad the drapes were drawn; now I could use my flashlight to find the filing cabinet, I found the drawer with the letters U.V.W. and opened it. I went straight to the W's for Wilkes and found her folder immediately. In it was her death certificate. Everything seemed in order except for the date of her death. It read May 17, 2002 instead of October 18, 1999 like Gert had said. Cause of death was a heart attack. In telling me of Beatrice's death, Gert never told me where Beatrice's grave was. Even though she was cremated Lewis had to put her remains somewhere, this was all very strange. There was one room Lewis purposely steered me away from, and I was going to find out why.

I held my flashlight beam down towards the floor and made my way slowly to the stairs that led to the lower level. I kept talking to myself saying that in less than half an hour I'd be out of here. Maybe I would find nothing, but at least I could lay Beatrice to rest. I found what I thought was the light switch for the stairs; instead it was the switch to the sound system. Its volume set on high with Frankie Lane singing "Ghost Riders in the Sky" It was loud enough to wake the dead…another bad joke, I thought to myself. I quickly turned off the switch and found the right one. I proceeded to the lower level;

the rooms down here had few windows so I felt safe enough to put lights on. When I had been on the main floor I could hear the wind blowing through the vents, but down here, there was almost an eerie silence, like being in a tomb. It was a stormy night when Beatrice was here, that fateful night, but she had heard the wind coming from somewhere, maybe they'd done some renovations since then? I racked my brain and tried to remember where the casket room was, because I knew the embalming room was right next to it. There were so many rooms down here. Earlier today Lewis kept talking and talking as if to keep my mind busy, did he know I was up to something? I had done such a great job remembering the layout, …or so I'd thought.

I found some swinging doors and pushed one door open, it was then I knew I had found the right room; the smell of formaldehyde was very strong. Suddenly I heard a creak; I stopped, held my breath and listened. I let a few minutes pass, and then figured it was just my imagination, or the building was settling. I proceeded to find the light switch to the embalming room. The florescent lights came on; I looked around and thanked Thomas Edison for inventing electricity. Even in places like this, a person can feel less intimated when there is the comfort of light. Everything in this room was stainless steel and very immaculate. It was just like I had seen on television or in the movies. It had cabinets on two walls; a stainless steel table was in the middle of the room with a huge moveable light above the table. There was a huge metal door that took a great part of a third wall. I had surmised that it was the cooler where they kept the bodies. I didn't think it hid any of Beatrice's and Lewis's secrets, but I figured that if I came this far, I might as well go all the way and investigate.

Aaron had just finished interviewing witnesses at the scene of the accident. He was relieved to find that it was not as serious as it could have been. The driver of the semi was injured as well as three children, but none seriously. The school bus was bringing the children back from a week's camp outing. There were a lot of distraught parents arriving at the scene, all of them asking about their children and what hospital they were going to. It was Aaron's job to interview, as well as to explain to the parents about the road conditions that might have caused the accident. The rain, mixed with build up of oil on the road caused very slippery conditions, almost like ice in the winter. This was an intersection, both vehicles tried stopping, but couldn't. The semi driver, seeing that he was about to hit the school bus, steered his truck into a plowed field. In doing so the bus only suffered minimal damage with three children suffering mostly whiplash and bumped heads. The fire department was also on the scene, cleaning up spilled gasoline from the semi. Weather did not make the clean up any easier, but little by little traffic was getting back to normal and the driver and injured children were whisked off to the hospital.

Aaron was very grateful that the outcome was as mild as it was. In his book, the semi driver was definitely a hero. He was going to make sure the Chief knew about this. Aaron tried calling Amanda, but when she didn't answer, he decided to call again when he returned to the station.

Hartger's Grove had a good size police department because it was the county seat. When the accident occurred, all available personnel were called to the scene. Officer Anne Bradley volunteered to stay and man the switchboard. As she watched everyone leave, she thought to herself how lucky she was that she didn't have to go out in the storm and mess up her hair. She felt a little sad that she couldn't be by Aaron's side, but that was life.

Anne was putting a coat of nail polish on her nails when the switchboard lit up. "Damn, who could that be?" she mumbled angrily. She turned towards the board and noticed it was the silent alarm system from Vormen's funeral home. When a silent alarm is triggered, a squad with back up is usually dispatched to the scene, but there was no one to go except Anne, now what was she going to do? If it was anywhere else, she would not hesitate, but to go to a funeral home that was situated next to a cemetery on a stormy night, well that only happened in horror movies. Next time she wouldn't be so fast to volunteer the switchboard. She picked up her hat and put it gingerly on her head so as not to mess up her hair. Next she buckled on her holster and checked her gun. Oh how she hated that thing, it was so unfeminine. While driving out to the home she wondered what made her choose the police department. The answer was simple; it was to be next to Aaron. She had loved him since high school. The only reason she married Ray Caplin, was to make Aaron jealous, but it just didn't work out that way. She played the meanest tricks on Amanda, but Aaron always came to her rescue. When Amanda broke up with Aaron, he was stationed in Chicago with their police department. He met and became engaged to the police chief's daughter. Anne thought there was no hope, but fate works in strange ways.

Anne thought about her ex-husband Ray. She met him while on vacation in New Orleans; he was rich and handsome and swept her completely off her feet. Two weeks after they met, they were married. It was a whirlwind courtship and marriage, which turned into a whirlwind disaster. No one in Hartger's Grove knew the real reason why Anne divorced Ray, and she wasn't telling anyone. How could a marriage survive, when her husband did not compare in any way to Aaron.

Anne sighed when she thought of Aaron. The steady swish of the windshield wipers was hypnotic as she slowly remembered the day. A couple of years passed before Aaron again came back into her life. That was her happiest moment. She took one look at him and just knew that she had to have him in her bed, forever. The trouble is that Aaron did not come back alone. She knew that Amanda and Aaron had broken off their relationship a long time before, and that she was teaching school in Milwaukee. She also knew that Aaron had been engaged, but she thought they broke up. Anne knew Aaron and she figured he would, sooner or later, miss his small hometown. He always loved it here, the friendliness of the people, the conversations at the Java Cup Café with the people he knew, and he knew just about everyone in town. When Anne thought about it, this town was like something out of a Norman Rockwell painting. Anne knew that in time Aaron would get sick of Chicago and come home, and she would be waiting for him. By the time he did she was also a police officer. She figured that it was another ploy she could use to snare him. She made it through the police academy and came back to her hometown.

By the time Anne came back and started to work for the Hartger's Grove police department, she had heard the rumor that Aaron was coming back, just like she knew he would.

Anne was busy at her desk when Aaron came into the station for the first time. He had his civilian clothes on since he hadn't started his job yet. All the officers were happy to see him; a couple of them were high school friends. They heard what a fine job he did while in Chicago. There was a lot of backslapping and hugs. He then saw Anne at her desk. She would never forget how she felt at that moment. She slowly stood up and thought to herself that this was the moment he would be hers forever. Anne felt like Aaron and she were the only two people in the world. Everything seemed to be in slow motion as they walked towards each other. In a matter of seconds that dream was shattered as she heard a very seductive voice inquire,

"Aaron Darling, aren't you going to introduce me to your fellow officers?"

As if in a daze, Anne could hear Aaron introduce his fiancé to everyone. She felt this woman's eyes on her as if they were daring her to infringe on her territory. Anne saw her arms tighten around Aaron's waist. She was warning Anne, without saying a word, that Aaron was hers. Yes, Anne knew all the signs; she had just met her match.

Aaron settled his fiancé into an apartment near the station and he started to work. Anne listened closely whenever he spoke of her. They had met at a dinner in the home of the police chief. The chief saw great promise in Aaron, so he thought his daughter had made a good catch in hooking up with Aaron. One thing led to another and before Aaron knew it they had become engaged. At first everything sounded like heaven between Aaron and his fiancé, but slowly the relationship started to crumble. Anne could not even say her name she hated her so much. First there was Amanda to contend with, now there was this…this person trying to take Aaron away from her. One day Anne came to work and heard one of the other officers talking about Aaron. It wasn't really about Aaron that they were talking about, but his fiancé. This really perked up Anne's interest. It seems Aaron's girl was introduced to Caleb. When she heard that he was a cop who became a lawyer she started pushing Aaron to do the same. Anne could see the change in Aaron. Even as shallow as Anne was, she could see how depressed he had become. With Aaron's sadness, came hope for Anne. Then one day it was over. Aaron, who never complained, said it was over for his fiancé and him and that she moved home to Chicago. That was the end of that chapter, until Amanda arrived for Beatrice's funeral.

Chapter 20

As Anne pulled into Vormen's parking lot she saw Amanda's car, the red mustang convertible, the one that she would just love to have. Anne was puzzled as to why that car would be parked here at this time of night. Anne shuddered at the thought of just being here, this place gave her the creeps. There were no lights on in the whole place and Anne noticed that the rain was coming down harder than before. She wished she'd brought an umbrella along but police couldn't carry umbrellas when on duty. Anne hurried to the entrance to get out of the rain. She looked over her shoulder as if she expected someone to be there. This was really getting to her; usually there would be back up, but because of the accident she was alone. She could feel the hair on the back of neck stand up. She pulled out her gun, and turned the doorknob, and found the door unlocked. Anne did not like this at all, who would want to break into a place like this? She walked in very slowly, hoping that this was just a false alarm. It was then she heard a voice somewhere behind her.

"Ah, if it isn't my favorite southern belle, I'm really lucky this evening."

Anne was about to turn around when she felt a sharp pain on the side of her head, and then nothing, as everything went black.

Aaron was the first one to come back to the station. He was surprised to find the switchboard lit up, but Anne was nowhere in sight. He noticed that there was a silent alarm going off at Vormen's and decided that Anne had responded to it. It wasn't safe for an officer to go out on a call without back up. He was surprised that Anne even went to this particular call. Maybe he was judging her too harshly. While driving to Vormen's, he tried calling Amanda again, but there still, was no answer. This had him worried, she was acting a little strange earlier this evening, and he knew that she didn't like storms, so why would she be out in this one? He thought that maybe one of the horses on the farm was acting up because of the storm and that Amanda was trying to help Katie with him. He would just keep trying to call her.

Amanda decided to try the cooler door and was surprised that it opened so easily. It looked so heavy that she expected a tug of war. After she found the light switch she noticed that there was one body that was covered with a sheet, laying on a gurney. She shivered but continued to push herself to do this last inspection, and then she would be out of there. She uncovered the body and it was a man, a very pale dead man. She was about to turn back when she saw the casket. There probably was a body in it and it was ready for burial the next day. Amanda walked towards the casket and recognized it as the Coventry five thousand model. This was the one Lewis was so proud of. Amanda's curiosity got the best of her; she wanted to see who could afford a casket like this. She was about to place her hands on the lid when she noticed something wasn't right. The casket was beautiful and shiny except where you would place your hands to open it. It was worn as if someone had been opening and closing it over a very long period of time. Amanda slowly opened the lid, not knowing what to expect. What she saw made the blood drain from her face. The corpse lay peacefully with her eyes wide open as if staring into space. Amanda could hear someone screaming in the distance, as the floor slowly rose to meet her, all she could hear was her own voice saying, "Beatrice!"

It was the rough ropes biting into her wrists that finally brought Amanda back to consciousness. Her head started to clear and she let out a sigh of relief when she realized that she was out of the cooler. But another shock set in when she realized that she was tied up to a chair and was about to watch the embalming of Anne Bradley. At first she thought she saw Lewis, no this was someone else, it was not Lewis. It had to be his son, Ronald. Now that she was conscious, Amanda had to think of a plan to put off the killing of Anne. She slowly lifted her head higher and saw that Ronald had completely undressed Anne, her uniform lying on the floor in a pile, and was about to wash her body. Anne was crying and begging him to stop. She promised him that she would not tell anyone if he would just let her live. Amanda thought she would never see Anne begging for anything, she had always seemed like a barracuda.

Ronald was not fooled by Anne's promises even sex, whenever he wanted it. It was then that he got very angry. He slapped her hard across the face and said with a sneer on his face,

"You bitch, you are all alike, you think I'm like my father."

That's when he noticed that Amanda was awake.

"Ah, Amanda, welcome back to reality, you do have a loud scream for a little woman, it was almost loud enough to wake the dead. Excuse the pun, but wait, you're not laughing, Amanda, I want you to laugh when I make a joke, now laugh, Amanda." Ronald demanded angrily.

Amanda realized that Ronald had slipped over the edge, so she had to play along with him. She also knew from Aaron that when an officer responded to a call they usually sent a back-up squad. She had to keep him occupied with questions to keep him from killing Anne. Amanda started to laugh and said, "Go ahead and kill the bitch, she's nothing to me but a shallow bimbo who thinks only of herself."

Ronald was taken aback by her vehement outburst. He knew that Amanda was going to be the new school teacher, and that she was suppose to be a real lady, so, to hear her talk like that surprised him. He looked up at Amanda and just shook his head, thinking to himself that he was right, all the time. Women were just no good, all they wanted was your money and sex, he was so glad that he wasn't like his father, with all those women, especially the one that's in the cooler.

Amanda realized that her outburst didn't faze him, as he continued to wash Anne's body, but now it was much slower as if he was listening to Amanda. She saw a little hope if only back up would get here soon, but she knew that the accident out on the highway could take quite awhile. After Ronald soaped up Anne's body he used a strong spray of water to wash off the suds. It must have been very cold because Anne started to shake and cry all the harder. Amanda wondered what kind of thoughts must have been going though her mind, realizing how close to death she was.

Amanda had to think fast. Ronald started to hum. He really was enjoying this.

"Ronald, what happened to Beatrice? Did your dad kill her and you're covering up for him?"

He stopped working on Anne, Amanda almost felt sorry for her, but then she remembered all the dirty tricks she had pulled on her while in high school. Still she didn't want Anne to die. Ronald's voice cut into her thoughts.

"Don't call him my father, he is nothing to me. He made my beautiful mother's life a total misery. He had so many women, but it was the one in the casket who was the worst, he was actually thinking of divorcing my mother and marrying her. When he dies, I will burn that dead bitch and send her to hell. Then I will burn this whole damn place to the ground."

"But, Ronald, this place is what keeps you and your mother in money, remember?"

Ronald became angry again,

"What do you think I am Teacher, stupid? I did my homework well. Didn't you ever hear of insurance? I bought lots of it in case something should happen to him or this place. My mother and I will be well taken care of."

Ronald then turned back to Anne as he said,

"Ok you little southern belle, I'm going to tell you and your friend there what's going to happen next. Amanda are you paying close attention? I hope so, because this is what's going to happen to you next."

Silently Amanda knew she had to think fast for both their sakes. Anne's cries turned into one continuous moan with her head rolling from side to side. Beads of perspiration started to trickle down Amanda's forehead. She knew she had to keep talking.

"Ronald, if Lewis didn't kill Beatrice, who did? Did she really die of a heart attack?"

He held a syringe with a very long needle. When Amanda asked him the question about Beatrice his hand stopped in mid-air. Amanda hoped, that if he talked, he would stop whatever he was doing, giving them both more time. She could tell that he was getting more agitated.

"Who killed Beatrice, Ronald, I know it couldn't be you."

Ronald started to respond as she had hoped. He put the syringe down, and with a glazed look in his eyes he stared towards the ceiling. It was as if he was going back to the day it happened, as he began to talk.

I always loved my mother, probably more than he did. He had so many women, women who, just the day before, had buried their husbands. Mother knew of most of them and it made her cry. She was very beautiful when she was younger, but her beauty left her, what with all the things she had to go though. Every woman, my father had an affair with, showed up on her face like so many hard lines. I told her that I would always be there for her. She would look at me as I knelt in adoration of her. My mother would put her hands on my face and say how much I looked like him, and then she would cry."

Ronald stopped talking for a moment, Amanda could see the tears running down his face, and then he started to talk again,

"I remember the day he phoned the bitch, Beatrice. He didn't know I was in the building; close enough to hear his every word. He said he was very lonely for her and that he needed her. He said that his wife left him feeling cold, and that my mother's beauty never would compare to hers. He begged to see her again, her answer must have been no. Shortly after he had hung up the phone, I left by the rear exit; he never knew I'd had been there. I drove home to my mother's. I never should have told her what I had just heard; she turned white and clutched her chest. She started to scream and scream and pounded her head against the wall. I tried to stop her I put my arms around her, but she pushed me away and called me Lewis. I knew, then, that I had to take matters into my own hands."

"What did you do then Ronald?" I asked bidding for more time. He looked at me and said

"You are a nosey bitch, aren't you? I saw you snooping in Lewis's office today, and I saw you take one of his keys. I figured you had something up your pretty little sleeve, and I was right. I'm like the proverbial spider and I have you both in my web. You won't be long for this world anyway, so why would you care what happened?" Ronald left Anne's side and paced back and forth, holding his head as if in deep pain, his words began in a quiet tone.

"After I quieted my mother, I drove to the bitch's house and parked my car a ways from her house. I decided to enter her house from the side door, but I had to break a window to get in. She had the television on so I knew she didn't hear me. Before I went in I looked through a window and could see someone sitting on the couch. I quietly went into the living room, but it wasn't Beatrice I saw, but an Angel. She looked like Beatrice, only younger. I walked up to her and it was then that she looked up at me. God she was beautiful. She didn't look surprised to see me; there was no emotion in her face, just a dark vacant stare. I put my hands through her hair. It felt like silk. I then grabbed her shoulders, and stood her up, she didn't resist. I stood there in shock, as feelings I never felt before surfaced. I went there to kill Beatrice, not this Angel. This one was very different than the women my father went for. She was so helpless and trusting, before I knew it, I had her in my arms, just to hold her. Her body was so warm and smelled so intoxicating; my breathing became heavy, and all thoughts of why I was there all but vanished. I just had to have her, she was so exquisite and she would never be able to tell anyone. You see it was at that moment that I realized I did indeed have my father's genes.

Beatrice came running into the room, she realized my intentions, and she started screaming, "No, no!" I pushed her away and noticed the fireplace poker near by. I picked it up, raised it, and hit her with it, all the hate I had for her came to a boiling point as I kept hitting her, so many times that I lost count. It was not only her that I was hitting, but my father as well. There was blood everywhere and she was lying in the middle of it. I looked at the other woman, as she sat down and started to rock back and forth. I left her there and went back to the funeral home. I was in shock; I didn't even realize how much blood I had on me. Lewis was there and turned pale when he saw all the blood. He asked me if I was in an accident. I looked at him and as cool as a cucumber, I said that I had just removed a thorn from mother's side; I then told him what I did. I enjoyed watching all the different facial expressions, surprise, shock, horror; they were all there just like I had hoped they would be. I wanted him to suffer the way my mother did for all those years. He asked me if there was anyone else there. I said, yes, and I told him about my intentions. In a fury he came up to me and struck me across my face. He then called me a low-lying bastard. I would have liked to have killed him right then and there, but I figured killing Beatrice was like killing him, too. I never saw him run so fast, as he grabbed his car keys and drove off. It was several hours before he returned. I watched him though the window as he opened the car trunk and removed her body. It was dusk and there was no one visiting the cemetery, so there was no one to witness him carrying her in. He cried as he took her into the embalming room. I never saw him cry before, I almost felt sorry for the bastard, so I asked him if I could be of any help. He turned toward me and, with a look of hatred, shouted that I had done enough damage to last a lifetime so and to get the hell away from him. He then added that if I ever told anyone about the younger woman, my Mother and I would never get a penny of his money. I had only one question to ask him. I asked him who the young woman was,

"Your half-sister Sarah!"

"Well girls, now that I told you my story, it is time for you to go to sleep, a nice long, permanent sleep."

Anne's eyes widened and she started to scream. Ronald shook his head and then slapped her hard across the face, he then said,

"Now if you are going to scream like that I'm going to have to put some tape across your mouth. You know ladies, I haven't embalmed a body since I left mortuary school, and that was so long ago. You see, I'm just a glorified doorman here, just so Lewis could use "Vormen and Son" above the funeral home door. That sign is a joke, I'm not his son, just like I'm not really a mortician to him."

It was then that Ronald started humming again. He once again picked up the syringe with the long needle. The syringe had a long tube connected to it, which led to a huge glass container.

"Now let me see, if I put this needle in this vein that should drain the blood from the lovely lady. Then this other needle should inject the formaldehyde into this vein, or is it just the reverse? Well it doesn't make much difference since you'll die either way. Now hold very still Anne, it will hurt for just a short while."

At this point Amanda saw Anne pass out. She could have kicked herself for not knowing there was a silent alarm, and for getting Anne into this. She closed her eyes and kept repeating Aaron's name and praying at the same time. She opened her eyes and watched, as the needle got closer to Anne's vein, and thinking how lucky that she'd passed out. All of a sudden she heard a slight noise in back of her. She turned slightly and saw Aaron. He put his finger across his lips and drew out his gun with the other hand. Ronald was so intent on what he was doing that he didn't notice Aaron. Just as the needle was about to go into Anne's vein, Aaron stepped out of hiding.

"All right, Vormen, stop right there, step away from the table, and put the needle down!"

Ronald looked up with the needle still in his hand, and looking very amused, said,

"Well, well if it isn't the boyfriend cop, you almost missed out on all the fun. Your little girlfriend is too nosey for her own good. She took the key to the funeral home this morning; she didn't know I saw her. I figured she'd be back tonight, but I forgot to turn off the silent alarm. I'm really sorry I got the police involved."

Ronald stopped talking and looked down at the needle; I hadn't realized I was holding my breath. Before Aaron could fire his gun, Ronald plunged the needle with the formaldehyde into his own jugular vein. He stood there for a moment with a big smile and very slowly slipped to the floor. Aaron ran around to where Ronald was lying, and felt for his pulse. He knew Ronald was dead. He pulled out his cell phone and called for backup, as well as for an ambulance. He then covered Anne with a sheet as she started to come to. Anne's eyes fluttered open, and she saw Aaron standing next to the table. She asked in a whisper,

"Have I died and gone to heaven? Or is it really you Aaron? Have you come to rescue me?" then she started to cry. She reached up for Aaron and wound her arms about his neck and held on to him. The sheet that Aaron had used to cover her was slowly slipping down to her waist. When Amanda saw this she felt as if a bucket of cold water had just been dumped on her. Jealousy coursed through her like formaldehyde. She wished it was her on the table instead of Anne.

Aaron looked at Amanda; she could see the disappointment as well as relief on his face. He came over to her and untied the ropes and said sternly,

"Amanda, you have a lot of explaining to do."

"Aaron I'm so sorry that I got Anne into this, but please, look in the cooler before you say anything else."

By this time she was feeling the effects of the whole day as tears started flowing down her face. She didn't try to stop them; it felt so good to ease the tension that was like a hard knot in her throat. Aaron put his arms around her and rocked her like a baby, until the tears stopped and the hiccups started. Aaron put his fingers under her chin and raised her face so she could look in his eyes. Amanda could see the gentleness and the love he had for her as well as concern.

"Amanda I don't know what I would have done if something had happened to you."

"Hey you two, what about me? I'm the one who almost died remember? Aaron, I need some hugs!"

Amanda looked at Aaron and then walked over to Anne. She gave a very shocked Anne a hug and an apology for almost causing her death. Then she asked Anne where her southern accent went too. Flustered, Anne started to stammer an excuse. Amanda then handed Anne her uniform to put on. Meanwhile Aaron had walked into the cooler. After a minute or two Amanda could hear him exclaim,

"Oh my God, I can't believe this!"

Amanda reached his side beside the casket. He asked her if she knew who did this. She just nodded her head, yes. She couldn't trust her voice because she knew the tears would start. This was her beloved teacher, who could now rest in peace. They could hear sirens in the distance. Anne was just finished putting on her uniform when she asked Aaron to help her tie her tie. Amanda wondered who did it for her when she was alone. She again had a moment of jealousy when she saw him oblige her. Men are so naive when it comes to women. When he finished, she quickly put her arms around his neck and kissed him, and then she said, in a low purring voice,

"That kiss was for saving my life, I am now yours forever."

Amanda did not like the kiss or the words "yours forever" but she wasn't going to let Anne see the green eye of jealousy.

In minutes the funeral home was filled with people, police, firemen, and newspaper reporters. Many came straight from the scene of the highway accident. Police Chief, Frank Smith, made his way over to Aaron and Amanda. He was a big man, imposing in stature, with his trademark cigar in his mouth.

"All right, Fischer, what happened here?"

Aaron told him what he knew and that he would have the rest on paper by morning.

"Humph, the whole town is going crazy, must be the weather. Well see that the report is on my desk before you go off duty."

"Yes Chief!" replied Aaron. He took Amanda by the elbow and told her not to say anything to the reporters, as he led her out of the mortuary. He took her to the car and asked if she was alright to drive, she nodded her head yes.

"I'm sorry that I can't drive you home and be with you tonight, but I'll be there first thing in the morning to bring you to the station for a written statement. Again Amanda nodded her head; she was too numb to ask questions.

The storm was letting up by the time Amanda reached the farm; it had been a long day, and a longer night. She felt bad for Beatrice and Sarah, but now, they can both rest in peace.

Chapter 21

The night was a restless one for me. I was very tired, yet sleep would not come. I tossed and turned; the scenes from the mortuary crossed my mind like passing scenery on a bus tour. I kept seeing Beatrice's eyes staring, but not seeing. Over and over the needle kept coming closer to Anne's vein. I could see the kiss between Aaron and Anne, and the words "I'm yours forever."

I knew the kiss didn't mean anything to Aaron, but I couldn't help but wonder if Aaron didn't enjoy it, even a little. The worst scene was the disappointment on Aaron's face whenever he looked at me. How could I ever vindicate myself?

Though the night was short, the dawn still came slowly. It was five A.M. and I had given up any chance for sleep. I looked at myself in the mirror and thought that Beatrice looked better than I did, and Beatrice had been dead for three years. Aaron didn't say what time he was coming to get me, but he did say early. I showered in hopes that it would revive me for what was going to happen next. I dressed careful, wanting to look my best for Aaron. I longed to see the admiration in his eyes, not the disappointment of last night. I could feel the tears start to build, "Damn it, I have to get a hold of myself, it's not the end of the world!"

It was around 6:30 when I heard a car pull into the drive. It was a police car, but Aaron was not in it. It was then that Anne Bradley got out and waved to me. Anne approached the house with a spring in her step; she looked as if she had twelve hours of sleep. I let her in and offered her a cup of coffee, which she refused, saying that's all Aaron and she were drinking through the night. I looked at her, unbelievingly.

"You mean you didn't go home yet?"

"Oh my goodness no! Aaron and I had to stay until all the T's were crossed and I's dotted. But I didn't think of it as work at all, not when I was with Aaron. He's so considerate of his fellow officers. We had so many reporters at the scene. I had just walked over to my squad car and I must have had my picture taken about a dozen times. Of course I couldn't say anything to them, but it was fun being a celebrity for fifteen minutes. But enough about me, I'm supposed to bring you down to the station. Are you done putting your make up on? You don't look so hot."

I did have one giant headache. If last night was a long night this promised to be an even longer day. Being with Anne wasn't helping. Finally I took matters in my own hands by saying,

"Look Anne, I appreciate you coming out here, but I'll take my own car."

"But Aaron said I was to bring you in, and you know our Aaron."

"Yes, I know my Aaron very well. I do have a lot of errands to run, mostly for our wedding, so I will need to bring my own car."

Anne looked at me with narrowed eyes. I wished I could have read her mind, but then again, maybe I wouldn't want to.

"Ok, suit yourself."

With that remark Anne left the house. As she drove out of the driveway, I let out a breath of gratitude.

It was hard for me to face Aaron at the station. I was hoping that we could talk things over on the drive there, but that wasn't to be. Everyone stopped doing their work and stared at me. I felt as if I was walking into a room full of strangers, when in fact I knew most of them. Aaron got up from his desk and walked toward me, it was hard to read anything in his face except that he looked very tired. He took my hand and led me into an empty office. Once the door was closed he took me in his arms and held me tight. He whispered in my ear,

"Oh Baby, I don't ever want to let you go. You are like my heart, if yours stops beating, so does mine. I'm asking you once and for all, please leave the police work to me. Two police officers in the family are one too many."

Before I could say anything there was a sharp knock, it was Anne.

"Aaron, Lewis Vormen just arrived to make his statement. The chief wants you to handle it."

"Tell him I'll be right there."

"Amanda, I want you in the next room listening to everything Lewis says. Write down any discrepancies you might notice."

Before I could reply, Aaron had me by the elbow and ushered me into the room next to the interrogation room. It was a room equipped with a two-way mirror, a table, and four chairs. It also had a speaker so that I could hear what the person in the next room was saying.

Lewis was seated at the table. He was impeccably dressed. If he had chosen another profession, I thought he could have been a male model.

Aaron questioned him for over two hours. Lewis was very calm and articulate in his answers. He had his lawyer with him. I listened carefully to all of his answers. He didn't seem very upset about the death of his only son.

Without warning the door swung open, it was Serena. I often heard the statement, "Hell hath no fury, like a woman scorned," well that certainly pertained to Serena. She came though the room pushing chairs aside, like a tornado when it goes through a town. Anne was trying to keep her from entering the interrogation room; I could hear Anne say,

"You can't go in their Mrs. Vormen."

"Like hell I can't! I'm going to nail that S.O.B. if it's the last thing I do!" Serena shouted.

Now Aaron really had his hands full, since Lewis and Serena started shouting at each other. I thought it was like watching a three-ring circus. Anne was trying to pull Serena off Lewis. Aaron was trying to put handcuffs on Lewis, and the fancy lawyer was cringing in the corner, trying to keep out of the way. Two more officers came in to help. A couple of seconds later Aaron had everyone in control and then turned to Serena and said.

"Mrs. Vormen, just what do you think you are doing here? This is a police station, not a boxing ring."

Serena, started to cry, Aaron handed her a tissue as she said,

"He killed my Ronnie and I want him prosecuted to the fullest extent of the law."

Aaron replied with patience and compassion,

"Mrs. Vormen, I am deeply sorry for the loss of your son, but we are not accusing your husband of murder. We just want all the facts; you will get to tell your side of the story next."

Serena was a petite lady, who took very good care of herself. Her hair was done up in the latest fashion and her nails were professionally manicured.

Her figure was still slender and she carried herself erect. Despite all of her careful grooming, the years of living with Lewis had taken their toll on her face. Deep sadness and greed had etched its way like so many deep cracks on a road. Once more she jumped up from her chair, almost tipping it over.

"Oh no, you are not shutting me up! I want my say now and in front of him and that fancy dressed lawyer of his!"

There was silence for a few seconds while Aaron mulled this over, then he walked over to Serena,

"Mrs. Vormen, if I take off your handcuffs, will you behave yourself?"

Aaron hated to see an old lady in cuffs, and finally Serena nodded her head yes, and the cuffs were removed. An officer offered her a chair, but she refused to sit down.

"Mrs. Vormen, I want you to sit down right now. One false move from you and I will put you behind bars until Lewis has his say and goes home. Do I make myself clear?"

Amanda could tell Aaron's patience was wearing thin.

"Before you start, do you want an attorney?"

"No lawyer, I didn't kill anyone, but I want to tell you how he killed my boy."

Aaron turned on a recorder over the objection of Lewis's high priced lawyer.

"Don't you listen to his lawyer, put on that recorder, now." demanded Serena.

Serena took a drink of water that Anne offered her, then took a deep breath, and started talking.

"Lewis and I were married five years, the other forty-two years where in name only."

Serena once again stood up, but this time he let her stand. She seemed to be in a dream world as she spoke softly.

"We met when I was eighteen and Lewis was twenty six and just out of mortuary school. There were eight years difference in our age, but that didn't matter to us. We were a prefect match, he was handsome and I, believe it or not, had beauty." Once again Serena became agitated,

"Look at me, you bastard, look at my face and see what all your women have done to me over all these years." I pretended not to know about these women, thinking to myself that he will get tired of them and they will all go away. And they did except one, Beatrice. Oh she went away for awhile, but then came back with a baby, his baby."

Lewis took a deep breath and said,

"How did you know?"

"There isn't much I don't know about you. I never told Ronald about her, I didn't want him to kill you, after all you were my moneymaker, and I had to hold on to my pride. My mother and I agreed on everything, especially money and beauty and how important they were to us women. There was only one thing she and I disagreed about, you marrying me. I see now that I should have listened to her. My getting pregnant was an accident, you were happy, I hated it, being sick every morning, and as the months went by, my figure disappeared as well. I couldn't even look in the mirror without crying and I hated you for that. The day Ronald was born I fell in love, real love."

Amanda could see the softness in Serena's face when she spoke of Ronald. The softness made her look years younger. Once more Serena took a sip of water and continued her statement,

"Lewis called him a mama's boy. By this time our fifth wedding anniversary was over and so was our marriage. I didn't care; I had lots of money, my beauty, and my son, Ronald. I knew Lewis was fooling around, but I figured they were one-night stands. Then he met the schoolteacher and I knew she was different. I confronted him about that woman. He looked at me as if he saw me for the first time. He started to laugh and said that I couldn't hold a candle to her. He said she was everything I wasn't. From that day on I hated her, and him, with a passion."

I watched her as she went on about her life with Lewis. I had heard from Gert how beautiful Serena was, and I could see it, despite the hard bitterness that now lined her face. I watched Lewis's reaction to what she was saying. Most of the time his head was down, but when he raised it, he showed nothing but contempt for Serena, especially when he heard how much she hated Beatrice. It was then that he spoke, his hands clenched on the table,

"You never were a real woman, like Beatrice. You were nothing but a well-dressed mannequin, who did nothing but spend money. God, you don't know how much I loved Beatrice. To this day, I don't know why I didn't leave you and go with her, but money meant a lot to me back then and this was where the money was. The night Ronald was born, was the night my daughter Sarah was conceived."

Amanda saw the shock on Aaron's face as well as Anne's. Lewis continued,

"At first I didn't know about Sarah. Beatrice took a year's leave of absence from teaching, telling everyone that she was going East to take care of an ailing relative. I felt bad that she would be out of my life for that length of time, but Ronald had just been born a couple of months before, and I was getting used to being a father."

Ever so often Lewis stopped talking as if to gather his thoughts of those by-gone days. His lawyer would turn to him and whisper in his ear, but Lewis shook his head and continued,

"I remember the day Beatrice called and asked me to come to her home. She said it was very important. I was excited, I thought that she might have changed her mind and wanted to start our relationship again. I hadn't seen her since the day we made love at the funeral home when Ben saw us together in the casket."

I looked at the disbelief in Aaron and Anne's faces. Somehow I knew that Gert and I would have a lot of explaining due to Aaron. Lewis cleared his throat and said,

"We made a date for that night. When I got to her house, I felt like a high school kid on his first date. Here I was, a thirty-four years old man, with butterflies in my stomach. When I saw her, she seemed more beautiful than ever. There was a new softness to her as well as confidence that she didn't have before. She ushered me in and told me that she had a surprise for me. I just wanted her in my arms, but she always was a step away from me. She left the room and returned a few minutes later carrying a tiny bundle of humanity. All she said was,

"She is our baby, Sarah"

It was at this point that Serena, looking very pale and shaky, rose from her chair, turned slowly, and left the room. All the fight seemed to have left her. She looked as if she had aged more since she first came into the room. Aaron followed her out of the room and went over to Amanda in the next room.

"Amanda, did you know about this?"

I nodded my head yes. He then returned to the interrogation room. He poured a cup of coffee and offered it to Lewis. He then asked Lewis to continue, and, again, switched on the recorder. Lewis asked if he could smoke, he then lit up a cigarette before continuing,

"She was the loveliest baby I had ever seen, just like an angel. It was when she opened her eyes that I saw the dark, vacant stare. I looked at Beatrice questioningly and she said that Sarah would be a baby, her baby, till the day she dies. To this day, I hated what I did to Beatrice. When I heard that Sarah would be mentally incapacitated, the horror of that fact must have shown on my face. I could not face imperfection in anything I had or did. Maybe if I had held her in my arms, and felt the warmth of her tiny being, things would have turned out differently, but I just turned and walked out of both their lives. Later I wrote a letter to Beatrice, telling her that I would support Sarah monetarily, but that there was one stipulation, she was not to tell anyone about this child or its relationship to me. She did tell Gertrude Greyson, because she was the one person who was to take care of Sarah, when Beatrice returned to work."

When Lewis mentioned Gert's name, Amanda could see Aaron tense up and look at the mirror where Amanda was. She knew that Gert and she would be on the hot seat for quite awhile with Aaron. Amanda's attention was once again on Lewis.

"What I did to Beatrice was despicable, and I will be damning myself for the rest of my life. When my son, Ronald, became a mortician, it was in name only. I could see that he had no interest in it, so I made him my glorified go-for. I ruined his life by not letting him do what he really wanted to do. It seems that I'm good at ruining people's lives.

One day he heard me calling Beatrice. I thought I was alone at the funeral home, but Ronald was just coming from the back of the chapel. He heard me begging Beatrice, to resume our relationship. I realized that time was going by too fast and that I was now seventy years old with no one to really love me. When Ronald heard me, he walked out quietly. He went home and told Serena. He later told me how she ranted and raved about killing herself, or Beatrice. Ronald could not take it. This was his beloved mother. He did not want any harm done to her. It was then that he took matters into his own hands. That night he went over to Beatrice's house and saw Sarah for the first time. Her beauty mesmerized him, but that's when Beatrice ran in with the intention of protecting Sarah. There was a fight and when it was over, Beatrice was dead.

Aaron stopped Lewis at this point and asked him what day in May of this year did Ronald kill Beatrice? At first Lewis looked at Aaron as if he did not understand the question, then he said November 7, 1999. Again Aaron had a disbelieving look on his face.

"You mean to tell me that she has been dead for three years, and you never buried her? Who did you bury in May of this year?"

Lewis rose from his chair and started to pace, his lawyer, a bundle of nerves. He lit up another cigarette, took a long drag, and let the smoke slowly out into the air.

"I buried Sarah."

By now his lawyer was just about ready to quit. He warned Lewis that this evidence would probably condemn him and it would not be his fault. Lewis silenced him and was almost relieved that this was all in the open. He then sat down directly in front of Aaron, and slowly said to him,

"I loved her too much to bury her. I embalmed her, and repaired the mess that Ronald made of her beautiful face. I then dressed her in one of my finest gowns. I made her look like she did in life, with her eyes open. I would put glycerin in each eye to preserve the spark of life. Each day I would bring her out of the cooler and talk to her.

Aaron turned off the recorder and told Lewis that he was under arrest for covering up the murder of Beatrice. He read Lewis his rights, and told him to write down everything he had just said. Lewis's lawyer chastised him for not keeping quiet. Aaron came out of the room and took Amanda by her elbow and asked her if she was hungry.

Amanda said that she had not eaten anything since last night; she had been too upset to eat. Aaron turned to one of the officers and told him to send Anne home for the rest of the day. He also warned all of the officers not to say anything about what was going on. He purposely was looking at Anne when he said that. He took Amanda by the arm and led her to his car, saying that they could pick up her car after they ate.

Not much conversation was said between the two of them. Both were caught up in their own thoughts. Aaron looked over at Amanda and took her hand, the warmth of his hand making her feel somewhat better. At the restaurant both ordered a half sandwich and a cup of soup. Amanda really didn't feel like eating, but she didn't want to worry Aaron anymore than she had, so she ate. Aaron was the first to break the silence,

"We pretty much got the whole story from Lewis, so there won't be too many questions asked of you. But I do want to ask you a couple of very important questions. How did you find out about all this and have you finally laid Beatrice to rest?"

It was then that I told Aaron about the diary. I mentioned that whatever he didn't know, the diary would tell him the rest and he nodded his head.

"Gert and you are quite the pair. I take it that Gert knows as much as you do about all of this?"

"Yes, she does. Beatrice and she were very close friends for many years. But she didn't know that I had planned to go to the mortuary last night. Otherwise you would have had three of us to rescue instead of just Anne and I."

Aaron just shook his head and mumbled under his breath about hardheaded women. The longer we sat there the more tired I was becoming. I had to fight to stay awake I pushed away the plate of food and apologized to Aaron, saying that I really had to go home. He took the check and paid the waitress, telling me that he was taking me home to his apartment. I did not argue I knew he lived fairly close to the station, and in case I needed him he would be at my side in a moment's notice. When we got to his apartment, much to my surprise he took off his jacket, gun and holster.

"Aren't you going back to work?"

"No Sweetheart, the chief is taking over from here. I think we both need some rest. Besides I always sleep better with a warm body next to mine."

As we both walked to the bedroom, piece after piece of clothing fell to the floor, his intermingled with mine. Aaron covered me with a soft warm blanket and then lowered himself down next to me. He took me gently into his arms and smoothed my hair. The last thing I heard was Aaron saying "My wonderful, brave, wife-to-be."

Chapter 22

When I awoke, it was dark in the room. I jumped out of bed when I discovered Aaron was gone. There was a note on the kitchen table from him, saying that he went back to the station to do some paper work, and that he would be back around 7 P.M., and that I should help myself to anything that was in the refrigerator. I showered and dressed and felt a hundred times better. I made myself an egg sandwich and took a can of pop from the refrigerator. As I ate I had a chance to look around his apartment. It was small but cozy and very neat. To my pleasant surprise there were a lot of photos of me. Some were taken when Aaron and I were in high school and others were newer pictures of Aaron and me together. I put down the pictures and decided to call Gert. I thought that perhaps she might be worried since I hadn't called her, and maybe she would have heard over the television what had happened at the mortuary. Before I could dial up Gert's number, I heard Aaron's key in the lock.

"Hi sleepy head, how are you feeling? You sure look terrific."

He picked me up and spun me around. I started to laugh and begged him to put me down. I saw that he was not in uniform, but in tight blue jeans and a snow-white t-shirt. I could feel my mouth watering just looking at him. Aaron saw it in my eyes and told me that he knew what I was thinking. He started walking towards the bedroom. He stopped and turned to look at me.

"Well aren't you going to join me?"

As much as I wanted to, I couldn't. It seems like I hadn't been home in ages and I did have a lot of things to do. I didn't want to get to close too him, because I knew were it would end. I looked at him with a pleading look and then told him about all the things that I had to do, and I still had to call Gert, in case she would be worried.

"Okay, I'll tell you what. How about if we go to your place first, then we'll both visit Gert? There are a few questions I would like answered and I would hate to bring her down to the station for that. Does that sound okay to you?"

I said yes, and then grabbed my bag and we both left the apartment. When we got to the farm, I saw that my car was sitting in the driveway.

"You know I forgot my car was at the station. Did you drive it home for me?"

I could see it was a question he'd rather not answer.

"I bet that it was Anne Bradley. That was very nice of her to do that, I'll have to thank her for driving it here."

I could see the immediate relief in Aaron's face as he said admiringly, "You really are a great gal."

He then gave me a great big hug. He knew that there was no great love lost between us two women. I gave the house key to Aaron and looked back at my car, thinking to myself, that next time she touches my car or puts her arms around my man, I swear I'll break both her arms.

While I changed clothes, Aaron called Gert to see if it was ok to come over at this time of evening.

An hour later, all three of us were sitting around Gert's kitchen table. Fresh coffee was brewing on the stove and Gert was slicing an apple pie that she had baked earlier in the day. It was so relaxing that Aaron hated to bring up the subject of murder and the funeral home. Gert sensed that this was more than just a social call. She hadn't turned on her television for the entire day, so she hadn't heard the news.

At first we talked about the coming wedding, the new apartment, and about my grandparents, who would be coming home in two weeks. I often thought that life was like a book with many chapters. The chapter involving Beatrice was on its last page. Aaron needed Gert's closure of that chapter. She left the room and a few minutes later came back holding the diary, she handed it to Aaron and said,

"Honey, I think Beatrice wouldn't mind if you read it. I only ask that no one else reads it and that you destroy it when you're finished."

Aaron could not promise Gert that nobody else would see it. He said it was evidence, and if there were a trial, the diary would definitely be part of it. Gert thought about it, and then agreed. Aaron asked Gert if she saw Beatrice's body when Lewis told her that Beatrice died. She told him she didn't.

'Lewis said it would be best if I didn't, he said that Beatrice had been dead several hours before he came to the house, and that her looks were already changing. I was very distraught and so I took him at his word. He asked me to take care of Sarah and that he would pay me double. I told him I would love to take care of her for nothing, but he insisted on paying me. If I only could have seen her one more time, then it would have made her death real to me."

Aaron looked at me and I knew that this was the time to tell her about what went on at the funeral home. Aaron did not tell her all the details, but he did tell her that she would get to see Beatrice one last time.

"Amanda probably would not agree, but to me she is a hero by saving Anne's life. I really think this will bring a great friendship between the two of them. Anne offered to drive Amanda's car home and I said that Amanda wouldn't mind at all. Amanda was so thankful that she is going to thank her personally, right hon?"

"Yes, I'll do that first thing in the morning."

When Aaron turned his back, I looked over at Gert who had one eyebrow lifted high as if in disbelief. I thought to myself how naïve men were. There never could be a friendship between women, when they both want the same man, there could only be a truce.

Chapter 23

The story of Beatrice Wilkes and Lewis Vormen never did reach the papers and there was no trial. Consequently the diary was destroyed without anyone else reading it. Everyone involved in the case was forbidden to let out any information concerning the case, mostly out of respect for both families.

Like all small towns, there was a lot of speculation about what happened at the funeral home that stormy night. Some stories were gruesome enough to be told around campfires.

Aaron and I made sure Gert got her wish to see Beatrice one last time. She found closure as she watched the casket being slowly lowered into the ground. It was dusk when Beatrice joined her daughter Sarah in their final resting places. They have no headstone except for a cross that bears the strange inscription "TWICE DEAD"

Sometimes I wonder if there is justice in the world, especially after I've seen what happened to Beatrice. But justice was served the night Lewis Vormen watched his beloved funeral home burn to the ground. His heart could not take the strain and he died of a massive heart attack. To add insult to injury, Lewis was laid out at a mortuary, sixteen miles from his hometown, with hardly a mourner.

Aaron and I had a lovely wedding that third Saturday of August. Aaron was breathtakingly handsome in his dark tux and I; well I was counting the hours until we would start our honeymoon.

My parents, believe it or not, had a great time. I think Grams had a talk with them, or maybe it was the champagne. I really don't know why, but Mom kept kissing and hugging Aaron and me, and it did make for one great time. Yes, I invited Anne to the wedding, after all she was Aaron's partner on the force and everyone from the station was invited. But to be truthful, I wanted our wedding to finalize her feelings towards Aaron. Do I think this will work? Only time will tell.

Of all the people at our wedding I think Gert had the best time, except, of course, for the Bride and Groom. Maybe people sense when their work and time on earth is about done, so they put every ounce of living into their remaining days. It was mid September, three weeks after our wedding. Gert died, happy knowing she had closure to her Life.

I love you Gert, it was wonderful knowing you, even for a short while.

Chapter 24

August 24, four days later
Damn Her! Damn Him!
How could they do this to me?

He must be blind not to see that I was the one for him. My beauty far surpassed Amanda's rather ordinary looks. I am his partner on the police force. His Amanda is only a simple schoolteacher. Aaron and I were made for each other.

Their wedding was like a sharp kick to my mid-section. I knew they were planning on getting married, and yet when the wedding invitation arrived in the mail addressed to "Miss Anne Bradley and Friend" it was like the proverbial "last nail in the coffin."

It's been raining steadily since their wedding four days ago. From one day to the next, the grayness of the day follows the darkness of the night. Still the rain continues.

With each passing day my pacing increases. I want to scream at the face in my mind. I want to strike out at her. If only the rain would stop, maybe then I could put this nightmare to rest. I left the window, tired of watching the streams of water cascading down the pane.

I lay on my bed willing myself to slip into a cloud of unconsciousness. Once again the dreams start. I can see his face, so dear and wonderful. His arms are outstretched; I could almost touch him he looks so real. He's coming closer and closer. I stand mesmerized at the sight of him. It's then that I see her. She was wearing her wedding gown. She runs into his outstretched arms. I scream, "No, No. You can't have him. He's mine!"

They both turn and looked at me and then smile. It's then that I hear the words, "I now pronounce you Man and Wife" Their lips meet in their first kiss as husband and wife.

This wasn't a dream; it's a never-ending nightmare. I awoke with a start, shaking. I pulled the covers tighter around my body, hoping to stop the cold that settled around my heart. Once again my tears, like the rain began falling. My mind would not let me rest. I squeezed my eyes shut in hope of keeping out that fateful day in August but it was no use.

Once again I was standing on the sideline watching the same scene unfold. I could smell flowers in the air, and hear the soft strain of music. My face was frozen in a smile that hurt every facial muscle. I wondered how fate could be so cruel. I watch as they receive congratulations from the quests, with the exception of mine.

How can I make this dream end? A voice softly whispered to let him go, that he was never mine. He never loved me, and he will always love Amanda.

I once more walked over to the bedroom window. I wiped away the moisture that had gathered on the glass, I stopped as my finger slowly wrote

"I Hate Her"

Hate was a harsh word, but I did indeed hate Amanda. It was then that I made the decision to make their marriage a very short one.

My roommate, Jackie, has been worried about me since the wedding. She watched my pacing and noticed that I didn't have much of an appetite. I think it was the constant use of aspirins that upset her. Of late I've been categorizing the types of headaches I have been having. Hopefully they will stop once Aaron is back with me.

Their honeymoon is over!!! Tonight ....I will be with him

Chapter 25

I started my shift at 11 P.M. It took me longer to dress than normal. I wanted to look perfect for him. This was the night that I was going to make my major move.

I decided to walk to work. It had finally stopped raining, and a warm evening breeze made the walk to work all the more enjoyable. Weather could be so changeable at this time of year. Wisconsin had four seasons with each one very different from the other.

I could see Aaron's car parked in the department's parking lot. Amanda and Aaron lived a short distance from town. I had heard through the grapevine that they had an option to buy her grandparent's farm. They were seriously thinking about buying it. I had to admit that Amanda was very different from that fiancé from Chicago. That didn't make me like her any more. Amanda was always a thorn in my side, but she possessed some qualities I wished I had. I would not tell this to anyone, not even my roommate, Jackie.

As I walked to the station, I could feel someone following me. I stopped and turned. Hartger's Grove is a small town. With the exception of Beatrice Wilke's murder, nothing bad ever happens here. The town is the county seat. We have a sheriff's department as well as a police department. We also have a major prison in a nearby town with more uniformed officers. Needless to say no one gives much thought to major crime in this community.

I took a few more steps and again I sensed someone behind me. I stopped. They stopped. It was then I realized it was my footsteps echoing in the night. I had to laugh, thinking my nerves were getting the best of me. I finally got to the station. I didn't see Aaron and I was glad. This would give me more time to compose myself. I knew all eyes would be trained on me. Everyone knew how I felt. Well, I'm going to fool them. This is going to be one cool chick. That is, until I could be alone with Aaron. I smiled and thought that maybe I missed my calling and should have been an actress instead.

An hour passed. Aaron finally made his entrance into the squad room. I was a total wreck by that time. Everyone was genuinely happy to see him. There was a lot of backslapping and little innuendos about his honeymoon. It was this whole male sub-culture that really amazed me. Some call it typical male bonding.

I didn't have to turn around to know he was behind me. I could smell his aftershave. It was a mixture of just coming out of the shower, and splashing just enough scent to drive me wild. I wondered if it affected Amanda the way it did me. The room suddenly became very quiet. I stiffened up and thought, "Ok girl, go for the Oscar." Nonchalantly, I stood up and extended my hand to him. I felt my face go warm as he took my hand in return. I meant it to be a handshake, but it turned out to be a hand holding instead. I cleared my throat and was the first to speak.

"Well hello, stranger, welcome home. I didn't realize you would be back so soon. Vacations, somehow I could not say honeymoon "can be so short." I could have kicked myself. I must have sounded like an idiot. Of course Aaron would know that I was aware he would be back. Every officer had to check the duty roster when coming to or leaving work to see if there were any changes in their schedule. I wondered why he made my insides turn to jelly every time he was around.

"I wish I could say it was good to be back, but our honeymoon was too short."

"I know what you mean. Ray's and my vacation seemed short as well."

There I go again. I vowed never to mention my husband to anyone, especially to Aaron. I had hoped that none of the other officers had heard me.

Police chief, Frank Smith, entered the squad room. He was a big, imposing man with a trademark cigar in the corner of his mouth. The cigar was never lit. I think he thought it made him look more in charge. Aaron and I were still standing when the chief said,

"All right you two drop the hand holding, this is company time."

I always had a quick come back, except for today. As we returned to our desks, the Chief issued orders for the day.

"This just came in. It seems that there has been vandalism at the cemetery. Tombstones are turned over and one of the crypts has been broken into. Kids could be responsible, so we are going to check this out. Old Joe, the caretaker, said he found nothing at the scene. If kids were making it a party place, I think we would find beer cans, pizza wrappers, etc. So we are going to keep an eye open for whatever. A lot of these crypts are very old and in need of repair. It would be easy to break into one of them. Aaron, we are going to make your homecoming easy. I'm going to put you on this detail. You will just have to keep a sharp eye and stay awake. I'm stressing the staying awake part in case your mind is still on your honeymoon."

Everyone laughed at the Chief's pun.

"I do want this to be a two-man detail. Anne, I know you are Aaron's partner but I think you have been though too much lately. I want you to stay back on this one. Does anyone else want to volunteer for the assignment?"

Before anyone else could say anything, I jumped up and protested,

"Chief, I'm Aaron partner for better or worse and I will be the one to go with him. After the mortuary incident nothing could possibly faze me." I sat down, satisfied, that I had made my point clear to the Chief. It was then that I realized how anxious I must have sounded to everyone around me, especially to the Chief.

The Chief looked at me and shook his head and smiled, his trademark cigar moved with the movement of his head.

"All right, Anne, have it your way. I was hoping you would want to go, women do talk a lot. I knew this would be one way to keep Aaron awake. By the way Anne, I don't want you to marry him, just be his partner on the police force."

Everyone laughed at my expense. The Chief walked toward his office then turned to us and said,

"Be ready to go by 1 A.M. Take your warmer jackets, it's usually coldest at dawn."

I looked at my watch; we had half an hour to get ready. Aaron went out to check the squad car. As I was passing one of the female officers she handed me a thermos of coffee, winked, and said,

"You might need this tonight, but I know if I was with Aaron I could think of other ways to keep us warm. But now that he's married you might have other feelings for him." I took the coffee thermos and hurried to the car. I was afraid she could read my feelings for him.

There was silence as we drove out to the cemetery, each of us in our own thoughts. As we approached the gates of the cemetery Aaron stopped the car, and turned toward me, and said,

"Anne are you sure you want this assignment?"

I just nodded my head in reply. He looked at me as if to say something but then changed his mind as he drove the car into the cemetery. I didn't trust myself to speak. I was afraid he might hear the huskiness in my voice and feel the longing I have for him. Aaron took my nod as everything being okay and turned his conversation to our work detail.

"The crypt that has been broken into is up on the rise and in the midst of a grove of trees. We will park behind the building away from the road. The fog is coming in so we'll have to be alert at all times."

I was shocked to hear him say fog. I was so engrossed in my thoughts of being here with Aaron that I hadn't notice the mist slowly rising from the ground and moving towards us.

"Anne, are you listening?"

Once again I just nodded my head. Aaron looked at me in concern. The lights from the dashboard of the car reflected on his face and I could see the worry lines etched on his forehead.

Because of my silence to his questions he thought I was frightened to be out here. God if he could only read my thoughts he might be the one to hurry back to the station...for a new partner.

"No, Aaron, I'm fine, please go on with your instructions." That response seemed to relieve him of his concern for me.

"Every half hour I will survey the area on foot. In this fog, they just might sneak past us. I want you to stay in the car, I don't want anything happening to you."

It was then that I realized what he said.

"No, Aaron, I'm sick and tired of you guys treating me like a delicate flower. I'm an officer, just like you so I'll do my share. Besides after what I've been through at Vormen's mortuary, this is a piece of cake." Aaron could tell I was starting to get angry.

"Alright have it your way, but I will take the first watch." He shook his head and said, "You women sure can be contrary." He said that more to himself than to me.

As we settled in for the long night ahead, I looked around and shivered. I thought about the incident at Vormen's funeral home, and just seconds away from being embalmed. I thought I would never be afraid of things that related to death, but I certainly would not want to be out here by myself. Aaron mistook my shiver as being cold. He asked me if I was warm enough. Before I could answer, he left the car and went to the trunk and returned with a blanket.

He waited until I opened the thermos of coffee before handing me the blanket. The aroma of coffee filled the car, making it seem so warm and somehow so intimate. We drank our coffee in silence, each in our own thoughts. My mind raced ahead as to how I would make my next move. It had to be slow and easy. I didn't want to scare him away. I knew how much he loved Amanda. What he didn't know was that I could be as loving as she, maybe even more so. I heard of other men loving more than one woman. I wouldn't mind playing second fiddle for a short while until…

"Penny for your thoughts, Anne. Do you regret coming out here? I know it's going to be a long night."

Now was the time to let him know how I feel about him.

"No, I feel safe here with you. It's just that when I'm with you…there is no one else that exists…I"

Before I could say another word Aaron jumped out of the squad. He threw his cup to the ground, and started to run toward the crypt, disappearing into the fog. I froze, minutes passed. I was about to panic when I saw a dark figure moving slowly though the fog. I knew it wasn't Aaron, or if it was, he was wounded. I exited the squad car silently. If only this fog wasn't so thick. I drew my gun and shouted,

"This is the police, stop or I'll shoot." I had wondered if I would ever use that statement.

"Please Miss, don't shoot. I'm Joe, the caretaker. I was making my rounds and heard a noise and thought I would investigate. I'm sorry if I scared you."

I brought up the beam of my flashlight to his face. He looked as scared as I felt. I asked him for some identification. While he was getting his I.D. from his wallet, I had a chance to study him. He looked familiar. I wondered what made him want a job like this. He seemed to be passed the age of retirement. He had a shock of white hair, and a face, weathered from years of being outside in the elements. I squinted to get a better look at him. It was then that I remembered seeing him at the Java Cup Café. Joe handed me his I.D. and said,

"I'd be much obliged if you would put your gun away Miss. Your hands are shaking as much as mine."

I put my gun in its holster and asked him if he had seen my partner.

"I did see someone running in the distance, but with this fog it was difficult to see who it was. Doggone kids, nothing is sacred to them anymore. What they do out here would make your hair stand up on the back of your neck. Of course I've never seen them, but I do see the mess they leave behind. They don't need a caretaker out here, they need security guards." With that comment Joe spit out a mouthful of tobacco juice.

"I have to find my partner, he's been gone too long."

"I'll go with you Missy. A cemetery at night is no place for a woman, even if she is an officer. You lead the way."

If I hadn't been so concerned for Aaron, Joe's last comment would have made me chuckle. I pulled out my gun and we carefully inched our way along the damp outer wall of the mausoleum, when I heard a sound. At first I thought it was the wind whispering through the trees, only there was no wind. I proceeded slowly to the front of the crypt when once again I heard the sound. This time, it was a moan. I knew it was Aaron. It was then that I threw all caution to the wind. All my training at the academy was all but forgotten as I raced to the front of the building. I could have gotten Joe, as well as myself, killed, but my only thought was to save Aaron. When I got to the door of the crypt I flashed my light into its interior. I held my breath as the cold and darkness surrounded me. The smell of rot hung in the air from something that had been dead a long time. I could not help but shiver as I saw the beam of my light focus on a casket sitting in the middle of the room. Decayed flowers surrounded it. I wanted to run back to the squad and call for backup, but the thought of Aaron dying cleared my mind as I proceeded deeper into the crypt. If only Aaron would make a sound it would help me find him, and then I'd know that, at least, he was still alive. I could feel cobwebs brush against my face and hands. Oh God this couldn't be happening to me again. Visions of Aaron bleeding to death kept me on my course. I just had to get to him in time. It was so quiet, except for the tiny creatures that I heard scurrying around my feet, and I thought how much I disliked mice.

I took another step when my foot hit a soft object. I aimed my flashlight toward the floor and found Aaron, lying in a pool of blood. Old Joe bumped into me as I came abruptly to a stop. He looked down and muttered, "Holy Mother of God," when he saw Aaron lying on the cold concrete floor in a pool of blood. As he turned to leave he said,

"I'll go and call and an ambulance."

I grabbed his arm to stop him as I bent over Aaron's body to assess the damage. After what seemed like an eternity, I found that Aaron had suffered an injury to his head and what looked like a knife wound to his arm. It was difficult to see the extent of the wound with just the beam of my flashlight, but I could see by the pool of blood that it was severe and that he needed immediate hospital care. Waiting for an ambulance would take too long. I removed my tie and made a tourniquet to help stop the bleeding. I turned to Joe and ordered him to help me get Aaron to the squad car. He was about to argue with me about moving Aaron, when I looked over at him and said,

"Look, he's my partner and I'm not about to lose him waiting for an ambulance. Please take his feet and I'll take the upper body, gently now." It was slow going but we managed to get him to the car. I ordered Joe to get into the back seat and loosen the tourniquet when I told him to. As I was driving over the rutted roads of the old part of the cemetery, trying not to hit the holes, I kept thinking that I had no choice but to move him. He was my love and as I felt his pulse growing weaker I knew I had made the right decision. I glanced in the rear view mirror at Joe and told him to keep the blanket around Aaron. It was the same blanket that I had planned to seduce Aaron on. Fate had a way of changing my life.

It seemed that it took hours to reach the hospital. I had radioed ahead and told them I was bringing in a wounded officer and what type of wounds they were so the staff would be ready for him.

I once more looked at Aaron. He was so deathly pale and his breathing was so shallow that I began to wonder about my decision to drive him to the hospital.

Chapter 26

The squad came to a screeching halt at the entrance of the emergency department. Medical personnel were ready for him. Within seconds they had Aaron on a gurney and were rushing him into one of the cubicles. I watched the scene as if in a trance. Questions were asked of me, I answered those though numb lips. I wanted to cry, thinking that maybe I would find some release. I had all but forgotten Joe until a cup of steaming coffee was offered to me.

"Here Missy, I think you need this," he said with what looked like tears at the corner of his eyes.

I think it was the kindness in his voice that bought the release of my tears. He awkwardly took my hand and said in a whisper,

"No matter what I said at the cemetery about waiting for an ambulance, I think you made the right decision. We old timers are always overly cautious and sometimes that's not always right.

It takes you brave young ones to show us the way. I think that young officer of yours will be just fine, and on that I am sure."

I gave Joe a hug. I glanced at my watch and realized how late it was. I turned back to Joe and told him that one of the other officers would drive him home and that I would call him first thing in the morning and let him know how Aaron was. Once more we hugged each other and although just two hours ago we were strangers, and now through an almost tragic incident we will be friends forever.

It seemed like forever before a nurse came out of the examination room where Aaron was lying. I went up to her to ask her how Aaron was. As the nurse was about to speak, Amanda came running down the hall and grabbed the nurse by the arm. She was in hysterics. I felt sorry for her and wanted to put my arm around her, to comfort her. She must feel like her whole world is falling apart. What would we do if we lost Aaron? No I can't think like that. I wiped away the tears; I could not let Amanda see them. The nurse gently told her that the doctor would be out shortly, and he would give her an evaluation of Aaron's condition.

Amanda turned and saw me for the first time. I saw the anguish and anger on her face. For the first time in my life I felt truly sorry for all the misery I caused her. If Aaron should die...I just couldn't think like that, not now, not ever.

"Anne you're are his partner, you were suppose to watch his back, what happened out there?"

I could not say a word because of the lump that sat in my throat. Just then the doctor called to Amanda and led her into Aaron's cubicle. I was left standing alone. A nurse saw how lost I must have looked. She put her hand on my shoulder and said,

"Sometimes doctors seem to be so callous. There first concern is for their patient then to their family. I know you brought in Officer Fischer, and I shouldn't be telling you this, but I know how you must feel." In a soft tone she whispered, "He suffered a concussion to his head and a deep knife wound in the forearm. Because knife wounds to the hand and arm bleed profusely he had to be given two units of blood. The concussion is what has the doctor worried. We will be keeping him in the hospital for a few days. Thanks to your fast thinking, I'm positive he will be just fine. He's young and in good physical shape."

The nurse gave my hand a gentle squeeze and left. All of a sudden I felt very tired, like I had aged ten years.

I was still in the waiting room when I heard the blustery voice of Chief Smith.

"Nurse, where is she? Where is Officer Bradley?"

I got up slowly from my chair and walked over to the swinging door. "I'm here, Chief."

The Chief looked at me and knew I had been though hell, his tone of voice softened immeasurably when he said to me,

"Anne, I know you have been though a tough night. I want you to know you did the right thing by not waiting for the ambulance. If he'd had different injuries, it might have turned out differently. Now, I want you to go home and come by the station later and give your statement as to what happened out there."

No sir, I'm going back to work. I'm on duty till 7:00. A.M."

The Chief twirled his unlit cigar, and said,

"By gum, you women are the most stubborn creatures on this earth," he grumbled as he walked toward the front desk to get an update on Aaron.

I was just passing Aaron's room, when the door opened. Amanda and I collided. Amanda's tear streaked face was puffy from crying. She looked as if she was at a loss for words when she saw it was me. I was the first to speak,

"How is Aaron?"

"The doctor said he will be fine. He's strong. I want to thank you for acting so quickly. The doctor told me what you did and that it saved Aaron from worse injuries. Thank you again."

Amanda seemed undecided as what to do next. She hesitated, then put her arms around me, gave me a quick squeeze, then turned and went back into Aaron's room.

For the first time in a long time I felt at peace with myself. It took a near tragedy to realize how important the people around me are, not just my feelings for Aaron, but Amanda's as well. This was the first time I felt a kinship with Amanda. I knew we would never be close friends, but I could try for acquaintances. I knew then that I would have to let go of all my feelings for Aaron, and that was not going to be easy. Then it hit me that just maybe I was starting to grow up. I was actually putting others feelings before mine, it was a new and different feeling for me, and I felt good.

I left the hospital and walked over to the squad car. It was just starting to get light and the stars were beginning to fade. I wondered what had happened to the fog. I looked at my watch. It had been at least five hours since everything happened. I took a deep breath and slowly exhaled, yes, it was the start of a beautiful day.

Chapter 27

When I got back to the station, all my fellow officers gathered around me. There were a lot of questions about Aaron and about the events at the cemetery. I looked at them and told them that Aaron would be alright. As far as the cemetery was concerned, I informed them that the Chief would have to be filled in first, and they understood. I sat down at my desk, and started to type my statement. I had a feeling there was a big problem out there, and it had nothing to do with teenagers. I really wanted to put my thoughts passed the Chief.

I looked down at my uniform and I saw it was covered with Aaron's blood. I had another change of clothes in my locker, but it was so close to the end of my shift that I decided not to change. Maybe there was another reason; maybe I still wanted to hold on to whatever I could of him, even if it was his blood. It sounds morbid, but he was so much a part of my past life, that it was hard to let go.

It was a few moments later that the Chief came into the squad room. I had never seen him looking so serious. For a moment I thought that Aaron had taken a turn for the worse. "All right people, I want you attention. First of all, I'm sure that Officer Bradley informed you that Officer Fischer will be fine, and will be in the hospital for a few days. But what she probably didn't tell you is that because of her quick thinking she saved his life."

I didn't think the Chief was going to say that, but everyone stood up and applauded. For the first time in my life I was actually embarrassed by all the attention.

"He will then be home for a couple of weeks. I want to be sure he won't be suffering any repercussions from his head injury. I'm sure his new bride won't mind an extended honeymoon."

Everyone smiled at the Chief's attempt at making a serious situation a little lighter.

"Secondly, we still have a problem at the cemetery. When we finish here I want to talk to Anne. Maybe she can shed some light on this matter. We almost lost an officer out there, so I'm upgrading this to a dangerous situation. We will keep up the night patrol there, it will always be a two-man detail."

The Chief looked over at one of the other officers and said,

"Tom, I want you to go over to the cemetery and bring in old Joe, the caretaker. Starting today, I want Joe at the cemetery only in the daytime, dusk comes, and he's out of there. I know he lives on the grounds, but he will have to move back into town for the time being. He has a sister that he can move in with. Also I want the whole area around the crypt barricaded; I don't want any evidence destroyed. All gates in the cemetery will be closed at dusk. Now that it is getting dark sooner not many people go there. By the way, the doctor informed me that Aaron can have visitors tomorrow, but only a few minutes at a time. Amanda informed me that you can visit Aaron at home as well. That's all people, have a good and safe day. Anne, can you come into my office please?"

Once in his office, he offered me a chair and then sat down on a chair next to me.

'Anne, I know you had a tough night, but the sooner we get information, the sooner we can close this case."

"Chief, I really don't know where to start, everything happened so fast. It was very foggy out there. I was looking over at Aaron and was about to say something when all of a sudden he jumped out of the car, ran and disappeared into the fog. After a few minutes a figure emerged from the fog, I drew my gun and got out of the car. It was just old Joe he said he saw someone running in the distance but they were too far away to know who it was. He thought it was kids, but I don't think so. My gut instinct tells me there is something else going on out there. Most of the kids in town know and like Aaron. They would never do that to him. I can't stop blaming myself for what happened to him. I should have been alert, like he was."

"Anne you just took a major step in becoming a good officer. That's why I paired you with Aaron I figured he could teach you more than any of the other officers. You will have a lot of chances to practice what you have just learned…you can never let your guard down. Now I want you to go home and relax. I want you back here later, rested. Tonight you'll be on patrol with a new partner."

The Chief stood up and opened the door.

"By the way, I thought you were very courageous for going to the cemetery in the first place, especially after what you went through at the mortuary. Now go home and rest, you don't look so good. I don't want the public thinking I use slave labor."

I should have felt complimented on what the Chief said about my bravery, but I felt that I had lied to him. I didn't tell him the whole story, that I was really more concerned about seducing Aaron than paying attention to my job. It was always about me, whatever I wanted, I got, except Aaron's love. My mind went back to the crypt; I thought I heard a sound, like breathing. I didn't pay much attention to it; I was too busy trying to help Aaron.

My shift was about over. I felt restless and decided that my day needed closure. I needed to see Aaron. With my uniform on I knew I would have no trouble getting in to see him. Amanda was not there, so I quietly stepped into his room. He looked so vulnerable lying there. When I thought he could have been killed, the tears started to roll down my cheeks. I pulled up a chair next to his bed and took his hand in mine. I hadn't prayed since I was a child, today seemed like a good time to start. What started as a prayer ended up as a one-sided conversation with Aaron. I looked up into his sweet face and wished with all my heart for him to open his eyes. I wanted him to know how sorry I was about everything I put Amanda and him through. I leaned close to him and whispered,

"Aaron, I should have been at your side every minute, instead of trying to seduce you. It seems like I'm always thinking of myself. You will never know how much I love you, but I'm finally realizing it was just a one-sided love. I was willing to play second fiddle to Amanda, but now I know that's not how you and I really want it to be. I will always be your friend but not your partner on the police force. I'm asking the Chief for a new partner. Tonight I was not a good partner to you. As a result I endangered your life....and it hurts to work so close to you. I know you'll understand and I know Amanda will be a lot happier with this decision."

Anne rose from her chair and wiped the tears that were streaming down her face. She bent over and kissed Aaron on the lips. She knew this was the last time she would be doing this. She walked out the door, without looking back. Aaron opened his eyes and watched her walk away. He had heard her every word. He knew with a sigh of relief that this was the way it had to be. It was time for Anne to let go. Once again, Aaron closed his eyes and fell into a contented sleep.

Chapter 28

It was around eight AM when I returned home. Jackie, my roommate, had made fresh coffee before leaving for work. I poured myself a cup and sank down into an easy chair in the living room. I couldn't believe it had just been eight hours since Aaron's life had hung in the balance, and how much my life had changed as well. I took a sip of coffee and let the much needed warmth slowly seep into my body. I realized how tired I was of playing the role of a blonde airhead who was out to get Aaron. It was a losing game on my part. The prize would not have been winning him but losing all the years of my youth and happiness with someone else. Starting today I had to give a hundred present to the police force and forget my need for Aaron. I knew this last part wouldn't be easy.

I was getting ready for bed when the phone rang. I wasn't going to answer it, thinking that it was probably reporters wanting information about the cemetery and Aaron. On second thought it could be the Chief wanting more information. I walked over to the phone that was sitting on my nightstand. I picked up the receiver, "Hello…Hello?" There was only the sound of deep breathing on the other end. I hung up without further hesitation, and took the phone off the hook. I always felt pride in myself for being a very calm person but something about this phone call was unnerving. Before I got into bed I double-checked the doors and windows. I could not sleep. I thought about my town of Hartger's Grove and wondered what was going on in this Norman Rockwell town. It was always a quiet town, but now I could feel an evil undercurrent spreading its poison right though the center of town. I was too restless to sleep so I got up and walked over to the window. Most people were starting their day, either going to work or running errands. As I was about to close the blinds I looked down and noticed an old dark green van parked almost directly in front of my building. I had never noticed it before and thought that maybe someone new had moved into the building. I couldn't see if it had license plates, I laughed, and thought I was getting rather paranoid. I shrugged, and closed the mini blinds, and turned down my bed.

I had been asleep for about three hours when the phone rang. On the fourth ring I was awake enough to answer it.

"Hello?" There was no answer, only silence, once again I said "Hello? Is there anyone there?" By this time my patience was wearing thin.

"Look I know there is somebody on this phone. If this is a joke, it's not a very good one."

I hung up the phone and took it off its cradle. I found it rather difficult to fall back to sleep. After tossing and turning for a half hour I decided to watch the news to see if there was anything about the cemetery escapade. There wasn't, so I switched to another channel, which happened to be a soap opera. It was when the actress reached to answer her phone that I remembered my phone was still off the hook. I hurried to my room and hung up the phone. It was only seconds later that the phone began to ring. I wasn't going to answer it, but then figured that it could be the Chief. I still hesitated about answering it, but then what woman could ignore a ringing telephone? Before I could say Hello, a wild sounding Jackie said,

"Anne it's about time you answered the phone, I've been so worried about you. I heard what happened to Aaron, being hurt at the cemetery, and I knew you were there with him. Are you okay?"

"No, I'm not hurt. Jackie, have you been getting a lot of phone calls where no one says anything?"

"No, why do you ask?"

"I got a couple of them today that's why I took the phone off the hook."

"It was probably some kids playing a joke. How is Aaron doing? I bumped into Peggy at the donut shop this morning. She's a nurse that works at the hospital. She was the one who told me what happened to Aaron. She couldn't tell me everything because she doesn't work in emergency, so she didn't have all the information. Are you sure that you weren't hurt?"

"Jackie if I was I wouldn't be talking to you from home."

Jackie gave a small chuckle and made me promise to tell her about what happened later. When she hung up I decided to go back to bed, I didn't think I would fall back to sleep, but before I knew it the ringing of my alarm clock told me it was three o'clock.

I jumped into the shower and my thoughts immediately turned to Aaron and how he was doing. I knew it was useless calling the hospital as they could not release any information unless you were family. I took the bar of soap and started to lather up when I started to visualize Aaron being here with me. I closed my eyes and could see every dimple and smile line on his face. I let out a small groan when I realized what I was thinking.

"Oh God, please help me to get over this fixation, it's so wrong!" I knew it was going to be an uphill battle trying to forget Aaron as my lover. He never was my lover, only in my mind. I sighed and stepped out of the shower. I reached for the towel. With one hand I dried myself and with the other hand I reached into the closet for my clothes. I was almost finished getting dressed when the phone rang. This time it was the chief inquiring on how I was doing.

"I'm fine. Is there any word on how Aaron is doing?"

"Well he's not being a good patient, and the nurses are just about ready to throw him out. If he keeps up his good recovery he should be able to go home in a couple of days. His arm will be pretty sore with all those stitches and I imagine he has a king size headache from the concussion. Anne, I'm not one to beat around the bush, but I'm lining up the schedule for cemetery patrol. I don't think you or any other female officer should be out there. This is a more serious situation than we originally thought. I'm keeping you behind the desk tonight."

"No, you can't do this to me. I'm an officer just like the rest of the guys. Please, I have to do this, otherwise, I might as well not be a police officer." The chief did not say anything for a moment.

'Well it's against my better judgment, but I'll put you on tonight. If anything goes crazy out there, there will be no women officers going out there. That's my final word on the subject."

"Thank you sir, I appreciate it."

"Anne, don't make me regret my decision. You are one brave officer, but don't push it."

After Anne hung up the phone the chief started going though some of his papers on his desk. There was an envelope addressed to him that he had not seen before. He recognized the handwriting as Anne's. She had a very distinct penmanship, very bold yet feminine at the same time. He torn open the envelope, he never did have time for frills such as a letter opener. Letter openers belonged on women's fashionable desks. He began to wonder if he could be considered a male chauvinist. But he knew that some of his finest officers were women, like Anne. He began reading the letter.

To Chief Frank Smith:

I'm requesting a new partner. I feel that if I had been fully alert at the cemetery last night, nothing would have happened to Officer Fischer. A good officer would have been at his side at all times. Please consider my request

Officer Anne Bradley

Frank sat back and thought about the letter he'd just read. He knew it didn't tell him everything. There was always gossip floating around the station. He didn't like gossip, because things were always blown out of proportion. But it was another way for him to find out what was going on in his home away from home. He knew his officers well enough to separate the truth from false innuendoes. He knew Anne had special feelings for Aaron. It probably wasn't his best decision to make them partners, but he figured that Aaron could impart a lot of his skills on Anne. Now that Aaron was hurt he was going to honor Anne's request. He made a deep sigh and wondered what was going on in his hometown of Hartger's Grove. Up to six months ago it would have been voted the best and safest town to raise a family. He was proud to be part of that tradition. He wondered if the outside world was finally catching up with them, maybe it was time for him to retire. But that wasn't like him, to give up when things started to get rough. He was going to straighten out this cemetery problem even if he, himself, had to go on patrol. His mind made up, he decided that he would be Anne's partner for tonight and this would give him time to find a replacement for her.

Chapter 29

It was at dinner that night that I told Jackie about what happened at the cemetery the night before. She listened intently to everything I told her. I was almost finished when the phone rang. She said she would get it since she was expecting a call. I heard her pick up the phone and say hello a couple of times, after a few minutes she walked back into the kitchen saying,

"Humph that was strange, I said "Hello" but nobody answered. I know there was someone on the other end, I could hear him breathing. Now that I think about it, I did get a call this morning. Have you gotten the same calls Anne?"

I nodded my head yes and suggested that maybe we should change our phone number as well as the locks on our doors, she immediately agreed.

We took our coffee into the living room. We were silent for a while, then Jackie asked me what my plans would be, now that I don't have Aaron as my partner. I hesitated before I told her that Aaron would never be my partner on the police force again that I had asked the Chief for a new partner. That surprised her. I told her I finally realized that Aaron would never be mine, on the force, or otherwise. I also mentioned that I would be on cemetery patrol tonight. I really don't know which shocked her more because her mouth hung open in disbelief.

"You are going on cemetery patrol again? Who's going to be your partner?"

"The Chief is going to give me a new partner. He was going to put me on desk duty, but I insisted on going, otherwise I might as well not be a police officer."

"Well, all I can say is that he has faith in your work. As for me, I think you are one very brave woman."

I didn't know what to say when Jackie praised me. In the old days I would have relished it, but now I was embarrassed by it. After a few minutes of silence I returned to the kitchen to do the dishes, Jackie followed me and took a towel to help. I turned to her and continued slowly,

"This wanting I have for Aaron...well I'm trying to get over it. Last night I thought he was going to die. It took all my will power to think clearly and decide my course of action. Here was a man I truly loved, bleeding to death. When I started this obsession over him, it was mostly out of lust and not love. I was like a spoiled child who wanted everything, and usually got it. When I saw Amanda come into the emergency room in hysterics and the doctor leading her gently into Aaron's room, I realized then that I will never be Aaron's wife, just his partner on the force. When all is said and done, I would sooner see him happy with Amanda then lying in a casket with me as his wife. If I can't beat this wanting him...then I'll have to leave Hartger's Grove.

Jackie gave me a gentle hug and said,

"I hope you won't ever leave, and I'll be here to help you every step of the way."

It was around 10 P.M. when I started to get ready for work. I was just about finished putting on my uniform when I heard the phone ring. Jackie answered it and again I could hear her say "Hello, Hello?" then I heard her say,

"OK jerk have it your way." She blew a shrill whistle into the receiver, and then slammed it down on the cradle.

"I'll bet his ear will be hurting for awhile."

I was becoming alarmed as more of these phone calls came. I didn't mention to Jackie that I thought I might have been followed to work the other night. I intended to walk again tonight, but this time I'll be ready for whatever happens.

Nothing did happen, maybe it was all my imagination.

Chapter 30

I had just entered the squad room when the Chief called me into his office.

"Please sit down Anne. First of all I want you to know that I read your request. Since Aaron is on sick leave and you still want cemetery detail. I am giving you a temporary partner for tonight. But before I tell you who it is, I want to know if you really want this cemetery detail?"

I looked at the Chief, and tried to read his facial expression. He was grinning from ear to ear. Before I could reply he said,

"I'm going to be your partner, I want to see for myself what's really going on there. Be ready to leave by 1 A.M. sharp, and dress warm."

It was a little before one when the Chief came up to my desk and requested me to get the car ready. I was all too happy to get the show on the road.

Within ten minutes we were on our way. I found myself in the driver's seat with the Chief keeping a running dialog about his family and asking me how I was doing after the murder in the mortuary. He wanted to know if there were any lingering effect. The NO came out too quickly, because he looked at me with a questioning look. He didn't say anything but settled further back into his seat. Before we got to the cemetery we passed the place where Vormen's funeral home once stood. It had burned to the ground the night Lewis Vormen had his fatal heart attack. I felt with the deaths of the Vormen men, Beatrice, and her daughter Sarah, it was an end to an era. It was just as fitting that the mortuary was destroyed as a final closure. The arson investigation was still going on.

I showed the Chief where Aaron and I were parked and what our plan was. The crypt was surrounded by yellow tape, to warn people away from the scene of the crime. The chief nodded his head and said we were going to follow the same procedure.

The night was overcast with a hint of rain. The moon was hiding behind the clouds making it a little difficult to see what was going on around us. The Chief and I took turns making our rounds. I could feel the hair stand up on the back of my neck when I heard the many night creatures moving about. Ever so often I could hear the hoot of a great horned owl as it sat on the roof of a neighboring crypt. The crypt door was in the process of being repaired, but anyone could still enter if they had any intention of doing so. The night passed slowly. It was on my last round, just before dawn, that I heard a sound I couldn't identify. I paused and shined my flashlight towards the crypt. A minute passed when I heard it again, it was not more than a mere whisper, but the clarity was there,

"Anne....Anne, don't be afraid I won't hurt you. Please come a little closer."

I froze, just then I heard the Chief calling me. But I heard the soft whisper again, this time a little louder almost sounding angry.

"Anne, that was not nice of your roommate to blow that whistle into the phone. Tell her that if it happens again I will be very upset with her."

I walked away quickly, actually I wanted to run, but I didn't want the Chief to know how scared I was. I should have told him about the voice and we both could have investigated the sound in the crypt. I didn't, I just wanted to get far away from there. I was shaking when I got back to the squad. What was wrong with me? I knew that now was the time to tell the Chief, but I just didn't want to go back in there again. I got behind the wheel and started the car. I put it in reverse and almost hit a monument in doing so. The Chief looked at me and said,

"If it wasn't so dark out there I'd say you look as if you've seen a ghost. This place gives me the willies, too. I don't know how old Joe lives out here. I suppose its cheap rent and over the years you get use to living without neighbors, but I still wouldn't want to live here."

As an after thought to what he had just said he added, "Not while I'm alive."

As Anne was driving out of the cemetery, a lone figure was left standing in the doorway of the mausoleum, a thoughtful look on his face. He found Anne Bradley's beauty captivating. Ever since he'd seen saw her naked that night at Vormen's, he knew he wanted her.

Chapter 31

The next few days were uneventful for Anne. The phone calls stopped, she hoped that since the perpetrator scared her that night, in the cemetery that would be all he wanted from her. Aaron was home from the hospital, and receiving visitors. She wanted to go and tell him what was going on, but she didn't want to upset him. Besides he was not her partner, and maybe this whole incident was over. But Anne's police sense knew something was going on. She had this sick feeling in the pit of her stomach that something was about to happen. Every day at work she asked the other officers who had been on cemetery detail, if they had heard or seen anything out of the ordinary. All had the same reply that everything was as quiet as a tomb, and they would laugh at their own puns.

She was glad that she had a few days off; it gave her time to recharge her mental batteries.

When she returned to work, she was again on the graveyard shift. Anne was hoping that the Chief would not put her on cemetery patrol since her nerves were just beginning to calm down. Anne walked over to the duty roster and as bad luck would have it she did indeed find her name on that list. She had just returned to her desk when her phone rang.

"Hartger's Grove police department, Officer Bradley speaking."

"Hello Anne, are you coming out to the cemetery tonight? I've missed you these past few nights. Anne it's a wise thing that you didn't tell your boss about me, otherwise he might have been the next officer to be in the hospital. How would it look to your fellow officers if you were never the one to get hurt, just your partners. They would think you're still shocked from the mortuary incident and are too unsteady for police work. Rest assured, Anne, I would never hurt you. You're very quiet, are you surprised that I know so much about you. Someday when you and I are together I will tell you everything I know about you. Behave yourself Anne, I will see you tonight."

Anne's hand shook as she lowered the receiver.

"Anne are you coming down with the flu? You don't look so well." Bruce, my new partner, inquired. I just shook my head and told him that I had a headache and that I would be fine after I took a couple of aspirins. I walked over to the restroom, it was empty. I leaned my head against the cool tiles, the cold felt so soothing. With shaking hands I took out the aspirin bottle from my bag, and shook out two aspirins. If only I could go home and bury myself under the bed covers. I knew I couldn't do that since we were so short handed in the department. Oh if only Aaron could be here, he would know what to do. Those days are over for good. I combed my hair and applied fresh lipstick, hoping this would add more color to my face. As I left the restroom I collided with Ernie the maintenance man. He was a strange man, tall, and very thin almost to the point of being anorexic. He wore glasses that were so thick that it made me think he should have had a seeing eye dog instead. His hair was thinning and his clothes looked as if they had seen better days. It was hard to say how old he was, but I guessed him to be somewhere in his mid to late forties. He was a man that could be easily overlooked, almost like a shadow.

"Excuse me, Officer Bradley, I hope I didn't scare you?"

"No Ernie, it was my fault, I shouldn't have been rushing like that."

I gave him a weak smile and walked to my desk. Ernie watched her walk away. With a smirk on his face, he knew he'd finally gotten her attention. Yes sir, before this is all over she's going to get to know him real good. He grabbed his mop and bucket and went into the women's restroom. He took a deep breath and inhaled the perfume that she was wearing. He could close his eyes and follow her because of the special scent she always wore. Ernie leaned against the wall, an amused look on his face and deep in thought.

"Anne, you are so beautiful, I wonder what you taste like. A woman like you should not be a cop, but a slave who lies in bed to await her master's demands, my demands."

Anne sat down at her desk, trying to compose herself. She shuffled some papers, as her new partner Bruce came over. He was just a kid, no more than six months out of the academy. Anne wondered who would be protecting whom when the time came.

"Well, Anne, I hear you are my senior partner?"

Anne could see the cockiness in him and knew that a few of the young officers didn't like being overshadowed by a woman.

"Bruce, this might seem like kid's play to you., but you're forgetting that an officer got hurt out there, so it has been updated to a serious and dangerous situation. When we get out there I will fill you in with all the patrol details. Whatever you do, the crypt is off limits, is that understood?"

"You mean I'm not going to be on crypt patrol? I've been looking forward to this patrol for awhile and you just want me sitting in the car?"

"No, not sitting, but patrolling the outer limits away from the crypt, is that understood? Besides I don't want to have to be taking another officer to the hospital."

The Chief was standing in the doorway of his office, listening to the conversation between the two officers. It seems that Anne was taking on the role of leader very well. Maybe pairing her with Aaron had been a good idea after all. With a satisfied nod he turned to go back into his office. To all of his subordinates, the closed door meant, "do not disturb" except in an emergency. Frank thought about his job here in Hartger's. No, job, was wrong terminology. These officers and the town's people were like family to him, and he swore an oath to protect them. But there was a nagging inside of him that kept saying he was neglecting his own family, his wife Sophie and their three daughters. Of course Sophie knew his dedication to his job, but both of them were nearing their golden years and should be thinking about retiring. In his mind he had already picked his new Chief, and he knew that Aaron would make an excellent one. He promised himself that once this cemetery caper was over he would hand in his walking papers. It was close to one A.M., Frank decided to see if everything was ready for the cemetery detail.

Anne decided to let Bruce do the driving. She figured these young guys had big egos and he would prefer to do the driving. There was also another reason not having to drive, when they got to the cemetery, she wanted to give all of her attention to what was going on around her. Anne felt that if Bruce heard a hint of a whisper he would forget her commands and go off to investigate. She had to be in total control of him. She shuddered to think that she would have to put herself in close contact with the stalker. Stalker…that was the first time she had called him that, but that was what he was turning into.

As the squad turned into the cemetery, Anne told Bruce where to park. She gave him instructions and once again reminded him to stay away from the crypt. Both officers settled down for a spell, not much conversation flowed between them. It was quiet, except for the wind that rustled the branches of the tall pines. The season of fall was just around the corner it would be a pretty time of the year. The leaves would be turning shades of yellow, orange, and brown. The days would still be warm, but the nights would be decidedly cooler. In town the aroma of burning leaves would be in the air. The kids were back in school and the high school was already getting ready for the first football game of the season. It really was a scene out of a Norman Rockwell painting.

Bruce looked over at Anne in awe, and said,

"For a girl, you amaze me. I've been watching you and you are as cool as a cucumber. It's like we are sitting at a drive-in movie just waiting for the feature to start. Aren't you spooked a little? I have to admit this is not what I thought it would be like."

"Yes I'm scared, although I'm getting used to it. Don't forget this is my third time out here. I try to imagine it as it would be in the daytime. Besides it's not the dead that caused Aaron's injury, but the living. I also vowed that I won't watch any horror movies, until this is all settled." They laughed at that. Again silence ruled, each in his own thoughts. I thought about what I had just told Bruce, about not being afraid of the dead. That was a lie, because I was afraid. Suppose, just suppose it was a phantom that I was dealing with. According to articles I read, strange things are always happening. I rubbed my forehead, and thought to myself that I have been out here too many nights. How could this thing hurt Aaron as bad as it did, when it seemed he really wanted me? Aaron could not remember a thing about that night, except that he was hit from behind. The next thing he remembered was being in a lot of pain and in the hospital. The Chief was about to close the cemetery patrol since nothing was happening. The Chief thought the perp was long gone, but I knew differently. If I had told the Chief what was happening to me, I would not be out here tonight. I feel that only I can put an end to this case.

It was time for our rounds. I knew I was going to hear from the stalker on one of my rounds tonight. Both of us had our flashlights on, I wanted to whistle in the worse way, I knew I had to keep my nerves steady. I stood in front of the crypt door listening for the soft whisper. All I could hear was the sound of my own breathing. I was about to return to the car, when I heard it. It sounded like a soft lullaby. It sounded so soothing, like a lovers caress.

"Hello Anne, I've been waiting for you, please don't be frightened." I could not see him, but knew he could see me.

"Why are you playing this cat and mouse game with me? Why are you hiding in the shadows? Why did you almost kill Officer Fischer? I didn't give him time to answer, then I noticed he was silent. After a long pause he said,

"I'm sorry Anne, that was not supposed to happen. I know a lot about you, but there is so much more I want to learn. Consider this the start of an old fashioned courtship. In time this place will seem like home to you. By the way Anne, that was very smart of you to keep that young officer away from here. You see, I'm never very far from you. You are what I dream of day and night."

I wanted to get away from this stalker, but there was one question I wanted to ask him. In a voice a little above a whisper I asked him,

"Why are you hiding in the shadows? Why don't you come out and face me like a real man?"

Again there was silence, I was about to leave when he said in a voice filled with such great sadness,

"Anne, you are my dream, and I'm your worse nightmare. I'm a phantom and will always be."

I was startled by what he said, but I also knew I had to end this conversation before Bruce came looking for me

"This is ridiculous I can't believe I'm talking to a bodiless voice, a phantom no less."

"Anne, I want your boss to send only you on these night patrols. You won't have to be afraid of being out here, I'll protect you. You show great courage and I admire that. Goodnight, my sweet Anne."

As I hurried to the car I could hear Bruce calling me in a hoarse whisper.

The rest of the night seemed like it would never end. Bruce talked a mile a minute, I think it was to cover up his fear of being out here. I tried to concentrate on what he was saying, but my thoughts kept coming back to the phantom. He was probably no more a phantom, than someone that had a sick twisted way of meeting women. While he was talking I tried to pinpoint the exact location his voice was coming from. The direction was from the crypt, but then again it seemed to come from all around me, like a swirling mist. His voice sounded different than the other night, almost like it was two different people. One was loving, the other cruel and vindictive. Tonight it almost sounded like he was apologizing for hurting Aaron. What kind of thing am I dealing with?

"Anne, Anne are you ok?"

"I'm sorry, I guess I was in deep thought."

"You sure were, I kept asking you questions but you just sat there like a zombie."

When we got back to the station, I sat down at my desk. My shift was about over, when Ernie the maintenance man came over. He asked me if I wanted a cup of coffee. I was so deep in thought that I jumped when I heard his voice.

"I'm sorry again if I frightened you, I have a habit of walking quietly. I thought that you might need something hot to drink after sitting all night in the cold."

"No thank you and please don't apologize, I was in deep thought and I didn't hear you."

He stood there looking down at me, a cat like expression on his face, and I was the bird in the cage.

"Is something bothering you Anne? Did you see or hear something out of the ordinary at the cemetery tonight?"

It was an odd thing to ask, so I pretended not to hear.

"Well you probably wouldn't tell me anyway." He shrugged his shoulders and walked away.

I watched him as he walked away and wondered why he asked me those questions? He certainly was a strange man. Earlier I had tried to think of a word to describe him, and cunning would be the word.

Chapter 32

The days of September went fast, before I knew it, it was October. There was not a word from the phantom, either to the police or me. It was almost as if he were a bad dream, but the injury to Aaron made him very real.

Aaron was back on the job doing mostly paper work. I figured the Chief was grooming him for his job. Every now and then I could hear retirement coming from the Chief's office, if that was the case, the Chief could not have picked a better replacement.

Looking at Aaron, he seemed very rested and happy. I figured that's what a happy married life did to a person. In my heart I knew that if I had Aaron's wedding ring on my finger, I would have that same look. I sighed and called it a day.

When I got home Jackie had not yet left for work.

"Good morning, how did your day go?"

I was busy taking my gun and holster off so I didn't answer her. She was always perceptive to my moods. She knocked before entering my room.

"Is something the matter? Did something go bad at work?"

"No everything is fine, why do you ask?"

"Well when you walked through the door I could tell by the look on your face, that something is bothering you."

I sighed and sank down on the bed.

"I do have a problem but I'm not at liberty to say anything about it." I could tell she didn't quite believe me.

"Did the Chief tell you not to say anything about it?"

"No I'm using my own discretion on this one."

"Oh Anne I don't like the sound of this. Look I have to leave for work, but maybe we can talk about this tonight. So think about it, Ok?"

I just nodded my head and watched her leave the room. I had to make up my mind if I really wanted to tell her about the stalker, or phantom. This past month had been very quiet at the cemetery. So quiet that the Chief let Old Joe the caretaker back into his house at the cemetery. One of the women officers thought she'd heard something, but it turned out to be an owl.

I took out my pajamas and robe from behind the bathroom door. Normally I take a shower before retiring but today I feel very tired, and I just want to go lie down. I checked the door to be sure Jackie had locked it, she did. I was about to climb into bed when I decided to see if the green van was parked outside, it wasn't. Lately I've checked to see if it's was there, and it never is. As I climbed wearily into bed the phone rang. With the ring of the phone I could feel every nerve and muscle in my body tense up. I hesitated, and then slowly picked up the receiver on the third ring.

"Hello? There was silence for a brief second when I heard a soft seductive voice.

"Good morning Anne, I've missed seeing you at the cemetery. Are you getting ready for bed?"

My hands turned cold and sweaty as I listen to the all too familiar voice. The voice that was barely above a whisper. If I closed my eyes I could almost feel his breath on my face and neck, warm with life, yet cool like a late fall's night. How could this be? Was I headed for a nervous breakdown?

"Anne, I know you're listening, I can hear your heart beating, and your breathing turning more rapid with every word I say. I just wanted to say Goodnight to you. Like you, I'm going to sleep that long sleep of day and awaken when the night calls. Please don't be afraid of me. Sleep my sweet Anne, I will see you soon."

I held the phone to my ear long after I heard the click. As if in a trance I slid under the bed covers and fell into a long dark dreamless sleep.

"Hey girl, wake up, don't you know what time it is? Its 5:30, didn't you go right to bed after I left for work?"

I sat on the edge of my bed, I felt so strange, like I had been drugged. All I took before I went to bed were two aspirins, so I knew it couldn't be that. I couldn't believe that I had slept ten hours. I sat, and tried to make sense about the way I was feeling. There was something about the phone that I should remember, but for some reason it would not come into focus. All I could remember was the overwhelming fatigue and the dreamless sleep.

"Anne, is there something special you want for dinner?"

"I'm not very hungry, I'll eat later."

Jackie would not take that for an answer. As she walked into the living room with her hands on her hips. She saw Anne was standing in the middle of the room as if she was in a daze. She knew there was a problem but until Anne was ready to talk there was nothing she could do to help.

"Anne, I'm going to order a pizza while you go and take a shower, which should make you feel better."

Jackie had that no nonsense tone of voice, like an old mother hen. While I was in the shower I decided to tell Jackie what was going on.

The pizza delivery guy was just leaving when I came into the room. Jackie took the pizza into the living room and laid it on a snack table. We were quiet for a couple of minutes, both of us relishing each bite we took. I guess I was hungrier than I thought. I took a few sips of my coke, when Jackie came right to the point and said,

"Ok Anne, I'm in the mood for some conversation. Are you going to tell me what's going on in your life?"

"I really don't know where to start except to tell you about the phone calls."

Jackie wrinkled her brow in puzzlement, but didn't say anything. I told her everything starting with the calls, about someone following me to work one night, and the bodiless voice at the cemetery. When I finished, I made Jackie promise not to blow the whistle into the phone, telling her that he said he would hurt her if she did.

"Who says they're going to hurt me?"

"The phantom or stalker or whatever you want to call him. He made himself known the night I went with the Chief to the cemetery. I can't explain it, but something happened to me that night. I found myself standing in front of the crypt, just standing there as if in a trance. It was then that I heard a sound, at first I thought it was the wind whispering though the trees. It was his soft voice beckoning me to come closer to the entrance of the crypt. I wondered if I would have gone in if I hadn't heard the Chief calling me. Sometimes I think I'm dealing with two different people. One voice is demanding and harsh, the other is like a lovers caress."

"My God, Anne, please tell me that you told the Chief all about this?"

I looked down at my can of soda, and that was enough of an answer for Jackie.

"Anne it's imperative that you tell the Chief all about this. This guy sounds dangerous, for Pete sakes, look what he did to Aaron. I really, really can't believe you didn't tell the Chief. What did they teach you at the Academy? Do you think you are a police force of one? Maybe there is more to this story then you're telling me?"

"The calls stopped coming for awhile, until this morning. No one on patrol heard or saw anything. If I told them my story they would think I'm crazy, or suffering from my near embalming at the mortuary. He keeps warning me to keep my partner away from the crypt, or he would end up in the hospital like Aaron. All he really wants is me, and I will be dealing with him my own way."

Jackie jumped out of her chair, almost knocking over the snack table, I never saw her so angry.

"If you don't tell the Chief, I will at least tell Aaron."

"No, Jackie, you won't tell anyone. If you do I'll deny everything and move out, to boot. Please give me your solemn oath that you will not tell anyone?"

Jackie thought a long time then sat back in her chair, and I knew that I had won for the moment. I told Jackie that I felt a headache coming on and that I was going to my room to lie down before I had to dress for work. She came up to me and gave me a big hug. She told me not to worry, that she would not mention our conversation to anyone. She squeezed my hand and walked slowly to her room. I knew there was something else she wanted to say, but thought better of it. She knew I disliked sermons.

I hated to lie to Jackie; I really did not have a headache. I just wanted time to think things over, like how tired I was this morning; it felt as if I had been drugged. I remembered a voice so rich and warm, and yet at the same time as cool as the fall night. There was something about a phone, it was then that I remembered the call from him. His voice was so mesmerizing. I loved the way he said my name. I was beginning to think I was having a total meltdown. Was I having feelings for a man living in the shadows? I don't know why he preferred to live that way, but I was going to find out. I lay on the bed trying to remember the whole conversation, but it was no use. I dimmed my bedside lamp and closed my eyes. I tried to visualize the man behind the voice. Soon, I felt as if I was in a swirling mist, with darkness all around me.

Minutes passed, and Anne was soon asleep. Her breathing began to slow down. This dream was different from the last one. Anne could see herself lying on her bed, at the side of the bed was a figure. The harder she tried to see his face the more elusive he became. She tried to reach for his hand, but he moved back into the shadows. She could feel her lips moving, but no sound came, it was like she was pleading for an answer. She could feel the coolness of being undressed, feeling the night air on her bare skin. The coolness woke her; she looked down at her naked body lying on top of the blankets. She sat up and quickly pulled the covers over her body, her eyes scanning the room around her. The room was empty, but the dream seemed so real. She laid back down, wondering what was happening to her. She wondered if all this was a delayed reaction from the mortuary incident. Were the cemetery patrol and the funeral incident finally taking a toll on her? One thing she did know was that she had to get a hold of herself before she loses it all together.

A hot shower put warmth back into her body. Her whole being had been shaken by the dream. She slowly applied her make up and finished dressing. As she walked into the living room Jackie looked up from the book she had been reading and said,

"You look a hundred percent better, your headache must have gone away. Anne, were you having a bad dream? I almost came in to see if you were okay, but then you quieted down. Oh by the way, I just saw the weather report on television; they are forecasting rain before morning. As I reached for my rain gear I thanked Jackie for the information. I decided to drive to work, it was only a short drive but I thought I would do some errands in the morning after work. No…that was a lie, who was I trying to kid. I was scared, like the night I had to answer the call at Vormen's funeral home.

I pulled the car into the station parking lot then ran into the building as the first few drops of rain hit the ground. The weather people were certainly wrong on this one. It wasn't supposed to start raining till morning. I was checking the papers on my desk when the Chief called me into his office. While I was closing the door he pulled up a chair for me. He shuffled some papers then cleared his throat before he spoke.

"Anne, as you know we have been patrolling the cemetery for some weeks now and haven't found a clue. Personally I think the perp is long gone. We are short of manpower, and it is too costly to have two officers sitting out there. I'm thinking of closing the case all together, but before I do I want your opinion."

The Chief searched Anne's face for any sign of relief or…hell he didn't know what to expect to see on her face. One thing he knew for sure was that Anne was holding back some vital information. Maybe this would be the time she would speak up.

Anne knew the Chief was expecting some kind of answer. Now would be the time to tell him everything, but something held her back.

"Your right, the perp is probably in the next county. But I think we could bring it down to a one-man operation for at least a week. Chief, I have the most time out there, I want to volunteer to go." I could not believe I was saying that.

This was not the answer the Chief was expecting from her.

"No that's definitely out of the question. I didn't like sending you with a partner, and for me to send you alone is ludicrous."

"But Chief you just said that the perp is long gone. Give me this last chance to atone for what happened to Aaron, otherwise I won't be a good officer to any of my future partners."

'Off the cuff Anne, aren't you a little afraid to be out there alone?"

"I'm afraid of the living, not the dead. It was the living that did that to Aaron. I had to say something to the Chief to calm his objections of my going out there. It looked like it was working as I watched him moving his unlit cigar around in his mouth. I was amazed at how easy it was to lie. This is what the phantom wanted, an end to the patrol. This is what I wanted, time alone with the phantom.

It was against his better judgment, but after a few minutes he gave Anne the okay. Frank watched Anne walk out of his office. The feeling that she was hiding something was stronger than ever. He remembered the night he was out there with her, she was gone longer than usual on her rounds. She came back looking as pale as a ghost and a little shaky. Anne didn't say if she'd seen anything unusual. She was turning out to be a good police officer. At first she seemed like a pretty desk ornament, flighty, and a distraction to the male officers. She's changed since Aaron was wounded. Her serious and responsible side has emerged, and that is what he wants in his officers. He couldn't say for sure, but he thought the infatuation with Aaron was over, time will tell.

Ernie watched Anne return to her desk. He wondered what Frank wanted with her. He slowly approached her desk and asked,

"Good Evening Anne, I saw you come out of the Chief's office. Is someone getting a promotion?"

Anne looked up at him, and thought to herself that his teeth needed a good cleaning. He had a big smile, she could see every tooth in his mouth. It was not a pretty sight. She was a little annoyed that he should be that nosey, but then she thought that maybe he was lonely and just wanted to make a little conversation. Most of the officers had very little to do with Ernie. More than once she caught him looking at papers on their desks.

"No promotion today, just orders for the night patrol."

Anne could tell that he wanted more conversation, but her body language told him shoptalk was over. He stood by her desk for a while then turned and walked away. If Anne could have read his mind she would have been shocked. He smirked as he thought she was nothing but a lying piece of baggage, who thought she was too good for the likes of him. Well, he'll show her and her boyfriend Aaron. Alive they make a beautiful couple, but dead, maggots don't care how beautiful you are. He chuckled to himself as he went about his business. Soon my lovely. soon.

Chapter 33

It was raining hard when I left the station. When I arrived at the cemetery, I got out of the squad and unlocked the gates. I drove in a few feet and once again got out and locked the gates behind me. I returned to my car and slowly proceeded to the crypt. My conscience kept asking me if I really wanted to do this. I could turn back right now, the Chief wouldn't think badly of me. He probably thought I was a glutton for punishment to come this far. I thought about the phantom and Aaron. At this point I don't think he intended to hurt Aaron like he did. For some reason he wanted me. The break in was a ploy to get me out here, but why here was the puzzle.

I decided to park in front of the crypt, I wanted him to know that I was here by myself. I was just settling in and poured myself a cup of coffee, when I thought I heard a sound. It was hard to hear because of the rain beating on the roof of the car. When I heard the sound a second time, I put my cup down and started the car so I could start the windshield wipers. Even the windshield wipers couldn't keep up with the rain. I made the decision to go out and investigate, I took my flashlight and made sure my gun was handy. It was then that I noticed the crypt door was partly open. I knew the door had been repaired so it should have been closed. The phantom knew I was here. I broke into a cold sweat, and began to wonder about the sanity of being out here alone. This was no time for regrets. I slowly opened the car door and preceded cautiously towards the open crypt door, my hands shook. The grass was getting slippery and the dead leaves didn't help matters either. From the corner of my eye, I could see movement coming from around the side of the crypt. Throwing caution to the wind, I started to run towards it. It was in a split second that I felt myself falling and felt a sharp resonating pain though my head, then nothing.

The sound of rain coming from a distance brought me to semi-consciousness. I realized that I wasn't outside, but somewhere where it was warm and dry. I tried to open my eyes. As hard as I tried I could only see the darkness and nothing else. My head hurt too much to move, but I fought to get passed the darkness and haze. It was then I heard a familiar whisper,

"Anne don't move, you will only hurt all the more. I carried you to your car, but I had to blindfold you to cover up my identity, please forgive me."

Anne's head hurt so much that it was hard to think clearly. She tried to take the blindfold off, but the phantom took her hands in his. His touch was warm and gentle, and somehow that touch felt so comforting.

"Anne I just want you to know that I didn't do this to you. When you started to run, you slipped, fell, and hit your head against a tombstone. You might have a concussion and should go to the hospital. I only wanted to get you alone so we could talk, I didn't want all this to happen."

Anne could hear his voice in the distance, and she wondered why he was talking from so far away. She wished she could see him, this phantom of hers. All of this didn't make any sense to her. Her pain was so great that she once again passed out.

It was a quiet night at the hospital emergency department. The heavy rain and the early morning hours found most people asleep. Suddenly a loud siren from a police car broke the stillness. In a matter of seconds medical personnel went running through the automatic doors of the emergency entrance, to find a squad car with it's hood touching the doors. A nurse called for a gurney she saw a female officer slumped over, with a small river of blood trickling from under her hairline and down her face. They carefully got her out of the car and placed her on the gurney. Once in a cubicle, they worked on her as carefully as they could. One of the nurses remembered Anne from when she brought another police officer into the emergency room. She thought to herself how lucky she was to be a nurse instead of a police officer. The hospital contacted the Chief. He was just about to leave the station for the night when he received the call. He listened for a moment and before the doctor could finish he was out the door and on his way to the hospital, sirens blaring. He came in like a whirlwind and demanded to know where his officer was. A nurse came from behind a desk and tried to calm him down, but it was no use. She finally led him into the cubicle where they were still working on Anne. He stopped short as he saw a very still and very pale Anne. Her head was already bandaged and another doctor was working on her leg.

"Doc, is she going to be alright? What happened to her? Who brought her in? "

The doctor continued to work on Anne, he looked up at Frank and saw the worry etched on his face. He knew the man needed an answer fast. He heard from the grape vine how much the Chief cared for his people; they were like family to him. He also thought that whoever did this to her, should get out of town fast. He suggested to Frank that he should go and wait in the lounge. It would be only a few more minutes and he would have an answer for him.

Frank was used to giving orders not taking them, but he knew he was hampering their work so he did what the doctor suggested. As he paced the floor, the next twenty minutes seemed like forever. He had sent Anne out against his better judgment. He wondered if he was losing his touch at being a good boss. Maybe this wasn't an open and shut case after all. Earlier he had a hunch about Anne knowing something, he should have followed that hunch. Just then the doctor came into the room and offered him a cup of coffee.

"You know what I can't understand Chief? I can't understand how that woman drove herself to the hospital. First of all she has a very bad concussion that will keep her in the hospital for a few days. Secondly she has a fractured right leg that would hamper her from driving. What was her duty tonight that put her in this condition?"

"I can't give you the particulars of this case, but we were in the final stage of closing it up. Can I see her now?"

She hasn't regained consciousness yet, we are monitoring her very carefully. She'll have one big headache when she comes to. By tomorrow morning we should know more. By the way, she keeps mumbling something about a phantom, do you know what that means?"

Frank shook his head in puzzlement.

"They are getting a room ready for her but she still is in the emergency section, so why don't you go and take a peek and we will call you in the morning with more of an update."

"Like hell you'll call me in the morning, I'm going to stay right here until she regains consciousness."

The doctor knew how bullheaded Frank could be so he just shrugged and laid his hand on his shoulder as he walked past him.

The hours of the night dragged on as Frank would ever so often inquire about how Anne was. He remembered to call his wife Sophie and told her what was going on. She knew him well enough not to ask too many questions. She knew that he would tell her everything when the time comes. Sophie told him that she missed and loved him and that he should drive carefully. Frank counted himself lucky to have such a loving and devoted wife. The have been married thirty-five years, and yet it seemed like just yesterday.

Once more he tried to sit but it was no use, it seemed like his legs had a mind of their own. Anne was now in her own room so he decided to peek in on her. There was a nurse by Anne's side taking her blood pressure. She nodded a Hello, and then left the room. Frank pulled up a chair close to the bed. Anne looked so fragile lying in the hospital bed. Ever so often he thought he saw Anne's eyelids flutter, but he thought that maybe it was just wishful thinking on his part. He settled back in his chair, he knew he would be in for a long night. But no matter how long it would take, he would be at her side.

Frank closed his eyes and thought back to the day she walked into his office, requesting an application to the police academy. He knew of her, in a small town everyone knows everybody else. If you didn't know them personally you at least heard of them. Frank didn't know if he should take her seriously. When she returned the filled out application, he overheard some of the men talking about her. They all thought she was beautiful, but an airhead. But Frank wasn't one to turn down a person without giving them a chance. He figured if they passed the academy's rigorous training they were half way home. Frank tried to keep his eyes opened but he'd had a long day and they had a mind of their own. He was just settling into a peaceful sleep mode, when a nurse gently touched him on the shoulder. He woke with a start. The nurse apologized and said that there was a phone call for Anne and would he mind taking it? Frank figured it might be Aaron inquiring on how Anne was doing. He walked over to the nurse's station and picked up the receiver.

"Hello, Chief Smith, how can I help you?" After a moment of silence, he repeated the message, but there was still no reply. He put the phone back on its cradle, turned to the nurse and told her that no information about Anne was to be given to anyone. She curtly replied that it was hospital policy and he didn't have to tell her that. He then told the nurse that he wanted to be told about any other phones calls that might come in for Anne. He had a hunch that the call came from the person that put Anne in this situation, and usually his hunches were right.

The hours went by slowly, Frank disliked not being able to plan the next step of the cemetery patrol. He had to talk to Anne first to find out what happened out there. It was just about seven in the morning when Frank got a call from the station stating that he was needed. He was about to tell them to contact Aaron for the problem, when he got an idea, and told them to send Aaron over to the hospital. He thought that Anne might confide in Aaron before she would tell him. He had a smug look on his face as he hung up the phone. He mentally patted himself on the back, thinking that maybe he hadn't lost his touch after all.

Within twenty minutes Frank could hear Aaron's footsteps coming down the hall. He stepped out of Anne's room so she wouldn't hear what he was saying.

'Chief, how is Anne?"

Frank could see the worried look on Aaron's face. He also knew that Aaron felt he owed Anne for saving his life.

"She is still in a coma, but her vitals are stable, so that's a good sign. The reason I have you here is that since you were her partner, I figured she would talk more openly about what happened out there. I think she is covering up some facts about what happened to her on a earlier visit to the cemetery. There was a phone call for her, but whoever it was refuses to talk to me. I will inform the nurses to let you answer the phone in Anne's room."

Frank was about to leave when he turned to Aaron and said,

"By the way the doc mentioned that she keeps mumbling something about a phantom. The night I was on duty with her she was gone a little longer than usual on her patrol. I had to call her and she came back looking as pale as a ghost. I asked her if everything was all right out there, she just said everything was fine. Maybe that call came from her phantom, this case seems to get more interesting as we go along. Our Anne seems to be a woman of many secrets, but we won't know how many until she wakes up. I think she will talk more freely to you and I already ruffled the feathers of the head nurse, so you have your work cut out for you." When he was through giving Aaron the information he slapped him on the back and walked over to the elevator.

Morning shift at a hospital is hectic. Aaron left the room when the aids came in to change Anne's bedding. He walked up to the nurse's station to check on Anne's progress. The nurse was just about to give him a progress report when a young aid came running out of Anne's room exclaiming that Anne was coming out of her coma. A doctor and two nurses went marching into Anne's room. Aaron stayed in the hallway until the doctor came out, he then approached him to inquire about Anne's condition. The doctor recognized him from his pervious hospital stay.

"Officer Fischer, it's nice to see you in the picture of good health, how can I help you?"

"I like to know about Anne's progress?"

"What kind of case are you people working on? First it was you, then Officer Bradley, I didn't think we had such evil people in this town that would keep putting our officers in the hospital."

"We didn't think we had those kind of citizens either, but it only takes one bad apple to change things."

While Aaron was talking to the doctor, Jackie came hurrying down the corridor. Aaron introduced her to the doctor. The doctor then gave them a good but cautious report,

"Right now she's awake but groggy. At this time we don't know how much of a memory loss she has. She knows her name but she can't remember what put her in the hospital. Like I said she is not totally alert but the memory loss should be temporary. It takes time for the brain to heal.

I would suggest that you let her know you're here then let her rest. By this evening we should know a lot more about her condition."

Aaron and Jackie tiptoed into Anne's room, her eyelids fluttered open and she saw Aaron standing near her bed. At first everything seemed blurred as she fought to clear her vision. She felt his warm hand take hold of hers. There was something that seemed so right about this simple act, but she couldn't understand what. She wondered why the woman had tears coming down her cheeks. This was all so strange; she knew she hadn't died because she had this bad headache. If you died you weren't suppose to feel pain, only peace. Slowly that peace in the form of sleep took hold of her. Jackie and Aaron nodded to each other and left her room. Aaron took hold of Jackie's arm and suggested they go to the cafeteria for a cup of coffee. First he had to call the chief and give him a progress report. Jackie knew what was coming but she didn't know how much to tell him. A few minutes later Aaron joined Jackie at a table where two cups of steaming coffee awaited. There were a few minutes of silence before Aaron started the conversation,

"Jackie, I'm glad you could join me for coffee this morning. You probably already guessed that I have a lot of questions I need answers to." Jackie nodded her head in response.

"As Anne's roommate, has she ever confided in you about what's been going on in this case?"

Jackie didn't say anything at first, she wondered how much she should tell him. Would she be putting Anne's job in peril? Anne could have been killed out there, but she did know that if anyone could help Anne and save her job at the same time, it would be Aaron. It was then she decided to tell him everything she knew. She mentioned all the phone calls, and about how upset Anne got after Jackie blew a whistle into the phone. And how the next day Anne told her the Phantom would harm her if she did that again. She also mentioned how she thought she was being followed to work one night.

"A phantom?" It was then that Aaron remembered Frank mentioning how Anne kept mumbling about a phantom.

"Yes a phantom, which was what Anne started calling him. She first felt his presence the night she was on patrol with Chief Smith."

Aaron could not believe that Anne would keep this from the chief and mentioned that to Jackie.

"I had thought about that, but then I realized Anne was afraid if she told the Chief he would think she was suffering from the effects of the mortuary case, and he would put her on desk duty."

Aaron knew that would have been quite possible, but at the same time she was putting herself in danger.

"Why didn't Anne tell me, I'm her partner."

"You were her partner." Jackie emphasized were and then continued,

"Aaron, you had just come home from the hospital and was in no position to help her. I think eventually she would have told Frank after she'd gathered more facts. The phantom told her that it was a good thing she hadn't told the chief, because she would have been bringing him to the hospital as well. She tried to do some investigating on her own, like trying to hear where his voice was coming from, but couldn't."

"Jackie, how many times did Anne talk with this person?"

"I really don't know, but after awhile it seems that she started to have feelings for him.

"What do you mean, feelings?"

"Perhaps feelings isn't the correct word, but when I would say something derogatory about him she came to his defense."

Jackie looked down into her cup of coffee, which was now cooling down. She looked up at Aaron, tears glistening in her eyes.

"I'm sorry Aaron that's all I can remember, the rest, if there's more will have to come from Anne herself. Do you think Anne will be in trouble if what I told you gets to Frank?"

"Frank is a fair boss, but he will be angry when he hears this. The fact is that Anne held back important information, which could have cost her life as well as the lives of other officers who were sent out there."

"But she was doing that for you, Aaron. She wanted to find the person who did that to you. She felt so guilty about not covering your back that night, you were a person she truly loved. When she got to the hospital with you, thinking that you might die, and then seeing Amanda's reaction, I think that was the night she finally gave you up, but at the same time vowed that she would find the person who harmed you."

Aaron covered Jackie's hand with his and promised her that he would do everything in his power to come to Anne's defense. After a few more minutes of conversation Jackie decided to go to work since she knew that Anne was in good hands here at the hospital and would probably be sleeping for the rest of the day. Aaron knew he had asked a lot of Jackie, to betray the confidences Anne told her, but he thought that somehow Jackie seemed relieved in telling him.

When Aaron returned to the floor Anne was on, he decided to call the chief to see if he was needed at the station house. Frank thought a moment then told him to wait until he sent another officer in his place. It was barely fifteen minutes later when Bruce Langston came to relieve him.

"Wow I couldn't believe what happened to Anne. I'll say one thing about her, she sure is one cool lady."

"What do you mean cool lady?" Aaron asked with interest.

"Well, the night we had cemetery stakeout Anne issued me a lot of orders. It almost seemed like she was trying to protect me from getting hurt. She told me not to get anywhere near the crypt but to patrol the outer perimeter which was as far away as you can get. She also told me that if she got hurt, I shouldn't come near her, just to call 911 and wait in the car for backup. Between making rounds, she would sit in the car as if she were watching a movie at a drive-in. She seemed so calm, maybe I watch too many horror movies, but I sure didn't like being out there. I can't believe that Anne went out there by herself, she should get a medal for bravery."

Aaron thanked him for the information and told him that this news would be told to the Chief. Aaron took one more look at Anne, seeing that she was still sleeping he left her in the care of Bruce.

Chapter 34

A pair of blood shot eyes followed Aaron's entrance into the police station. Ernie made sure nobody saw his interest in the officer as he went right into the chief's office. He slid his pail and mop closer to the office and pretended to be cleaning. He strained his ears to hear what was being said on the other side of the door. He muttered to himself about the good soundproofing they'd put in these building. Damn, he couldn't hear a single word, so now he would have to devise a way to get his information. That damn Mike should not have been at the cemetery last night. He really screwed everything up, now the police will have their noses behind every tombstone in the cemetery. He was beginning to think that Mike was starting to have some feelings for Anne. Looks like he'll have to put some fear into him. Mike had him so worked up that he forgot to figure what kind of plan he needed to get the information. It couldn't be too obvious, mind you, just a very clever question that would give him all the information he wanted. Ernie didn't have to wait too long before Aaron came out of the chief's office. Ernie still hadn't thought of a question so he would have to wing it.

"Ah, excuse me, Officer Fischer, I heard that Officer Bradley is hurt pretty bad, is she going to make it? I hope you guys get the guy who did this to her."

"Anne is out of the coma and as soon as she's fully awake she'll be able to give us more information as to who did this to her."

Ernie pretended to agree with him, and then went back to his work thinking that Fischer should just know how much he hated him. His pretty boy image, plus his spit and polish and brains will be of use to him by the time he was finished with him. Yes, Siree, Ernie could taste his revenge, it was so sweet. The next plans will be carefully made, he will meet with Mike as soon as possible. But something bothered Ernie; he kept wondering why Mike had been where he wasn't suppose to be. Usually he had enough liquor in him that he couldn't even leave his apartment at night unless Ernie sent him on a job.

Even then, Ernie had to keep all booze away from him for at least a day. Again he had a gut feeling his partner was falling for Anne Bradley, and this would not do at all. If anyone was going to have her, it would be him. Ernie almost found himself drooling just thinking about her.

It was two nights later when Ernie met with his partner in crime. Ernie decided to meet him in a town twenty miles away from Hartger's Grove. It was a small bar, the interior was dark and smoke filled. Ernie was the first to arrive and chose a table in a corner away from prying eyes. He muttered to himself about people smoking and not knowing the dangers of cigarettes. Ernie looked around, the barmaid noticing his nervous actions. With no drink in front of him she walked up to his table to take his order.

"What can I get ya sugar, beer, whiskey, or me?"

Ernie looked her up and down, and thought that he would have to be pretty hard up and blind, to boot, take her up on her suggestive offer. Not wanting to draw attention to himself, he held back his wise crack and ordered a beer. Waiting for his beer he once again started to look the place over. He figured it must have been built around the 1920's like everything else in the town including the waitress. Being that it was mid-week there weren't many patrons in the bar. There was one lone couple sitting at a table at the far corner of the room. Ernie figured they weren't married to each other, because ever so often the guy would look nervously at the door especially when someone entered. Ernie decided to sip his beer slowly, money was tight for him since the police didn't pay their cleaning people, namely him, too much money. The beer was warm and flat. He was halfway though his beer when his partner entered. Talk about a fish out of water, this guy stood out in a crowd that is if you didn't notice his messed up face. Ernie wondered how the two of them could be brothers. He figured his old lady must have been stepping out on the old man. Both Mike and he were complete opposites of each other. The barmaid noticed Mike also, as she just about set a record to get to their table. Mike turned his face away so she could not see the damaged side. He nodded at Ernie then gave the woman his order. She stood for a moment just starring at him trying to really get a good look at him.

"Are ya a celebrity or sumptin? Ya sure are handsome, at least the side I can see. We never had someone as good looking as you in here before. Ya voice is so soft and sexy, it almost seems like ya propositioning me…are ya? Are ya on television?"

By this time Ernie had it with her and he told her to hurry up and get his buddy a beer. She couldn't tear her eyes off of her movie star. As she turned, she gave Ernie a drop-dead look. He decided that she'd just lost her tip. Not that he was going to give her one, but you just never know when a miracle might happen. He leaned over toward his brother and with a smirk said,

"The dimwit broad should just see the side of your face, she wouldn't think you're so handsome." In reality Ernie would give a king's fortune to have that face, until the accident happened. Since he was small he wanted to be the center of attention. In school he tried to be the class clown, the kids would laugh at him but not with him. He tried out for sports in high school but was too clumsy. He tried hard to fit in with the jocks and they made him their go-for instead. Well that was better than nothing, but someday he would show them all how smart he was. Many times he would curse who had made him the way he looked. He was tall in stature, but far too thin for his frame. His hair was thinning and a mousy brown in color. He had one outstanding feature and that was his eyes, which were dark and piercing like a bird of prey. He needed glasses, so he squinted, which made him look mean. He consoled himself with the fact that however short he might be in the looks department, his brains made up for it. Nobody knew how smart he really was, not even his former teachers, they just thought he was a conniver. He prided himself on that attribute.

Neither Mike nor he said anything until the waitress brought Mike's beer. She was just about to turn away when she turned to Ernie and said caustically,

"Ya just can't sit here all night with one beer, I'll be back in ten minutes with another beer so drink up." With a flip of her hair and a wink to his partner she returned to the bar. Ernie chose to ignore her remark.

"Ok Mike, what the hell happened out there, evidently you didn't follow my orders to stay home last night. Anne is out of her coma and might be able to talk to the police about what happened. If she mentions you, you'll be dead meat. So I'm asking you, what happened out there? Did you have rough sex with her, she's pretty banged up. If you had just stayed at home like you were suppose too, we could have gone on with my plans. But no, you had to fall for a pretty face, and play the hero by driving her to the hospital. I know it was you who drove her there cause she was in no shape to drive herself there. A hero nobody will ever know except to call you a phantom because that's what they're calling you...a nothing. You owe me big time Mike, for saving your life in the fiery inferno that was Vormen's funeral home. So now we are going to make new plans, plans that you will carry out to the fullest. You know if Anne saw the way you look, she would just turn away in disgust."

Ernie gloated at the last comment he'd made, it was like jabbing in a knife and twisting. Brother or not, Mike was another one Ernie hated intensely. Mike was afraid of Ernie, not what he could to him, but what Ernie might do to Anne. He took a drink of his beer, more for courage, than thirst. He wondered how he could protect Anne from Ernie. Ernie was now on his second beer, and was downing it in one big gulp. He never could handle his drinks, not even a plain beer.

"Ernie, I think we should just forget about this for awhile, at least until we find out how much the police know."

Ernie jumped up from his chair. In doing so, he knocked over Mike's beer, which spilled onto the floor. The waitress saw that it was Mike's beer, came hurrying over with a fresh one and a cloth to wipe the table.

"That's okay honey accidents happen, this beer is on me. Are ya pants wet? Ya dressed so nice I wouldn't want any stains on those nice pants of yours."

Mike could see Ernie was about to explode with anger and call attention to them, so he said everything was fine and apologized for the mess. Mike stood up from his chair, careful to keep his back to the waitress. He tried helping Ernie to his feet. The barmaid saw that they were going to leave and she would lose her chance at getting to know a celebrity. In her mind, Mike was a celebrity, she had a feeling she knew him from somewhere. It wasn't so much his face, because she could only see one side of it. It was his voice that sounded so familiar. She figured he was hiding his face so his fans wouldn't bother him. If only she could see his entire face. Mike put a generous tip on the table for her and led Ernie out of the bar.

Once outside he said,

"I think you have called enough attention to us, get in your car and go home.

"Not so fast buddy boy, who do you think you're ordering around? You are the one that screwed up remember?'

Mike knew that Ernie was feeling his beer, and nothing he could say to him would sound reasonable.

"Look Ernie, you're a little drunk so I'll drive you home. We can discuss our new plan in my car."

Ernie thought a moment then opened Mike's car door and slid in. He disliked not having the upper hand, especially from his younger brother. He was the one who was supposed to be giving orders, but those warm beers really affected him. He vowed never to come to this place again. Meanwhile, Mike went back into the bar to get permission to leave Ernie's car overnight. When the barmaid saw him come back into the bar she thought her prayers had been answered. Almost panting she came so close to him that he could smell her breath, which was a mixture of stale booze and sweet mints. Mike thought that maybe he should show her his face, that would keep her away.

"I knew you would come back handsome, how can I be of service to ya?"

When Mike told her he wanted to speak to the owner she put a pout on her face, which only added more wrinkles to it. She pointed to the man behind the bar. She overheard every word Mike said to the owner. Before the owner could reply she ran up to Mike and said,

"Honey my shift ends in ten minutes, if ya could wait, I'll be happy to drive his car home. Then you could drive me back here, how does that sound to ya?"

Mike could feel the eagerness in her as she clung to his arm. He knew he would have to let her down easy.

"How sweet you are, but I couldn't possibly make you go out of your way. Especially since you've already put in a long night with my friend and me. The bar owner knew he was about to spoil his waitress's night but his customers were more important to him.

"Sorry Sally, it's your turn to mop the bar tonight."

He then told Mike that he could leave the car here until the next night, hoping that he could drum up more business from him. He was puzzled by the way Mike kept one side of his face turned away from the light. Well that was his business. He did get a lot of strange ones in here, he thought, as he walked to the other side of the bar. Mike heard the owner call her Sally so he used her name in thanking her for her generosity. She sighed as she watched him walk out of the bar and her life…again.

"Well it's about time, what were you doing, making out with the slut? That's all you can get, is worn out baggage that you have to pay for. Maybe if you don't tow the line I should tell that lady cop who the phantom really is. How would you like that?"

Mike wanted so badly to wipe the smirk off Ernie's face, but he thought now was not the time. He didn't want to jeopardize Anne's life, he knew Ernie could turn mean very fast. He chose to ignore Ernie's remark and started the car. There was a lot more Ernie wanted to say, but he wasn't feeling so well as he opened the car window, just in case he had to get rid of that damn rotten beer, he ought to sue the place.

"Well what do you have planned for us?"

"I don't want to talk plans tonight, I'm not feeling too well. By the way, your not falling for that cop, are you?"

Ernie knew the answer without Mike having to say a word. He didn't like that at all, because more and more he was entertaining the thought that if, that was the case, he would have to sever their relationship sooner than he thought. Brother or no brother he wasn't going to jail for Mike's stupidity. That's another plan he would have to work on, but right now he just wanted to get home,' cause he sure wasn't feeling too good.

Chapter 35

It was a week before Anne could come home from the hospital. After Jackie got her settled, she ran down to the pharmacy for Anne's medication. Before she left the apartment, she placed the phone next to Anne's chair so she wouldn't have to struggle out of the chair to answer it. Anne snuggled under the blanket that Jackie draped over her. Anne sighed with contentment and thought how good it was to be home.

It was now the month of November. The days were considerably shorter as well as colder. Occasionally Wisconsin would get a day of reprieve and the sun and its warmth would shower down upon the state. Today however, was not that day, so an extra blanket would have to suffice.

Anne's leg was not broken, just a minor fracture. Still, it was enough to keep her off her feet for a while. She had crutches and as soon as she could handle them she would be back at work.

Her memory was another problem, while most of it had returned there were still bits and pieces that were in a fog. As hard as she tried she could not recall what had happened that night at the cemetery. Maybe she was trying too hard, give it time she kept telling herself. Anne closed her eyes and was about to drift off to sleep when she heard the phone ring. She answered it on the third ring. There was no sound at first just silence. She became anxious, she remember this happening before.

"Please answer, I know there is someone there."

"Hello Anne, welcome home."

"Who is this? What kind of sick game are you playing? Do you love tormenting people?"

Mike could tell that Anne was getting upset and that was one thing he didn't want to do to her. Somehow he would have to gain her confidence.

"Anne, please don't get upset, I just want to be your friend." He really wanted to say that he wanted to be her protector, but most of all, her lover, but he could never tell her that.

"You say you are my friend but I don't even know your name."

His voice brought back a memory, it was so soft and caressing, like a dark night breeze.

"A name, is that all you really want to know? How about a helping hand when needed, or a drive on the wild side, to save your life?"

"Stop! You are talking in riddles. You're confusing me! All I want from you is for you to stay away from me."

Anne felt so helpless she started to cry, which made Mike sorry that he had called her. He had no intention of causing her more pain. It was then that he realized she was still having trouble with her memory. He had missed seeing her when she was in the hospital. At least her cemetery patrols gave him a few moments of time with her, even though it was one-sided. Ernie never gave him any information about her condition, and Ernie must have known how she was doing, from listening to the other officers. He would be leaving in a few days, but he didn't want to leave Anne without talking to her one more time, to explain everything. He knew there was more than just that, he really wanted to take her in his arms and tell her that he had deep feelings for her. He really had no right to this woman. She was a good person as well as courageous and beautiful. Who was he? At one time he had a promising future, but that was in the past. God, he was so lonely, he desperately wanted a normal life just like he'd had before. With his face so scarred, and his addiction to drugs and alcohol, he knew his life was over. Then he saw Anne Bradley, and in a short space of time knew that maybe she could see passed his face and love him just a little.

'Anne I'm going to hang up for now, but I will call you tomorrow, and I will try to explain everything."

Before Anne had a chance to respond he had hung up. This was all so perplexing for her, who was this person? She remembered receiving calls in the past, if he had given her his name before, she couldn't remember. She would just have to wait till tomorrow, when he said he would call.

Anne felt herself getting sleepy, she fought against it but it was like she had no control over her eyes as they slowly closed. The dreams started with a soft voice, his voice calling to her. What is he trying to tell her? Try as she might, she could not hear his words. Anne struggled to come out of her dream, but it was no use, the darkness held her down. The voice that sounded so soft and sensual suddenly changed to a harsh laugh. She tried to see him but it was no use, all she could see was a shadow of a man walking away from her as she begged him to stop.

"Pease don't go, tell me who you are!" Slowly he turned and it was then that she saw his face, and started to scream. Her scream brought her out of her dream, and she bolted upright from her chair. Sweat dampened her forehead and her hands shook. She tried to wipe out the bad part of the dream, but it would not go away. She put her shaking hands under the blanket, hoping the warmth of the covers would control her shaking. She squeezed her eyes shut to erase the face in her dream, no it wasn't a dream, but a nightmare. How could a soft sensual voice turn into this mockery of a human being? The tears started to trickle down her face, Anne felt so hopeless she knew that somewhere in her very being she had feelings for this shadow. Pity was a better word for this man. Anne started to rock back and forth, like she was trying to hold on to her sanity. One thing she did know was that she could never have feelings for the harsh laughing face of someone who had so much cruelty written across it…never.

Anne reached for the bottle of pain pills that were still left over from the hospital. She was in so much pain, but was it her head that hurt? Or was the pain coming from her heart? She laid back against the chair, but this time sleep did not come. That was okay, she needed time to think. The phantom in her dreams was always in the shadows, why? His voice sounded like he was two people in one body. There was tomorrow and his phone call, maybe then she could find all the answers to her questions.

The next day passed too slowly for Anne as she waited for his phone call. She planned to meet with the phantom, and she knew she had to get her strength back in order to do that. Jackie noticed the change in Anne as soon as she came home from work. Anne was using her crutches; she was a little clumsy as she set the table for dinner. All in all she was doing a 100 percent better than in the morning. "Wow, what happened to you? You're dressed and actually look happy. Something smells delicious in the kitchen. All right, Anne, what happened, did you win the lottery or did Aaron come to visit you?"

As soon as the words left Jackie's mouth, she knew she had said the wrong thing, as the happiness left Anne's face.

"I'm sorry, Anne, I shouldn't have said that, you know I wouldn't hurt you for the world. Sometimes I don't think before I talk."

Anne touched Jackie on the shoulder and replied softly,

"That's alright I know you didn't say that to be mean. I guess I have been in a slump lately, I thought I was finally over Aaron but it's hard to forget. I really want to return to work as soon as possible, I left the chief shorthanded." Once again the smile came back, as she said,

"Today is the first day of the rest of my life."

"Good for you Anne, and if you need any help, I'm here for you. Now what's for dinner?"

That night, sleep didn't come easily for Anne. Her leg was aching; she knew that she had over done it with the housework. Once she had her mind set, there was no stopping her. She took a couple of aspirins to ease the pain. She didn't like the medication, from the doctor, it made her rather groggy. Despite the leg pain she found she still had some nervous energy that made it difficult to rest comfortably. It was eight in the evening and he hadn't called yet, she thought that maybe he was the reason she felt this nervous energy. Waiting, waiting, waiting at the cemetery, now, it's waiting for a phone call. This is probably just a big game to him, and she is his toy.

The apartment was quiet, Jackie was out on a date with a fellow from the local newspaper. She had been dating him since Aaron and Amanda's wedding. Anne sighed as her thoughts turned to Aaron. She really hadn't thought too much about him since all the commotion at the cemetery. But it seemed that tonight was going to be one of those long nights where a million memories popped into her mind. Anne knew that Aaron and Amanda were very happy, especially now that there might be a little Fischer on the way. Kelly, one of the other police officers, had stopped by for a short visit to bring Anne up to date on the department gossip. Anne, listened with an eager ear, she missed work a lot. Kelly saved the news about Aaron till last. She mentioned that the baby news was not official yet, but the girls noticed a change in Amanda's figure, and how she glowed when she came to pick up Aaron at work.

"I'm not upsetting you, am I? You look a little pale. I probably shouldn't have told you since you waited for Aaron all this time, only to lose him to Amanda. Oh, one more thing that you might find interesting. I think you might find that you have a new admirer when you get back to work." Anne's ears perked up at what Kelly said.

"You know that creepy janitor we have at the station? Well he's has been asking a lot of questions about you."

"What kind of questions?" Anne didn't know if she could take any more shocks for today.

"Oh like when are you coming back? He wanted to know if you could recall anything that happened to you that night. He asks these questions in a round about way, almost sneaky like. He also asked Bruce if you are receiving visitors at home. I shudder anytime he comes near me, it's almost like he's undressing me when he speaks to me. I sure hope he doesn't come to visit you, if I were you I would keep my doors locked." A short while later Kelly left, saying that she hoped Anne would be back to work soon.

Anne went over the visit in her mind, especially the part of Amanda glowing. She slid her hand over her stomach, trying to imagine how it would feel if she were in Amanda's shoes with Aaron's baby inside of her. No, she can't think like that, it would only hamper her recovery of mind and body. She once again closed her eyes, this time Ernie popped into her mind. Why was he so interested in her? She never said much to him in a conversational way. Now as she thought about him, all she could see were his squinty eyes and very scummy teeth that looked as if they hadn't been brushed in over a month. There was something else about him that bothered her. She didn't know him very well; he had been at the station a long time before she started working there. If Anne had to describe him in just two words, she would have to say he was a fake and was very mean. One day she happened to walk out to her squad car and saw Ernie coming from behind the station holding a cat by the tail. The cat was very dead and blood was dripping from his slit throat. Ernie held a knife that he had used on the animal. He was surprised to see Anne, but she could see the glee on his face. When he saw Anne he muttered an excuse on how the cat was always sneaking into the station and causing a mess for him to clean. She wondered at the time why Ernie hadn't found a better way of disposing of the animal instead of slitting its throat. Now Anne wondered if Ernie could be the stalker, especially since he seemed so interested in her. No, maybe not, since he was at work the nights the phantom was on the prowl. Besides how can one so strange have such an alluring voice, like her phantom? Anne thought about the voice, a voice that sounded so calm and assuring. It was so sensual that she might have followed him into the crypt if he had asked. Just then a voice in her head said,

"Anne, Anne why are you thinking this way? Are you that lonely that you can't handle reality? Are you mourning the loss of one love, and making up another one?"

Anne bolted upright in her bed, and ran her hands though her hair, she did not like what she was thinking. She always had taken pride in herself as a levelheaded person, but doubts started to take root in her mind. Maybe this phantom was a figment of her imagination. Anne knew the only way to find out, was to see and touch this shadow and to know that he indeed was real. When he calls, she would make sure she would get to see him.

The next day came and went, and so did another two days without calls from the phantom. Every time the phone rang Anne quickly hobbled over to the phone. It was never the call she expected. It was on the fourth day when Anne once again heard the sensual sound of his voice. Anne was a little out of breath when she answered.

"Hello Anne, I hope I didn't get you at a bad time?"

"No you didn't, I thought that maybe something might have happened to you, since you didn't call when you were suppose to." Anne could have kicked herself for sounding so anxious to hear from him.

"Were you worried about me, Anne? I just thought since I upset you so much with the last call, I would give you time to straighten out your thoughts. How are you feeling, Anne?"

"I'm feeling much better." Anne couldn't believe how normal this conversation was sounding. Her legs felt wobbly, she reached for a chair that was close by and sat down.

"Have you thought a lot about us, Anne? I want you to know that you are constantly on my mind. I'm just sorry that we had to meet the way we did, but I won't be bothering you much longer, since I'll be leaving in a few days."

With those words Anne felt as if a knife had just been plunged into her heart,

"No, please don't go, at least not until I have a chance to straightened out what's in my mind. Please, I have to see you, I must talk to you before you go."

"Do you want to talk to me as a police officer or as a woman?"

His question surprised her; she almost forgot that she was this other person, who was to uphold the law at all times. Had she forgotten how he had injured Aaron, and maybe injured her? Her thoughts were in turmoil that she didn't answer his question immediately.

"Anne are you still there?"

"Yes, I'm still here, I was thinking on how to answer your question."

"Well, Anne, what have you decided? If it is as a police officer, I will just say I'm sorry for everything and hang up. I will be out of your life forever."

Panic set in, as Anne pleaded,

"Please don't hang up, there are so many questions I would like answered."

Anne hesitated, then said,

"I'm asking them without my uniform on." Anne waited for what seemed like an eternity before he answered.

"Okay, Anne, that sounds fair, where do you want to start?" Anne sighed quietly, as she relaxed her hold on the phone.

"First I want to know your name."

"What have you been calling me, Anne?"

Anne felt her face getting warm as she said in a soft tone of voice,

"I've been calling you a phantom,. my phantom."

"Phantom, I like that name, it sounds better than the stalker."

"Oh, I've called you that a few times, plus the shadow, but what is your real name?"

Mike thought for a moment, he didn't know if he should open the door to his life. True, she was just asking his name, but she was a police officer, and a beautiful one at that. Her beauty and courage are what could make her dangerous to him, but that was a chance he would have to take.

"My name is Mike."

Anne rolled his name over her tongue, she liked that name, and it sounded manly like his voice.

"Mike, can't we meet somewhere?"

'I'm sorry, Anne, that can never happen."

"Mike I will meet you anywhere, even the cemetery if need be, you owe me that. In the last few weeks my life has been turned upside down by you. The phone calls, and your voice sounding caring one minute then turning harsh with the next phone call, it's almost as if I'm dealing with two different people. Please say you will meet me, you owe me this."

Mike was afraid of this and he wondered how he was going to handle it. He could just hang up on her and never see her again. But he had too many feelings for her, and she deserved more of an explanation rather than him just walking out on her. A few minutes went by before he found the answer she wanted to hear.

"All right, Anne, you win, I'll meet you, but it will have to be on my turf."

Anne held her breath with anticipation.

"Meet me at the wayside, south of town, tonight at eleven. I trust you Anne, if you breathe a word of this meeting to anyone, my life will be on the line."

With that, Mike hung up the phone. Anne couldn't believe she would finally meet her phantom, but she wondered what he meant by his life being in danger?

The rest of the day dragged on, as I checked my watch every half hour. I felt Jackie's eyes on me, but she never said anything. At the dinner table I asked her about her date. She mentioned that she was going out again tonight to me that sounded very serious and I mentioned it to Jackie. Her face turned a little red as well as serious.

"I like to think it's serious, he's a wonderful guy, someone I could really settle down with. But I think it's a little too soon to foretell the future. Anne I feel so guilty leaving you home alone, maybe I could have Bill fix you up with one of his buddies."

'No, Jackie, please don't do that. I appreciate what you're are trying to do, but I'm really not ready for dating. Why I couldn't even go dancing with this leg of mine, wouldn't I look great hobbling around on the dance floor?"

"Yes I guess you're right on that one, but on the other hand we could go to a movie. Any guy would be wild to sit next to you in a dark theatre, you know the routine, starting with handholding. The arm around the shoulder would be next, the soft kiss on the neck, then…both women started to laugh at Jackie's portrayal of a movie date.

"Jackie, just go and have fun on your date, it will be peaceful to have this apartment to myself for awhile. There will be no one to harp at me about doing my exercises. I will have the television remote all to myself. Oh Jackie, by the way, when you get to the part were he kisses you on the neck and the breathing gets hot and heavy that's the time for a pop corn break."

Again both girls laughed as Anne pointed to the door, Jackie shook her head and left. In a way I envied Jackie, Bill and she seemed to be heading in the right direction. Jackie didn't have the phantom hang up as I did. In other words, her life was simple and direct with nothing to clutter it. If only my life could be like that. Who knows, maybe after tonight it will be? Maybe the phantom…Mike will answer all my questions."

Chapter 36

The hour of eleven was fast approaching. I pulled into the wayside, it was the first time I drove since my accident. There was no moon just the darkness, the only thing missing were the tombstones and crypts. I made sure my doors were locked, I missed having my gun along. I won't need it because of Mike, but just in case someone other than him appears. I pulled up my jacket collar, and slipped my hands into my pockets for warmth. The highway was not heavily traveled at this time of night, just a few trucks that had to get to their destination fast. I always felt better when I saw headlights coming down the highway; it broke the darkness of the night. This was one of the older waysides that hadn't had electricity installed. Not many travelers used it because of its proximity to town, at one time there was talk of closing this wayside down.

It was close to eleven thirty and Mike was late. I looked into my rear view mirror and spied a slow moving car approaching the wayside. I had planned to wait only another ten minutes before leaving, when the car pulled into the parking lot. I automatically tensed up not knowing who it could be. The car was an older model Chevy with tinted windows. It pulled up next to mine. I watched with bated breath as the passenger side window slowly slid down. In turn I lowered my window, it was then that I heard the now familiar voice.

"Hello Anne, I'm sorry I'm late, but I had to be sure you came alone. I was watching you from the other side of the road."

I didn't care that he was late, I was just glad he came. I'm so close to him, yet so far. When a passing car drove by I caught his side profile before he quickly ducked his head. He didn't make a move to get out of his car.

"Mike, can I come into your car? It would make it a lot easier for conversation."

Mike anticipated this question.

"Anne, I'm going to hang this scarf on the window. I want you to tie this over your eyes before getting into my car."

I thought it a strange request, but under the circumstances with me being a police officer he had every right to be leery of me. I did as I was told and I could hear him opening the car door for me to climb in. If someone were to ask me how I felt at that time I would have to reply "VICTORIUS." I knew that I was invading this man's very private and very strange world and he was letting me.

'Hello Mike, I appreciate you meeting me."

I could smell his after-shave, it was a clean scent yet mixed with an outdoors fragrance. The car was warm and the aroma of coffee prevailed throughout the car. I could feel his hand shake as he offered me a cup, which I gladly accepted. I didn't realized how chilled I was until I held the warm cup in my hand. Neither of us spoke for a few moments, it gave me time to gather my thoughts. I remembered sitting with Aaron on a very dark night at the cemetery. It was a different lifetime and this was now. The coffee was good and I asked Mike if he had made it, he replied that he had. More silence… finally I asked him if I could remove the scarf.

"I'd prefer if you didn't, Anne."

I was about to object when I thought better of it. I figured I would go one step at a time, it was then that Mike spoke.

"Well, Anne, where do we start?"

"Mike, are you really my phantom? A phantom that could hurt a human being? What was the purpose of meeting at the cemetery? You sound as if you have some feelings for me, yet I was hurt by you. How can you explain all of this? I'm asking you this not as a police officer but hopefully as a new friend."

Mike took a deep breath, how was he to answer her questions without involving Ernie? He had to give some kind of answer because he didn't want her to think he could possibly hurt her. He had heard from Ernie how she had deep feelings for Aaron. If he could have Ernie within reach he would have wrung his neck for getting him into this situation. Every time he saw Anne his feelings for her were getting stronger. He had loved his wife deeply… Mike stopped there with his thoughts, after all this time he still could not say her name. He didn't want to think about her, it hurt too bad. Right now he wished he was in a bar, drowning his grief. It was then that he heard Anne's voice calling his name.

"Mike, answer me, is something wrong?"

190

Anne's hand reached out and found Mike's, at that moment it was like a surge of electricity had passed through him. He quickly withdrew his hand that only seconds before was covered by Anne's.

"Mike, I'm very sorry if I have invaded your life. If you will just answer my questions, I'll be out of your life, if that's what you want."

He really didn't want her out of his life. He was beginning to realize how much he needed this woman. He looked at Anne's profile, it was dark in the car but his eyes were adjusted to the darkness. She was turned in his direction, God, she was beautiful. He didn't need light to see her classic beauty. He couldn't figure why she went into the police force for a profession, when she could easily have been a model. Ernie mentioned that her former husband owned a top fashion house, God, he was a fool to let her go. He would have gone to great lengths to keep her as his own. He thought of his own marriage and the love he had for his wife, only to lose it all within seconds.

"Mike, please answer me." Mike shook his head as if trying to clear the mist of years past.

"Yes of course, first I want you to know that it wasn't me who was in the cemetery that night Aaron was hurt. I'm not the kind of person who likes to hurt people, and I know how much you cared for Aaron."

Anne groaned when she heard him say that, she wondered if the whole town knew of her feelings for Aaron"

"If you didn't, then who did?"

"I'm not at liberty to tell you."

"Then who hurt me?"

"Nobody did, if you remember that night, it was raining steady and there were a lot of leaves on the ground. When you started running, you slipped on the leaves, which were very wet. You fell and hit your head on a monument."

"But you admit that you were out there that night?"

"Yes I was, my partner knew every move that you made so he would tell me when you would be out there on patrol. That night he didn't want me to go out there, but I had to because I wanted to see you again. When your head hit the stone and I saw all that blood start to trickle down your face I almost panicked. You had passed out so I carried you to your car and drove you to the hospital. It was the longest two days before I learned that you would be alright."

"I still don't know what the purpose was for all this?"

"My friend hates Aaron immensely, this was his way of getting even with him. He thought he had killed Aaron that first night. When he found out that he hadn't, you were his next best target." Mike paused and then continued,

'Anne I would never, never hurt you, you are so much like her."

Mike hadn't meant to say what he did, somehow it just slipped out about his other love. He was hoping that Anne hadn't caught what he had said, but she did.

"Mike who is this other person, is she your partner or wife? Is she also part of this whole comedy of errors?"

Mike's face paled at this remark, but how could he tell her without letting her in on his private life? But again, he would have to start putting his trust in her, but not today.

"Look Anne I can't tell you everything, I have to do some deep soul searching before I do."

"Alright, I won't push you, I appreciate you meeting me here tonight. I believe what you told me so far about your part in this whole affair, I really don't know why, but I do. Right now I just want to go home and give a lot of thought to what you told me."

"Anne, are you going home as my friend, or as a police officer?"

"I would lie if I told you it would be as a friend and not as a police officer. What you told me will not go any further than this car, you can rest assured of that. When this puzzle has all its pieces, only then will you know if it's as a friend."

Mike got out of the car and helped Anne to hers.

"Anne, when you hear my car start up you can remove your blindfold, and drop it on the ground beside your car. I will follow you home to be sure you get there safe. Meet me here tomorrow at the same time, if you're still interested in what I have to say."

Mike didn't want to take a chance of them running into Ernie. He was sneaky, and of late has been very wary of Mike. He didn't mention anything about what was happening at the station. Mike just had to see Anne again and try to clear his name if that was possible.

It was way past midnight when Anne walked into her apartment. Jackie was already home and drinking coffee at the kitchen table. When she heard Anne's key in the door, she jumped up and walked rapidly into the hall.

"Anne, where have you been? I've been worried about you."

"I'm sorry, I was just tired of being cooped up in this apartment and decided to go for a ride."

Jackie didn't really believe that excuse but left it at that, she knew Anne could be close lipped when she wanted to be.

"How was your date, was the movie good?"

Jackie spent the next half hour telling Anne about the show and how great her date with Bill was. Anne couldn't wait to go to bed so she could mull over her conversation with the phantom. Everything was so sketchy, since he didn't give her all the things she needed. One thing she knew for sure, was that there were two people involved. She knew that she would have to make him tell her the whole story at the next wayside meeting. He would be leaving soon and she would be returning to work within the next couple of days. She would have to work fast to get all his information. When Anne thought of him leaving she felt a twinge in her heart, she wondered if fate was once again playing games with her?

Chapter 37

The following day dragged on, just as the day before. It wasn't so easy to leave the apartment with Jackie staying home that night. Around 10:30 Anne started to pace, after trying to think of a good excuse, she finally told Jackie that she was going to the station to see how things were coming along.

"Anne, I can come along if you would like some company?"

"No I'll be fine, besides I don't know how long I'll be there and you have to get up early for work tomorrow."

Anne couldn't look Jackie in the eye, she was afraid that just maybe Jackie could see the lie. Anne slipped on a jacket and reached for her cane as she headed out the door. Her leg was getting much better, but when she got a little tired her leg would weaken, so the cane did come in handy. Jackie watched from the front window as Anne drove off. She knew that she was up to something, she had a deep feeling that it had something to do with the phantom. God, now she was calling him the phantom, if her hunch was right this could be putting Anne in a very dangerous situation. She was tempted to call Aaron and let him know what was going on. No, Anne would never forgive her if she told Aaron. On the other hand it could be entirely what Anne said, a visit to the station. Jackie sighed as she turned from the window thinking to herself that she was becoming too paranoid. All she could do was hope that everything would go okay in whatever Anne was up too.

When Mike got back to his small one room apartment, he did not turn on the lights. He preferred to sit in the dark, maybe he was more phantom than he realized. Mike walked over to the refrigerator and started to reach for a beer. He decided he would just have one beer, it would taste so good going down. In disgust he slammed shut the refrigerator door, who is he trying to kid? One beer, that's a laugh, you can multiply that by six or eight beers until he was in a drunken stupor drowning in his own vomit. He really could not blame Ernie for getting him into this type of life. He was a grown man who should have made his own decisions, but Ernie took advantage of him when he was at his lowest point. For the rest of his life he would always be just one drink away from being an alcoholic. He plunked himself down on the one chair in his apartment; this was what his life had come to. Just like the chair, he was worn out, and felt old beyond his years.

Mike's thoughts turned to Anne, his one reason for trying to stay sober. He remembered the night he first saw her at the mortuary. God, she was beautiful lying naked on the embalming table. In his drunken haze he wondered if all corpses were as lovely as she was. Ernie had dragged him to the funeral home. When they got there they noticed a red convertible and a squad car parked near the mortuary's front door. Mike remembered that the weather was very stormy, with the wind and rain, he thought that the rain had helped sober him up to a small degree. Ernie started swearing when he saw the two cars. Mike was hoping that Ernie would call off the whole thing. Whatever he drank that night made him sick to his stomach, but Ernie shoved him to the back of the mortuary. He remembered stumbling to the ground and seeing light coming through a cracked window near where he fell. It wasn't much of a hole, but it was enough to see the embalming table and who was on it. The beauty that lay on the table mesmerized Mike. It was when the corpse screamed that he realized she was not dead. She started to squirm as the man went toward her with a needle, and then she fainted. The last thing Mike remembered was looking up, shocked, as a rock in Ernie's hand came down hard on his head. It was hours later when he awoke in his hole of an apartment, thinking that this beautiful creature was, by now, dead. Somehow he felt just as dead as the girl probably was. Alcohol and drugs were again a steady diet for him. Now he felt he had two deaths, no three deaths on his hands. He kept asking Ernie about the girl, but Ernie just gave a shrug and told him to forget about her.

It was a few weeks later that Ernie once again started to make plans. He was always happiest when he felt he could get even with his enemies, Aaron being the biggest thorn in his side. He knew when Aaron was coming back from his honeymoon and that he would be back to work that same night. Ernie didn't tell him about the cemetery caper until after the first visit, when Aaron was injured. Mike remembered how Ernie was beside himself with glee, although he later admitted that it was too bad that Aaron was still alive. Mike listened as Ernie told him how he had injured Aaron and that he would be in the hospital awhile. One day the name of Anne Bradley was mentioned, and how Ernie was going to make her his next target. In his mixed up brain he blamed Anne for messing up his plans to kill Aaron. He told Mike how she was going to suffer big time, and how he was going to help. Mike was to be the phantom, this would take the pressure off Ernie, in case someone at the station house would get suspicious. Even in Mike's fog he felt sorry for the woman, he knew how vindictive and mean Ernie could be. Part of his brain revolted at what he was hearing. He wanted to ask Ernie about this Anne, but his mind and speech were still under the influence of alcohol and painkillers. Ernie took away his liquor and told him that he wanted him clear headed for the next visit to the cemetery.

"All right Mike, you are going to do a job for me, and you better not screw it up."

Mike lowered his head as all these memories came flooding back to him. The shock of seeing Anne and realizing she wasn't dead and that she was a police officer. Ernie told him what to say to Anne,

"Yeah, Mike, you will probably get an Oscar for playing the phantom. With your face you fit the part perfectly. Just stay sober for a couple of hours and you won't screw up."

If he just had the strength to walk out of this mess, but he was weak in mind and body. He remembered the shrill, insane laughter that echoed through the night air. He didn't know what Ernie was planning for Anne, but whatever it was Mike knew it wouldn't be good.

Night came and their second meeting was just minutes away. Mike was already parked at the wayside when Anne arrived. As far as he knew he didn't think Ernie had any idea of their meeting. He still didn't know how much he was going to tell her, he decided just let her take the lead and go from there. She was very punctual as she pulled in and parked right next to his car. He had the blindfold draped over the door, and without a word she tied it over her eyes and climbed into his car.

"Hello Mike, thanks again for meeting me."

Forgetting that she couldn't see him, Mike just nodded his response.

"Mike I spent most of the night trying to understand what happened, to make you do what you did. Perhaps if you tell me a little about yourself, the puzzle will start coming together."

Mike figured she would ask him about himself, but he didn't want to tie himself to Ernie in any way. He hesitated and she took this as a refusal on his part.

"Mike, it would be a big help to me if I could understand you, and by really getting to know the personal side of you. You could start by letting me take off this blindfold."

"No Anne, I can't let you do that. If you take off the blindfold this meeting is terminated and you will never see me again." Mike knew what he said was a lie, he wanted to keep seeing her for the rest of his life. But he had to keep her from seeing him until he thought she could handle seeing his face. His feelings for her were growing stronger but he didn't know if they were reciprocated.

'I understand, I won't take it off."

"Okay, Anne, now that's understood I will tell you a little about myself."

Anne settled comfortably into the car's cushioned seat, because of the blindfold she felt like she had closed her eyes and was listening to a drama on the radio. At first Mike talked very slow as if his heart wasn't into telling it. He told her about his childhood, and his family, he was careful not to mention Ernie. It was when he got to the part of meeting a girl by the name of Dana that Mike stopped and said nothing for a few moments. Anne took his hand in hers and held it on her lap, he didn't resist her this time. She couldn't see him, but it was like she knew something had happened to this girl. As he tightly clenched her hand she could feel his raw emotion spill out in the shudder that followed.

"Mike, if what you're going to tell me will be too hard on you, you can tell me at a later time."

Mike knew there might not be another time after tonight.

"No I have to tell you in order for you to understand." Mike took a deep breath and continued slowly,

"I met Dana while working at a television station. I was an anchorperson in the news department, and she just started working in the front office of the station. I guess you could call it love at first sight, Dana was everything I ever wanted in a woman. She was beautiful, like you, she was gentle, kind, loved to listen to my stories, it seemed like we could talk for hours. After dating for a couple of months we decided not to waste anymore precious time and got married. Two wonderful years passed and we welcomed our little Amy into the world. She was the spitting image of her mother."

Again Mike stopped talking, Anne could feel him trembling. Forgetting that she was a police officer, Anne moved a little closer to him. She knew this man was hurting and needed compassion and understanding. It was amazing to her how this man could turn from a phantom to a human being in such a short time. Anne knew that in order to be a good police officer you have to listen intently, but as a woman you also have to listen with your heart as well.

"Mike you don't have to go on."

"I have to, I can't sleep nights reliving that day in my dreams. It's like I locked it away inside and it's killing me a little each day. Our little Amy was so tiny, so sweet but she could fill a room with sunshine just by walking into it. Her calling me daddy made me feel on top of the world. I often wondered if God had a mean streak because not only did he decide to take Amy, but he looked down again and decided that old Mike didn't need a loving wife either, so he took Dana, too."

Anne wanted to take Mike in her arms and soothe him, but she knew that Mike wasn't finished talking. She kept silent, besides it would be too difficult to talk with a lump in her throat.

"It started with me going on an assignment to a neighboring city, it was a simple job and I knew that it wouldn't take but a few hours, so I asked Dana to come along. It would be good for her to get out of the house. Amy had just gotten over the measles and needed some sunshine on her little cheeks. I was very proud to be driving with my two beautiful girls. We were a couple of miles from our destination, my camera crew was traveling in a van behind us. We got to a railroad crossing that had no gates. Amy was chattering away the whole trip, she had just learned to talk. She called to me to show me something, I remembered looking over my shoulder, and I was totally distracted by her. I could hear Amy giggling mixed with a train whistle and Dana's high-pitched scream. It was over in seconds, my whole life, how I wish I could have gone with them."

It was then that Mike started to cry, almost like a wail of an animal that was badly wounded. Anne never heard such heart wrenching sobs, she slid up to Mike and put her arms around him and rocked him like a baby. Minutes past and Mike started to talk, with Anne still holding him close.

"It was three days before I regained consciousness, I thought I was in the most pain that I could ever stand. I was so wrong, because that's when they told me about Dana and Amy. That's when the real pain started, it's like someone put a knife into my heart and kept twisting it. I heard someone in the distance screaming and I wished they would stop because I wanted to die in peace. It was later that I learned that it had been me screaming. It was because of the loss of my family and the physical pain I was in. My camera crew pulled me out of the wreckage but the flames were too intense to get Dana and Amy out in time. I know it wasn't the fault of the crew but I still cursed them for not letting me die. I missed their funerals, my folks had died before I was married so it was up to Dana's family to make all the arrangements. I often wondered why God didn't let me die along side Dana and Amy? I had two surgeries to the side of my face, I was supposed to have more surgery. One day I'd had enough of needles and hospitals and just walked out. It wasn't my body that hurt but my soul and no hospital could cure that. I had medications that I took religiously because they put me into another world. One day they ran out and so did my refills. The hospital wouldn't give me another prescription unless I came in and talked to the shrink. I took the next step, liquor, and poured it down my throat like it was water. I moved out of our old apartment, I couldn't stand being there without them. Everything reminded me of Dana and of the times I would never have again, besides I only needed one room to die in. I have a partner, he supplies me with all the liquor I need. I lost my friends and job and I really didn't care, until I saw you. You are not only beautiful, but you had the courage and the will to fight a phantom on your cemetery patrols and to lay on an embalming table while a madman threatened you."

Anne was aghast when she heard Mike say that, then anger set in as she said, "You saw me at the mortuary? If you saw me there why didn't you try to save me?"

"I was just coming out of a drunken stupor, at first I thought you were a corpse. Then I heard you scream and saw him coming at you with a needle. I looked up at my partner and the next thing I knew I woke up with a big lump on my head. Please believe me, Anne, if I hadn't been in a drunken haze I would have been there to save you. I thought for sure you had died that night, only to see you again on your second night at the cemetery. It was at that time that I knew I had to save you from my partner. Seeing you with all your courage made me feel ashamed of my cowardice in facing life. Even now my hands are shaking for want of a bottle."

Anne had a hard time absorbing everything Mike told her

"Mike, what were you doing at the mortuary?"

"We came to burn it down, but my partner told me that he had changed his mind when he heard the police sirens."

"Mike there was a fire weeks later, did you and your partner do that?" Anne held her breath until he answered.

"The fire that night was my fault, I keep trying to deny it but I was really out of it. My partner told me he handed me the match after we poured gasoline around the place. I have no recourse but to think that it was I who threw the lit match into the gasoline soaked ground."

Anne pondered his answer for a moment then asked him who his partner is, hoping he will tell her.

"I can't tell you that, but what I will tell you is that when you go back to work, watch your back. He wants you, Anne, for himself."

Anne was deeply concerned that it could be someone in the department. Yet it didn't seem possible, everyone was like one big family, but she still had to ask the dreaded question.

'Please tell me who he is, is it one of the officers?"

"I'm sorry Anne, I really can't tell you. I wish I could be there to protect you, but I can't even help myself."

I could tell Mike was through giving me any more personal information. I didn't want him to leave. I really didn't know what I felt for him, but the more I knew of him the deeper my feelings for him became. We talked though the night, there were times when Mike mentioned his family and once again I could feel him shudder. I really wanted to tear the blindfold off to let him see the anguish I felt for him. It had been two years since he had lost his family but the wounds were still very raw.

"Mike are you going to be my phantom forever? Will I always have to remember you as a man without a face? I put my hands up to the blindfold, it was then that he stopped them in mid-air."

"Okay Anne I think its time you see for yourself what I didn't want you to see."

I lowered the blindfold and slowly turned in Mike's direction, he didn't look at me. I wondered what thoughts raced though his mind. I didn't have to wait long as he asked me,

"Are you ready for this, Anne? You can still get into your car and drive away."

I held my breath but didn't say a word. He took my silence as consent. I could see his side profile and thought to myself how breathtakingly handsome he is. It was when I saw the whole face that I let out a gasp. I hadn't meant too, but it was too late to take it back. It was like someone had thrown acid on his left side of his face, leaving the right side prefect. An artist couldn't have done a better job dividing his face in half. There was no emotion in Mike's voice as he said, "This is why I didn't show you my face from the beginning, but I figured that since you now know my story, you would be ready for this freak show."

Mike turned his face away from Anne and quietly told her to go back to her car and drive away.

"Mike, please don't send me away, at least not until I have my say. Suddenly Mike grabbed me by the shoulders and shook me as he said,

"Damn it Anne, get a real good look at me, you are looking at a monster. You can say anything you want but when the talk is done and its bright daylight, would you walk down Main Street with me? You don't have to answer that, Anne, in the early days after the doctors took off the bandages I would look in the mirror and think to myself that God was really a comedian at heart to make my face the way he did. Half of it was handsome the other half was like something from a horror movie, it was like a Jeckel and Hyde face. If I'm ever invited to a Halloween party I won't have to look for a costume because I always have mine on. Or better yet we can both go as Beauty and the Beast, well Anne what do you think?"

"Stop it Mike, it was shocking when I first saw your face, I'm sorry that I gasped. To tell you the truth right now I'm thinking how much courage you have in surviving the fiery crash and the deaths of your loved ones. You say how brave I am but it's nothing compared to you, and for what it's worth I don't think you are responsible for that fire. I think your so-called partner is using you for his own gain, and I'm saying this as a police officer. Mike, you have been in tremendous pain in body and soul, other people would probably have taken their own lives going though what you did."

"Oh don't think I haven't thought about doing away with myself, but something always stops me. One day I took an overdose of pills, but my partner came in and called 911, he saved my life and I hate him for that. I am thankful for one thing, and that's meeting you, and because of that I have to try and repair my own life, I know Dana would want me too. I am leaving tomorrow; I have to see what the doctors can do to repair what the fire did to my face. There are also the drugs and alcohol to deal with, sometimes I wonder which one will be toughest to beat."

Anne put both hands on his face and turned it towards her and said,

"I wish I could take all your pain away, and I wish we could have met under different circumstances. Since we haven't, stay and let me help you.

I will try my hardest and I know that Aaron would also help, to get to the bottom of this. You might not like what I have to say next, but I think your partner saved your life for a reason. It's not because he is a true and caring friend but because he is not done using you. Please stay, problems are always easier to face when there is someone to help."

Anne moved closer to him, and as she did Mike groaned, he knew what was coming next. Her kiss, something he dreamt about, but never thought possible. He stared at her lips as they came closer to his, a warning in his head urged him to pull away, but his body betrayed him. He wanted her and he wasn't going to fight it any longer. He gathered her in his arms, somehow she felt like she belonged there. Neither fought it as their lips met for the first time. She felt and tasted so good that he wanted the kiss to go on forever. It had been so long since he felt such giving from another human being. It was when he felt other body stirrings that he abruptly pulled away from her. Anne looked startled when he roughly took hold of her shoulders and said,

"God, Anne I shouldn't have kissed you, not now. You are a police officer and I don't want to confuse your thinking. I want you to fully believe in me, and in time help me clear myself with the law. Anne I would give my soul to take you in my arms and love you forever. Not like this, not with my face the way it is, and in a car at a deserted wayside, you deserve so much better. Maybe what you feel is nothing but pity and some day you will wake up and look at me in disgust. That would be reliving the worst part of my life. Maybe even more so, worst since I've tasted your sweet lips and felt your warm body against mine. Anne I want you to leave right now before you regret it."

"Please Mike don't send me away because of something that you think could happen, I really don't know how I feel about you but I do want to help you. I just wish you would listen to me and we could work this out together."

"My sweet Anne, I admire your tenacity but I have to leave tomorrow and you are just making it harder for me. Goodnight Anne, someday we will meet again."

Anne looked at him as he leaned over to open her door, she could smell his fresh after-shave, in some strange way he reminded her of Aaron. She inhaled deeply; she wanted to remember him forever.

Chapter 38

It was around four in the morning when Anne walked into the apartment, she was hoping Jackie was asleep. She didn't want to face anyone at the moment, she felt wrung out as if she had been in a tornado and lost the fight. Luck was not on her side, as soon as she put the key in the lock a wild looking Jackie pulled it open.

"Oh my God, Anne, where have you been all night? Wait don't tell me I know where you've been, with him, weren't you?" Jackie didn't give Anne a chance to answer.

"Anne are you crazy? You don't know this man, he could have killed you and hid you in one of those crypts he's so fond of."

"As you can see I'm perfectly fine, give me credit to know who I'm dealing with."

"Okay then tell me, you were a little afraid weren't you?"

Anne hesitated, she had to admit she had been afraid that first night, but not on the second night. If Jackie were to know what had almost happen between Mike and she, she'd probably have her committed. So Anne made up her mind not to tell her dear, concerned friend everything, as a matter of fact she wasn't going to tell her anything at all.

"I'm sorry I had you worried, time went by so fast that I didn't realize how late it was. Look, Jackie, I have to be at work by seven and that only gives me an hour and a half of sleep. I will talk to you when we come home from work, good night Jackie."

Anne walked into her room and closed the door. Sleep didn't come to her, somehow she was expecting the phantom to call. The phantom, he didn't seem like a phantom when his lips met hers, but she had known him by that name a lot longer than by his real name, Mike.

Everyone was happy to see Anne back at work. Her desk was all in order, on closer observation it looked as if it had been polished. She could smell the wax, she made that comment to one of the other officers, who said,

"Somebody here is especially happy to have you back, he was almost spit polishing your desk. He kept asking when you would be back, he also asked if you'd gotten your memory back. He was overly concerned about you."

Anne was getting a little tired of the cat and mouse game, but she held back her sarcasm and asked who it was. She had a feeling she knew who it was.

"It's Ernie, who else cleans around here?"

Anne felt a shiver go down her spine, Mike mentioned that he had a partner, could it be Ernie? He's in the perfect position to know the entire goings on around here. Anne made a mental note not to let her guard down around him. Just then Ernie walked into the room and headed over to Anne's desk.

"Hello Ernie, thank you for polishing my desk, it looks great. I almost hate to use it." Anne could feel every one watching them as Ernie bent over and whispered in her ear,

"I'm glad you like it, it has to look great for a beautiful woman like you." She stood up abruptly, in doing so Ernie fell back against the next desk. Everyone in the room started to laugh. Ernie didn't like anyone laughing at him, right then and there he made up his mind to get even with each and everyone of them. He'd show them that they can't get away with making fun of him. As if Anne didn't have enough embarrassment, Aaron walked into the station and greeted her with a big hug, saying,

"Gosh, partner, it's about time you got back to work, we all missed you."

Ernie took as much as he could, suddenly he pushed himself between Anne and Aaron and with a sly grin on his face he said out loud so the other officers could hear,

"I'm sure Anne knows how you feel about her, especially when your pregnant wife isn't around."

With those words said, Ernie walked out of the room. Everyone turned back to what they were doing, and pretended not to notice the uncomfortable situation surrounding them.

"Whatever got into Ernie this morning? I know he doesn't like me very much, but that was a pretty low down thing to say."

"Forget it Mike...I mean Aaron, it seems I didn't give Ernie enough accolades on the good job he did on my desk." Aaron stepped back to admire the work Ernie did on the desk,

"Yeah it does look like new, he must have spent all night just getting it ready for you. By the way how are you feeling? And who is this guy

Mike? Somebody special you met at the hospital?" Anne chose to ignore Aaron's questions about Mike.

"I'm feeling fine, I now use a cane instead of crutches."

"Good for you Anne, you'll be on desk duty for a couple of weeks, Chief's orders. By the way have you seen the chief yet?" Aaron sensed that Anne didn't want to discuss a guy named Mike so he didn't pursue it, but he'll keep that name in mind.

"No I haven't, I don't think he's come in yet." with that answer Aaron went back to his desk.

Anne started organizing her desk when a thundering voice filled the station, making every head turn in that direction.

"Okay where is that officer? I want to see her in my office immediately."

Anne, knowing he meant her, followed him. As she hobbled into the chief's office he closed the door behind her and pulled out a chair for her to sit on.

"Well Anne how are you feeling? I see you are now using a cane, that's good. Aaron probably informed you that you will be on desk duty for awhile."

"Yes he did sir."

"Good, good I'm going to bring you up to snuff on what's going on. First of all the cemetery patrols are over, there hasn't been any activity since before the night you were hurt. The doctors at the hospital told me that what happened to you was just an accident. I also had some of the other officers' check the area where it happened, and they found your blood on a tombstone where you had hit your head. Now Anne before I officially close this case I want to hear if there is anything else you might want to tell me about this case."

Frank had a feeling that she was hiding something, he watched her face for any signs that might tell him his hunch was right.

Anne made a mental thank you to Mike for telling her what had happened.

"I know I slipped on the wet glass and hit my head on a tombstone and when I went down I did a number on my leg, end of story." The chief was not done questioning her,

"Do you remember how you got to the hospital?"

"That part is not entirely clear, I know I tried to walk over to my squad but I was in a lot of pain, so I had to drag myself to the car. I believe it was sheer will power, and the fact that I had my squad parked almost in front of the crypt. When I got to the hospital it was then that I passed out."

Frank didn't say anything more, but if Anne had looked at his face at that moment she would have seen skepticism written all over it. Frank knew she was covering up something but he knew better than to push, instead he would have Aaron watch her very carefully and to let him know if his hunch was right.

After talking a few more minutes Anne started to walk towards the door when she stopped and turned to look back at the chief,

"Chief I want to thank you for all your concern during my time at the hospital and after. I know you were at my side when I was unconscious, having no close family I appreciate your concern more than you can imagine."

Anne walked over to the chief and gave him a hug that made him turn a bright red. Once again she was about to walk out of his office when she stopped and looked back at the chief.

"Chief what do you know about Ernie, our cleaning man? How long has he been working here?"

"Well let me see." Frank rubbed his chin while trying to remember the exact time when he had hired Ernie.

"He'd been working here at least a couple of years before you got here, always does his job, and hasn't taken off too often. Why do you ask? Is there a problem with him?"

"No, not really, I was just curious, but he does seem to have taken an unusual liking to me. He said a few rude words to Aaron today when he saw Aaron and me talking. It's probably nothing but a bad day for him."

Frank watched Anne limp back to her desk. He thought her asking about Ernie was rather interesting and made a mental note to dig a little deeper into Ernie's past. The one thing Frank could not tolerate in his second family, was discontent.

Frank was not the only one to watch Anne, Ernie watched her every move, and he wondered why she spent so much time in the chief's office. He hadn't seen his partner today and that was puzzling to him, because Mike always checked in with him. He also noticed that Mike was cutting back on his demand for liquor and drugs. Ernie was starting to get a little uneasy about not hearing from his brother. He started to wonder if Mike had something on the side with Anne. Maybe she was trying to help him beat his addiction. No, what would a beautiful creature, like Anne, be doing with an ugly scarred up bum like Mike. Maybe he should ask the chief for a half day off, he did have some time coming. Yeah that's what he was going to do, he was going to take the rest of the day off. He was going to tell the chief that he wasn't feeling well, the fact that he wasn't feeling well would also cover up his stupid behavior between Aaron and him.

Ernie congratulated himself on being so clever, now he will have the time to take care of Mike once and for all. The more Ernie thought about Mike the angrier he became. His mind started playing tricks on him, like seeing Mike and Anne making love and then laughing at him. He could hear Mike telling Anne all the bad things Ernie made him do. He was so upset about the things that were going on inside his head that he inadvertently spilled a pail of soapy water in front of Anne's desk. He forgot himself and let out a string of vulgar words just as the chief was coming out of his office to see what all the noise was about.

"Are you having a bad day, Ernie?"

"No Chief, but I guess I am a little clumsy today. I'm not feeling very good, I would like to take the rest of the day off, I have time coming."

"Sure Ernie just clean up so nobody slips on the wet floor."

Ernie cussed under his breath, since the water was soapy it was going to take more time to clean it up. He blamed this all on his brother Mike, brother or no brother he couldn't wait to get his hands on him. It took him a good half hour to clean up the mess. With every stroke of his mop he wished it had been Mike's face he was doing this to and not the floor. When he was finished he quickly stored his cleaning equipment, punched his time card and left the building. He knew his day was ruined when he saw Aaron hugging Anne, and that it should have been him doing that instead of Aaron. Things had gone from bad to worse, but he will take care of all of them in due time.

When Ernie got to Mike's one room apartment he tried the door, it was then that the landlady came up from behind him saying,

"If you are looking for the man who lives here, you'll have a long wait. He left early this morning. If you are Ernie he asked me to give you this message."

"Did he say when he was coming back?"

"He's gone for good, paid me his rent and said that he would send me his forwarding address when he gets one. "

Ernie was in a state of shock as he walked back to his green van. When he got into the drivers seat he opened the note.

Ernie,

I'm going for medical help, don't bother to come looking for me. If I find that you harmed Anne in any way I will, come looking for you.

Mike

Ernie wadded up the note in a tight ball, he gritted his teeth as he threw the paper on the floor. He couldn't believe how his day was going. If Mike thinks he can make it on his own, he's in for a big surprise. In time he'll come crawling back to me, to his big brother.

Chapter 39

The first day back on my job seemed to drag. I felt so tired, I guess I was used to lounging around the apartment. I would have rather been patrolling in my patrol car instead of pushing a pencil around. I was glad that Ernie left for the day, but I wondered what he had up his sleeve. Maybe thinking that he might be Mike's brother, and partner in crime, was all in my mind. My mind kept going over that last night with Mike, and wondering if he really did leave. I wished he had told me were he was going. I hope that he finds all the help he needs. Somehow my life now seems empty, what direction I was going to take will have to be decided on very soon.

That night when I came home from work I found a note from Jackie, stating that she had a dinner date with Bill. I let out a big sigh of relief. I knew Jackie meant well but sometimes she was to controlling, especially since the whole cemetery incident. I turned on the television, for a couple of minutes, after channel surfing, and finding nothing of interest, I turned it off. I went over to the refrigerator, there again I found nothing of interest. After moving several dishes around I closed the refrigerator door. It seems like I can't get interested in anything. I began wondering why I was so restless, if my leg had been feeling better I probably would have gone for a walk. Since a walk was out of the question, I decided that maybe a shower would be soothing. The shower did help and my bed did look inviting. I decided that I would lie down for a half hour, maybe that would take some of the pain from my leg and I could then take my walk. I was about to close the blinds when I noticed the green van, parked in front of the building. I just shrugged my shoulders and went to the bed that looked so inviting. I didn't bother to slip into my nightgown, the sheets felt so smooth against my bare skin. I closed my eyes, it didn't take long for my thoughts to turn to Mike. I wondered where he was and smiled as I remembered his kiss. I could still smell a hint of his after-shave as I nestled down under the warm blanket. The sound of a persisted ringing awoke me. I searched for the switch on my bedside lamp, and looked at my watch, it was nine P.M. I must have been very tired to have slept that long. I tried to wipe away the cobwebs from my mind, when I realized it was the ringing of the phone that woke me.

"Hello?" There was only silence on the other end.

"Hello? Mike, is that you? Have you decided not to go after all?"

When there still wasn't any answer, I grasped the receiver a little tighter, "Who is this?"

"This is the phantom, Anne, calling to see how you are."

"You aren't him, you are his partner." There was hesitation on the other end. Finally the voice that sounded like it came from a long empty tunnel replied,

"So Anne you know about my partner, and you think he went away, but he didn't, you know. I have him locked up in one of my favorite places. If you want to see him again, come and get him. I will meet you in one hour and come alone. If you bring Fischer or any other cop you will never get a chance to say goodbye."

I didn't even have to ask him where, because I already knew it was the crypt. I only thought a second before I swung into action. I went into the closet and pulled out a black sweater and slacks and dressed in record time. The only thing on my mind was to get to Mike in time. The voice on the phone sounded so sinister, yet so familiar. As I drove out to the cemetery I tried placing the voice, but no one came to mind. Since the cemetery patrol was called off, the gates now remained open, so I drove straight through. It was now early December and the nights were very cold, there was a full moon so it was easy to see what was around me. I parked a short distance from the crypt. I shivered as I remembered what happened the last time I was here. I've been out here so often that it should have felt like old home week. I took a deep breath and found myself thinking that I was only out here to save Mike's life, which gave me a little more courage to do what I have to do. I was approaching the stone structure when a very familiar voice behind me asked,

"Anne, what are you doing out here?"

I spun around and collided into Aaron, I found myself grabbing him by his jacket collar and whispering in a low voice.

"Aaron, go home you can't be out here." I no sooner got the words out of my mouth when an explosion ripped apart the stillness. I screamed as the tool shed some yards behind the crypt exploded and sent flames high into the air.

I started running towards what was once the shed when I felt Aaron's hands pulling me back and landing us both on the ground. I heard myself screaming Mike's name over and over, all the while trying to push Aaron away from me.

"You killed him Aaron, you killed Mike by following me here."

Aaron shook me until I could here my teeth rattle.

"Anne what are you talking about? Who is this Mike? I was here on final patrol before we closed the case."

Aaron put his arms around me, trying to comfort me, but it was no use. Deep down in my jumbled thoughts I was thinking how ironic life was. Here I was pushing him away, and just a few months ago I would have given anything to be in his arms. Life just seemed so cruel to me.

Aaron kept his arms around Anne. The flames were slowly simmering down but he could still hear Anne's quiet sobs amidst the crackling of the dying embers. He gently picked her up and carried her to his car. As he drove her home he kept looking at her and knew that he had to get to the bottom of this. Her sobs were now a whimper, as she stared out the windshield. She looked as if she were in a trance, all the while saying, in a barely audible voice.

"He's gone, he's gone forever." Her face drained of all emotion.

"Anne, I'm going to take you home, I don't want you to come to work tomorrow, and I'll cover for you. I will be over sometime during the day, maybe then you can tell me a little about Mike."

When they got to the apartment, Jackie met them at the door.

"Anne, Aaron what happened?"

Anne didn't speak, she hurt beyond anything she had ever felt before. Aaron explained some of the details to Jackie as they both watched her walk like a zombie into her room. Jackie started to follow Anne but Aaron pulled her back.

"No, Jackie, just leave her alone for tonight, she will be alright for now. I told her to stay home tomorrow and that I'll be dropping by to see if she wants to talk then."

Jackie's face was red with anger.

"I know it was the work of the phantom, he just won't let her alone."

Aaron heard the word phantom before, but he didn't want to keep Amanda waiting at home. He pretended not to hear, Jackie, he thanked her and left. As Aaron walked to his car a dark figure in a green van watched him pull away. A gleeful chuckle sounded deep in his throat as he still could hear Anne's screams amidst the crackling of flames. "This was a job well done, only it's too bad both of them couldn't have been in the fire as well. Tomorrow is another day." and with that thought he slowly drove away.

The next morning, Jackie looked in on Anne and found that she was fast asleep. She hated to leave her alone but she knew that Aaron would be here to look in on her, so she felt a little better leaving her alone. Anne opened her eyes as soon as she heard the front door close. She looked at the clock and saw that it was 7:30. She lay there for a few moments in deep thought. She thought about Mike and that just maybe he wasn't in the shed after all. Mike told her that his partner had a mean streak, but would he pull that kind of trick on her? Once again the tears flowed from her swollen eyes. She buried her face into her tear soaked pillow and let the tears turn into loud crying, she didn't care if the whole world heard her. She never thought she had so much sorrow in her, but she did. Someone once said that sleep was the best healer for pain, and she hoped that was true because she wanted to sleep her life away.

Anne awoke shortly before noon, she dragged herself into the shower, hoping the water would help her come back to some kind of normalcy. After putting on her robe she heard a soft knock at the door. Anne went to answer it and was surprised to find Amanda standing in the doorway.

"I'm sorry to bother you, Anne. May I come in?"

After a second or two Anne, still in shock to find Amanda standing there, nodded her head and stepped aside to let her in.

Anne led the way to the living room motioning for Amanda to sit on one of the easy chairs. She was a little puzzled as to why Amanda was here. Amanda sensing this in Anne spoke first,

"How are you feeling Anne?"

"I'm getting better with each day, my leg still feels a little stiff, but the doctor says the more I use it the better it will become."

Again there was silence, when Amanda said,

"Anne, Aaron told me about last night and I want to assure you that Aaron will surely get to the bottom of this."

When Amanda saw the surprised look on Anne's face she quickly said,

"Aaron came home last night looking rather worried, when he worries, I worry. He usually doesn't tell me much about his work, especially now that I'm pregnant." Amanda stopped talking when she realized what she said.

"I'm sorry, you probably didn't know that since you have been out of work for awhile."

"I did know, one of the girls from the station visited me when I was laid up and brought me up to date on what was going on. She mentioned that they thought you might be pregnant. Congratulations." This time it was Amanda's turn to be embarrassed to be the talk of the station. She let out a small chuckle and said,

"That's a small town for you, sometimes it seems everyone knows the news before the newspapers. Thank you for the congratulations, Aaron and I are very happy about the coming baby. He wants at least six children." It was then that she noticed the sad look on Anne's face. She remembered how badly Anne had wanted Aaron, and now she might have lost another chance at happiness.

"I'm sorry, Anne. That was thoughtless of me, talking about my happiness when you have suffered much at the hands of this monster in the cemetery, and not to have anyone to talk to about it."

"No need to apologize, Aaron probably told you about the phantom, actually his name is Mike."

Anne stood up and walked to the window, she looked out and could see the same green van. When she saw it, she lost her train of thought and became silent. She looked over at Amanda who was a picture of health and happiness. For a short minute Anne became her old self that was filled with dislike for and envy of this woman. She quickly erased the thought from her mind and felt like she was on the verge of crying.

"Amanda I'm sorry but I have to lie down, ever since the accident I've been getting these headaches. I want to thank you for dropping by, it was thoughtful of you."

As she escorted Amanda to the door, Amanda gave her a hug and said,

"Anne, I really do want to become your friend, nobody should have to go though this alone. If you want a shoulder to cry on or want to talk, I'm here for you."

Anne felt emotionally drained, she walked over to the window again to watch Amanda get into her car and as she drove away Anne watched the green van again. It was then that she realized how mixed up her life had become. If her life had been normal, she, as a police officer, would have checked out the van immediately. She turned to find a paper to write down a reminder to check into this van, when the phone rang.

"Hello?"

"Hello Anne, naughty, naughty I told you to come alone last night, now you've gone and done it, he's gone for good. But then again maybe he isn't, what do you think Anne? Do you think I'm really that bad, as to kill my own brother?"

"Mike is your brother?"

"Oh he didn't tell you that? I'll have to talk to him about that when I see him, if he's still alive that is."

"Why are you doing this to me? I don't even know you."

"That's true you don't know me but you will when the time comes. I know you so very well, I know your past, present, and future. I especially know your future because it will revolve around me. I love the way you look, the way you walk and talk, even the way you smell. Sometimes I'm so close to you that I want to reach out and touch you. I must say, you really turn on a guy without realizing it. I remember one night in particular, when you walked to work. I think you suspected that you were being followed. You turned and looked back, I was there, and I could have had you, but the time wasn't quite right. I wanted to play with you for a while to see what you were made of. I like my girls not only to be beautiful but gutsy as well. Then there is Fischer, I know your feelings for him. Him with all his spit and polish, rugged good looks and brains, you don't know how I hate him. I would sell my soul to the devil if I could get rid of him right now. I saw how he helped you up from that embalming table, and how he covered your beautiful body with a sheet. You see, Anne, I'm drooling this minute just thinking about that scene. How I wished it could have been me that you gave that lingering kiss." There was silence for a moment, Anne thought that he had hung up until she heard heavy breathing,

When my bother Mike fell for your charms it was more than I could stand. Even with his ugly face he could still make you fall for him, leaving me no chance. Well, I'm still going to have my way only it will take a lot longer than I had hoped."

"Please whoever you are, just tell me if Mike is alive. I will do anything you ask, just don't kill Mike."

Ernie could not believe that he had her on her knees, begging him,

"Hmmm, that sounds interesting, you say you will do anything I ask? Let me think on that, I will get in touch with you later. Goodbye, my Darling, oh you don't mind if I call you Darling, do you? Before long, you will be mine in every sense of the word."

With that remark he laughed a harsh laugh and hung up. Anne slowly sank down in a nearby chair, still holding the receiver in her shaking hand. Who could be that close to her, to know her every move? What kind of policewoman is she that something so obvious is eluding her? The phone conversation did give her hope that Mike might still be alive. A moment later she hung up the phone then it rang again. She reached for the phone thinking it was Mike's brother again, quickly grabbing the phone and all but shouting into the receiver.

"Now what do you want? Why are you taunting me? Didn't I say I would give you anything you wanted?"

"Anne, this is Aaron, who is bothering you?"

"I'm sorry, Aaron, I just had a crank phone call."

"It's that phantom again, isn't it? Never mind you don't have to answer that. Anne I have to talk to you. Are you able to meet with me at the Java Cup Café say in twenty minutes?"

Anne hesitated, but then said,

"Yes, twenty minutes is fine."

Anne put on a red turtleneck sweater, and a pair of jeans, she dressed warm. Snow hadn't arrived yet but the temperatures were down in the 30's. When Anne stepped outside of her apartment building the raw wind wrapped its fingers around her. She pulled her long coat closer to her body. She was going to walk the few short blocks to the café, figuring it would do her leg some good. But after feeling the effects of the wind she decided to drive over.

It was in the middle of the afternoon and in between the lunch and dinner crowd, which made the café just about empty. Anne was glad about this because she knew how talk, no matter how innocent, goes through a small town. Aaron was already there, sitting in at a booth. When he saw her come in, he stood up until she was seated.

"You are looking much better than you did yesterday. Are you feeling as good as you look?"

Her heart skipped a beat as her eyes saw the admiration in his. In the past she would consider this to mean something more inviting, but that was the old Anne. The new Anne was a lot more serious and level headed, who didn't want to play second fiddle to anyone. She knew that something happened to her during the cemetery patrols and seeing Aaron almost die. She felt she was far better off for it. Before she could answer Aaron the waitress came up to take their order. She recognized Anne and admonished her for not coming in more often.

"And you, Officer Aaron, I see you enough with your pretty little wife. By the way when is your baby due?"

Anne had a feeling that she was warning her, "Hands Off."

Aaron gave her the due date and then ordered coffee for both of them. As the waitress walked away Aaron saw her look over her shoulder at them, with a knowing eye.

"Aaron you better tell Amanda that we had coffee together, otherwise our waitress is going to have us eloping by the time we finish our first cup. There was silence for a brief time when Anne looked at him and asked him in a quiet tone of voice,

"Aaron, what did you tell the chief about last night, I know he must have heard about the fire."

"First of all I didn't tell Frank too much except that someone lit the tool shed on fire. Old Joe, the caretaker, came in and made the same report, saying that that he had seen some kids making out on the cemetery road last night. I also told him that you were not feeling well, and that working full time on your first day back was not the best thing. He agreed and said that he might put you on part time for awhile."

Anne felt a little guilty about deceiving the chief, but in truth she was very tired when she had came home. She also felt bad putting Aaron in the middle of this whole mess. She watched Aaron take a small notebook and pen from his shirt pocket.

"I assume you are turning into a cop, I thought this conversation was just between you and me."

"Anne, you know why I'm here. I see my friend and partner; by the way Frank made you my partner again, put herself into a very dangerous situation. I want to know all about this phantom, or Mike, I'm assuming here's one and the same. Please start from the beginning. The chief might have officially closed this case but he did ask me to keep an ear and eye open. I know that it wasn't a ghost that hit me over the head, and I'll wager it wasn't kids either. There is something definitely going on in that cemetery, and I aim to find out what, on my own time, with your help or not. So Anne, what's it to be?"

Anne cleared her throat and thought about how much she should tell him. Aaron watched her facial expression, as if he was trying to read her mind.

"Everything Anne!" he said in a commanding voice.

"It started that first night of cemetery patrol when you got injured and I rushed you to the hospital. It wasn't Mike that did that to you, it was his partner that almost killed you. After that first night he sent Mike on the rest of the patrols and no one was hurt."

Anne told Aaron everything, how Mike worked in television and was married to a woman named Dana. She told him about Mike's little girl Amy, and how his family was killed in a train accident. She told him about how Mike escaped being killed but how terribly disfigured the left side of his face was. Aaron watched Anne as the tears flowed down her face, he handed her his handkerchief. He took her hand in his to comfort her. This did not go unnoticed by the waitress, as she memorized every little detail of what she saw. Anne continued Mike's story about the alcohol and drugs that kept his life numb, but somewhat functioning. She mentioned how his partner, who really was his brother kept him in these vices just so he could make him do all the things he wanted. She told him how his brother, made him burn down Vormens. At this point, Aaron made Anne stop, he couldn't believe what she'd just said.

"Anne, how did you get all this information, and why did you keep this from the police?"

It was then she told Aaron that she'd made a deal with Mike at the wayside. If he told her everything she would not go to the police until hearing the whole story from him. Then at that time she would make a decision."

"You met him at a wayside, alone? What if he wasn't the nice guy you thought he was? Do you realize what a chance you were taking? Did you forget everything you learned in police training?"

Aaron was dumbfounded at what she just told him.

"Anne, you are first a police officer, so you have to think as one, and not with your heart."

"Yes I knew I was taking a chance with him, but the world is filled with chances and risks. Besides, I had phone conversations with him and I felt I knew him to some degree."

I knew I was stretching the phone conversations a little, but I had to make Aaron see my logic and Mike's side of the story.

"When I met him for the last time he told me about his partner and that I should watch my back. He also told me that he was leaving the next day, but that he would be back when he straightened out his medical problems."

"Did he also mention his problems with the law?"

"Yes, I believe that too. Anyway, I think if we can get his partner, Mike will not have that much trouble clearing himself.'

"What do you know about his partner, Anne?"

"Not much, except that he has a mean streak and he will stop at nothing to get what he wants. He seems to know our every move. He called me just before your call."

"Was that the crank call you received?"

"Yes, I begged him to tell me if Mike was still alive, and that I would do anything he asked as long as he told me if Mike was still alive. You see, he warned me that I should come alone to the cemetery, if I didn't I would never see Mike alive. Then you came up behind me and there was the explosion in the shed. He also mentioned that he knows a lot about you and me."

Aaron looked puzzled at that comment,

"What about us?"

At this question Anne's face turned red as she looked down at her coffee cup, she quietly answered,

"He knew how much I once wanted you and lost you to Amanda."

Aaron didn't know what to say, after a few moments he said,

"He does know a lot. Have you tried placing his voice?"

"Yes I have, but it's no use, he disguises his voice, it sounds like it comes thought a long tunnel."

"When you told him that you would do anything he wanted, what was his comment?"

"He was amused at first then said he would think about it and would call me back."

"Ok that sounds good, and no doubt he will. Anne when he does I want you to call me immediately and we will plan from there, okay? Oh, by the way, here are my home and cell phone numbers."

As Aaron was giving her his numbers the waitress came over to see if they wanted more coffee, which they declined. The waitress smacked her lips at all the interesting things she will have to tell her best friend. As she got back to the counter she looked back at them and saw Aaron take Anne's hand in his, she could not believe this was happening here in public. Oh that poor Amanda and her with a baby on the way. That Anne was always a hussy. She could not wait till they left so she could call her best friend and tell her what just took place. Aaron took hold of Anne's hand, even the warm cup of coffee she had been holding hadn't taken the chill out of them. Anne closed her eyes, she didn't want the strong feeling, and she had at the moment for Aaron, come to the surface. She took her hand out of his and pretended to dig in her bag for a handkerchief.

"Anne, I have one more question for you, do you have feelings for this Mike? If you do, this might cloud your judgment"

"I don't know what my feelings for Mike are. When I'm with him and see I see his poor face, I want to take him in my arms and hold him there forever. I think of all the bad things that brought him down to this level and I admire his courage for going on with life. Maybe he is on drugs and alcohol, but he was given them at his lowest time of his life. After the train accident, he lost his job because of his face, no one wants a freak on their payroll. I wondered what we would do if we were in his shoes, have you wondered that Aaron? Just imagine everything you love, gone in a split second."

Aaron did not have to think about it, he knew he would want to die right along with Amanda if that had happened to him. Anne wasn't finished talking,

"I know he is alive, last night I didn't think he was, but after I talked to his partner I have a gut feeling he is. He told me he was going to leave the next day, so maybe he got away from his brother in time. I know they didn't live together. His brother might have set up that fire to get my attention, and to warn me to do whatever he wants."

What I didn't tell Aaron was that Mike promised to see me someday, and I hope with all my heart he does. Aaron had asked me about my feelings for Mike, it has been only a day since I last saw Mike but I'm missing him as if it has been years. When the explosion happened I felt as if my life was gone with Mike's. If that is love, I would love him forever, scarred face and all.

It was quite late when Anne and Aaron left the Java Cup Café. The dinner customers started to arrive for their evening meals. Myrtle, the lunch waitress, was about finished with her shift and was on her cell phone with her best friend, spreading her gossip. Aaron decided that just Anne and he would be involved at this time, just in case Mike's brother had an inside plant at the station. What they were planning was against department policy. He hated to do this to Frank, but they had to be careful that the brother didn't get wind of their plans.

That night at ten the phone rang, and Anne jumped up to answer it. Jackie was gone for the evening, which made it easier for Anne and Aaron to carry out their plan. Of late, Jackie didn't ask Anne too many questions, she was becoming more involved with Bill. Jackie also knew that Anne could be very closed mouth when it came to this phantom. Anne took a deep breath before answering the phone.

"Hello Darlin, are you happy to hear from me again?"

When Anne heard his voice, it took all her stamina not to get sick.

"What do you think?"

"Now that's not a nice way to start up a beautiful relationship. But I will ignore the sarcasm in your voice, in fact that kind of turns me on. Tonight will be our first night together. When you come to meet me I want you to wear something real seductive, like you would like to wear meeting Aaron or maybe even Mike. I won't go into a long explanation of what I'm planning to do to you, but be ready for a good time. Oh by the way, I know you were with Fischer today, if you want him to go on living, don't plan an ambush. Meet me in 45 minutes, at our usual place." With that Ernie hung up.

Anne decided not to inform Aaron, she didn't want him killed. Being a police officer herself, she figured she could handle Mike's brother, but she did have to figure out what to wear and still hide her gun. This would not be easy with the type of clothes that perp wanted her to wear.

Anne was sitting in her car next to the crypt, when her cell phone rang.

"Hello Anne, I'm not going to meet you at our usual crypt. I want you to go to the crypt in the old part of the cemetery, the one under the weeping willow tree." With that he hung up. Anne did not like this, she wasn't familiar with that part of the cemetery, and there wasn't a way for her to run if she had too. She decided to wing it and hoped that she could dissuade him from doing whatever he had planned. Anne had a hard time finding the crypt. She kept on driving slowly until she found it. It was in the oldest part of the cemetery, almost hidden by two tall weeping willows. She had been in this cemetery a lot lately but never this part. She shivered as she looked at the tumbled down tombstones that surrounded the crypt. She thought of those poor souls, many were forgotten by the living.

By the looks of the graves Anne could not but help feeling sad for them. She could see Old Joe's house in the distance, she could see the lights on. Somehow this made her feel a little better. She parked her car and slowly limped over to the crypt, the tree branches brushed against her face as she made her way there. Her leg always hurt more at night, she supposed it had something to do with the cold weather. She stood close to the crypt, hoping that the prep. wouldn't keep her waiting too long. But he did, minutes ticked by, and the pain in her leg intensified. When she thought about it, she was glad Aaron wasn't with her. She didn't want him getting hurt again or maybe even killed. Anne wanted to test her police skills, but prayers wouldn't hurt at this point. It was then that Anne heard a sound and then a voice.

"Well Darlin, I'm sorry that I'm a little late, but I had to make sure that you were not followed by your boyfriend. Damn, you smell so good, let me feel what I can't see."

When he moved to the front of her she was shocked to see that Mike's partner and brother was Ernie. She was surprised by the fact that the suspect was right under their noses the whole time, and they never caught on. "You're speechless Anne, I was always there by your side, but you never gave me a second look. You would rather make love to my grotesque brother than have a cup of coffee with me, well that's going to change tonight. First I'm going to frisk you up, is that what the police say when they are feeling you up for weapons?"

Anne felt repulsed when she felt Ernie's hands travel slowly up and down her body. She closed her eyes and tried to will him away to another planet.

"Darlin, I'm so glad that I told you to wear something sexy, it makes looking for a gun so much easier. Baby, you're shaking, are you cold? Let me get a little closer and I'll make you hot."

Ernie's hands got as far down as her waist, he started to lick his lips in anticipation. He was like a cat and she was the mouse trapped with no way out. He slid his hands under her skirt, and traveled up her thighs until he found her gun. With great satisfaction, he withdrew the gun, and slipped it into the back waistband of his jeans. Anne started to gag.

"No need to rush the evening, I'll wait till you compose yourself."

It took her a few minutes to get herself in control, and to figure out what she should do. All she could think of was to fight…fight don't let him get the best of you.

"Ernie this is ludicrous, let's talk this over."

"Sorry Baby the time for talk is over, now I take what I want, is you. Besides you had your chance to be nice to me, now see me as your captor. You know Anne when we were at the station and you looked at me, it was like you were staring at a bug. I have feelings just like Mike. Mike liked you a great deal. When I realized that, I knew I had to act fast. Even with half a face he could still win women's hearts, but he never tried. The barmaid in a bar would have given her eyeteeth to have him. Of course she didn't get to see the ugly side of his face. She kept asking him if he was on television, she didn't know how close she came to the truth. But enough about him, lets talk about us, and what I'm going to do to you. I want you to take off your clothes, you don't have too much on so it won't take too long to undress."

"Ernie please, don't do this, just let me go and I'll forget this ever happened." Ernie laughed at her plea. She started to back away from him, all the while looking for an avenue of escape. She wondered why she thought she could handle a deranged monster all by her self. She tried to remember her police training, but her mind, like her body, felt numb. All of a sudden she stopped backing away, Ernie started to reach for her. It was then that she raised her knee and got him in the groin. Because of her bad leg, the knee barely connected, but it did give her a few seconds to start running. Ernie recovered quickly, she could hear him breathing close behind her. She cursed her bad leg as the pain caused her to slow down. All she could think of was "Her car, I've got to get to my car." Another second and she would be there, it was then that she felt herself falling as Ernie tackled her to the ground. He grabbed her by the hair and then flipped her over onto her back. He straddled her, as he tried to get his breath. Even in the dark Anne could see the hatred marring his face, as saliva dripped from his mouth onto her. She felt his fist come smashing into her face and the word bitch resonating in the air, and then blackness.

When Anne came to, she wondered how long she had been unconscious, was it minutes or hours? She was so cold and sore and had the copper taste of blood in her mouth. As she tried to clear her head she realized that she was in some kind of panel truck, and she was totally nude. Ernie was bent over her but he was so busy running his hands over her body that he didn't realize she had regained consciousness. Gently he touched her breasts, then her stomach, all the while smacking his lips, as if he was about to engage in a great feast. It was almost dark in the truck except for a dim light in the front of the vehicle. He was startled when Anne said, in a snarling voice,

"Get your dirty paws off me, you poor excuse for a man!"

She then realized that it was the wrong thing to say, as Ernie reared up and slapped her so hard on the face that she thought he had broken her jaw.

"Well my girl wants to play rough, I love that, it's puts more excitement in the game."

Ernie reached over her to check the ropes that held her down, finding them tight, he grunted with satisfaction. Anne could feel every muscle in her arms stretched to the limit. She watched as Ernie started to undress, he kept wiping the drool that kept running out of his mouth with his hand, then running the same hand over her body. It was only a matter of time before she would throw up.

"You little bitch, what's coming next should be nothing new to you. After all you were married a few months, and then there was Aaron. How many times did you do it with Aaron, bitch? Was it six times, twenty times, or more?"

Anne closed her eyes as his face slowly descended, she imagined his green teeth that never seemed brushed. She could smell his foul breath as he tried to pry open up her mouth with his tongue. She just knew she was going to drown in her own vomit if he didn't stop. Then he stopped as she started to heave. He started slapping her, telling her to stop. Anne didn't care if she did throw up, then maybe she could drown before he could do anything. He stopped slapping her as she fought for air. It was far from over as Ernie laid his body on top of hers, getting ready to penetrate her. All she could think of was 'Please God let this be over soon!"

Ernie drove into her body and rode her mercilessly, till Anne started screaming from pain. It was then she passed out. When she came to, Ernie was fully dressed and had his jacket on. She wondered how many times he had taken her. All she could remember was the constant grinding and stopping and then the sequence starting over again.

"That was good for me Anne, how was it for you? You must be cold, your nipples are hard, or is it because of me?"

He bent down, and took one nipple in his mouth, and bit down hard, and repeated the act with the other nipple, the pain was horrific.

'That's just a little something to remember me by." She never heard a laugh so evil.

Anne didn't remember him untying her, but she was free. He watched her with greedy eyes as if he was memorizing every inch of her body. She tried to gather her clothing but couldn't find any. If she thought she was hurting before, it was nothing like she hurt now. When she tried sitting up, Ernie pulled her roughly from the truck and dumped her hard on the ground, next to an open grave. She could feel something warm trickling down her face and knew that it must be blood. She felt so dirty and violated that she wanted to crawl into the open grave. Ernie must have read her mind. The next thing she felt was Ernie's foot crashing into her side. The pain was excruciating as her body rolled into the open grave and hit the hard cold floor. Ernie looked down into the grave and said,

"You can tell your pal, Fischer, that you were a good piece, and if you see my brother Mike, tell him that his big brother had you first. Someday I'll be back, just don't walk down a dark street, it just might be me behind you, wanting another taste of revenge." As an after thought he added,

"You're lucky I don't have a shovel in my truck, otherwise I would have buried you."

Ernie turned away and his laughter could be heard throughout the cemetery.

Anne tried to get up but her legs just didn't want to support her. She never realized how deep graves were. She was so cold, that her teeth were actually chattering. She had to clear her head and think, because it wouldn't take long for her to freeze to death. Anne remembered seeing a light in the caretaker's house, maybe if she could scream loud enough he would hear her. It was an effort for her to open her mouth and scream, but she had to try.

Joe was watching the late night news when he went into the kitchen for a cup of coffee. He was thinking to himself how lucky he was to have a job like this. The peace was so soothing. No nosey neighbors asking to borrow something or other. Yes sir, he sure was one lucky guy. Joe was about to return to his television when he remembered to put his cat out for the night. Fondly he picked her up and thought that even his cat, Josie, was prefect, no trouble at all, not like those darn dogs or a wife. Although a month ago he sure would have liked to have one of those Doberman dogs, it would have probably nipped the problem right in the bud, better than the cops had done.

Joe hated living with his sister, Clara, even for a few days. Nag, nag, no wonder nobody would marry her. No man in his right mind would have that danged old woman. Old Joe would gladly have taken his chances out here, but the police gave him no choice. Yes sir, there was no good or bad neighbors out here. He put Josie down on the back porch when he thought he heard a sound. He stopped and listened, he thought it could have been an owl, plenty of those around. He was about to go into his house when he heard the sound again. It was hard to say what direction the sound was coming from, since sounds carry on the night air. The sound seemed like it was getting weaker, he had to decide if he should call the police. No, he was not going to do that, they would just send him back to Clara's. Heck, he'll just investigate it himself. Joe went inside and put on his weather beaten coat, and retrieved his trusty old fireplace poker, just in case it's not an owl. He muttered to himself wondering what the world was coming to, there is no peace, not even in a graveyard. Joe climbed into his truck and slowly drove in the direction he thought the sound was coming from. After a short distance he backed up his truck and changed course. The wind was coming up and that seemed to change the direction from where the sound was coming from. A short time later Joe stopped his truck and decided to walk, maybe then he could hear the sound that now changed to a soft cry.

"Who's out there? Where are you? This is no place to play around in, you dang kids."

"Please help me, I'm down here." came a weak response.

'Where, down here?"

"I'm in the open grave."

Thinking that kids were still playing a prank on him, Joe was about to chastise them. The beam of his flashlight shone down into the grave and onto a blood soaked head of what was once blond hair. Joe was in shock when he passed the hair with the beam and looked into the face of the young policewoman. He remembered that she was the one who saved her partner's life when all of this chaos started. As he was helping her out of the hole he realized that she had no clothes on.

"Oh my God, missy, how did you get into this mess? Never mind, here's my jacket, put it on."

When he saw how weak she was and how much difficulty she had just putting on the coat, he helped her with it.

"I'm sorry I don't have a blanket, but I wasn't expecting this." In Joe's mind he made a vow that from now on he would always have a blanket in his truck. With this world turning upside down, you never know what equipment might come in handy.

He drove her to his house, all the while thinking, what a beautiful woman she was, even though she was messed up. He was no saint of a man, so it was hard for old Joe to keep his eyes off her. When they got to his home he offered her a pair of small jeans and shirt that he wore in his younger and thinner days. She thanked him, then he told her where the bathroom was so she could change. When she finished dressing she came into the kitchen where he was making her a cup of coffee. He pulled out a kitchen chair for her to sit on, he could see she was still trembling. Her hands shook as she tried to bring the cup to her swollen mouth, but it was no use, the liquid dribbled down her chin. Joe offered to take her to the hospital; she shook her head and in a hoarse voice replied, that she was enough trouble to him and that she could drive herself. Old Joe knew that this girl had courage, but driving in her condition was doubtful. He sure would like to get his hands on the louse who did this to her. With all the bruising she had on her body, somebody must have really had it in for her. Since she would not let him drive her, he insisted that he would follow her as far as the gates, just in case that demon was still around. He wondered what he was thinking when he thought he lived in a peaceful and soothing place.

Anne drove a mile down the road when she pulled over to the side and stopped the car. She laid her head against the steering wheel and the tears started to flow. It felt good to cry, no one was here to see or listen to her as she kept asking the question, WHY, WHY, did he do this to her? Anne didn't think that she ever intentionally hurt Ernie. Maybe some people don't need a reason, but it was just beyond her reasoning. She looked out the window and noticed snowflakes starting to fall, it was the first snowfall of the season. Soon the snow would cover all the dirt that covered this part of the world, her world. Anne sat awhile longer, her crying quieted down to sobs. It was getting cold in the car as she gathered old Joe's coat tighter around her body. She didn't know what Ernie did with her clothes, and she really didn't care, she would have burned them anyway. She didn't want any reminders of tonight. It was then that she knew what she had to do. She turned the key in the ignition and drove to the hospital. She hoped they had a rape kit on hand. In a small town like Hartger's Grove rapes don't happen very often or they just aren't reported. Anne wondered why she thought she could handle him by herself, but it was no use thinking about that, since it was over, and she was now paying for it.

Anne parked her car in the hospital parking lot and slowly made her way into the emergency department. It was a quiet night and Anne was glad for that. The nurse on duty took one look at her and immediately brought over a wheel chair. Anne's legs were about to buckle as she lowered herself into the chair, where they quickly wheeled her into a cubical. She told them about the assault as well as the rape, without hesitation the nurse helped her undress and helped her onto the table. While the nurse was helping Anne with paper work, the doctor entered the room. Anne lay on the table, looking up at the ceiling, tears sliding down the sides of her face. She closed her one eye, the other was already swollen shut, she was trying hard to shut out what the doctor was doing and saying. She knew the doctor was a professional and was only doing his job, but she still felt dirty and humiliated. The doctor mentioned that it was good that she did not go home and shower. When she was at Old Joe's house she wanted so badly to jump into his shower and scrub and scrub, but common sense made her stop. It seemed like an eternity before the doctor was finished. The nurse tried to make light of the situation and mentioned that they should charge the police department extra since they always seem to be here as patients. They asked Anne if they could call anyone. She thought a moment, she really didn't want Jackie; she always got too emotional. She then asked them if they would please call her partner, Aaron Fischer.

Anne looked as if she had been in a fight and lost. One eye was entirely swollen shut, the E.R. doctor told her that when the swelling goes down she would have to make an appointment with an eye specialist to see if there was any eye damage. Both cheekbones were beginning to swell, but after they were x-rayed they found that the bones were not broken. The doctor at first thought that her nose might be broken but then again Anne lucked out, the x-ray was negative. As far as her body was concerned, that was another story. Her whole body was one big black and blue mark, and hurt like the dickens. The doctor prescribed her pain pills to ease the pain and stiffness for the next couple of days. She asked him of he knew how many times she had been penetrated since she was passed out at the time. The doctor said he could not tell for sure, but knew it was more than once. There was tearing and a lot of abrasions in the vaginal area. The only real good news was that her bad leg did not suffer any break, especially after Ernie tossed her into the grave. While waiting for Aaron, Anne thought back to the cemetery when Ernie pushed her into the grave. He could so easily have buried her right then and there. Anne shuddered when she thought about it.

It was a few minutes later when Aaron came rushing though the swinging doors, he took one look at Anne and swore under his breath. He put his arms around her and her tears started flowing. His arms tightened around her as he rocked her like a baby. The two nurses that were present left quietly, each thinking what an understanding wife he must have. Aaron took Anne's arm and helped her down from the table and led her into the lounge so they could talk in private. He took her cold hands in his and leaned forward.

"Do you feel like talking Anne?" Anne could hardly talk above a whisper, her voice was hoarse from calling for help, and from Ernie pressing down hard when he was kissing her. At that thought Anne gagged and Aaron went and got her a emesis basin in case she did throw up.

"Anne, I know you are hurting, but there are some questions I have to ask you. I have to know where this attack occurred, and I have to ask, did Mike do this to you?"

Anne looked shocked when he asked if Mike did it.

'Oh no, Mike, could never do this to me, I don't even know if he's alive."

Anne hesitated for a second when she said,

"It was Ernie who did this to me."

Now it was Aaron's turn to look at her questioningly.

"You mean, Ernie, our maintenance man, did this to you?"

"I just found out tonight that he's Mike's brother."

"So that's how our plans leaked out. Anne, why didn't you call me when Ernie got in touch with you? I gave you my home, as well as my cell phone number, you could have told me where you were heading."

"I thought about calling you, but I thought I could handle him myself. If it wasn't for my bum leg I think I could have, besides I didn't want anything happening to you. Mike warned me about what a mean streak Ernie has. I should have listened. I think he suspected you might have been following me so he changed the location when I was already at the cemetery. Aaron, he raped me. He was so strong. I just couldn't remember any of my police training. My mind drew a blank. I tried to give him a knee to the groin but my bum leg didn't have the strength and fell short of its mark. Oh Aaron, I'm so ashamed of what he did to me. I thought I was a better police officer than this."

This time Anne's sobs shook her whole body. Aaron once again took her in his arms to comfort her. After awhile when Anne was once again able to talk she looked up at Aaron and said.

"There is one thing I did find out from Ernie, it's that Mike might not be dead."

"What makes you think he isn't? Was it something he said?"

Anne blushed; she knew she would have to tell Aaron, she began slowly,

"When Ernie threw me into the grave, he looked down at me and said that if I see Mike I should tell him that his big brother Ernie had me first." Anne did not mention what Ernie said about Aaron and her.

Just then a nurse came by and handed Anne her bottle of pain pills and told her how and when to take them. Aaron helped Anne out to his car, Anne started to refuse the ride from Aaron, but he would not take no for an answer.

Anne was quiet all the way home, which left Aaron to his own thoughts. When he would get home he would tell Amanda about his long coffee break with Anne and the conversation between them. He knew Amanda, being in a delicate condition, would be upset about it if she had heard it from someone else. He knew that he could trust his wife not to breathe a word of what he told her. When they got to Anne's apartment it was dark inside, Aaron insisted that he walk Anne right to her door, and make sure that everything was okay. She didn't refuse, she was just so tired that it was very difficult to talk, she felt as if her lips were swollen to twice their size. As Aaron gave back her keys, she took Aaron by the hand to thank him. As he turned to leave, he stopped and said,

"If you feel up to it tomorrow, we should meet with the chief and give him the whole report."

Anne took a deep breath and nodded her head yes. She was thankful that she didn't have to face Jackie. She went into her bedroom, undressed, and went straight to the shower where she scrubbed and scrubbed till her skin was raw. She then took a pain pill and went straight to bed.

The next morning she awoke to hear Jackie singing in the kitchen. Anne lay there for a minute and tried to hear what she was singing, it was "Here comes the Bride." As the title dawned on her, Jackie came rushing into Anne's room and said,

"Wake up sleepy head, I have some great news for you. You are going to be my matron of honor."

Jackie could not see Anne's face because the blinds were still drawn shut. She went over to the window and opened them, she wanted to show Anne her ring. She turned to face Anne and turned pale as she rushed over to her and gently took her in her arms and started to cry.

"Anne what happened, were you in an auto accident? It was that phantom wasn't it? Do the police know about this?" It was hard for Anne to talk, but she finally replied,

"Jackie, please get a hold of yourself, it wasn't Mike who did this, it was his brother, Ernie."

"Oh my God, you mean that cleaning guy at your station? That whole family must be insane."

It was difficult for Anne to talk, so she had to talk slow. When she finished a much shorter version of her story, with a lot of things left out, Jackie was somewhat convinced that it wasn't Mike, and reluctantly left for work. The apartment was quiet, as Anne slowly got out of bed. She didn't think it was possible, but her body felt stiffer and more painful than the day before. After eating a liquid breakfast she dressed and was ready to see the chief. Anne was going to drive herself, but again Aaron insisted on picking her up and driving to the station. She wondered how much of this Amanda was going to take. It took a very broad-minded woman to share her husband with a woman who once wanted him as much as his wife did. She wondered where Ernie was, she hoped he rots in hell.

Anne was waiting when Aaron pulled up to the curb. She asked him if he minded that they come in through the back entrance of the station. Her leg was giving her more of a problem than usual, it also had snowed heavily during the night, which made it more difficult for her to walk through. Aaron called ahead to Frank, so he was expecting them. The chief was standing in the office doorway, when he saw Anne his face blanched at the sight of her, he uttered

"God, Anne, Aaron told me you were beat up, but I never expected you to look this bad."

He pulled out a chair for Anne and she sat down in gratitude, he then went back behind his desk. Anne could not believe how nervous she felt, it reminded her of her first day of high school. She looked up at the chief, and saw him shake his head in pity and disbelief.

"First of all, I want you to know we are going to catch that son of a bitch, excuse my language, if it's the last thing we do. Now Aaron told me some of the facts, but I want to hear the rest from you. Anne started to fidget, she was sore between her legs, the doctor said she had internal abrasions, and that in time she would heal. Physically she would, but mentally, that was another problem. Every time she thought of Ernie she felt sick to her stomach. Anne had thought she had a strong fortitude, but then she had never been raped before. The chief's voice broke into her train of thoughts.

'Anne, do you want to give me your statement another day?"

He had noticed her silence.

"No Chief, today is fine, we might as well get it over with, but I would like a cup of coffee if you don't mind."

Aaron jumped up to get it for her. Anne didn't really need the coffee, it was so she could hold the cup in her hands, they were so cold. She wondered if they would ever feel warm again. After Frank and she got their coffee, she start her story. The chief already knew about Ernie being involved, but he did not know that Anne was raped, until she told him.

"You know that doesn't surprise me, he liked all the girls here at the station, especially you. Sometimes I caught him staring at you, but I couldn't do anything about it. Not as long as he wasn't a bother to you. We already have an "all points bulletin" out on him. When you went to the hospital, did they do a rape kit on you?"

Anne blushed when he asked her that question, she nodded that they had. The questioning took another hour before the chief was satisfied, he then had Anne write down everything she had told him. Frank stood up from behind his desk when Anne said,

"I know what I did was against department rules, but I'm stubborn and I thought I could handle this myself."

"I don't know what else to say to you, Anne. I'm going to put you on suspension, with pay, until I can talk to the board of inquiry. You put yourself at risk and we don't take that lightly. Anne, considering what you have been through, and the fact that we now know who we are dealing with, I think the board might go easy on you. Why don't you go on out and let the crew know you are still living, they heard some gruesome stories about what happened to you. I also want them to know that I didn't flog you with a whip."

Anne knew the chief went easy on her, but she also knew that the board of inquiry's ruling could swing the opposite way. She was still in the hot seat. Everyone at the station was shocked to see the condition she was in, but they were not surprised to hear that it was Ernie that did it to her. Everyone had their own negative story about him. When Frank finished talking to Aaron, Aaron drove her home.

"Aaron, how long do you think I'll be suspended?"

"I really don't know, it just depends on when the board meets."

"I'm just happy I didn't involve you last night, you are too good of an officer to be suspended. With a new baby on the way, you can't lose your job or a future promotion. Congratulations on the coming baby. Amanda came to see me yesterday afternoon, she looks good, pregnancy agrees with her."

"We both are delighted with the prospect of a baby in the family."

Anne turned away and looked out the window, wishing…wishing that she could have been in Amanda's shoes.

"Well Anne here you are, safe and sound."

Thanks Aaron, I appreciated having you on my side, it made it a lot easier in facing the chief."

Aaron took Anne's hand in his and answered, "That's what partners and friends are for."

She got out of the car and limped into her building.

As she entered her apartment the phone started to ring, she took her time in answering it. When she did answer it, she was sorry she did.

"Well Anne, I didn't think you were going to answer, and I know you are home, I just saw your lover boy dropping you off."

When Ernie said that, Anne limped to the window to see if his green van was out there, but the street was empty of cars.

"Now you don't think I would be right outside your window do you? I was waiting for you to give him a kiss goodbye, and you were wise not to, you see I'm insanely jealous."

"What do you want Ernie? Haven't you done enough damage to me? You know the police have an "all points" out for you."

"Do tell, but as clever as think they are, they will never catch old Ernie boy. I will always be a step ahead of them."

Anne just about had enough of him and was about to hang up when he said,

"Now, Anne, you really didn't go and tell everything I did to you, did you? That was naughty of you, I will be leaving town as soon as I hang up. I do want to warn you not to hook up with Mike, because you are mine, now. If you do, watch for me in some dark alley or cemetery, you will never be safe."

Anne slammed down the phone, and limped to the bathroom to throw up.

Jackie came home an hour before dinner, and asked Anne about her meeting with Frank. She told Jackie about her suspension, with pay, until the board of inquiry meets to decide her fate.

"Jackie, I've been doing a lot of thinking about my job. It's like I'm always making a wrong decision, I think more with my heart then my head and that could jeopardize another police officer's life."

"Anne, what are you talking about? You are one of the bravest officer in the department. I'll bet there wasn't another woman there that volunteered for the cemetery detail. You saved Aaron's life, by driving him to the hospital, and not waiting for the ambulance. You met with the phantom at a wayside late at night, and also found out who was behind all this, that took a lot of courage. True, you are a little stubborn and bull headed, but I never doubted for a minute that you are our police force's greatest asset."

Anne did not know what to say except to give Jackie a hug in gratitude. The conversation then changed to a happier note, and the coming wedding event.

That evening Jackie went out to make arrangements for their wedding. Anne was glad to have the apartment to herself. She was still hurting physically, and every time she passed a mirror she cringed at what she saw. Again she wondered how some people could have such a mean streak as to enjoy hurting another so drastically?

I did not expect Jackie back until late. When I heard a soft knock on the apartment door, thinking that it might be Jackie and that she might have forgotten her key, I went to the door and was about to unlock the deadbolt when I stopped. The image of Ernie with his leering face made its way into my memory. My hand was poised in midair, as I looked though the peephole and saw no one. I laid the side of my face against the warm wood of the door and quietly asked who it was. At first there was silence, and then the deep familiar voice of Mike came through like a beacon in the night. I closed my eyes and took a deep breath, "Dear God he is alive!"

"Anne please let me in!"

It was then that my hands flew into motion, as I quickly opened the door for him. I stood there for what seemed like an eternity, my eyes drinking in the sight of him. The shadows of the hallways softened his facial scars. He made the first move and opened his arms to me. I flew into them and buried my face into his wet jacket, and at the same time frantically kissing his sweet face and crying that I could not believe he was alive. I wanted to remember this moment forever, somewhere deep inside I had a feeling that if I let go, I might lose him again. But he was here, his hair wet and glistening from the melted snow that was blanketing the world outside. I took his hand and gently pulled him into the apartment, locking the door. Neither of us said a word as he again took me in his arms, it just seems so natural to be in his warm embrace, and here I will always want to be. Tenderly he kissed away the tears that had trickled down my face. He pulled away in shock when he noticed Ernie's handiwork, his hand moving up the side of my face that had suffered the worse punishment. In a choked voice he asked me what had happened.

"My God, Anne, what happened to your face?" I didn't answer his question; it was then that I could see an expression on his face that bordered between disbelief and hatred, as he answered his own question,

'This is my brother's work, isn't it?" I still did not answer him as I pulled away and limped into the living room.

"Anne, for God's sake, talk to me, I know it was my brother who did this to you. And since it was my brother who did this, then you must know the rest of the puzzle as well as his name."

Mike put his hands on my shoulders making me look into his eyes, demanding that I tell him his brother's name.

"Yes, yes I do know his name, its Ernie, who is your brother!" I screamed as a flood of tears burst loose. I walked away from him and went over to the window, if someone asked me what I was seeing I could honestly say that I did not see the snow that was accumulating. But what I felt I could indeed relate too. The bitterness and anger I felt were like a boiling pot threatening to spill over. I felt Mike's hands on the back of my shoulders as he turned me around to face him.

"Anne, this is entirely my fault, I should have told you about him right from the beginning. I knew how mean and cruel he could become. I should have gone right to your friend, Aaron, and told him, but I thought you would be safe once I left town. He knew that I started to have feelings for you, but I think when I left the note for him to keep his hands off you was what really set him off. Anne please believe me when I say how sorry I am, I only wish he would have taken his hatred out on me instead of you."

"No, Mike, not you. You've suffered enough, I'm just so happy he didn't kill you as he threatened."

I looked up into Mike's eyes, and the kisses started all over again, I wanted a lifetime of them. It was later when our feelings for each other settled down to hand holding that I told him everything, except for the rape. Somehow I just couldn't tell him that, I knew that would anger him to the level of wanting to kill Ernie. No, that would be my secret till the day I died. I took hold of both his hands and made him promise me that he would do nothing that would be against the law. After a moment I could feel his body relax. I wrapped my arms around him to comfort him as well as myself; this is what we both needed for now. Time passed and once again I looked up into his sweet face, as if reading my mind he lowered his lips to mine. Suddenly he jerked away and turned his face away from me, in an anguished tone of voice he asked me,

"How can you kiss this scarred mess of a man?"

He started to get up off the couch but I pulled him down next to me, he ran his hands though his hair and in a voice riddled with emotion he continued,

"I shouldn't even be here, I had planned to be miles away from you, I have messed up your life enough as it is. But deep inside me I could never leave you forever because you are my only chance of being a human being again. I never thought I would love again, but then you came into my life, and I know now that there is hope for me. You see Anne I love you with all my heart and soul, I guess there is a, God, to give me another chance at love."

I stepped back and looked up into his wonderful face and realized how much I really loved this phantom. Fate has strange ways of dealing with people.

"Mike, when I kiss you, it's not the face I kiss. It's you, the man I love and kiss. Please let me love you, I want so much to drive away all your sorrow."

Mike groaned and swept Anne into his arms, never wanting her to get away. He had heard the beautiful word 'love' it was like someone offering him water in the middle of a desert.

The phone started to ring, Anne tensed up for a moment, afraid that it could be Ernie. She picked up the phone slowly and it was then that she heard Jackie's voice.

"For goodness sake Anne, I thought you would never answer. In case you don't know we are in the middle of a Wisconsin snowstorm, the roads are not in very good driving condition so Bill and I are going to stay in the city. I hate to leave you alone like this but I'll leave you our number in case you have a problem."

Mike moved behind Anne and put his arms around her and started to rain tiny kisses down the nape of her neck that made her shiver.

'No, Jackie, you don't have to be concerned about me, I'll be just fine. Just have a good time and I'll see you when the snow stops, have a good night."

After putting the phone down Anne turned to face Mike, putting her arms around his neck she whispered,

"We have this whole night to ourselves, please love me, my sweet, wonderful phantom."

She slid her arms down his chest and led him by the hand into her bedroom. One by one the lights throughout the apartment were extinguished, except for one lone bedroom lamp, which cast a soft glow on the bed. It was a perfect setting for what Anne and Mike both knew was going to happen. They stood, looking at each other, holding their breath, each with there own thoughts. Mike wondering if he was messing up her life even more with his wanting her, and Anne thinking she found true love with her phantom. The distance closed between them until each could feel the others breath. Anne was the first to act as she reached for his hand and placed it on her breast. She just stood there. Seconds seemed like hours as Mike looked down to where she had placed his hand, his next question barely audible,

"Anne you are so beautiful, are you sure you want to do this? If you are not sure, or just feel pity for me, just turn away and I'll quietly leave and be out of your life forever."

"Oh Mike I have never been more sure of anything in my life. I need you as much as you need me and all the love you can give me."

With every piece of clothing he removed from Anne, he kissed her until she was standing in all her naked glory. He stepped back and thought that she was as beautiful on the outside as she was on the inside. He drew her to the bed and laid her gently on the soft coverlet, neither said a word for fear of breaking this magic spell. Anne watched him with half closed eyes and saw the awe and sense of wanting in his eyes. She slowly raised her arms and beckoned him into her private world, saying,

"Mike I need you now."

With those words Mike quickly removed his clothing. Anne, watched in admiration at the powerful built body that was slowly emerging from beneath his clothes. The accident and fire had not touched the rest of his body, and for Mike's sake she was glad. He joined her on the bed, and laid on his side studying her sweet face and beautiful body. He wondered why she had joined the police force when she so easily could have become a model. His brother Ernie often made lewd remarks about her and her partner Aaron. As he secretly got to know her, he knew Ernie was only talking from envy and spite. He trailed his fingers lightly across her face and neck trying to memorize each soft spot. He knew this would be the only night for a long time that they would have for themselves. His fingers traveled down to her breasts, they were so perfect, she was more endowed than a model would have been. He felt her sharp intake of air as he softly caressed her breast. Memories started to materialize as he remembered the night he laid in bed with Dana. They had just finished making love when she told him they were going to become parents. He covered her breast in wonderment because he knew that soon they would be the source of his child's food. He then leaned over and kissed each mound. He thought how women were God given creatures to be cherished and protected, and he would always protect his Dana.

Anne sensed his withdrawal from her as she put her hand over his.

"Mike, is something wrong? Maybe we should just lay here and let nature take its course."

Mike let his hand slip off her breast, as he got off the bed and walked over to the window, he pulled back the curtain and drew open the blinds. Jackie was right, Wisconsin was in the middle of its first snowstorm of the season. He could hear movement behind him, as the perfume Anne wore floated like a fine mist around him. She slipped her arms around him and rested her face on his back. He moved aside to bring her next to him so they could watch the swirling snow together. Tears slid down his cheeks as he quietly said,

"Beautiful isn't it, like a winter fairyland, so unsettling and when it's over, the calm returns with a sense of peace and awe. My little Amy loved the snow, she only had two seasons of snow in her short life, but every snow flake was pure enjoyment."

Anne looked up into his face and saw the tears slowly slide down his cheeks, she stood on her toes and kissed the scarred side of his face. She made a vow to herself that it would be the last tear he would ever shed. He wrapped his arms around her as they gazed out the window, each in his own thoughts. The room temperature started to drop, when Anne shivered Mike picked her up and carried her to the bed.

"My wonderful Anne I want to share my love with you, but it's been a long time since I've been with a woman, show me how you want it to be."

Anne put her arms around his neck and looked up into his face and slowly kissed his face, to Mike they felt like the breath of an angel. With her kisses came soft words whispered into his ear almost like a lullaby, it was then that he felt his soul and heart begin to heal. She moved slowly as her lips moved from his cheek to his chest. When she felt his hardness she settled over it, never letting go of his lips or body. He moved his hands to her breasts and marveled at the softness of each mound, his tongue played with one nipple then the other coaxing them to hardness. He moved down to the flat plateau of her stomach, excitement was building in both of them as his fingers explored the depths of her very being. Just when Anne thought she could not stand it any longer she felt his male organ enter the opening that just two nights before had been so defiled by his brother. Anne tensed up for the fear of pain she knew was going to come. Mike sensed something was wrong as he gently said,

"Don't worry my sweet Anne, I'll take it slow and if it hurts too much I'll stop."

When Anne heard those gentle words she didn't care how much pain there was, she would never let him know. She found out that night that Mike was a gentle lover, his concern for her made him patient and if possible more loving. To her relief there was very little pain after the severe rape she'd suffered at the hands of Ernie. Anne promised herself that she would never tell Mike what Ernie had done to her that night at the cemetery. That was going to be her secret and her hell.

When they could make love no more, they lay side by side on top of the coverlet, sweat glistening on both their bodies. Mike, realizing the coolness of the room, reached for Anne, gathered her in his arms, and covered them both with a blanket. He looked at her face in the now soft shadows of night, he thought that surely this must be what heaven was like. He closed his eyes and thought back to the dark days after he had lost his family, and the first time he had seen the hideous side of his face. In the days that followed he often wondered how God could have put so much cruelty in his life. It was at that time that he stopped believing in this person they called a loving God. But now as he looked down at the sleeping angel, who had just told him that she loved him, despite his messed up face and life. He realized it was time that he again question this man called God. Anne opened her eyes and pressed her lips to his.

"My darling Anne, you are exquisite, I don't ever want this night to end."

She whispered that it didn't have to end, as she snuggled into his arms and again drifted off to sleep. As he did earlier that evening, he tried to memorize her soft and lovely face and body. He knew that all too soon he would be leaving, but this time he knew in his heart and mind that he would be coming back to her. But that was tomorrow and they still had a long night ahead of them to love, and make love they did.

The snow came down for two days without stopping, locking Mike and his love in their own warm world. More than once in the extra days he spent with Anne did Mike think that there indeed is a man called God. With a deep contented sigh he snuggled Anne closer and slowly closed his eyes.

On their last day together Mike made a huge breakfast and served it to Anne in bed. He bowed to Anne and said that it was the least he could do for his mistress, she laughed at that and called him her sex slave. There was enough food for both of them, and they ate like there would be no tomorrow.

The snow had finally stopped and Anne felt a sense of sadness, she knew their long nights of love were over for a long time to come. She also knew that Jackie would soon be home, and that Mike would be gone. A melancholy overtook her as she watched him shower and shave. She begged him to stay as she slipped into the shower with him and wrapped her arms around his waist, all the while reining kisses on his chest.

"Anne you are making this so hard for me, if you could know how I ache to stay, but I can't. Right now I can hardly support myself, let alone a wife."

Anne heard the anguish in his voice, but it was then that she realized he had used the word wife.

"Mike, did I hear you say wife?"

A slow grin spread across his face,

"Of course you sweet young thing, you didn't think I only wanted you as a sex goddess do you? I want you for my wife, to cherish and love forever. Right now I'm going for medical help, after that, maybe your friend Aaron can help me straighten out this mess I'm in. But then again, I might never go if you stay here in the shower with me."

"Oh Mike, Aaron can help you, trust me. You're not even gone and I miss you already"

Her tears mingled with the water that flowed across Anne's face.

'Don't cry, my angel, I will always find you no matter where you are. When we are parted and there are many miles between us just lay your hand across your heart and feel the love we shared these past two nights. Then close your eyes and you will feel that I'm doing the same."

Anne and Mike held each other while they talked for another hour. When all was said, Anne knew she was going to quit the police force and move to New Orleans. She told Mike this as they both clung to each other. Mike kissed her tear-stained face, feeling that his heart was again being wrenched from his chest. Gently he removed Anne from his arms and quickly left the apartment, he didn't look back. He knew that if he turned around he would see Anne tearfully looking out the window. The urge would be to fly back into her warm loving arms. The thought of a future with her was what kept him going. He also knew the sooner his health and accounting to the police was taken care of, the quicker he would have a future with Anne. He pulled up the collar of his pea coat against the biting cold that followed the snowstorm. Mike knew where he had to go, and with Anne's love in his heart he kept going forward with each determined step.

I sat by the window until I could no longer see Mike. I let out a wistful sigh, knowing that once more he would be my phantom. A phantom I could only have in my dreams. It would only be in my dreams, that I would again, hear his sensuous voice. I knew it would be months before I would get to see him again. If I could only be at his side to help him straighten out his life, but he was as stubborn as I was. I walked though the apartment and I could still smell his after-shave. I walked into the bedroom and broke down as I looked at the crumpled sheet and coverlet. It was a bed full of love and dreams. I knew then the sooner I left Hartger's Grove the closer I will be to my future.

It was going to be hard leaving everyone I knew, especially, Jackie, my roommate for so many years. But I have the feeling that now that she has Bill, maybe our parting won't be as hard. Aaron, how was I going to break the news to him that I was leaving Hartgers and the police force? My sweet Aaron, deep down I knew that he never loved me, but I had this fixation about him. I could never have him but that made me try all the harder to try and change his mind about me. I knew that Amanda would be happy to hear that I was leaving. Who wouldn't be happy, having a thorn removed from one's side? I let out a long sigh, I never realized how often I did that lately. As I walked through the apartment, my thoughts and prayers were with Mike, to keep him safe on his long journey.

Chapter 40

I knew I had to keep busy, but my heart felt so heavy. I missed him so much that I just wanted to go to bed and sleep my life away, I sighed again and decided to clean the apartment. When I finished, I once again started my pacing, wishing that Jackie was home, conversation was Jackie's strongest trait. Suddenly I stopped and realized that it would be best if I would be out among people. I dressed for the biting cold that I knew usually follows a snowstorm and left the apartment.

I walked slowly down Main Street, the snowplows had already cleared the streets and the salting crews were doing their share. Wisconsin was always prepared when a storm was on the way. The hardware stores were doing a brisk trade of selling snow shovels to people who didn't think we would get this kind of snow until mid-January. Christmas was still two weeks away but there was a holiday feeling in the air as shop owners were decorating their store windows. Schools were closed, since many of the children were bussed in from rural communities. I spotted boys having snowball fights, their laughter ringing though the clear, cold air. I thought how all this reminded me of a Norman Rockwell painting. I wondered if Mike and I would ever be walking down this street, happy and so much in love.

I was just about to go through the Java Cup Café doors when I heard a familiar voice behind me,

"Hi partner, shouldn't you be home, resting that leg?"

"Hi Aaron, actually I'm doing my exercising, and if I stay in that apartment any longer I'll go stir crazy.

"Would you mind some company, it's my lunch break?"

Aaron ushered Anne into the cafe and led her to a window booth. Myrtle, the waitress, was again on duty, the same waitress who found their last visit very interesting. She smacked her lips, anticipating more juicy gossip for her friends. She grabbed a couple of menus and walked over to their booth.

"Hi Aaron, Hi Anne, how are you all doing? How is your little pregnant wife doing Aaron?"

"She is just fine Myrtle. We will have your lunch special, and decaf coffee please."

Aaron thought it was funny that she only asks about Amanda when he's with Anne.

"How about some delicious apple pie for dessert, I made it myself?"

Anne declined the pie, but Aaron could not pass up homemade pie. Myrtle could not wait to tell her friend that "they" were here again. As a matter of fact she might even make a little side bet on how long they were going to stay. Yes, this business can be very interesting at times. Myrtle chuckled as she walked back to the kitchen to get their order.

Neither Aaron nor Anne spoke until their coffee was served. Anne was the first to speak,

"You know Aaron, I'm very glad we met today. I have something to tell you and I wanted you to know before you heard it from the office grapevine. You, being my partner, should be the first to know."

Anne took a deep breathe before going on, Aaron took hold of her hand. Somehow he knew what she was going to say and he wanted her to know she had his full attention.

'Oh God, Aaron, my life is such a wonderful mess." Anne could not say anymore because the tears started to trickle down her cheeks. She wondered where all those tears came from? She thought about her past and how she'd never shed a tear, until the night of Aaron's accident. Now it seemed like a daily occurrence, but today just being able to talk to a friend about her problems broke the dam that held the tears back. Myrtle didn't miss a trick, she was so happy that she didn't have to wait on customers and miss all this. She edged a little closer to where they were sitting and pretended to be cleaning the counter just so she could hear them.

"Anne, just take your time, I have all afternoon if you need it."

Anne blew her nose in a handkerchief Aaron had given her. It took a couple of minutes before she was able to talk.

"I'm so sorry, Aaron, I feel like such a fool, breaking down like this, but I needed to talk to someone and I'm glad its you. You see I'm leaving the department, even if the inquiry board overlooks my indiscretions." Anne finished the last sentence in a rush, just to get it over with.

Aaron was about to object but Anne stopped him,

"Please, Aaron, hear me out. You see it is very hard for me to say this, but I have given it a lot of thought. First of all, I never really wanted to be an officer, it was you I wanted. By joining the department I could be at your side, even though you were in Chicago at the time, I knew you would be back sooner or later, and I was willing to wait. When you came back and married Amanda, I was crushed but as you know I don't give up that easy." Anne stopped and took a deep breath, she knew the next part would be even harder for her to tell him.

"Your marriage to Amanda didn't mean anything to me, because I was willing to play second fiddle to her. I had big plans for you and me the night you came back from your honeymoon, especially after I heard we would be together on patrol at the cemetery. My life changed that night, after you almost lost your life. I waited outside the emergency room, thinking that when you opened your eyes I would be the first person you would see. Then Amanda came running in, and the doctor led her into your room immediately. It was like a slap in the face, and I realized that as far as the world was concerned, Amanda, not I, was the most important person in your life. I stood outside of your room as it slowly sank in. I think it was then that I started to grow up. For the first time in my life, I put someone else's feelings before mine. I saw how hysterical Amanda was, and then not knowing if you were going to live, or die. I saw how shallow and vain I had been. I can't believe I have the courage to tell you all of this, but I want to set the record straight with you before I leave Hartger's Grove."

Aaron started to interrupt her, but once again Anne held up her hand to silence him.

"Please Aaron, there is more I have to say. I never was a good police officer, although Jackie keeps telling me otherwise. After that person almost ended your life I made a promise to myself that I would get him if it was the last thing I would do. To my surprise and shock I found not one, but two suspects. One was pure evil, and the other because of circumstances beyond his control, a victim to the others' evil demands, yet they were blood brothers. I started to look forward to the phantom's calls, he became a challenge to me. I met him twice at the wayside, the first time he would not let me see his face. The second time I got to really know him and saw his face. I was horrified to see the damage that the fire did to him. One side was so handsome, the other side a mask of scars. I gasped at the sight and Mike took that as a sign of rejection, it wasn't, but it took a while to convince him of that. I saw the sadness in him as well as the torment when he told me about the loss of his family. I wanted to hold him in my arms and soothe away all his pain. We talked for most of the night and it was when I kissed him that my deeper feelings came to the surface."

Anne stopped talking as fresh tears flowed down her face. She tried swallowing the lump that made it so difficult for her to talk. Aaron came over to her side of the booth to comfort her, he put his arms around her shoulders. Myrtle could not believe her eyes when she saw the scene unfolding in front of her. Just then a customer came into the café and sat on the farthest side of the room away from Aaron and Anne. She softly muttered under her breath as she grabbed a menu and walked over to where the customer sat. She didn't care if she was rude to him, he wasn't a good tipper anyway. The scene between the two cops was like watching her favorite soap opera, maybe better. She kept her eye on them, ever so often she could see Anne crying, wishing she could hear what they were saying. She started to make up her own dialog to what she thought they were saying. She quickly dialed up her best friend Mabel and whispered into the phone.

"You will never guess what I'm watching! No, not on television, here at the restaurant." she replied. "Yep, they're here again." She was rather disappointed that Mabel guessed almost immediately.

"I don't know how you knew, but this time he's actually sitting right close to her on the same side of the booth. I can't hear what they are saying but she's doing a lot of crying, he even gave her his handkerchief to blow her nose on. You don't think she's pregnant, do you? Oh, did I mention how bad she looks? Someone must have given her a real good beating; she's black and blue all over. Her one eye looks pretty bad, it's almost swollen shut. First she comes in with a bad limp, now this. What's that police department of ours coming to?"

Without waiting for a reply from her friend, Myrtle said in a haughty voice,

"It seems the vows of matrimony just don't seem important to some people like it does to us, right Mabel? Our husbands are just so lucky to have such loyal and steadfast wives, right Mabel? I have to go, I'm going to offer them more coffee and see if I can hear some of their conversation, call you later."

Aaron had his one hand over Anne's, this did not escape Myrtle's attention. She heard Anne say, "We had the two most wonderful nights imaginable."

Myrtle almost dropped her coffee pot. Aaron looked up at her and asked her what she wanted, since her mouth was still hanging open.

"Could I get you more pie or coffee?" she stammered,

"No thanks, but you can leave us a pot of coffee so we won't have to bother you. Walking back and forth like you do has to be hard on the feet and ears."

Myrtle's face turned beet red as she muttered that she would be right back. She wondered if Aaron had heard her on the phone with Mabel. Poor Amanda should just know what's going on between these two. She sighed and thought that the wife was always the last to know.

Anne told Aaron everything, she wanted him to know why she was leaving and that she loved Mike, with all her heart.

"Aaron, there is a favor I want to ask of you. When Mike straightens out his medical problems, he's coming back to ask your help. Would you please help him?"

Aaron thought a moment, and for Anne's sake he hoped that Mike would come back, but he did have reservations about that. Aaron looked at Anne, even with her face badly bruised she still looked lovely. He also saw the hope in her eyes, and he knew he could only have one answer for her.

"When he comes back I certainly will go to bat for him, now that I know the whole story. When are you going to give Frank your resignation? You know I still think you are doing the wrong thing by leaving town. I know you're going to survive the board of inquiry, thirty years from now you will retire with your full pension in hand."

"Thank you, Aaron, for being such a true friend, but I have to get away from here and start a new life. New Orleans will be my new home, besides I don't know were Ernie is, but I don't think he will find me there."

"Anne if you ever need my help, never hesitate to call me. Amanda would agree with me on that."

She thanked Aaron for listening and being so understanding, but in her heart she knew that Amanda would not be that understanding. What woman would, when they have a wonderful man like Aaron, giving help to a woman who at one time tried seducing him at every turn? Anne knew that the person she once was, was all in the past, now she must look toward a new future.

While Anne was putting on her coat, Aaron took their check to the counter to pay it. When Myrtle reached for the check, Aaron took her hand and held it. She looked inquiringly at him and was about to ask him if anything was wrong when he said softly,

"Myrtle, my wife is going to have a baby very shortly. If she should hear any gossip that would upset her, I personally would look for that person and cause them hell here on Earth, do you understand?"

For once in her life she was at a loss for words, but Aaron knew she got the drift of his message.

"Great, I'm glad we understand each other, now you have a great day. Oh by the way, your pie was delicious."

Aaron and I met with Chief Frank Smith the following morning. Aaron was ushered into his office while I waited my turn. My fellow officers had heard about the inquiry and wished me luck. As I sat there, so many thoughts were going though my mind, a lot of doubts as well. No matter what Jackie and Aaron said about my bravery and what an asset I was to the department, I felt I let them down because of the way I handled the cemetery detail. Maybe I was too thin skinned about the way I felt, but when a fellow officer's life hung in the balance it was time to sit back and take stock of the situation I handled so poorly.

When the inner door to Frank's office opened, both men came out with big smiles on their faces. As Aaron passed me he touched my arm and gave me a wink as if to say, "Everything is going to be okay, hang in there." Whatever the out come, I knew I was leaving, but I wanted to leave under the best of circumstances.

Frank offered me a chair, and shuffled some papers he had sitting on his desk before looking at me. He cleared his throat before speaking, I think that was a nervous habit of his,

"You know Anne, Aaron was almost in as much trouble with the board as you were. He told us that he knew pretty much of what was going on with you and this phantom of yours.

"Chief, please let me explain."

"No Anne, you listen. Aaron told me what happened out there. Even if he knew only the smallest detail, he used poor judgment by not informing us. Both of you were wrong on how you handled this situation, and I blame him more because he was the senior partner. Fortunately he is an excellent officer and we will not hold him accountable for this. We also knew that we could not afford to lose two valuable officers, so as of tomorrow you will be on first shift with no more cemetery patrols…ever."

I was very pleased that they were willing to give me another chance, but now I had to break the news that I was leaving Hartger's Grove, and it was very hard. We sat in his office for a half hour and talked, all the while he would ask "Are you sure you want to do this?" He reached into the desk drawer and pulled out my shield and laid it on his desk for me to take. I looked down at it as I reached out my hand in a handshake of goodbye. He then came around his desk to put his arm around my shoulder,

'I still think you are making a mistake Anne but I trust your gave this a lot of thought. No matter how you feel about being a police officer, I want you to know you are a damn good cop, and your badge will always be here waiting for you. Have you made any plans?"

I told him about going to New Orleans and taking up the offer that Ray had once made. Frank thought that it was good idea and that I could use a change of scenery. Maybe after living in the hustle and bustle of New Orleans I would look forward to coming back to a small quiet town in rural Wisconsin.

Epilog

In the remaining weeks I had left in Hartger's Grove, I had time to think about my life here in this small Midwestern town. Some people will probably not think too highly of me, while others, hopefully, will say, "Gosh that police officer Anne Bradley really was a darn good cop."

I will definitely miss my roommate, Jackie, with all her concerns and caring of a mother hen. I think now that she is getting married, it will soften the fact that I'm leaving. I did promise to come back to stand up in her spring wedding.

Then there is my sweet wonderful Aaron, I think I will always call him that. It hurt to say goodbye on that last day, but not as much as it would have, before Mike, "My phantom" came into my life.

I will miss Frank and the whole department; they were the family I never had. I was in foster care since I was eleven. Most of the placements were good homes, but the department, with the chief, being the patriarch, was my real family. Yes, I'm really going to miss all of them, but it's time to move on, and find my phantom once again. I know I will find him, no matter how long it takes. All I need to remember is, "When we are parted, lay your hand across your heart, and feel the love we have shared. Then close your eyes, and you will feel that I'm doing the same." I WILL CONTINUE MY SEARCH!